D1471973

The item should be returned or renewed by the last date stamped below.

Dylid dychwelyd neu adnewyddu'r eitem erbyn y dyddiad olaf sydd wedi'i stampio isod.

Newport
CITY COUNCIL
CYNGOR DINAS
Casnewydd

Newport Library and
Information Service

0 2 DEC 2022

To renew visit / Adnewyddwch ar
www.newport.gov.uk/libraries

Harper Sloan, *New York Times* bestselling author

'This tense, sensual romance is chock full of headstrong, admirable characters who will appeal to romance and suspense fans alike' *Publishers Weekly*

'A heart-pounding narrative . . . Twists and turns abound as this whodunit builds up to revelations that will surprise even longtime suspense readers' *Shelf Awareness*

'Jay Crownover hits it out of the park with this sexy and suspenseful enemies-to-lovers romance . . . You'll be on the edge of your seat and thoroughly entertained while cheering for this sassy, feisty heroine and grumpy, swoonworthy cowboy as they bicker their way to happily ever after' *Frolic*

'Crownover writes cowboys that make you want to pack your bags in search of a small-town ranch! Alpha and broody, they hit all the right buttons' Melissa Foster, *New York Times* bestselling author

By Jay Crownover

The Loveless, Texas Series
Justified
Unforgiven

JAY CROWNOVER

Unforgiven

HEADLINE
ETERNAL

Copyright © 2020 Jennifer M. Voorhees
Bonus Novella *Cowboy to the Rescue* copyright © 2019 by A.J. Pine

The right of Jay Crownover to be identified as the Author of
the Work has been asserted by her in accordance with the
Copyright, Designs and Patents Act 1988.

Published by arrangement with Forever,
An imprint of Grand Central Publishing.

First published in Great Britain in 2020
by HEADLINE ETERNAL
An imprint of HEADLINE PUBLISHING GROUP

1

Apart from any use permitted under UK copyright law, this publication may
only be reproduced, stored, or transmitted, in any form, or by any means,
with prior permission in writing of the publishers or, in the case
of reprographic production, in accordance with the terms of
licences issued by the Copyright Licensing Agency.

All characters in this publication are fictitious
and any resemblance to real persons, living or dead,
is purely coincidental.

Cataloguing in Publication Data is available from the British Library

ISBN 978 1 4722 5427 6

Offset in 11.85/14.23 pt TimesLTStd by Jouve (UK), Milton Keynes

Printed and bound in Great Britain by Clays Ltd, Elcograf S.p.A.

Headline's policy is to use papers that are natural, renewable and recyclable
products and made from wood grown in well-managed forests and other
controlled sources. The logging and manufacturing processes are expected
to conform to the environmental regulations of the country of origin.

HEADLINE PUBLISHING GROUP
An Hachette UK Company
Carmelite House
50 Victoria Embankment
London EC4Y 0DZ

www.headlineeternal.com
www.headline.co.uk
www.hachette.co.uk

This book is dedicated to anyone who has loved someone, and their demons, no matter how hard it was or how badly it hurt.

Unforgiven

Unforgiven

PROLOGUE

∞

My little brother had been my best friend.

It was common knowledge around our tiny hometown of Loveless, Texas, that where one Gamble brother went, the other followed.

Our home life wasn't the best. Our parents had a complicated, volatile marriage. They loved each other deeply, passionately, almost obsessively... They hated each other with the same intensity. At times it felt like Aaron and I were nothing more than props in some overly dramatic soap opera. So my baby brother and I learned early it was better to be anywhere other than home. I never minded him following me around. I liked being his hero. I enjoyed being the one who taught him the basics, like how to play catch, how to fish, and how to drive. I also indulged him by passing along my tips and tricks when it came to getting girls. Although I tended to stick with sports and extracurricular activities that might help me get into a good college, girls were always Aaron's favorite distraction from what was happening at home.

It helped that Aaron was a good-looking kid. Tall, lanky, and filled with that unpredictable teenage angst that made him broody and unpredictable. He cruised around Loveless on a battered old dirt bike I'd helped him fix up and had just enough disdain for authority to place him squarely in the "bad boy" category. Teenage girls found him irresistible, adults found him uncontrollable. He was a quiet kid, often lost in his own thoughts, but he never had a problem opening up to me. I didn't think there was a single secret between the two of us.

I was wrong. Very wrong.

I had no idea Aaron was cutting himself. Leaving scars on his body to hide the ones that refused to heal on his heart.

I never guessed his wild mood swings were anything more than puberty and testosterone taking their toll on a growing boy.

I didn't have a clue my younger brother was silently suffering, internally agonized every single day. His mind was telling him lies, twisting him up and dragging him down... His mind was his worst enemy.

Unfortunately, I also never in a million years would have predicted that Aaron and I would end up falling in love with the same girl. Or that she would be the reason our relationship fell apart.

Kody Lawton had been the center of Aaron's entire world for as long as I could remember. The Lawton kids, Aaron, and I were all friends growing up, but Aaron and Kody were thick as thieves, almost inseparable, and forever up to no good. Kody was a troublemaker, a fearless rebel, a sassy, smart-mouthed brat my brother thought the sun rose and set upon. But it wasn't until Kody's mother passed away, right as she was about to enter high school, that my brother realized his feelings for her went deeper than friendship.

I'd graduated by then. But before I left for college, I asked Kody's brother Case to keep an eye on Aaron. I knew the death of their mother had hit all the Lawton kids hard. Kody was devastated, and Aaron, even though he was emotionally fragile at best, was whom she leaned on the hardest. Almost overnight they went from best friends to something so much more. For Aaron there was no other girl besides Kody Lawton; and for Kody, Aaron was always going to be the first boy she loved. He adored every untamed inch of her and made her feel accepted and special.

By that time I was too far away—too engrossed in finally finding some freedom and getting to live life on my own terms—to recognize the warning signs. But I did know the way Aaron loved Kody wasn't unlike the way my parents loved and hated one another. There was zero balance, and little mattered in my brother's life other than the girl who had stolen his heart. They got engaged the day before Kody graduated high school and started living together soon after. To the casual observer it appeared to be young love flourishing, but on the inside things were a mess. Aaron needed help, but he was too scared to admit it to anyone...even Kody.

She was the one who called me in the middle of the night, crying because she found Aaron huddled in a ball on the bathroom floor slashing his skin. Kody was the one who texted me in a panic when Aaron was so listless and drained he wouldn't leave bed for days and days at a time. She begged me to come home. Pleaded with me to fix my brother, but I blew her off over and over again. I didn't know how to fix Aaron, didn't have the tools required to convince him that he needed help. I tried to comfort him from afar, but I kept my distance. I was selfish, and deep down, I was jealous. Because even with all the turmoil and upheaval Aaron brought into her life, Kody adored him.

She loved him like it was the only thing keeping him alive, and maybe it was.

When I did go home to check on Aaron, it felt like visiting a stranger. I was no longer his hero. In fact, I had somehow morphed into his number one enemy. Aaron acted as if he hated me for leaving, for living my own life. It made me wonder if he knew how hard I worked to be a good brother while also hiding my attraction to his one true love. Time and distance didn't matter. I was in love with Kody Lawton, and I hated myself for it.

I didn't want to find her beautiful and vivacious. I didn't want to be charmed by her sharp tongue and no-holds-barred attitude...but I was. On my first visit back home, it suddenly hit me that Kody was no longer a little girl but a young woman. One who was strong, savvy, and endlessly patient with my baby brother. I'd spent my entire life taking care of Aaron, and I couldn't deny that I was envious of the kindness and compassion she was always showing him. It was an inconvenient crush, especially since I couldn't distance myself from her emotionally, since we were tied together by our growing concern for Aaron. The many late-night phone calls talking to her about how much she worried about my little brother often left me hurting—for her and for Aaron—but I suffered through, caught between my love for her and my love for him. What other option did I have?

Knowing my feelings for Kody could never go anywhere, I focused on my life away from Loveless. I graduated college, joined the United States Border Patrol, and eventually worked my way up the ranks of law enforcement until I had the opportunity to apply to be a Texas Ranger. I dated here and there. Told myself I couldn't settle down because my career came first, because I didn't have enough to offer anyone just yet. The truth was, my whole heart was never invested in finding a new love. It was stuck back home, hung up on my little brother's soon-to-be wife. I distanced myself more and more from Aaron and Kody, not knowing Aaron's issues were escalating. I eventually forced myself to stop taking Kody's calls. I needed to make a clean break, but I never stopped caring about my brother. I called him directly, urged him to get help, and begged him to see someone about his emotional unpredictability. I tried to connect with him, urged him to get out of Loveless, to experience the world outside his own dark, suffocating bubble. I even tried to get my parents involved, but as usual, they were more concerned about themselves than about their children. No matter what I said, or how hard I tried, Aaron brushed off my concern and assured me he would be fine. And I selfishly believed him. It was easier for me that way.

But he wasn't fine. Far from it.

A couple of days before Aaron and Kody's wedding, I received a call from Case Lawton, who was working as a deputy for the Loveless sheriff's office. Someone who lived next to Aaron and Kody had called in a disturbance complaint. When Case got to the house, Aaron was nowhere to be found. The small home they rented was trashed, and Kody was sporting a fat lip and a sprained wrist. Case was pissed at the state his sister was in, and even angrier that my brother was missing and unable to answer for his actions. I was tangled up in an extremely complicated sex trafficking case at the border, so I hadn't planned on making it home for the wedding as it was. Not that Aaron had bothered to invite me. The distance between us felt insurmountable at that point.

Nevertheless, I knew there was no way Aaron would hurt Kody if he still had some sort of control over his condition and his actions. Worried in a way that could not be ignored,

I called in someone to take over my case and went back to Loveless for the first time in years.

I found Kody before I found Aaron.

Seeing her tearstained, pale, horrified face did something to me. All the emotions I'd learned to deny did their best to burst free. I couldn't resist pulling her into my arms, and couldn't stop myself from touching my lips to her forehead and apologizing for not taking better care of my brother...and her. As far back as I could recall, it was the first time in my life I felt like an absolute failure. It was also the first time Kody went out of her way to get so close to me. It was an accidental, or playful touch but one with purpose and filled with emotion, making it a memory seared in my mind forever.

I will also never forget the look of absolute betrayal and utter devastation on Aaron's face when he suddenly appeared. I let go of Kody like her skin had suddenly sprouted thorns and stepped toward my brother.

"It takes *her* getting hurt for you to give a shit, Hill? What about me? I hurt all the time and you pretend like I don't exist." He was gaunt, his eyes wild, and far too pale. He was shaking uncontrollably, and his arms were covered in thin white scars. He no longer looked like the sullen kid who'd followed me around, but like a man with too many demons to count.

Kody pushed me out of the way and reached for him, pleading, "Aaron, we have to talk about this. You have to let me help you. I love you, but we can't go on like this."

My brother lunged for his pretty, blond fiancée. His hands were curled into claws and I swear that if I hadn't gotten between the two of them, he would have wrapped those shaking hands around Kody's neck.

I put a hand on the center of Aaron's too-thin chest and

pushed him back. I didn't expect for him to land on his ass, or for him to immediately leap to his feet and bolt for his motorcycle. He'd long since upgraded from the dirt bike to a sporty foreign design that was faster than lightning. He disappeared before I could get my scattered thoughts together. Kody's hand locked on my arm as she yanked me around to face her.

"You have to find him, Hill. If something happens to him..." She trailed off, head shaking sadly from side to side. "I'll never forgive myself."

I nodded absently. I wasn't going to let anything happen to my little brother, and it was high time I forced him to get the help he so obviously needed. I was a pro at pushing my feelings aside and would continue to push them aside so that Aaron and Kody could have the happy-ever-after they'd always dreamed of. Well, as long as Case didn't murder my brother for roughing Kody up before I got my hands on him.

I made Kody text me a list of places Aaron might go and asked Case to help me track down anyone he might be close to. But it was almost as if Aaron had disappeared into thin air. Kody called every fifteen minutes asking for updates, even though she was turning Loveless upside down trying to find him as well. The last place to look was my parents' house. I couldn't fathom why Aaron would go to the one place he'd spent so much time trying to escape, but sure enough, his bike was parked out front when I arrived.

It took my mother forever to answer the door, and she blinked at me like she didn't recognize me.

"Hill? What are you doing here? I thought you were skipping the wedding." She narrowed her eyes at me. "Aaron was devastated when you told him you weren't coming."

I highly doubted Aaron had shared anything so personal with her, but the well-aimed barb did sting.

"Is he here?" I maneuvered around her before she could answer me.

"Yes, he is. He showed up a few hours ago. He said he was spending the night here while Kody was at her bachelorette party." She reached for my arm, but I was already running up the stairs, headed toward the small bedroom Aaron and I had shared growing up.

I smelled it before I reached the door.

The coppery, metallic scent of blood. There had to be a lot of it for the smell to be as strong as it was. Freaking out, I kicked the door open and rushed into the room, my heart immediately sinking into my stomach.

Aaron was slumped on the floor, head bent, sitting in a pool of blood. There was an empty bottle of pills on the floor near his legs, and a bloodstained razor blade abandoned on his lap. I had no idea how long he'd been there, but it had been long enough for his skin to turn a faint gray and for his breath to be incredibly shallow and ragged.

Shouting Aaron's name, I fumbled with my phone to call 911.

I pulled a pillow off the bed, wrenching the case off so I could wrap it around Aaron's wrist. I did the same on the other side, barking orders into the phone.

The commotion brought my parents into the room. My mother immediately burst into hysterics, while my father stood stoically.

Refusing to take my focus off Aaron, I growled, "Neither one of you bothered to check on him. He showed up out of the blue, looking like a zombie, and you left him alone. How can you be so thoughtless? So careless." It was a pointless statement. Neither one had ever had the first clue what to do with either of us. Aaron and I had always been bit players in their theatrics.

My heart skipped a beat when Aaron's eyelids suddenly fluttered. He looked at me through hazy eyes and tried to say my name. Everything inside me froze, then burst into panicked flames a moment later when he stopped breathing.

Time ceased to exist.

I have no idea how long I sat on the floor of my childhood room after the paramedics left. I stayed there covered in my brother's blood, crying, agonizing over all the mistakes I'd made.

Eventually I pulled myself together enough to drag myself to Aaron and Kody's so I could tell her what had happened.

Only I didn't get a chance to get a word out. Kody took one look at the dried blood on my hands and clothes and collapsed into a boneless heap of grief at my feet. I wanted to comfort her, to tell her we could face this together. No one loved Aaron the way we did. No one understood him the way we did.

Twenty-two years old was way too young to die.

However, as soon as she was able to speak through the tears and violent shakes, she smacked me in the face and sobbed. "This is all your fault. All he *ever* wanted was to make you proud. He did everything he could for your time and attention. Why weren't you here when he needed you most?" Her voice was cold as she told me flatly, "I never want to see you again, Hill Gamble. I hate you."

I had never known words had the power to wound so deeply. Their impact stole my breath and turned my heart inside out. My knees went weak, and it took every ounce of self-control I had to stay upright. If she'd thrown a punch it would've hurt less.

I watched her heart break right in front of my eyes. I could see that she believed I'd let Aaron down. And I didn't disagree with her. All I could do was walk away, because I knew that if I touched her she really would try to hit me.

After the funeral I silently promised I would stay out of her life and move on with my own, but it was hard. I still cared about her more than I should. So I kept our contact to a minimum when I was back in town. It was easier for both of us, and eventually things between us got less hostile and awkward. We matured and learned a little more about ourselves, and a whole lot about bipolar disorder and depression. We grieved separately, but the pain over losing Aaron tied us together indefinitely. I buried myself in work and became even more of a chronic bachelor, and Kody, she committed to being an even bigger pain in the ass than she already was. I resigned myself to the fact that we would never be friends, but we would always be almost family.

It was my unfortunate luck that fate was determined to have love, death, and Kody Lawton pulling my strings for an eternity. I'd never wanted to tell her she'd lost someone else. Never planned on being the guy who continually trampled her heart. But here I was, so many years later, getting ready to explain to all the Lawton kids their father had been murdered. And it was my job to find his killer.

CHAPTER 1

∞

KODY

I skipped over the first stage of grief after hearing about my father's murder and went right to stage two . . . anger. I had little use for denial, bargaining, depression, or acceptance. The last time I'd lost someone I loved, I'd suffered through all the stages and still ended up feeling lost and alone. This time I knew anger served me well. Anger kept me going. Anger was a comfortable, familiar feeling when it came to my father. It was an emotion I had no problem embracing when word of his murder made its way around the small town where our family had lived for generations.

Loveless was a tight-knit community, one with a lot of secrets and a history of looking the other way when bad things happened. However, those bad things were forever discussed in hushed voices after church and in low tones in passing. The fact that Conrad Lawton, my father and the town's sheriff for many, many years, had been found murdered just outside of Austin was bound to be the only topic of conversation for months to come. The thought made my skin crawl and fueled the silent fury I'd been clinging to since I'd gotten the news my father was no longer around to be a major thorn in my side.

But my anger was complicated. I didn't want false sympathy from the folks who whispered when my back was turned that the old man had deserved it. I didn't want to hear the gossip about how Conrad Lawton's notorious misdeeds had finally caught up to him. I didn't want to see the curious looks weighing and judging how I and my two older brothers were dealing with the loss of the man who had demeaned and emotionally terrorized us throughout our childhoods. If I showed any sort of regret, the busybodies and rumor mill would start churning out theories that tales of our tortured youth had been exaggerated. Yet if I wasn't sad enough that Conrad had met a violent, brutal end, I would never hear the end of *that*.

People in Loveless already questioned my motives, sanity, and capability. If they decided I wasn't responding appropriately to the news that my father had been murdered, I would become more of an outcast than I already was. And my bar, which was barely staying afloat as it was, would undoubtedly go under.

So anger it was. We were old friends anyway.

I lived it. I breathed it. I spread it around to the point that my brothers and everyone else who loved me were walking on eggshells, not knowing when or where I was going to explode next. I was unpredictable and volatile. Which wasn't exactly new, but I'd gotten better at controlling myself as I'd gotten older. But after I got the news about my father, all my old, uncontrollable impulses seemed to roar back to life, and I was back to being a prickly, easily provoked mess. It didn't help matters that the person who came bearing the bad news was the *last* person on the planet I wanted to hear such devastating words from.

It felt like every single time my disorderly world was finally righting itself, Hill Gamble and his stupidly handsome face would show up and send everything spiraling chaotically out of control once again. I'd started to associate Hill with everything bad that had ever happened in my life, so naturally, where my unchecked anger was concerned, Hill always seemed to end up being the main target. Since he'd delivered the news of my father's death, I had a hard time recalling a single second when I wasn't absolutely furious at the gorgeous Texas Ranger. It should've been exhausting, but the warmth from the rage Hill sent swirling through my blood was the only heat I felt anymore.

I grew up in a house mostly devoid of love and affection. Sure, my mother doted on me and my brothers, but she did it knowing she would have to bear the brunt of my father's temper anytime he thought she was being too soft on us. There was no love between them, only fear and impossible expectations. My older brothers, Crew and Case, loved me unconditionally, but sometimes that love leaned into their being overprotective and overbearing. Especially after our mother died. I'd had to push them back in order to breathe, in order to live any kind of life of my own. Their love was tinted with several shades of pain and remorse and always came with the dark shadows of our shared history. It was ultimately a cold, and slightly savage, upbringing.

When I was a teenager, I thought I'd finally found the kind of love that would chase away the chill that always lingered inside my heart. When Hill and Aaron Gamble came crashing into my life, they brought the sun and the promise of better days ahead with them. Hill reminded me of my oldest brother, Case. He was serious, steady, focused on the future and a life outside of Loveless, Texas. He was reserved and thoughtful, always watching and evaluating the world around him. He was also too beautiful for words. I literally had a hard time forming words around him. Luckily, Aaron Gamble was far easier to approach. He was quiet, moody, and sweet enough to give a girl cavities. He was the first boy who made me smile. He was the first boy brave enough to be my friend. Neither my brothers' warnings nor my father's ugly reputation was enough to scare Aaron off when I started to cling to him. He was my first best friend, and later on my first love. I wanted to believe the warmth he brought into my life, and into my heart, would last forever, but things were never that simple. It wasn't until I promised to marry Aaron Gamble that I realized exactly how cold I could be on the inside.

Loving him forced my icy heart to thaw. Losing him froze it right back up and shattered the brittle block of ice into a million pieces. I was certain I was never going to be warm again. I got used to living with a frigid void inside my chest. I tolerated the constant chill embedding itself deep into my bones.

From the start I never knew what to do with the heat Hill brought with him when he crept into my thoughts. I would never be as angry at anyone as I was at my father, but Hill owned the second spot on my shit list. I refused to think about *why* he was the only person who always managed to make me forget I was frozen solid on the inside. It bugged me to no end that Hill didn't even have to try to make me feel like my insides were kindling for an impending inferno. He just *did*.

I hated that he was the one who was going to be investigating my father's death, not because he wasn't good at his job, but because it meant he was going to be hanging around

Loveless and my family far more than I was comfortable with. It grated on my last nerve that with little effort, Hill still managed to make my whole world spin off its axis. I didn't want him to have that kind of power in my life. I didn't want *anyone* to have that effect on me.

But Hill always had. And still did…

When he calmly and coolly informed me that my dad was dead, I hit him.

Was it fair? No.

Did he deserve it? Absolutely not.

But once again, I couldn't control my anger around him. It was the second time Hill was the one explaining to me that a man who had fundamentally changed me had been taken away. Since there was no way to take out my frustration on my father, Hill was the target. Just like he'd been when Aaron died.

He absorbed my misguided anger, my misplaced blame, in the exact same way he had when Aaron passed away. The man was a sponge. Taking all my insults and hastily hurled venom without saying a word, never letting a drop of my ugly, unjust emotions spill out and infect the other people in our lives. He suffered in silence, but I could see the way my words affected him in those sharp silver eyes of his.

"Whose job is it to cut the bartender off when they've had too much to drink?" The question laden with sarcasm came from across the bar.

There was only one person not related to me who was daring enough to talk to me that way. I had a zero-bullshit policy in my bar. I didn't take lip or attitude from anyone. My regulars knew not to mess with me, but this particular regular was braver than most and one of the few actual friends I had. My brothers hated that I was close with Shot Caldwell. Mostly because he was the president of the local outlaw motorcycle club, but also because I could confide in Shot in a way I couldn't with them.

This bar was my safe haven. It was also the only place I was comfortable enough to let my guard down. I'd spent the last few days in a fog, trying to figure out how I really felt about Conrad Lawton being gone and what his death meant to me, all while drinking myself into a stupor. Both my brothers had been by to check up on me, but I wasn't in the mood to be coddled or critiqued. I chased both Crew and Case away with my bad temper and continued with my bender, trying to drink myself numb.

It wasn't a surprise the gruff, good-looking biker had made it a point to come check on me. Not that I was in any mood to entertain his concern.

"No one is cutting me off. Not if they want to keep their job." All of my staff had been giving me a wide berth the last couple of days. I couldn't blame them. I'd snapped at each and every single one of them for no reason. I was going to have to apologize once I came back to my senses.

Unfazed by my snarky warning, he reached a tattooed hand across the bar and snagged the rocks glass with a double shot of Crown Royal from my hand. I made a clumsy grab for my stolen drink but ended up watching as the dark-haired man tossed it back and finished it in one swallow. He wiped his mouth with the back of the same tattooed hand and lifted a dark eyebrow in my direction.

If I were sober, I would've cut him down to size with a witty retort or ordered him out of my bar. Since I'd been three sheets to the wind for a solid two days and was hovering on the precipice of a sharp emotional drop-off, it was all I could do not to burst into tears or climb across the bar and strangle him.

Letting my wild temper loose on Shot wasn't a good idea. He was a good friend and had been, at one point, something more, but he wasn't Hill Gamble. He wouldn't just accept my anger. Shot's temper ran almost as hot as mine. He was one of the few people in my life I had a healthy dose of respect for. I went out of my way to avoid pushing his buttons most days.

I rubbed my tired, dry eyes with the heels of my palms and sucked in a painful breath.

"I'm not in the mood to play with you, Shot." My voice was raspy and the words burned on their way out. Maybe I'd had enough to drink. It wasn't like the booze was helping me forget the look on Hill's face when he told me my father was dead, or the sharp pain in my chest at the thought of my father no longer being around. It didn't matter how much I'd disliked him.

"You in the mood to tell me what's going on with your old man's case? Or how about you tell me what you need, Trouble. You know I've got your back, no matter what." He tapped his fingers on the bar and pushed the empty glass in my direction. I poured him another shot on autopilot and nearly lost my balance when I pushed it back in his direction.

I sighed and rubbed at the painful throb in the center of my chest.

"You need to get gone. I'm sure one of my brothers will be in to try and bully me into going to one of their houses so they can hover over me until the funeral. I don't have it in me to play referee between you and them right now. You know if I need anything I'll let you know." And I would. Shot was often the person I turned to when I was at my wits' end. He never judged me. His unwavering acceptance was something I had fallen back on time and time again. It was also the reason I refused to cut him out of my life, even though my brothers and even my worthless father had pushed for me to do just that.

"You want me to look into who might be behind his death?" His midnight-colored eyebrows lifted again. "You know I can go places and ask questions your brother and the boys in blue can't."

My father had been the sheriff in Loveless for a very long time. The job had passed into Case's hands after my oldest brother did his best to bring our father down. Dad had been a dirty cop. Corrupt as hell. The man had left a list of enemies a mile long, and it wouldn't surprise me if Shot was among them. It was no secret the biker and my father never saw eye to eye on what was best for the town, or for me. If I hadn't known down to my soul that Shot would never do anything to intentionally hurt me, I might have wondered exactly what he was up to the night my father was killed. Fortunately, I knew his fondness for me ran much deeper than most people, including my family, believed.

"Stay away from it, Shot." With the Rangers on the case, nothing good could come of it. Especially considering Shot wasn't involved in exactly legal activities. "Case won't be involved in the investigation. He can't be. They called in the Texas Rangers to investigate since Dad was a cop." And because there were more than a handful of people who'd wanted him dead. I came by my knack for making enemies naturally, it seemed.

I poured Shot another drink and got myself a glass of water. I was dizzy and starting to feel a little queasy now that I wasn't pickling my insides with liquor.

Shot blew out a low whistle and gave his head a little shake. He was a good-looking guy in a dark and danger-ous way. I was drawn to his rebellious attitude and his complete disregard for what anyone else happened to think about him. He reminded me of the man Aaron might have grown into if he'd given himself the chance. There were moments when I wished I'd tried harder to make things between me and Shot into something more than they were, but even his good looks and our easy compatibility weren't enough to melt all the frost gathered inside my soft, secret places. Shot never warmed me up from the inside out, even though he tried his best. I always wondered how badly I'd hurt him when I let our brief romance fizzle out. It made me feel uneasy when I thought about it... but that might have been the booze.

"The Rangers, huh?" He finished the drink with a grimace and knocked the wooden bar top with his knuckles. "They bring in the guy who's friends with your brother?"

I gulped down another glass of water and wavered on my feet a little. "How did you know that?"

Shot flashed a grin. "Makes sense. He's familiar with your old man's history and knows both the family and this town."

I nodded, my head flopping around sloppily. "He's assisting. He can't be lead on the case since he knew Dad personally." I swallowed again and rubbed my forehead. "Case trusts Hill. He believes he'll find whoever killed our dad."

Shot leaned on the bar and stared at me intently. "What do *you* believe, Kody? Do you think he'll find whoever took out your old man? Do you think the justice system is going to work in your favor if he does? Conrad had some of the dirtiest hands I've ever seen. You sure whoever killed your dad is going to get what's coming to them, or will everyone view them as having done Loveless a favor by taking out the trash?"

My breath locked in my lungs. I knew Shot was just being brutally honest, but hearing him voice some of my biggest fears when I was in no place to hear them made my knees turn to water and sent my head throbbing painfully.

I reached out to brace myself on the bar. I heard one of the bartenders ask if I was all right and heard Shot call my name. My vision blurred out for a second, but not before I caught sight of a very tall man wearing a gray Stetson coming through the front door of my bar. Considering this was Texas, a man in a cowboy hat was nothing to write home about. But when that man practically glowed in a golden light of perfection and wore a shiny badge that was impossible to miss, people stopped and took notice. I couldn't miss him, because suddenly, in all the places where I had been ice-cold, a fire burned.

Scowling, I let go of the bar and tried to wave both my employee and Shot off when they made sounds of concern. It was a mistake. Too little sleep, too much to drink, too much stress and sadness all combined with gravity sent me toppling to the ground. My knees hit the hardwood behind the bar with a jolt and I heard loud exclamations burst out from somewhere above my head.

I put both my hands on my chest and tried to hold my pounding heart in place. I wasn't used to the normally frozen thing getting such a hefty workout. I closed my eyes and ordered myself to get it together. I tried to remember I was angry...and that was it. Anger was all I was going to allow myself to feel.

Suddenly a pair of boots hit the floor in front of me. Not the heavy black motorcycle boots I knew Shot wore, but an expensive pair of gray ostrich boots that matched the Stetson on Hill's head when he walked through the door.

When I pried my eyes open they met a soft, dove-gray gaze filled with simmering concern and something else. Something I'd always been terrified to acknowledge.

A warm hand landed on my shoulder and I felt the brush of his thumb along the side of my neck.

"Are you okay, Kody?" The question was quiet and asked in a familiar drawl.

That damn heat he brought with him crept across my skin, and before I could stop myself I burst into tears, crying for the first time since I'd learned my father was dead.

CHAPTER 2

❧

HILL

Kody Lawton and I had a lot of unspoken rules between the two of us.

She knew I was going to call her occasionally to check on her, but she never called me back.

I wasn't supposed to show up unannounced. She claimed she needed to brace herself to deal with me.

We never mentioned Aaron or the past. At least not to one another, which was sad. We were the only two people in the world who knew just how great my younger brother had been...and just how troubled.

I wasn't supposed to ask her brothers how she was doing, and I certainly wasn't supposed to worry about her. I broke those rules all the time. And I was breaking the "don't show up unannounced" one right now.

It was common knowledge to those close to the Lawton kids that their sweet and calculating mother had wanted each of them to have an out. When she was gone, she'd made sure her kids all had a way to escape the tyrannical rule of Conrad

Lawton. They were supposed to use the money she left them for college, to get out of Loveless, but none of them had. Kody went into the bar business. Crew bought a stallion and a small plot of land to raise horses on. And Case, well, he lost all of his to his first wife in a bitter divorce, so he had the least to show for it. None of them had managed to escape this small town, or the long shadow their father cast.

I'd never been inside the bar Kody purchased with the money she received after her mother passed away. I knew neither of her brothers liked the fact that she'd opened the rowdy dive bar on the outskirts of the city. I also knew Case frequently paid visits to the bar in his official capacity as sheriff in order to break up fights and keep the peace. But I always thought the occupation suited her. Kody was never cut out for the nine-to-five life. I was also proud of her for making her own way in the world. She called her own shots, played by her own rules, and lived her life on her own terms, which was ultimately the best revenge when it came to showing Conrad Lawton he'd never managed to quell his daughter's fighting spirit.

I tried to convince myself I was breaking Kody's firm no–unannounced visits rule because of the murder investigation. She was the only Lawton sibling I'd yet to interview. Case had informed me she was having a rough time coming to terms with Conrad's murder, and I was far from her favorite person on a good day. He'd warned I wasn't in for a warm reception, but I had a job to do. And frankly, I needed to see how Kody was doing with my own two eyes. I'd never managed to convince myself that worrying about her wasn't my problem.

I'd assured my partner in the investigation I would handle all the interviews and questioning of the people in Loveless and those closest to the former sheriff. It was likely that the

people in this close-knit community would be more open
with me, since I had roots here. Not that it was any kind of
secret that Conrad Lawton had courted trouble for years and
was due for a reckoning of some sort. But I needed to narrow down who might have information about what Conrad
had been doing in Austin, and who had gained the most from
his death. This case had a lot riding on it, not only because
Conrad was so well known in the area, but also because Case
wasn't going to let me breathe until he had answers he was
satisfied with. I didn't want to let him down.

I also needed to give Kody answers. I would never forgive myself for not being more aware and proactive with
Aaron when his mental state started to decline. To this day
I wondered if I could have saved him, if I could have done
something to prevent the agony he'd put Kody through. Her
relationship with her father had been complicated and often
ugly, but she was going to need closure, and the only way
she could get there was for the person, or persons, responsible for Conrad's murder to be brought to justice. It was the
least I could do for her.

As I stood in the doorway, I took in the bar. It had a
decent-size crowd considering it was a Tuesday night. The
mix of patrons was as eclectic as the decor. It was all very
Kody. The building was an old barn, so the interior had a
lot of western elements, including old whiskey barrels for tables. But there were also brightly colored artwork and neon
signs brightening up the space. Instead of the big lighting
fixture in the middle of the bar being made out of antlers
or wrought iron, it was an intricate mix of colorful glass
beads. The whole thing was very country and western meets
boho chic. The people filling up the seats were mostly Loveless residents. They included the guys gathered near the
bar dressed in leather, covered in tattoos, and rocking club

colors. The Sons of Sorrow motorcycle club had moved into the hill country on the outskirts of Loveless years after I'd left town. Now their flashy bikes and intimidating presence were as commonplace as pickup trucks and horse trailers. It made sense they liked Kody's bar since it was between town and their clubhouse, but I didn't have to like it.

I *really* didn't like the way the large, dark-haired man leaning across the bar looked at Kody. I knew from Case that Palmer "Shot" Caldwell was the current president of the Texas branch of the club. I'd taken it upon myself to learn more about the man when he ended up in the middle of the last case that brought me home. Shot was a former marine, a decorated sniper, the son of the founder of the club, and someone Kody was inexplicably close to. Everything about her relationship with the biker set my teeth on edge and had me wanting to make a claim I had no right to stake.

As I stepped forward, the heavy wooden door shut with a bang behind me and drew the eyes of the people sitting closest to me. I saw a couple of looks of recognition, and some people purposely looking away. I nodded and touched the tip of my finger to the brim of my hat in a fairly polite greeting. These people weren't my friends. No one in this town had tried to help my brother when he needed it the most, and I would never forget that. Unlike the Lawton kids, I'd left Loveless in the rearview mirror and planned on never looking back. All of my worst memories were here. So was the one person I wanted more than anything but knew I could never have.

Under the dim bar lights, I met Kody's gaze across the room. She looked pale. Her wild mane of multicolored blond hair was messier than usual, and she appeared to be swaying slightly every time she let go of her hold on the bar. Her eyes narrowed, and at first I thought she was giving me a dirty look, but the next instant her entire body lurched and she toppled over, listing to the side and disappearing behind the wide, long bar.

My heart stopped for a split second and I had to bite my tongue to stop from screaming her name. I often found myself in dangerous, deadly situations due to my job, but I couldn't recall a single instance when I had been as terrified as I was in that moment Kody went down.

I heard the biker shout her name and was vaguely aware of him kicking back his bar stool as he jumped to his feet. I was moving before I had time to weigh whether it was a good idea. Kody didn't like when I was in her space. She'd told me she hated me and ordered me to leave her alone on more than one occasion, but none of that stopped me from reaching the bar in record time. It didn't slow me down when I planted a hand near the biker's empty drink and vaulted over the top of the bar.

I landed on the floor in front of Kody, ignoring the shouts and commotion coming from all directions. I waved off the bartender hovering uncertainly behind Kody and quietly asked, "Are you okay, Kody?"

The answer was obvious when, instead of biting my head off, her big, bright-green eyes flooded with tears and her shoulders started to shake with silent sobs. Having people burst into tears as I was talking to them was a pretty common occurrence considering my line of work. I'd developed a natural immunity to tears of all kinds. But not to Kody's. Hearing her breath catch and watching her eyelashes get spiky and damp as she struggled to hold the tears back made my heart twist painfully in my chest.

"Is there someplace quiet I can take her for a few minutes?" I asked the question over Kody's head as the bartender pointed to a set of stairs that led to what I assumed used to be the hayloft when the building was an actual barn.

"Her office is up there." The bartender twisted a white towel between his hands and muttered, "Is she going to be all right?"

Kody gave her head a shake, but a sob broke free. Before she could fight me, or push me away, I reached for her, wrapping her up in my arms and lifting her off the scarred, battered floor.

"She'll be fine. It's been a rough few days." I was responding to the bartender, but I was also telling Kody she would be okay. I was sure she'd heard it from her family and the people who loved her, but I wanted her to hear it from me as well. She would be fine even if I had to move heaven and earth to make it happen.

I stood, Kody clutched in my arms, her wet face turned toward my shoulder. I was getting ready to move toward the stairs when I heard a thump and was suddenly face-to-face with a pissed-off biker.

Shot was an inch or two shorter than I was, but he was bulkier. If it came to throwing fists there was no guarantee I would be the victor. And I figured the badge I carried would do little to deter the man if he felt I was standing in his way.

"Put her down. I'll take care of her." His voice was low and void of any kind of accent. His eyes were dark and unwavering. A tic jumped in his cheek, indicating he didn't like my being close to Kody any more than I liked his easy familiarity with her.

I lifted an eyebrow and regarded him from under the brim of my Stetson. The guy was fearless, I'd give him that. But he didn't know me, or the history I had with the difficult woman in my arms. If he did, he would've known the only way I was handing her off to anyone else was if they pried her out of my grasp as I lay dying.

"Move." I inclined my chin and narrowed my eyes. "If you don't get out of my way I'll arrest you and the rest of your minions for interfering with an active investigation."

It was a stretch, but I wasn't above playing dirty if I had to.

The biker let out a snort and took a threatening step toward me. "Did you just call my brothers 'minions'?" The words were bitten out on a growl, and the rising tension could be felt throughout the bar.

The bartender cleared his throat and shifted uneasily behind the biker. "Umm...guys...take it down a notch. This place can get out of hand when Kody's not on her game. If you start something while she's out of it, the troublemakers might burn the place to the ground, and that would piss her off even more."

I wasn't about to hand Kody over to the tattooed thug, and it was obvious he wasn't going to let me get past him without a fight. I was weighing my options, trying to find a solution that would lead to the least amount of bloodshed—and property damage—when Kody suddenly let out a loud sniff and lifted her head from where it had been tucked next to the side of my neck.

Eyes the color of a ripe Granny Smith apple gazed up at me. They were partly questioning, with a good dose of desperation clouding them. She sniffed loudly and turned her head to look at the angry biker.

"Back down, Shot. I'm not in the mood to bail you and your crew out of jail tonight." Her voice sounded strained, and her words were slightly slurred. Her gaze shot up to mine but flickered away just as quickly. "Put me down, Hill. You're both overreacting."

The biker and I growled in protest almost simultaneously, but we both complied with her wishes. I didn't want to let her go. It was the closest we'd been in years, and I reveled in the way she seemed to fit perfectly in my arms. Every single place where we touched felt like it was alive with an electric kind of fire. My skin sizzled and my heart raced. Letting go of her was one of the hardest things I'd ever had to do, so I held on just a little bit longer, until she squirmed to be put down.

I gently put Kody back on her feet, keeping a hand low on her spine as she swayed slightly, leaning against me for balance. Shot took a step to the side and crossed his arms over his chest as he continued to glare at both of us. I ignored the big biker's ire because a sudden chill skated across my skin where it had lost contact with Kody. There was a void, a consuming emptiness that only she could fill. Too bad she had zero interest in the spot inside my heart reserved solely for her.

"Shut the bar down early, Trouble. Go home and take a day off. You can't keep going this way, and you know it." The effortless way the other man issued the concerned commands had my back teeth grinding together so hard I was worried they might crack.

Kody weakly waved a hand in his direction and heaved a deep sigh. "Don't worry about me. I already have two older brothers who think they can order me around. I don't need another. Be good, and keep your boys in line. I'm sure Agent Gamble is here for business and nothing else, right?"

The implication was clear. I better have a damn good reason for breaking her hallowed rules.

I shrugged a shoulder. "I do need a couple minutes of your time." For the investigation and for my own peace of mind.

Kody nodded, but the movement seemed uncoordinated

and sloppy. I agreed with the biker. She needed to leave work for a few days and get some rest. However, I knew that if I suggested such a thing, she'd freeze me out and ignore the advice out of pure spite. One surefire way to get Kody Lawton not to do something was to tell her she should be doing it.

Very subtly Kody reached for my arm. I felt her fingers curl into the fabric of my shirt, showing a vulnerability she rarely allowed. The mere fact she hadn't kicked me out of her precious bar was telling. She was putting on a brave face, but on the inside she was crumbling, finally reaching her breaking point and having to face her emotions.

I shifted my weight just enough to block her small movement from view. These people didn't need to smell blood in the water. If there was even a hint that Kody was no longer in control of the unpredictable crowd, all hell would break loose.

"Let's go to your office. I promise to keep things quick and get out of your hair as fast as possible." It was on the tip of my tongue to apologize for showing up unannounced when she was so clearly at the end of her already frayed rope, but I didn't. There was no doubt in my mind that she would've ordered me to stay far, far away from her if she had known I was coming. Then I would have been denied the opportunity to touch her, to hold her, to take care of her in some small way.

It would have been obvious to anyone who knew her that Kody was not in her typical fighting form when she quietly nodded and wordlessly allowed me to guide her to the stairs. The woman wasn't one to capitulate to anyone, let alone someone she openly despised.

The wooden stairs creaked under my boots, but once the intricate barn-style door slid shut, all the sound from the noisy bar down below went quiet. The office was set up more like a living room than a stuffy place for a boss to work. There was a huge teal couch against one wall, a television mounted to the one across from it, and a wooden coffee table complete with fashion magazines and abandoned soda cans on the surface. There was also a desk covered in scattered paperwork and a fancy computer setup in one corner. Once again the design seemed to be a perfect reflection of Kody's personality. She was determined to do things in her own way. She ran her business with little to no help from anyone else, but she was still a free-spirited, dynamic soul. She liked color and comfort, even while she was being the boss.

As soon as we were inside the room, Kody released my arm and stumbled her way to the couch. She threw herself onto the soft-looking fabric with an exaggerated groan and covered her eyes with her arm. Her feet landed on the coffee table with a thud as she whispered, "I don't want to talk to you about my father, Hill. I don't want to talk to you about anything, but especially not him."

I took my hat off and used my free hand to pull at my flattened hair. "You're going to have to talk to me about him in an official capacity sooner or later. Right now I think you need to get some rest and sober up. You're no use to my investigation in the state you're in now."

She let out a bitter-sounding laugh and peeked at me from underneath the bend of her arm. Her eyes were bloodshot and her skin pale.

"You hated my father, Hill. Everyone did. Is there anyone who isn't a possible suspect in his murder? Are you actually going to try and find the person responsible for killing him, or are you going to say good riddance like everyone else is whispering behind my back?"

I sighed and shoved my hat back on my head with more

force than necessary. This woman...she made me want to
hug her and strangle her.

"I'm going to do my job. A victim is a victim regardless
of who they were or the things they did while they were
alive. My personal feelings don't have any place in finding
the truth."

She snorted again and re-covered her eyes. "Aren't you a
little close to this case? Do you really think you can remain
impartial?" She sounded doubtful. The same way my boss
had when I insisted on assisting in the official investigation.

"I'm not the person in charge of the actual investigation.
I'm just lending a hand because everyone knows people in
this town are more likely to open up to a local. No matter
what you think, I'm here to help." It felt like I was forever
trying to prove myself to her. I wouldn't be the one making
the arrest or getting the Lawtons justice, but I could help the
process along. I was damn good at my job.

I waited for her rebuttal or another snarky reply, but after
a few seconds of silence and no response, I called her name
and got nothing back.

A moment later a soft snore drifted up from where she
was sprawled.

"Did you really fall asleep in the middle of our argument?" I asked the question to her still form, biting back
a grin as her head suddenly flopped heavily to the side. "I
guess you're going to get the last word no matter what, aren't
you?"

Shaking my head, I found a colorful blanket folded up
next to the couch and grabbed it. I debated taking her boots
off for her, but decided against it. She obviously needed
the rest, and I didn't want to do anything that might wake
her up. Tucking the blanket up around her chin, I took a
minute to look at her face. Even in her sleep there was a

tiny furrow between her brows. She was always scowling at me, always looking at me with scorn and disdain. There were times I honestly felt I would give up a limb just to see her smile at me.

When she was a teenager, I was drawn to her when I realized she immediately saw through all of Aaron's swagger and defense mechanisms. She saw the kind, soft heart he harbored. I admired the way she remained unfailing Kody in the face of constant criticism. She never hid how hard her life was or how she was hurting, and that unfiltered honesty was beautiful. Especially when I was avoiding my own hardships at home like my life depended on it...Unfortunately, I fell into using the same tactics when things starting going south with Aaron.

When we got older, it was her unwavering loyalty, and the way her love never changed, no matter what my brother did, that hit my heart hardest. Kody never once gave up on Aaron, or even thought about walking away, even when it was pretty clear he was going to hurt her. I loved her love, and was envious none of it was meant for me. I'd never had anyone I could rely on like that. Never had anyone accept me wholeheartedly, faults and all.

It was a question that had haunted me to this day. What would it be like to be loved by Kody Lawton?

Rubbing a hand over my face, I turned and headed back the way I had come. There would be time to talk to her about the investigation when she was in better shape. Right now I wanted to make sure her bar stayed in one piece so she didn't find another reason to hate me when she woke up.

CHAPTER 3

∞

KODY

I wasn't sure what time it was when I finally pried my eyes open, but the sun from one of the windows was hitting me in the face. I could hear my staff clinking glassware together downstairs, letting me know the day shift crew had already shown up. I stretched my arms above my head, which was pounding. My eyes were scratchy and my neck was stiff. My stomach was angry at being empty, but also felt like it would revolt if I dared put anything inside it. All in all, it was a hangover for the record books. Thankfully I was no longer dizzy, and some of the hollow emptiness I'd been trying to fill with whiskey had dissipated. I was still mad my father had gone and gotten himself killed. And I was still pissed Hill was right back in the middle of the tragedy taking over my life.

Thinking of Hill caused my entire body to freeze for a split second, right before it melted. In the haze of my horrendous hangover, I didn't have a clear recollection of how I'd ended up all cuddly in my office. But I did remember Hill vaulting over the bar like some kind of hero in an old Western. I also clearly recalled him picking me up off the floor like I was something precious and dear to him, and the tender way he held me to his chest. I purposely kept my distance from Hill because I was always terrified I would no longer be able to keep my complicated feelings secret if he put his hands on me. It was easy to let him see the anger and resentment that I used as a shield when there was space between us. But if he got too close...I didn't doubt he would see right through me—see the undeniable attraction I felt toward him, and the guilt that accompanied it.

I would never be able to forgive myself for having had feelings for Hill since I was young. I might have fallen in love with his brother, but that didn't stop my heart from being torn in two the entire time it was happening. When I was young and naive, I was drawn to the goodness in Hill Gamble. He was a stand-up guy. One who wouldn't be swayed from doing the right thing. He didn't put on an act the way Case did, didn't rebel and create chaos the way I did. He simply owned his lot in life and made the best out of a bad situation. I was envious of his ability to compartmentalize the different parts of his life. Later I was jealous because he actually made it out of Loveless and left everyone and everything who'd hurt him behind. I wished I'd been brave enough to do the same.

When I got older, and things with Aaron became impossible to handle on my own, Hill was the one I leaned on the most. I was terrified of losing the boy I loved, and his brother was the only one who understood that blinding, consuming fear. At least I thought Hill understood. Slowly, over months and eventually years, I realized Hill was pulling away, shutting both me and Aaron out. He wasn't as quick to answer my middle-of-the-night calls, and his patience for the mess Aaron was making of both our lives eventually ran out. Aaron was slipping through my fingers, but Hill effectively cut me out of his life, and the empty ache of that abandonment still echoed inside my chest.

Grumbling about the sunlight nearly blinding me, and the reawakened feelings for one sexy Texas Ranger, I stumbled to my desk and found a hairbrush and small bottle of mouthwash I kept stashed there for emergencies. Last night wasn't the first night I'd crashed on the couch in my office, but it was the first time I'd allowed anyone else into my private space... the first time in a very long time that someone else had put me to bed. I didn't like the shiver that shot down my spine when I recalled how gently Hill had handled me. My memories were a little foggy still, but I definitely remembered him covering me with a blanket. Considering how argumentative I was whenever I was around him, I had no idea how Hill continually treated me with consideration and kindness, instead of acting like I was the enemy.

Once I was as freshened up as I could be, I headed back down the creaky stairs and into the mostly empty bar. We were open for lunch, but the place never really picked up until happy hour. It was the day shift employees' job to keep the bar cleaned and stocked, not that the young, single mother I kept on for sympathy more than her skill did a great job at either. Which was why I was stunned at the sight of my bar sparkling and so clean it looked like a different place. The worn floors gleamed. The bar top was spotless. The glassware sparkled, and each and every table was polished. The place hadn't looked this good since I first bought it and renovated it.

Looking around with wide eyes, I grabbed a glass of water and asked Shelby, the daytime waitress, "Did you do all this? I'm impressed."

Shelby was perpetually stressed and constantly on her phone during her shift. She was in an endless custody battle with her ex-husband, and half the time I ended up taking care of the customers during her shift, since she was so distracted. We'd gone to high school together and had been acquaintances. When Aaron died, Shelby was one of the few people in town who offered genuine condolences and asked what she could do for me. So when she came begging for a job after her husband left her high and dry, I couldn't help but hire her. I sometimes regretted my decision, but I couldn't bring myself to fire her. Looking at the bar, I wondered if she'd finally managed to turn things around.

The other woman shook her head, platinum blond ponytail swinging. "No way. This wasn't me. Apparently your friend stayed until close last night and asked the staff to stay until the bar was spick-and-span. Lorenzo was pissed, but stuck around anyway. I woke up to a string of very angry text messages."

Lorenzo was my lead bartender. He'd been working crazy hours the last few days while I drank away my feelings. I relied on him a lot and could only imagine the way he would have gotten riled up when asked to stay late and clean by someone who wasn't me.

I gulped down a second glass of water and made my way over to the back of the bar, where I kept a bottle of Tylenol. Tossing a couple of pills back, I shook my head a little. "I'll call Lorenzo and apologize on behalf of Shot. I'm sure he was just trying to help out."

Sometimes Shot forgot we were nothing more than friends and business associates. There were times he tended to be even more protective than my older brothers. This wouldn't be the first time I'd had to warn the biker to back off. Lord only knew if he was ever going to listen.

"Oh. It wasn't Shot. It was the guy in the gray Stetson. Lorenzo said he had a badge, but didn't think he was with the sheriff's office. I think the only reason Lorenzo stayed was because the guy was in law enforcement." Shelby smiled brightly as the door to the bar opened. "You know how he is."

The smile dimmed some when she realized the customer was Case's live-in girlfriend, Aspen Barlow. Aspen often popped in for lunch with her clients. She was an attorney, and I think she liked that the low-key, rustic feel of the bar often put the people she was representing at ease. Aspen was originally from Chicago and had never really managed to blend in with the locals. My bar was familiar and neutral territory. Plus, we'd become very good friends ever since she'd managed to mellow my uptight, stern oldest brother. She was a perfect match for Case, no matter how different the two of them were. She was also a wonderful addition to our fractured, disjointed family. She'd done nothing but try to pull us all together from the start.

I waved at the tiny, dark-haired attorney and glanced at Shelby from the corner of my eye. "You're telling me Hill stayed until close last night and made the night shift crew clean the bar before they could go home?" I couldn't keep the surprise out of my tone.

Shelby shrugged a shoulder and pulled her cell phone out of the pocket of the short, black apron she was wearing. "He didn't *make* them stay. He asked, and no one felt like they could say no. He's intimidating, and has a badge." She rolled her eyes as if that explained everything. "I need to go see if the burger for the guy in the back corner is done. I'm sure Lorenzo sent you a bunch of angry messages as well. He's the one to ask about what happened last night." She nodded at Aspen, who had to hop in an adorable way to get her small frame up onto one of the bar stools. "Good afternoon, Counselor."

Aspen smiled politely in return and watched as Shelby disappeared in the direction of the kitchen. "Is she still mad that I'm now representing her husband in their custody dispute?"

That was the thing about small towns. Everyone seemed to be connected in one way or another, and there was very little anyone could do to escape the ties that bound us all together... and to the past.

"Probably. She's mad about anything that has to do with that guy." I rubbed a hand over my face and blinked my tired eyes. "Did Case ask you to come check up on me? I told him I would be fine, and I am." Well, I was my own version of fine, which meant I was holding it together, barely.

"Her ex isn't a bad guy, and he really does have the best interest of the kids in mind. I think after enough time passes, Shelby will recognize that." Aspen lifted a midnight-colored eyebrow and tapped her fingers on the polished bar top. "As for your brother, no, he didn't ask me to check up on you. He didn't need to. Everyone's been worried sick about you since you bolted from Hayes's graduation party. I had a client cancel on me this afternoon, so I decided I would come and see how you were doing for myself." She cocked her head to the side and gave me a slight grin. "I'm also starving, so I figured I would kill two birds with one stone."

"You want your usual?" When she nodded, I turned and entered it into the point of sale system and poured her a glass of sweet tea. "How is Hayes doing?"

I loved my nephew. It was totally unfair that the news of my father's murder had come at the same time my family was supposed to be celebrating Hayes. He'd recently graduated high school and was moving out of state to play college football. There were a lot of big changes happening in the kid's life, and he shouldn't have to deal with the upheaval my father's death was bound to bring when his future was so bright.

Aspen shifted on the bar stool and traced the drops of moisture on the outside of her glass with her finger.

"I think Hayes is doing the same as the rest of you are. Confused and sad. Angry that something like this happened, even if it isn't a huge surprise. Men like your father." She shook her head. "Nothing in their lives is peaceful. Including the way they leave us."

I rested my forearms on the opposite side of the bar and nodded. "My dad always knew how to ruin any good memory we were trying to make. We're supposed to be sending Hayes off in style and planning a wedding, now we're all focused on a murder and planning a funeral instead."

Our middle sibling, Crew, had recently gotten engaged. His fiancée was another city girl like Aspen. Della was a classy chick with expensive taste. I liked her—I wasn't as close to her as I was to Aspen, but she made my restless, troubled brother happy. I wanted them to have the wedding of their dreams and not have their happy moment overshadowed by my father. Even in death he was spreading darkness over our lives, and frankly, I was sick of it.

Shelby swung by the bar, dropping Aspen's plate with her favorite fried chicken sandwich on the wood in front of her. She swished away without another word, causing both Aspen and me to roll our eyes at her behavior.

"I helped Case get everything together to lay your father to rest properly as soon as Hill and the Rangers release his body. No matter how awful Conrad was, all of you need to say goodbye and get some kind of closure. We need to do it as a family, united, the same way you survived him when you were growing up." She gave me a curious look as she picked up a French fry. "Hill mentioned he still hadn't had a chance to talk to you yet and that he was going to come by the bar. Have you seen him?"

I let my head drop so that I was staring at the floor. "He came by last night. I wasn't exactly up to answering questions." Or behaving like a civil human being. "I'll track him down sooner or later." If he had been the one behind the spring-cleaning of the bar, I owed him a thank-you. If I managed to get the words out.

Even when I had good intentions where Hill was concerned, they always seemed to go south on me. It was always hard for me to see around the sense of betrayal Hill made me feel and the blame I couldn't seem to let go of. If he hadn't shut me out, if he hadn't turned a blind eye, maybe things would have ended differently . . . for all of us.

Aspen took a big bite of her fried chicken sandwich and let out a little hum of delight. She always ordered the same thing when she came in. I had no idea how she stayed as petite as she did.

Aspen gave me a knowing look. "I don't blame you for not wanting to answer his questions. When he got involved in my case, he didn't hold back when he was questioning me and brought some very painful truths from my past to light. He doesn't play nice, which is what makes him good at his job. I can also see why he's one of the few people Case trusts and believes in. They're very similar in some ways."

Case and Aspen had fallen in love during a tumultuous few weeks when my brother had been trying to figure out who wanted the sassy lawyer dead. After many bullets and more bloodshed than I wanted to remember, Aspen's own mother was revealed as the mastermind behind all the attempts on her daughter's life. The Rangers sent Hill in to help Case manage the media coverage of the case, and to help track down the shooter who'd put the entire town at risk while trying to take Aspen out. It didn't surprise me in the least that Hill had grilled Aspen and dug up every secret she had. He was ruthless when it came to getting to the truth of a matter, which was why it was a bitter pill to swallow that he hadn't been able to see what was happening with Aaron. He managed to dig up everyone else's secrets, but had remained oblivious to how serious his younger brother's struggles were.

I knocked my knuckles on the bar and muttered, "They're alike in all the annoying ways. They're both bossy, demanding, stubborn, and always think they know best. Anyway, I need to make some calls and smooth out ruffled feathers. Hill took it upon himself to wrangle my staff into deep cleaning this place late last night." I made sure my annoyance at his high-handedness was clear in my tone.

Aspen chuckled behind the napkin she was using to wipe her mouth. "I was wondering why everything was so spotless." She arched her dark eyebrows in my direction. "I think it's kind of sweet he went out of his way to help out. He obviously knows how much this place means to you, and I know he's been working crazy hours on your father's case. He was probably exhausted, but he stuck around to make sure your bar was taken care of, and in even better shape than you left it."

Scowling at her, I pointed at her now-empty plate. "You wanna pay in cash or put that on a card?"

She grinned at me as she reached for her purse. I typically never charged her, even though she always insisted on paying and leaving a tip, no matter how bad the service she'd received. "So you're making me pay today?"

I snorted and crossed my arms over my chest. "When you're Team Hill, you pay full price."

Aspen tossed her head back and let out a loud laugh. I snatched her credit card up as she pushed it across the bar in my direction. "I'm always Team Lawton, but I can appreciate a good play by the opposing team."

I sniffed in annoyance, reaching for the phone when it started to ring, more to save my pounding head from this discussion than from any real desire to speak to whoever was on the other end.

"Thanks for calling the Barn. What can I do for you?" I popped a hip on the back bar and tossed Aspen her credit card. She deftly caught it in one hand as I put the receipt in front of her and slammed down a ballpoint pen with more force than necessary. I ignored her quiet chuckle and turned my attention to the phone call.

"Hey. I've been calling your cell phone for hours. Why aren't you picking up?" Shot's deep growl thundered through the earpiece and made my head throb. I squinted against a bolt of pain and tightened my grip on the receiver.

"I must've left it on silent. It's upstairs somewhere, and I'm down in the bar... working." I was snippier than I usually was with him, but I didn't like the accusation in his voice. "I would've called you back as soon as I saw your missed call. You know that."

He swore, and I could easily picture the familiar scowl that usually accompanied the frustrated sound.

"I was worried about you. Didn't care for that cop butting in last night." Shot grunted and quietly reminded me, "You need to be careful who you let get close, Kody."

I sighed and rubbed at my forehead. It was a warning I didn't need. It was hard enough to keep Case and Crew out of my business dealings with Shot and the Sons of Sorrow. I knew Case had his suspicions as to how exactly I kept my bar up and running, but he never asked. It was for the best he didn't pry. He would be greatly disappointed at what he found. As for Hill, there would be no forgiveness and no looking the other way if all my complicated ties to Shot Caldwell and his club came to light.

"The last person you need to be worried about getting too close to me is Hill Gamble." There was too much history and hurt between the two of us for the gap to ever be bridged. "He's investigating my father's murder. He's Case's friend. He's Aaron's older brother. That's all he's ever been to me." I refused to see him as anything else, even if my heart complained loudly at the thought.

"He wasn't acting like a friend of the family when he jumped over that bar last night. Just tread lightly, Trouble. You have a knack for finding yourself in bad situations. And take better care of yourself, since you won't let anyone else do it."

The biker hung up without saying goodbye, which was probably a good thing. It was on the tip of my tongue to tell him Hill had taken care of me and I hadn't fought it at all. I swore under my breath and let my head fall forward until my forehead banged on the bar in front of me.

Depending on Hill would end badly, so I refused to do it. I'd already learned that lesson the hard way...

CHAPTER 4

∞

HILL

I'm releasing the body to the family so they can move forward with the funeral. Have you managed to pin down the daughter to ask her if she might have any idea why Lawton was in Austin? Nobody seems to know why he was there or who he was meeting."

Johnny Hearst was a good cop. Younger than me by several years, he'd moved up the ranks and made it into the Rangers with single-minded focus and determination. I didn't mind him being the lead on Conrad's case, because he listened when I had something to add in my role as unofficial consultant. Unfortunately, I was coming up empty when it came to prying anything out of the locals or the Lawton siblings. It was clear the former sheriff had been up to something in his last few days, but figuring out what it was seemed impossible.

Running on minimal sleep and fueled by high-octane coffee, I swore I could feel my bones vibrating under my skin when Hearst brought up Kody. Dragging my hands over my face, I cringed at the sandpapery texture of the scruff.

"No. But Kody isn't the type to be pinned down, regardless of the situation. I was holding out hope that if I gave her some space and didn't pressure her, she would come find me." Wishful thinking. She was so used to running in the opposite direction when she saw me coming, I should've known I would never be able to stop chasing her.

"I need a formal statement from her on file. Both the brothers stated all the kids had limited contact with the old man for various reasons. I'd like the sister to confirm." Hearst leaned back in his metal chair until it was balanced on two legs. He kicked his sneakered feet up onto the table, and I watched out of the corner of my eye as he rocked back and forth.

"If you fall and crack your head open, it's your own fault."

The other man shot me a grin, and I silently wondered if there had ever been a moment in my life where I'd been as laid back and carefree as the young investigator. I always felt like I'd been born into the middle of an emotional tornado and the winds had never stopped.

"We know Conrad was comfortable here in Loveless. He had his own little network, had people scared enough of him to look the other way, no matter what he was up to. It doesn't make any sense to take his schemes outside of town. His reputation doesn't stretch very far past the Loveless city limits, which makes me think someone or something forced him to make the trip to Austin. I don't think he went because he wanted to."

I nodded in agreement, squeezing my eyes closed and rubbing the corners. We'd already gone over Conrad's property with a fine-toothed comb. There was nothing indicating why he had suddenly taken off for Austin, and no sign he'd been forced out of his home. Conrad was a big, mean son of a bitch. There weren't many folks I could think of who had been capable of making the man do something he didn't want to do. This case was one dead end after another, which was frustrating to me as a cop, but even more so to me as a friend of the grieving family.

"Do you want me to take a crack at the daughter? I know the two of you have history. She might be more amenable to speaking to someone without any ties to her past." Suddenly the legs of the chair hit the floor with a loud thump, and the younger man leaned forward. "I'd like to know exactly how tied into the local motorcycle club she is. That bar of hers was barely hanging on a couple of years ago, then boom, the club shows up in town and her bar is back in the black. Something tells me the timing of those two events isn't a coincidence."

No, it probably wasn't. Especially seeing how protective and proprietary the leader of the club was when it came to Kody. I'd never expected her to stop living her life after Aaron died. In fact, I'd spent many sleepless nights wondering if the relentless infatuation I had for the problematic youngest Lawton would finally go away if she settled down and found someone who made her smile. She deserved a relationship that made her happy. She had earned the kind of love that came without expectations and restrictions. I could never exactly figure out why it felt like my ability to find my own happiness was directly linked to her ability to find hers.

Groaning and climbing to my feet, I stretched my arms above my head and winced as my spine popped loudly. I was getting too old to burn the candle at both ends. Constantly moving so I could outrun my mistakes and the ghosts of my past was starting to take its toll. I was tired in a way that felt suffocating. No amount of sleep was going to chase away the lethargy.

"Give me another day. I'll track her down tonight and see if I can get her to talk. She might give me some leeway knowing we're releasing the body and they can move forward with the funeral. Conrad was a grade-A jerk. He was a bully and a dirty cop. But he still managed to bring some really good kids into the world." I tried to keep my voice even, but I could hear the exhausted, strained rasp in it.

I didn't know if Kody had calmed down since I'd last seen her a few days ago, but I knew for certain my heart couldn't handle seeing her so close to the edge again. I'd been giving her time, but I'd also needed the distance so I didn't do something I knew I would instantly regret. I was careful to stay on the other side of the invisible lines Kody drew between us, but I couldn't stop myself from crossing them when her hurt was visible and screaming out for someone, anyone, to do something about it.

"One day, Gamble. I'm tired of banging my head against the wall. We've given the family more leeway than we would anyone else in the same situation, since you vouched for them, and because of Case Lawton's spotless service record. But something's gotta shake loose, or this case is going to go cold."

Hearst clapped a hand on my shoulder and reached for the open laptop on the table in front of him.

"I think we're done for the day. I'll update the bosses. Get some rest. You look like shit." He bumped his shoulder against mine and walked out the door, sneakers squeaking on the linoleum floor. I'd never worked with a Ranger who didn't wear cowboy boots or polished dress shoes. Hearst was a different breed, but he got the job done.

And he was observant as hell. I'd learned a long time ago

how to hide the soul-deep exhaustion I lived with. It annoyed me that the younger man had no problem seeing through the iron mask I'd worn since I was a child.

I swore under my breath, but the swearing almost immediately turned into a yawn. I blinked bleary eyes and headed out of the small conference room. The motel where Hearst and I were staying had let us take it over and turn it into a makeshift office. The motel was by no means five-star accommodations, but it wasn't the worst place I'd had to stay during an extended investigation. And even if it had been roach infested and falling down around me, it would still be preferable to the house where I'd grown up and where my brother had died. I avoided my parents' place like the plague. I wish I could say the same for the memories tied to that house. Those were never too far out of reach.

I nodded absently to a couple as I walked down the hallway, and lifted a hand to rub my eyes again. It would be nice if I could catch a quick nap, but if I wanted to try to catch Kody before the bar got busy, then I needed to shake off the dull fog hanging around my head and get my ass in gear. I had my doubts I was going to be welcome, especially after the way I'd strongly "encouraged" her staff to stay late and clean the bar. But I had a job to do, and giving Kody her space was no longer an option.

I drew to a sudden stop, nearly tripping over my own feet, when the profile of a figure sitting against the closed door of my motel room came into sight. While I wasn't currently undercover, I wasn't exactly making the fact that I was back in Loveless known. The last thing I needed was for either of my parents to show up and make a scene. The only people who should know my exact whereabouts were the employees of the motel, Hearst, and Case. The long legs, unruly blond hair, and sharp green eyes glaring up at me didn't belong to any of those people. I had no idea why Kody was sitting on the floor in front of my room, but I couldn't stop the way my heart lurched at the sight of her.

I took the last few steps required to get to her. I braced myself against the railing dividing the walkway from the parking lot and crossed my arms over my chest while we silently sized one another up. She looked a lot better than she had the other night, but any of the softness she'd shown toward me while drunk was long gone. Her green gaze was as hard as glass, and her pretty, plush mouth was pulled into a tight frown.

"I promised Case I would come and talk to you before the funeral, so here I am. Let's get this over with." Kody pushed back against the door to my room and levered herself up to her feet.

She was wearing a pair of coral-colored jeans and a bright teal top. It should've looked garish and tacky, but for some reason, all the bizarre color combinations she favored worked for her.

"Case tell you which room was mine?" That would make me feel a lot better than the motel staff randomly giving out the information to anyone who asked for it.

Kody nodded. "He called and told me one of the reasons we haven't been able to lay Dad to rest yet is because you haven't interviewed the whole family. I was properly chastised for being a brat and told him I would come talk to you as soon as I could get away from the bar." She crossed her arms over her chest and tapped the toe of her silver cowboy boot on the concrete. "I don't have all night."

I dipped my chin down and tried to hide a yawn. "Give me five minutes. We can meet at the diner across the parking lot. I'll buy you a cup of coffee and keep the questions quick."

Kody gave a stiff nod and moved to the side so I had a clear path to the door. I pushed off the railing I was leaning against and sucked in a surprised breath when the ground tilted suddenly and my vision went blurry for a split second. I must've lost my footing, because the next thing I knew, small, soft hands were braced on the center of my chest, keeping me from toppling over. I blinked rapidly and slowly gave my head a shake.

Instinctively I wrapped my fingers around Kody's slim wrist and tried to ignore the way her pulse was racing underneath my touch.

I cleared my throat and took a step back. "Sorry about that. I guess I need that cup of coffee more than I realized." I let go of her when she gave her hand a little tug.

Kody's gold-tinted eyebrows furrowed into a frown as she cocked her head to the side. "When was the last time you slept? And I don't mean a nap."

I shrugged and fished the key to the room out of my pocket. "I'm in the middle of an investigation. I left in the middle of another one to come back to Loveless. I'm used to the lack of sleep. Strong coffee is enough to shake most of the cobwebs loose." I grunted when I felt her slight weight bounce off my back as I stopped once I was inside the room. Surprised, I looked at her over my shoulder.

Kody pushed her wild fall of hair out of her face and scowled up at me. "How effective can you be at your job if you're practically a zombie? Everyone is all up in my face because I'm not taking great care of myself lately, but what about you? You look terrible."

It wasn't exactly what I wanted to hear, but considering she was the second person in an hour to say the exact same thing, maybe I needed to do a better job at hiding just how run down I was.

"I'm going to change my shirt and splash some water on my face. After we talk, I'll come back and try and catch a couple hours of sleep." I figured she would run the other way when I told her I was about to start taking my clothes off. Instead she wordlessly followed me into the small motel room, reminding me that all she ever saw me as was Aaron's older brother and that she was still reckless when it came to her own safety. She shouldn't be following *any* man into his motel room so casually, even one she'd known forever.

Throwing my Stetson on the bed, I tried not to react as she closed the door behind her. Sighing, I made sure there was nothing she shouldn't see relating to her father's case lying around and started to unbutton my shirt. I'd had the patterned button-up on for over twenty-four hours and was ready for a T-shirt and a cold beer.

"Neither Case or Crew have any idea why your old man might've been in Austin the night he was killed. I know he tended to have a soft spot for you. You have any clue why he made the trip out of the blue?" I pulled the tails of the shirt out from my jeans and crouched down to dig through my open suitcase for a somewhat clean tee. Once I found a black one I shook the button-up loose and stood so I could make the switch. "Conrad wasn't much of a sharer, didn't like anyone in his business, but maybe he mentioned something in passing, something he wouldn't say to the boys?"

The question was greeted with absolute silence. Surprised, since she was in such a hurry and was never particularly fond of my company, I turned to see what had her distracted, and was stunned to find her staring at me wide eyed, her mouth slightly open.

Lifting an eyebrow, I asked, "Kody, did you hear me?"

Her mouth snapped shut with an audible click, and even in the dim light of the room I could see her blush. "Uh. What are you doing?" She waved a hand at my exposed chest and slammed her eyes closed. "Put a shirt on."

I snorted and pulled the black cotton over my head. "I told you, I needed to change."

She cleared her throat loudly. "Oh...umm...I wasn't listening. I'll just meet you over at the diner."

She turned on her heel and fled the room so fast I was surprised she didn't leave a cartoon-style cloud of smoke behind her.

That woman was difficult to figure out. Grumbling at the never-ending day and the embarrassment of nearly falling in front of Kody, I brushed my teeth, washed my face, and debated running a razor over the stubble that was fast approaching full-on beard status. Deciding it was better not to keep Kody waiting, I snatched my hat back up, hurried out the door, and made my way to the diner.

The place hadn't changed at all since I'd left town. In fact, I was pretty sure the waitress and the guy slinging hash in the back were the exact same people who had run the joint when I would bring Aaron here after a football game for milkshakes. I was greeted by name as soon as I stepped in the door, and had no problem picking Kody out of the crowd. She was ensconced in a booth toward the back, a carafe of coffee already on the table in front of her, as well as a plate of onion rings.

She looked up at me from under her thick lashes when I slid into the seat across from her, the vinyl squeaking under my weight. I was tired, but even so, I didn't miss the flush on Kody's face or the way her bright eyes briefly skimmed over my now-cotton-covered chest. Before I could let my mind run wild with possibilities, her expression shifted to one of practiced indifference as she pushed a dark coffee mug in my direction.

"Dad didn't have a soft spot for me. He just knew if he treated me half as badly as he treated Crew and Case, they would make his life miserable. They protected me my whole life, from Dad, from everyone." Her voice was low, and her eyes darted around nervously. I realized she was worried about her personal business getting around town. I could have kicked myself. I should have known the last place she would want to talk about this was in a crowded place filled with locals. The diner was a breeding ground for gossip.

I nodded to let her know I understood and matched my tone to hers. "When was the last time you spoke with Conrad?"

Her lips twitched into a frown as she wrapped her hands around the mug in front of her. It was close to a hundred degrees outside, but she looked like she was freezing.

"I went to see him the week before Hayes's graduation party. I told him he better do something to congratulate his only grandchild before Hayes left Loveless for college. I told him he should try and make an appearance at the party, or at the very least send a card stuffed with money. I warned him that Case would completely disown him if he didn't acknowledge Hayes's accomplishments." She lifted a shoulder and let it fall. "He told me to mind my own business. Actually, he seemed like he was in a pretty big rush to get rid of me that afternoon. Usually, when I made the trip out to the farm, he tried to rope me into stocking his fridge and cleaning the place from top to bottom." A sneer crossed her delicate features. "You know, woman's work he wouldn't lower himself to do."

"Did he mention if he was expecting visitors, or if he was planning on going somewhere?" Conrad's body had been found the night before Hayes's graduation party. As far as we knew, Kody was the last person who had seen the former sheriff alive.

"He didn't say anything, really. He bitched about Hayes going out of state for school, but that was nothing new. He was one of those people who thought there is no life worth living outside of Texas. If you left Loveless, you were a traitor in my dad's eyes. If he was having problems, he wasn't the type to share. He always thought he knew best and could handle anything without help." She rolled her eyes and slumped down in the booth. "He always had more enemies than he did friends."

I arched an eyebrow. "Runs in the family."

I grunted when the toe of her boot connected with my shin under the table. Bending down to rub the spot she kicked, I asked, "Anything else about that visit stick out in your mind? I've got to be honest, we aren't having much luck tracking down anyone who knows Conrad's whereabouts before the murder. Your dad was good at playing it close to the vest." When cops had secrets they wanted to keep buried, it was damn near impossible to dig them up without help.

She rapped her nails on the side of her mug as she thought. After a moment she shook her head. "There really was nothing special about that day. Dad was surly and rude as usual. The farm and the house looked the same. He pissed me off without trying, just like always. I was so mad at him I almost took out one of his neighbors on my way back into town."

I set my mug down and leaned on the table. It was a long, barren dirt road leading up into the hill country to get to Conrad's property. There was very little traffic out there, so the fact that Kody had passed someone was highly suspicious.

"Was it a neighbor you recognized? A vehicle you were

familiar with?" It was a battle to keep the spark of excitement out of my voice. I didn't want to pressure her. The memory was fleeting, and if she lost it right after finding it, I was back at square one.

Kody pushed her coffee away and lifted a hand to push her hair back. Her eyes narrowed slightly, and I felt her watching me intently. "No. I don't know his neighbors. He always kept us isolated out there on the farm. You know he didn't like anyone poking their nose in what was going on in our house. He had an image to keep up. I just figured it was a neighbor since they were out on the road in the middle of the day."

I nodded and asked, "Do you remember what kind of car it was? Did it have Texas plates?"

She stiffened, and I could practically see the wheels turning in her head. She closed her eyes briefly, and I watched as her breathing slowed as she concentrated. A moment later she brought her hand up to her mouth so she could tug on her lower lip.

"It was a Tesla. I remember thinking I was going to be super screwed if I did run into it, because there's no way I could afford to fix something like that. I can't remember if it had Texas plates or not, but I do think I remember the driver being a woman." Her eyes flew open and her palms hit the table, rattling both our cups and the untouched silverware. "I can guarantee none of Dad's neighbors drive a Tesla. No one in Loveless does. A car like that would stick out like a sore thumb. People would be talking about it for days."

She banged her hands on the table again and came up out of her seat. "Are you telling me I drove past my father's killer and didn't even know it?"

Heads started to turn in our direction, and the waitress stopped near our table to ask if we needed anything. I offered up a weak grin and reached out to forcibly pull Kody back into her seat. "We're fine. You can drop the bill anytime."

Once she was gone and Kody's breathing evened out some, I leaned across the table and told her, "You don't know that. We don't know who was in the car, or if the car was even headed to the farm. But you finally gave me a lead to follow. If a car like that came through Loveless, someone was bound to notice." It was also certain it would pop up on any one of the surveillance cameras from the shops around Main Street, which would lead to a license plate number. "No use getting worked up until we have the facts."

She growled at me and jumped to her feet. Her palms landed on the table once again, making some of the leftover coffee in her mug splash out.

"Don't tell me not to get worked up. I'm not a heartless robot like you, Gamble." With a flip of her hair, she stormed out of the booth, leaving practically everyone in the diner staring after her. Whispers erupted as soon as she was gone, and I had to bite back a groan as attention turned my way.

She knew how to make an exit, that was for sure.

The accusation that I was cold and unfeeling was nothing new. But the words hurt, and they weren't true. I was far from being a robot where she was concerned. I felt too much. Always had, and that was the problem. The more she'd called me, heartbroken and heartsick, when Aaron was going through a rough patch, the more I'd struggled to keep my feelings for her in check. I wanted to protect her. I wanted to save her—from my own brother, which made me feel guilty as hell. I had to pull back before I did something I regretted. Yet here I was, years later, and I still wanted to save her, to hold her and tell her that everything would be fine. I wanted to chase after her, wanted to explain *why* I'd behaved the way I had all those years ago, but I stayed in the booth, my eyes focused on my cooling coffee as my heart twisted itself into painful knots. She still blamed me for what had happened to Aaron, and I couldn't dispute that I should've handled things better. Maybe if I'd been honest about how I felt, she would have understood why I had to walk away. But it was too late to turn back the clock, no matter how desperately I wanted a do-over.

Slurping down the rest of my coffee and smothering a yawn, I told myself I could sleep as soon as I tracked down any footage I could find of the Tesla. Hearst was going to be pissed when I called and told him we were looking at another all-nighter.

CHAPTER 5

∞

KODY

The weather on the day of my father's funeral was beautiful. Bright and sunny. Hot as hell, without a cloud in the sky. It was almost as if the universe were mocking what was supposed to be a sad and somber occasion. The temperature also made dressing in head-to-toe black seem ridiculous, so I refused to do it. I didn't own very many dark, single-colored garments as it was, and there was no way I was making a special trip into Austin to buy something new in order to say goodbye to the man who had ruined my mother's life and made mine a living hell. I settled on a long maxi dress striped with varying shades of gray and light pink. It wasn't as in your face as most of my outfit choices, but it was still vibrant enough that I didn't feel like I was toning it down to appease the busybodies and curious onlookers who were bound to show up for the viewing.

Initially I'd planned on skipping everything having to do with the funeral. None of us really understood his instructions to leave him for eternity on the land that had been in the family for generations, instead of next to my mother in the cemetery on the outskirts of town. I, for one, was grateful my mother's eternal peace wasn't going to be tainted by her having to share her resting place with the man who had made her living days miserable. But I also wanted nothing to do with the property if my father was going to be forever a part of it. Last night over too many beers, Crew drunkenly mentioned that was probably the old man's plan all along. None of us had any good memories of that farmhouse, and we wouldn't want to keep it in the family. But how could we get rid of the property if our father was buried there? The man was always just as clever as he was mean.

However, when Aspen mentioned how hard the day was going to be for my brothers, especially Case, I realized I couldn't take the easy way out. Case and Crew had both gone above and beyond for me whenever I needed them to. I couldn't justify hiding away from the rest of the world because I was uncomfortable with my feelings. Luckily I wasn't required to play hostess. Della and Aspen slipped into the role easily enough, having no trouble faking smiles and accepting false condolences from the nosy townsfolk. My brothers picked the women they were going to spend the rest of their lives with wisely. When the time came for Della and Aspen to protect their men from the outside world, they didn't hesitate to do it. If those loving, protective instincts had been operating under any other circumstances, I would have been glowing with pride. Our family was growing in the best way possible.

"Here." I looked up at Crew when he suddenly appeared by my side. While both my brothers resembled our father, Crew had an easy, careless charm about him that he'd clearly inherited from our mother. He was the risk-taker in the family. The daredevil. And up until he met Della, he was the one I worried about the most. Now he was the one worrying about me as he stealthily passed me a small silver flask he'd had hidden somewhere in his dark gray blazer. I wasn't the only one who refused to wear black.

"Thanks." I took a sneaky drink and tried not to wheeze as the whiskey burned on the way down. Clearly our father's funeral didn't call for the top-shelf stuff.

"Who are you waiting for?" Crew took the flask back and tucked it away just as Aspen cut us a curious look from where she was hovering protectively between Case and Hayes.

Surprised, I turned to face him. "What? I'm not waiting for anyone. I'm anxious for this circus to be over so we can get on with our lives."

Crew arched a black eyebrow as he tucked his thumbs in the front pockets of his dark jeans. "Oh. I noticed you keep looking at the door whenever someone new comes in. I thought maybe you invited that biker friend of yours."

I blinked in surprise. "Shot? No. I didn't ask him to come today." He'd offered, but I'd firmly told him not to come. While riling my brothers up and pushing all their buttons was typically my most favorite pastime, I knew today wasn't the time for it. There were too many emotions running high and far too much testosterone in any scenario involving Shot and my brothers for it to end well. "I guess I'm wondering if Hill is going to show up. Don't you think that would be part of his investigation? Doesn't the killer usually show up at the victim's funeral?"

Crew gave a soft chuckle so as not to be overheard by the lurking busybodies. "I think that only happens on TV. He's been out of town for the last few days. I know Case has been trying to track him down for info on the investigation, but it's been tricky. Sounds like he's working himself to the bone on this case."

I reached up to tug on my lower lip, remembered the way he'd stumbled and fallen in front of his motel the last time I saw him. Hill had had dark circles under his eyes and looked like he hadn't slept a full night in weeks. Somehow concern for his well-being got buried under the alarm at my visceral reaction to seeing him shirtless in the small room. The sight of all those rippling back muscles, some marred by very visible and prominent scars, made me forget why I'd absently followed him into the room in the first place. He'd always been too good-looking for my peace of mind, and now I knew for certain it wasn't just his artistically carved face, with its sharp cheekbones and chiseled jaw, that had aged with superiority. The man was built like a professional athlete, big, strong, and capable. I had to get out of that room before I did something stupid like reach out and touch him.

"He's not going to do anyone any good if he burns out at the start of this case." I muttered the words, which were eerily similar to the ones he'd said to me when he picked me up off the floor of the bar.

Crew shrugged. "Hill's been doing this a long time. I'm sure he knows his own limits. I know all of us will breathe a little easier once he has a suspect. Case is practically chomping at the bit to butt in. You know it's got to be torture for him to watch the investigation from the sidelines."

I nodded absently in agreement as the door to the viewing room opened once again. I didn't realize I was holding my breath until an unknown woman entered the space. I let it out in a whoosh as the stranger looked around, slowly making her way into the room. I guess I'd been waiting for someone after all. Only I hadn't known it until each new arrival had proved to be someone other than the grouchy Texas Ranger.

"Who is she?" Crew's voice was louder than called for, causing several heads to turn in the direction of the new arrival.

The woman was probably around my age, dressed in a sharp black suit and a pair of sky-high heels. She was carrying a designer purse, the kind I couldn't afford even if I saved for a year, and her strawberry-blond hair was pulled back in a chic twist at the base of her neck. Even though she'd come into the viewing room, she'd left on a pair of very dark sunglasses that covered half of her face. She looked like one of the executives who worked for Della at her cosmetics company. She definitely wasn't a local, and almost as soon as she crossed the threshold, whispers and low murmurs started up. Apparently Crew wasn't the only person wondering who the woman was and where exactly she came from.

"I have no idea who she is. Should we go ask?" I took a step forward, only to be brought up short by Crew's hold on my elbow.

"This is a funeral. Don't start shit today, Kode. If she's someone we need to worry about, we'll find out sooner or later, but there's no need get worked up over it today." He shifted his hold so he could pat me on top of the head, much like he had done when we were little. "Let's find a place to sit down and get this show on the road. The sooner this is over, the better." He tilted his chin in our older brother's direction. "Case is about to grind his teeth into dust. I'm going to tell the funeral director to move things along before he ends up needing dentures."

I nodded and made my way to the rows of chairs. We didn't expect much of a crowd. Sure, half the town had come to poke their heads in and offer quickly spoken words of condolence, but the number of people sticking around for the actual service was minimal. Which was why I found it odd that the redheaded, well-dressed woman unobtrusively took a seat toward the back. My father had made a lot of enemies in his time and burned a lot of bridges. I supposed she could be one of the victims of his shortsightedness and corruption. It wasn't much of a reach to imagine the folks he'd screwed over wanting to hang around and wish him a speedy trip to hell, but something about this woman made me uneasy. I wanted her to take her sunglasses off so I could at the very least meet her gaze head-on.

I jumped in surprise when I was suddenly surrounded by my family. Crew and Della sat on one side, Case, Hayes, and Aspen on the other. Before I could tell my brothers I was fine, each grabbed one of my hands and held on tight. It took me back to all the times we'd hidden in the dark when our dad came home in a foul mood. We'd huddle together, quiet as we could be. Back then they'd hold on to me like this and promise me everything would be all right.

I swallowed back against the emotion crawling up my throat and blinked at the moisture collecting in my eyes. God forbid anyone mistake the tears for signs of sadness over the loss of the old man. That simply wouldn't do.

The funeral director droned on about our father's legacy and the perceived good things he'd done for the town of Loveless. He mentioned Conrad being survived by us, and how his kids were his greatest accomplishment. With so few people in the room, Case's loud snort of disgust echoed. I had to bite down on the tip of my tongue to keep a laugh back and felt Crew's hand tighten on mine. All in all the service was short, but filled with enough bullshit about Conrad Lawton's accomplishments to fertilize several football fields. When the funeral director asked if anyone had any memorable stories or anecdotes to share about our father's life, it was no surprise absolutely no one came forward. My brothers and I had been trained from birth not to share what happened inside the farmhouse walls with anyone. Our stories about growing up under

Conrad's thumb weren't the kind to be shared. They were the kind we'd survived . . . barely.

I was glad when it was all over. And if the deep sighs both my brothers exhaled were any indication, so were they. Now all that was left was to move Dad to the farm and lay him to rest.

When I got to my feet and looked around the room, I noticed the well-dressed redhead was gone, but a new addition had snuck in during the time the funeral director was talking.

Leaning against the back wall dressed in black jeans and a black button-up, with his Stetson in his hand, was Hill. He was standing next to another man, one who was younger, probably Crew's age, and who also just happened to be ridiculously attractive. He didn't look like a guy from small-town Texas. He had slicked-back hair and wore skinny jeans with a hole in the knee, a light pink V-neck, and a pair of Air Jordans. He looked like he should be onstage as part of a popular boy band, not standing next to the glowering, grumpy-looking Texas Ranger.

Strangely enough, some of the tightness and unease locked in the center of my chest felt like it loosened when my eyes met the soft gray of Hill's. Why I could breathe easier when he was around was a mystery. One I didn't plan to investigate too thoroughly because I knew the answer would scare me to death.

We filed out of the chairs and all slowly made our way to the back of the room, where Hill was waiting with the other man.

Hill nodded at us and said, "This is Johnny Hearst. He's the special agent heading up Conrad's case." Handshakes went around as I studied Hill.

He looked even more tired than he had a few days ago. The whites of his eyes were lined with red, and the skin under his scruffy silvery-blond beard was pale, with alarming shadows making his eyes look sunken in and his cheekbones gaunt. Someone needed to put his ass to bed and keep it there.

I flushed at the heated image the thought brought to mind and pulled myself together when it was my turn to greet the Texas Ranger in charge of finding my father's killer. The younger man had an easy, charming smile that I would have appreciated under different circumstances.

"Did you find out who the driver of the Tesla is?" I didn't mean to sound so snappy and abrasive, but I was holding on to my composure by the skin of my teeth. I wanted this day to be over with, and for things to go back to normal as quickly as possible.

The younger guy with the slicked-back hair gave a quick nod. "We did. I think we're both cross-eyed from watching endless hours of surveillance footage. Tracked the owner to a small suburb of Austin, but she hasn't been home, and according to her neighbor she took a leave of absence from her job a few weeks ago. Still trying to pin her down. But it puts us one step closer to getting some answers."

Hill put his cowboy hat back on his head and stifled a yawn behind his hand. "We can save all the updates for later. Y'all go ahead and finish laying Conrad to rest. I just wanted to stop by and pay my respects."

Case reached out to clap Hill on the shoulder at the exact same time I reached out and grabbed a handful of his shirt. My body was moving faster than my brain, and my emotions were all over the place, making it impossible to keep up.

"Can you come out to the farmhouse with us?" I wasn't exactly sure why I needed him to come, but I suddenly knew I did.

My oldest brother gave me a questioning look, and I

quickly dropped my hand. I cleared my throat and reached up to tuck some of my hair behind my ear.

"I mean, if you don't have important investigative stuff to do. You're practically family. I think you have as much reason as the rest of us to be there." I felt like I might bolt out the door and not look back if he didn't agree to come. I wasn't supposed to rely on him anymore. He'd proved that was a bad idea in the past, but I couldn't seem to stop myself. As great as my brothers were, they didn't make me feel like everything would eventually be okay again the way Hill did. Regardless of the past, Hill was the one I always believed would be able to fix whatever was broken. It was a lot to put on his shoulders, and totally unfair. No one could live up to those expectations, not even Hill, which was why his fall from the pedestal I'd had him on back in the day had been so heartbreaking.

Slowly Hill nodded, all while covering up another yawn. I felt terrible. The guy needed to sleep, not to hang around as my underappreciated security blanket. But putting Conrad into the ground and saying goodbye to my complicated past forever seemed much more manageable when I knew Hill was going to be there while I did it.

We all followed the hearse out of town in a long procession of pickup trucks. Once again my lime-green Jeep Wrangler stuck out like a sore thumb and defied convention. My father had hated the brightly colored vehicle, often referring to it as a death trap. His disdain made me love the thing even more.

The finality of things eventually hit me as I watched my brothers, my nephew, and Hill each take a corner of the casket and start to move my dad to his final resting place. Case had picked a spot under an old cottonwood tree at the back of the property. It was far enough away from the house that a person would have to make a special trip out to pay their respects. It would keep whoever ended up living in the farmhouse from having my father's ghost lingering right over their shoulder.

It was a somber, serious walk to the location. I think all of us realized we no longer had to live in fear of Conrad or be oppressed by the secrets of our childhood. Our father's transgressions were no longer our cross to bear, and maybe now we could finally grieve not only for him, but also for our mother.

When she passed away, Conrad did his best to eradicate every trace of her from our lives. She was never spoken of, never cried over, never outwardly missed. She was snatched away and became a hazy memory before any of us could do anything about it. So while we were coming to peace with Dad being gone, we also now had the space to mourn the loss of the woman who had done her best to counterbalance all his hate.

I didn't realize I was crying until Aspen wrapped an arm around my waist and discreetly handed me a tissue. She also handed me a white rose and muttered, "Take your time."

I didn't want to get any closer to the grave. I didn't want to admit I was sad and maybe a little lost. I wanted to pretend none of this was happening... the same way I had when Aaron died.

Thinking about my mom, then Aaron, as well as my father suddenly made the tight grip I had on my composure shatter. It felt like so much had been taken away from me, and it was hard to breathe through the agony of that loss.

My shoulders shook as silent sobs racked my body. Aspen tried to pull me closer, but I jerked away, covering my face as I struggled to rein my emotions in. Both the tissue and the rose hit the ground at my feet as the flood of tears blurred everything into a hazy kaleidoscope. The sobs were no longer silent as I gasped for air and wailed at the unfairness of it all. Sure my dad hadn't been great, but he had been mine. Sure my mom had been sick and suffering, but she'd also been mine. And Aaron, God, I'd never wanted to let him go. He was the one person I'd honestly believed would never leave me, and he was gone as well.

Strong arms wrapped around me, and my forehead hit the center of a strong, broad chest. I knew immediately the man holding me wasn't Case or Crew, but the man who had also lost Aaron. I liked to delude myself into thinking Hill and I had nothing in common, but the truth was, our grief was exactly the same. He was the only person who really knew what it was like to live with that gaping hole inside your heart.

I fisted handfuls of his shirt and cried until I was hoarse and could barely stand. I felt his hand cup the back of my head, but he didn't say anything. He simply stood there, holding me, shielding me as my feelings were finally allowed to run free. I had no idea how long we stood like that, but my knees felt weak and my throat was completely raw by the time the tears dried up.

Wordlessly, I looked over at the now-covered grave and silently picked up the abandoned rose. I tossed it on top of the freshly dug dirt and rubbed my burning eyes with the palms of my hands. I wanted to apologize, to make up some excuse, but as always, Hill seemed to know I was at my breaking point. He didn't question me, didn't push.

Instead he inclined his scruffy chin in the direction of the old farmhouse and softly stated, "You need a glass of water and a few minutes to sit down. Let's head back to the house."

All I could do was nod weakly and walk next to him. I stumbled slightly and didn't protest when his arm shot out and wrapped around my shoulders, pulling me tightly to his side. I felt like a deflated balloon. I was always so full of hot air and bluster, but it took next to nothing to break that thin shell and show just how fragile I was.

I walked next to Hill in silence, wondering how he always had a knack of showing up just when I needed him. I really wanted to rest my head on his shoulder but held back. It was scary, really, how attuned he was to me, when all I'd ever done was push him away and throw up roadblock after roadblock when he tried to mend the wounds of our shared past. The hurt I had was comfortable. I wasn't ready to let go of it yet, no matter how tempting unloading all my baggage was.

"It never gets any easier." His voice was low and I could feel the vibration where I was pressed against him.

"What doesn't?"

"Saying goodbye." He sighed, and his hold on me tightened a fraction. "I still think about Aaron every single day. I can still hear his laugh and see his smile." Hill cleared his throat. "All these years later, whenever my phone rings, I still think it might be him. Time does help, but I don't think it's enough to heal some wounds. Some we just have to accept as being part of us forever."

I sucked in a breath and felt tears threaten once again. I swear I never cried, but lately I was like a damn faucet. I rarely talked about Aaron, and never brought him up when Hill was around. I always thought it would be too painful, too much to bear, but his words brought a flood of happy memories to the surface. Things with Aaron had been so bad at the end, I'd repressed almost everything about my time with him, including the good moments. He did have the world's best smile, and I hadn't thought of it in so long, and wouldn't have if Hill hadn't brought it up.

I put a hand to my chest and felt my heart pounding. "I

don't know if time has helped me, but it is nice to think of happier times."

Hill nodded and I shut my mouth, not wanting to go any further down memory lane. I remained silent as we continued to walk. I should've told him he could let me go, but I didn't.

It took about twenty minutes to wander back to my childhood home. Hill yawned and apologized for basically sleepwalking no less than five times. I was going to bully him into bed and order him to sleep for at least twelve hours when he came to an abrupt halt as soon as we rounded the side of the run-down house.

Coming down the long dirt road leading into the property was a flashy car, one that had no reason to be pulling up to my father's home.

"Isn't that a Tesla?" The question tumbled out as I instinctively put my hand on the muscled expanse of Hill's broad back. I felt him tense at the touch.

"It is. Does the driver look familiar?" He kept the question low as I squinted into the setting sun to see if I remembered seeing the person behind the wheel before.

I gasped and practically pushed Hill as I exclaimed, "She does!"

The woman driving the Tesla was the same well-dressed redhead who'd been at the viewing.

I still had no clue what her connection to my father was, but it looked like I was about to find out.

CHAPTER 6

∞

HILL

I instinctively moved in front of Kody in a protective stance. She'd been on the verge of an emotional collapse not long ago, but now her entire body was vibrating with tension and anticipation. She was a wild card on a good day, but today, when her restraint was stretched thin, I could spot the impending disaster from a mile away.

"Wait here. Let me go talk to her." I tried in vain to keep Kody a step behind me, but she shook off my hold, stepped around me, and marched toward the now-stopped Tesla. "Kody, goddammit. If she's involved in my case I need to talk to her. If you scare her off you're going to set the investigation back. If you say the wrong thing..."

It was foolish to think logic of any kind would get through to her when she had a target in her sights. She'd stopped hearing anything I had to say the minute she recognized the woman and realized she had probably been one of the last people to interact with Conrad. Kody was looking for a place to lay a whole lot of blame, and this stranger was the perfect target. The woman had no idea what she was in for.

Kody reached the expensive car just as the driver's door swung open. An elegant woman stepped out, looking surprisingly composed considering the way Kody was bearing down on her.

"Who are you? What are you doing here? What do you want?" Kody barked the questions out rapid fire, coming to a halt in front of the other woman, her hands curled into threatening fists at her sides.

The other woman didn't even flinch. Instead she cocked her head to the side and simply stared at Kody with a look of utter disbelief slowly creeping over her features.

She lifted a shaking hand and covered her mouth as a whispered "Oh my God" slipped out.

When I got close enough to physically put myself between the two women, I could see why the newcomer was rendered speechless, even in the face of Kody's unchecked fury.

The two women looked startlingly similar when they were standing face-to-face. The redhead was slightly taller, built along leaner lines, but their eyes were the same unusual shade of bright green. They had the same tiny, upturned button nose and the same pouty, heart-shaped mouth. They also had matching freckles across the bridges of their noses and their cheeks. They weren't identical by any stretch of the imagination, but they looked enough alike that it made me do a double take.

I felt Kody's hand on my back, trying to push me out of the way, as she barked, "How do you know my dad? Did you kill him?" Her voice rose with each question to the point that she was starting to sound hysterical. I knew it was only a matter of time before the rest of the Lawtons joined the party, and there was no way this woman would be able to handle all of them. If I wasn't careful, she was going to be in the wind again, and I'd have to track her down all over. I had too many questions for her to let that happen.

The other woman lowered her hand and cleared her throat. She blinked those startlingly green eyes and tried to peer around me to get a glimpse of Kody. "I'm sorry. I didn't realize anyone would be here. I thought the property would be empty."

"This isn't your first trip out to this farm, is it?" I asked the question lightly as Kody continued to push at my back and try and slip around me. If she would calm down for five seconds, she would see there was more going on here. But she'd always been one to act first and feel bad about it later.

The redhead clutched at the lapel of her obviously expensive blazer, which was total overkill in this heat. She blinked up at me and nervously shifted her weight on her heels. She might look similar to Kody, but the energy she put off and the way she carried herself were entirely different. Kody was a live wire, electric with all her defiance and fight. This woman was the opposite. She seemed cold as marble, like a statue. She moved deliberately, carefully, and there was an unnatural awareness surrounding her. It was a cautious alertness I'd only witnessed in fellow soldiers and police officers. She was a woman aware the situation could turn bad in a second and was prepared for the worst.

She cleared her throat and stiffened her shoulders. Tilting her head back slightly to meet my gaze directly, she stated, "No. I've been here before."

"Son of a bitch!" The exclamation slipped out when Kody's fist drove directly into my back, aiming for my kidney. Damn, those Lawtons knew how to fight dirty. The blow forced me to jerk to the side, leaving Kody and the stranger facing off once again. This time Kody must've noticed the similarities between the two of them, because a loud gasp ripped out of her, and her eyes popped open to twice their normal size.

"Who are you?" When she asked the question this time there was less accusation in her tone and more terror.

The other woman visibly pulled herself together. The tremor in her hand stopped, the shock in her expression slid away. Her face went expressionless and her spine stiffened. She looked untouchable. It was weird to see those eyes so like Kody's go dull.

This situation kept getting weirder and weirder by the minute.

"My name is Presley Baskin." She took a deep breath and watched Kody unblinkingly. "Earlier this month my mother passed away." Her breath hitched slightly, and some of her polished veneer seemed to chip slightly. "It was always just she and I. I never had any clue who my father was. She never answered when I asked. In fact, she made it pretty clear she never wanted me to know his identity."

"No way."

"When I cleaned out her home after she passed, I came across the key to a safety deposit box. My mother went to great lengths to keep the identity of my father hidden, but I'm sure you can guess where I'm going with this."

I swore under my breath and once again put a hand on Kody's shoulder to keep her in place. "You're saying Conrad Lawton is your biological father." It wasn't so much a question as it was a statement. "You found out he was your dad and you came out to the farm to confront him."

The redhead gave her head a shake and sort of slumped back against the side of her car. "Yes. I found out Conrad Lawton was my father, but I didn't come out here to confront him." Her gaze shifted to Kody, and she sighed. "I came to apologize to him."

"What!?" The word burst out of Kody on a broken laugh. "Why on earth would you apologize to him?"

The other woman sighed again and lifted a hand to rub at her forehead. I could see the way her brow furrowed and the way a flush climbed up her neck and into her face.

"I came to apologize because my mother had been blackmailing Sheriff Lawton for years."

Kody shot a stunned look over her shoulder in my direction. My mind was spinning, trying to put pieces of this ever-expanding puzzle together. If this woman's mother had been blackmailing Conrad, he would be the one with reason to kill, not the other way around.

"Was Conrad surprised to see you when you showed up on his doorstep?" I let out a little grunt when Kody suddenly leaned back into me, as if she could no longer stand on her own strength. I wrapped an arm around her and held her far more tightly than the situation called for. I knew I would never forget the feel of her slight frame pressed along the length of mine.

"No. He didn't seem particularly surprised, not by my sudden appearance or by the death of my mother. She was diabetic. She developed kidney disease when I was in my teens. Her health was never the best, but she hung in there much longer than anyone expected. After medical school, I knew exactly how costly her treatments and dialysis were. When I was younger it never occurred to me to ask how we could afford it all. I started asking more and more questions as I got older. She refused to answer, which caused a rift in our relationship. When she passed away the truth finally came out." The other woman looked at the ground. "Conrad Lawton was the only reason my mother lived as long as she did."

Kody's body tensed in my hold, and I could feel the way her heart was racing. "He kept your mother alive, but did nothing while mine died. You have no idea what kind of man my father was."

The redhead, Presley, gave a sharp nod. "Well, considering we appear to be about the same age, which means he slept with my mother while he was still married to yours, I think I do have an idea of what kind of man he was. The day I tracked him down, he didn't want anything to do with me. He said that it no longer mattered if his children and the town found out about me because his wife was no longer alive, he was no longer sheriff, and all his kids hated him as it was. I offered to pay back the money he'd given my mother over the years, and he laughed in my face. He told me the money was the only good deed he'd done in his entire life. And he wondered if it was enough to buy his way into heaven."

Kody scoffed. "That doesn't sound like my father at all. He knew he had a special place in hell just for him."

I squeezed Kody closer and absently laced the fingers of my hand through hers. "Did Conrad seem stressed or out of sorts the day you visited him?"

The woman lifted a rust-colored eyebrow and considered me silently for a long moment. Realizing I was asking pertinent questions without an introduction, I told her, "My name is Hill Gamble. I'm a longtime friend of the family, as well as a Texas Ranger. My partner and I are the ones looking into Conrad's murder. We actually tried to track you down in Ivy, but heard you took a leave of absence from work."

"Oh...uh...yeah. The work thing is unrelated. I needed time to deal with my mother's estate, and I wanted to pay proper respects to Conrad." She looked at Kody and something soft worked its way into her familiar green gaze. "I wanted to introduce myself to his family and say thank you, even if it isn't wanted."

"How did you know he was dead?" I kept my tone calm, but I was curious. There seemed to be something more behind her sudden leave of absence than she was saying. I could tell by the way her eyes shifted and how her fingers twitched involuntarily. The woman was hiding something.

"I work in the medical examiner's office in Ivy and sometimes in Austin when they're shorthanded. News travels fast in the morgue. Conrad Lawton had a reputation. When his body hit the slab, everyone was talking about it. It was sort of a double whammy. I found out Conrad Lawton was my father and that he was dead all within a couple of weeks." The fact that she was surrounded by death every single day explained a lot about her composure and coolness. A person had to be able to keep their head and stay focused when faced with the horrors humans could inflict on each other day in and day out.

I felt Kody cringe when she mentioned the word *slab*. It was a good reminder that while she liked to pretend she was tough as nails, there was a very soft and tender interior under all that armor.

Presley pushed off the car and smoothed a hand down the front of her suit. "I can see now is not the time to make amends. I'm sorry I intruded on a private family moment. I'm not exactly sure why I felt the need to come back here. I'm not usually so impulsive." She cleared her throat again. "I'll just be on my way."

"Can you give me a number to reach you and let me know where you're staying? I have more questions. You can consider yourself officially part of the investigation into Conrad's death." It wasn't the most tactful I'd ever been, but I had a feeling this woman was smart, and if she decided she didn't want to be found it would be a problem.

"Uh. Sure. Let me just get you my card." She opened the car door and rooted around for a second before coming back with a business card. She handed it to me and pointed to a hastily scrawled number on the front. "I changed phone numbers recently, so use that one. I'm currently staying with a friend in Austin and don't want to impose on her. So if we need to meet, call me and we can set something up." Again I got the strong impression there was more to this woman's story than she was letting on. Hearst and I had been by her very nice house in its upscale community when we initially tried to make contact. There had been no signs of renovation or other work being done, so why was she staying elsewhere? "I'm sorry I showed up unexpectedly. I was only thinking of myself. I didn't stop to consider how any of this would impact the children who grew up knowing Conrad as their father."

Kody snorted and jerked herself out of my loose hold. I wanted to kick myself for immediately missing the heat of her body against mine. The only time she was ever going to get that close to me was when her defenses were down. The thought stung. I wanted her in my arms more than anything, but she seemed to constantly remind me they were the last place she wanted to be.

"Be glad you don't know what it's like to have him as a dad. Caught between love and hate every single day of your life. Your timing does suck, but once things calm down, I'll tell my brothers what you told me. We'll decide together if we want to discuss anything further with you in the future. We make all those kinds of decisions as a family."

Kody was only speaking the truth, but the other woman flinched at the word *family*. Her icy mask of indifference slipped back in place as she nodded. "Okay. Sorry to intrude and bring such shocking news. I'll just be on my way."

"I'll be in touch, Ms. Baskin." It sounded more like a threat than I'd intended, but something about this woman made me uneasy.

She didn't respond. She simply got into the Tesla and backed out of the long dirt drive. Kody and I watched the car in silence until it disappeared. Once it was gone and the dust had literally settled, I asked, "Are you okay?"

Finding out you have a long-lost sibling who looks eerily like you has to be a shock, and it couldn't have happened on a worse day.

Kody let out a string of really dirty words and kicked at the ground in front of her. She looked like a toddler throwing a fit. The comparison almost made me smile. Maybe I would've if I hadn't been so tired that staying on my feet actually took a fair amount of concentration.

"My goddamn dad. Just when I think there's an end to his jerking us around and messing with our lives, this happens." She raked her hands through her hair, pausing to tug on the wild strands. "Am I surprised he cheated on my mother? No. I am shocked he didn't use the affair to torture her and embarrass her, though. He really was the worst, wasn't he?"

It wasn't a question she needed an answer to, so I kept quiet and watched her as she started to pace with short, sharp strides in front of me.

"Only Conrad could make his funeral even more awful than it already was. Do you think she had something to do with his murder?" Kody's head whipped around as she pinned me with a hard look.

I shrugged and lifted a hand to cover a massive yawn. "I don't know, but I'll find out." There was definitely something off with the other woman, and my natural curiosity would not let up until I figured out what it was. "Want to fill your family in now, or later? I'm sure they're all huddled around the front window wondering what in the hell is going on."

Kody looked toward the old house with the faded paint and dead rosebushes. Sure enough the curtains flicked. "I'll go in and tell them. You go find the closest bed and get some sleep. You looked exhausted earlier, now you look like you're dead on your feet."

Maybe not the best turn of phrase at the moment, but she was correct. I was at my limit for being able to function properly. I needed an hour or two to recharge, but still, if she needed someone to lean on while filling her family in on Conrad's latest transgression, I would muscle through and be there for her.

"If you need me, I'm here." And even if she didn't need me. I'd always been there.

Kody shook her head and reached out to give my shoulder a little shove. "Go to bed, Hill. I'm serious."

I grunted in agreement and turned to start walking toward my truck. I was brought up short by her hand landing so lightly on my forearm I had to double check to make sure it was there.

"Thank you." Her words were so soft I strained to hear them.

"For what?"

She shrugged. "For everything, I guess. For letting me cry all over you. For showing up in the first place when you are obviously exhausted. For being my punching bag...in more ways than one. You're far better to me than I deserve."

I was so tired I started to wonder if I was dreaming. Kody Lawton did not speak to me this way. She never acknowledged that I let her get away with things I would destroy anyone else for. Not once since I'd known her had she ever acknowledged she might know just how special she was to me.

Convinced my foggy, exhausted mind was playing tricks on me, I gave her a crooked grin and tipped the brim of my hat down in her direction.

"Half the time I don't know if I'm helping or hurting things where you're concerned. I'm always trying my best to do right by you, Kody, trying to be all the different things you need me to be. I failed at that task once before. I don't want to let you down again." I cleared my throat when her eyes widened in shock at my unfiltered honesty. It was the first time I'd let even a sliver of the truth out. Pulling my gaze away from her shocked expression, I looked toward where the Tesla had disappeared. "Things sure are never boring around you Lawtons."

And my heart was never going to beat normally when I was around this particular Lawton.

CHAPTER 7

∞

KODY

I can't believe someone put one over on the old man. I never thought anyone would beat him at his own game."

Case mumbled the words into the nearly empty rocks glass he was drinking from. We'd left the farmhouse not long after I sent Hill on his way. My brothers had demanded to know who the stranger was, which was a conversation I knew was going to require hard liquor and infinite patience. I had plenty of the first at the bar, and not much of the second. I called Lorenzo and asked him to kick the regulars out and shut down the bar early so my family had a quiet, safe place to digest the news that our father had been so much worse than we'd thought.

"Do you think Mom knew?" Crew asked the question quietly. He was sticking to beer and didn't seem nearly as far gone as Case was, but he was twice as pissed. Neither had taken the news that we had a half sister very well.

I handed him another bottle of Corona with a shrug. "I don't know. If she did, she never let on. She was great at hiding what was going on at home from everyone, even us sometimes."

Case finished his drink and set the glass on the bar with a thump. He was lucky it didn't shatter under the careless force. "Blackmail." He shook his dark head and rubbed a hand across his mouth. "Part of me wants to believe the reason he ended up on the take in the first place was to cover the cost of that woman demanding money." He huffed out an exaggerated sigh and reached out to clap Crew on the shoulder, nearly knocking him off the bar stool. "But Dad was an asshole from the minute he came into this world until the minute he left it."

Crew grunted in agreement. "Why would he pay to keep things quiet for so long? It's not like he cared what anyone thought about him, especially his own family." The bitterness was thick in his slightly slurred words.

I pushed back my hair and leaned my forearms on the bar. "Because the position of sheriff is still an elected one, and Loveless still likes to pretend it's based on family values. If news of an affair and a child out of wedlock made the rounds, the chances he would keep his position—and retain the fear and respect he spent his whole life cultivating—would be slim. There's no chance Conrad Lawton would risk letting some woman, *any* woman, take his power away." He was far too misogynistic and hardheaded for that.

"So he paid to keep her quiet." Case tapped the glass and I reluctantly refilled it. I wasn't reluctant because I was worried about him drinking too much, but because he was so big, it was going to be a pain in the ass to haul him to the car when Aspen showed up to take him home. "Or she had more on him than the affair and the baby, and he had no choice but to pay up."

"More?" Crew leaped to his feet, sending the stool flying to the floor. "What else could there be?"

Not realizing Crew was at the brink of being pushed too far, Case lifted the glass and muttered, "Who knows? Maybe he coerced the woman into having sex with him? Maybe he forced her? Maybe she threatened to tell Mom about the affair and the old man knew his house of cards was about to come tumbling down? There doesn't seem to be an end to Conrad's misdeeds."

Crew lifted his hands and tugged violently on his hair. "This is crazy. How could we have a sister we know nothing about? How could Dad provide for that woman—save her life—and not even shed a single tear when our mother, *his wife*, died? I thought things would be easier with him gone, but now everything seems even more complicated. Are we supposed to welcome this stranger into our family? Are we supposed to like her, to feel sorry for her since she also lost her mother and got stuck with Conrad Lawton as a father? I don't know what to think."

Watching Crew work himself up, I knew he was on the verge of making a bad decision. We shared that trait, letting our emotions rule us and lead us into trouble. Crew liked to gamble, liked the risk and the thrill. What had started out as a hobby ended up with him in the grip of a full-blown addiction and in deep with some very bad, very dangerous people. He'd been on the straight and narrow since meeting Della, realizing there was more to life than the next bet, but I could see he was losing his grip on his restraint, and I refused to let him backslide.

Discreetly texting Della that it was time to collect her man, I made my way around the bar and stopped in front of Crew. I reached up and put my hands on his shoulders, meeting his wild stare with a steady one of my own.

"We don't have to do anything tonight. It's been one hell of a day and I think we've all held up as well as could be expected. Yes, this was a shock. We'll deal with it together, just like we always do. I think it's too early to worry about how this woman fits into our lives. She might not want anything to do with us once she gets the full picture of who Conrad was. Right now, he's a man she feels indebted to. She doesn't know he was a monster. Once she does, she very well could decide to steer clear of us."

The Lawtons were a lot to take on. You really had to have a lot of love for one of us to be willing to embrace our never-ending drama and disorder. The baggage we all carried around was heavy and unwieldy. You never knew when a piece of it was going to topple and crush whatever good thing we had going on in the moment. That woman with my eyes, my father's eyes, didn't seem like the warm and fuzzy type. I doubted she had a lot of patience for anything as high maintenance as the Lawtons.

My brother continued to pull at his hair until tears filled his pretty blue eyes. "I feel like I'm going crazy. I swear this is all some kind of messed-up dream."

Case let out a dry, brittle-sounding laugh. "A nightmare. Hey, maybe we won't want anything to do with her. Her mother was a blackmailer. Her father was a soulless, corrupt cop. Maybe she's just as bad as them."

This was spiraling out of control. "Enough." I gave Crew a little shake. "We don't know anything about her, and she doesn't know anything about us. That isn't going to change tonight. We all need a breather. We can decide what we're going to do when our heads are clear. Right now you need to go home to your women. Let them take care of you."

I would be forever grateful they'd both found women up to that task, because it was never going to be easy.

Case clumsily got to his feet and stumbled his way to where Crew and I were standing. He nearly knocked Crew over when he tossed a heavily muscled arm across the other man's shoulders. Crew was no petite flower, but Case was a giant in comparison. A big, drunk, sloppy giant. Aspen was going to have her hands full when she got here. Luckily she'd sent a text not too long ago saying she was on her way. I figured Della must have sent out an SOS. Thank goodness for future sisters-in-law.

"Who's going to take care of you, Kode? That used to be our job, but you don't let us do it anymore." Case sounded sulky and put out. He'd definitely had more than his limit if he was openly talking about his feelings. The man was usually a brick wall when it came to discussing emotions.

I sighed and struggled to stay on my feet as his other arm wrapped around my neck, pulling me in for a hug that was nearly strangling.

I pushed ineffectively against his broad chest and called his name. "Case! Let me go. I can't breathe."

A smacking kiss landed on the top of my head, and I felt him rest his cheek on top of my curly hair. "I worry about you, kiddo. No matter what, you're always going to be our baby sister. I only want you to be happy."

I thought I heard him sniff. If Case started crying, I had no idea what I was going to do. He was the strong one. He was the one always in control. He was the one who refused to show weakness. Crew was right, this was like some kind of dream where everything was upside down.

"You and Crew did a good job raising me and loving me. I don't need anyone to take care of me because you guys taught me how to take care of myself." I liked being independent and self-sufficient. It felt less risky than relying on someone else. I'd trusted Aaron to stay by my side and help me navigate the treacherous waters of growing up and building a life together, and in the end he'd left me alone to figure it out by myself. I'd also believed that Hill would be there forever to make sure nothing bad happened to his brother...or to me. It was honestly devastating when he proved me wrong. As a result, I tried not to lean on anyone. That way the only person letting me down and disappointing me was myself.

Case pulled back and grabbed my face between his hands. He squished my cheeks and made my mouth pucker in a way that had Crew cracking up and me trying to shake him loose.

"What about Hill?" Case's clearly unfocused gaze suddenly had a dangerous gleam sparking in its icy blue depths. "He'd take good care of you if you let him."

I froze instinctively. There was no way Case could know that relying on Hill Gamble again was my greatest fear, something I'd fought against since I'd lost Aaron. I still remembered the heavy, sinking feeling deep in my gut the first time Hill didn't answer one of my panicked calls in the middle of the night. I could tell something was different when we talked. I always tried to ask how he was, checked to see if he was taking care of himself and enjoying life outside of Loveless, before diving into whatever was going on with Aaron. But Hill had been curt, making each call shorter and shorter. He would listen to whatever I had to say about Aaron, would offer his opinion and advice, but the easy conversation, the friendly touching base, was withering away. Eventually I felt like I was bothering him, even harassing him each time I called, so I started sending him text messages instead. He always responded, but often with one-word answers that came hours later. I missed having contact with him. Missed his voice. Missed his promises that things with Aaron would work out. I flat-out missed him, and felt horrible anytime Aaron asked what I was sulking about. I was trying my best to save one brother while secretly wondering why the other was forcibly pushing me out of his life. They were both breaking my heart, and I couldn't tell either one why.

"Of course you think that. He's your best friend. Hill and I have nothing in common, and he rubs me the wrong way. I'd kill him before he got around to taking care of me." I scoffed and shook loose of my oldest brother's hold. "Plus, did you get a good look at him today? He's barely taking care of himself right now."

It hurt, somewhere inside my frozen heart, when I remembered how tired and haggard Hill had looked today. I never really gave much thought to the fact that he was a few years older than me, but today each of those years had shown on his handsome face. He hadn't complained, had not fought when I begged him to stay with me today. I didn't want to read too much into his actions, or into the fact that he was reliable no matter how bratty and immature I acted toward him. Hill was a pillar of strength, just like Case. It was in their DNA to take care of others, to protect. Which was why it drove me nuts that Hill had never seemed to know exactly how fragile Aaron was. In the back of my mind, I always wondered: If Hill had paid more attention, would Aaron still be here? It wasn't fair to lay that on him, I knew it, but that didn't stop the thought from popping up whenever Hill was exceptionally good to *me*.

Since we were always in sync, it was no surprise when Crew chided a very inebriated Case. "She was engaged to Hill's younger brother. She loved Aaron, Case. Don't you think it would be a little awkward if she was suddenly gaga over his brother?"

I shot Crew a grateful look, but it quickly faded away when Case threw his arm over my shoulder and grumbled, "She only picked Aaron because he was as messed up as we were. She didn't think she deserved better, didn't think she deserved a good guy like Hill."

I gasped in shock. I felt like his words were a physical blow. The sting from the truth in them made my skin burn and set my ears ringing.

When I suddenly pulled away from Case, his blurry eyes widened as he landed on his rear end on the wooden floor of the bar. His Stetson fell off, making him swear up a storm as he glared up at me and Crew.

My middle brother shook his head at the man on the floor and reached out to pull me into a tight hug. He rubbed a hand on my back and barked at Case, "I know you're drunk, but that's uncalled for. Some things are off-limits. We don't talk about you getting tricked into knocking up the prom queen when we all know you're smarter than that, and we don't talk about the man Kody *chose* to spend her life with, the man she loved, with anything other than respect. You get a pass because today has been shit, but next time it won't be Kody putting you on your ass, it'll be me, and you won't get up so fast."

Case groaned, flinging his arms above his head and flopping on the floor on his back. He was lucky Hill had played drill sergeant and made my staff clean the place. Usually the floor of the bar was the last place I would recommend anyone getting comfortable, but right now it was clean enough it wouldn't do him any harm.

"Remind me of this the next time I offer to be your private bartender." I kicked the bottom of Case's cowboy boot with the toe of my sandal. "You better get a damn good apology ready."

I was still scowling at him when the door to the bar opened and revealed a statuesque blonde and a petite brunette. Della and Aspen couldn't be more opposite in appearance, but they both had a quiet, steady core to them that I admired immensely. Neither one had lost who she was or given up on her own goals when she fell in love with one of my brothers.

Della waved at Crew, while Aspen jerked to a stop when she caught sight of her man sprawled on the floor like a felled tree. One of her midnight eyebrows shot up as she gave me a questioning look.

"I see the conversation went well." She made her way over to Case, bending down so she could brush her fingers across his forehead. "You all right, hero?"

Case looked up at her, eyes still unfocused and slightly watery. "I just wanna go home with you."

Aspen gave him a lopsided smile and nodded. "You got it." She looked over at Crew, who had his head bent close to Della's and was talking in a low voice. "I assume since you're on your feet that you can help me get him to the car?"

Crew gave a grunt and narrowed his eyes. "We should leave him on the floor for the night. He deserves it."

Aspen straightened and gave Crew a knowing smile. "But you won't."

Della dug her elbow into my brother's side and told him flatly, "He won't."

I watched in silent amusement as all three of them wrestled a very uncooperative Case to his feet and out the door. I was going to lock it behind them so I could enjoy a drink or two in silence but was interrupted when Aspen suddenly stuck her head back inside.

I went still as she launched herself at me, wrapping her arms around me in a hug so tight, it rivaled the ones I'd just escaped from my brothers.

"If you need anything, let me know. If you don't want to be alone tonight, come stay at the house. You know we have room." Aspen and Case had recently moved into Aspen's newly renovated Craftsman in the center of town. The house had nearly been destroyed by a fire not too long ago and was now a quirky work of art. Aspen insisted I had my own room, even if I never used it. It was a sweet thought.

"Thanks. I'm fine. I'm going to clean up here, have a drink, then go home and sleep for a decade. You worry about my idiot brother. He's going to feel terrible in the morning." I squeezed her back and told her honestly, "I'll be okay."

She pulled back, giving me a look I swore saw all the way down into my frozen soul. "I want you to be better than okay. But I'll settle for okay for now." She turned back to the door, pausing before she stepped outside. "The lawyer handling your father's estate e-mailed me to set up a meeting. I can handle it all if you think that would be easier, or I can arrange for all of you to meet with him. You don't have to decide right away, but give it some thought."

I let out a little snort. "Is it bad if I say I don't want anything he might have left behind for us?"

She shook her dark head and gave a sympathetic grin. "I think that's perfectly reasonable considering that what he *did* give you while he was around was abuse and bad memories. We'll talk soon."

Once she was gone, I locked the door, hit the lights, leaving only the ones behind the bar on, and took the same seat Case had been sitting in. Sighing heavily, I let my head drop until my forehead was resting on the polished wood.

Even three sheets to the wind, my oldest brother saw too much, and it was exhausting. Back when we started hanging around the Gamble brothers, Hill was the one I'd noticed first. Hill was the one I'd been drawn to and fascinated by, even though I was pretty sure he viewed me as nothing more than a little kid at the time. However, when my mom got sick, Aaron was the one who seemed to understand how bad watching her wither away hurt. He not only recognized the pain, he was comfortable with it, embraced it. He never tried to tell me how I should act or how I should process my grief. He never cared when I lashed out, even if he was the target. He really was as messed up as me.

Hill, on the other hand, remained calm, cool, and collected regardless of what was going on around him. He was the one who quietly told me my actions might end up hurting the people closest to me. He was the one who questioned my motivations and asked if I *really* wanted to be the kind of person who acted without thinking first. At the time I was angry at what I thought was him unfairly judging me. When I got older, I finally understood why Hill had been warning me of the consequences of my actions. He was trying to get me to think things through when all I wanted to do was rage. When I wanted to burn the world down, Aaron was right beside me with matches and a can of gasoline. Hill was the one standing behind both of us with a fire extinguisher and the reminder that we could be burned by the flames.

They were as different as night and day, and I knew I wouldn't be the woman I was today without the influence of both of them. But I also knew, and had known even as a kid, that there could be nothing between me and Hill. When you were born a Lawton there was no room for perfection. We didn't know what to do with it, and we just ended up ruining it. So I purposely tried to stay away from Hill, and fell in love with the Gamble boy who made the most sense. Aaron and I were imperfect together, but at least we loved each other. I'd always been okay with that, or thought I was.

Yet here I was once again in the center of circumstances that were so far from perfect they felt impossible. And standing on the sideline, being his infallible, endlessly reliable self, was Hill. It was far too tempting to fall back on how we used to be. I wanted to believe he would be there for me when I needed him. But he'd let me down on that front once already. Wouldn't it make me utterly foolish to expect him to keep showing up when things were ugly and complicated? And what would happen this time if I leaned on him and he let me fall? I wasn't sure I had it in me to get back up from that kind of blow. I was sick and tired of pulling myself back to my feet, so I'd rather just stay standing.

CHAPTER 8

∞

HILL

Hold on a second." I hollered the words as I hastily wrapped a towel around my waist after scrambling from the shower.

Someone was pounding on the door hard enough that I was worried the wood was going to splinter under the force. I figured it had to be Hearst with a break in the case. No one else would be trying to beat down my door with such enthusiasm. Generally folks weren't that eager for my company.

Pushing my wet hair back from my forehead, I padded to the door, wishing the shower had been longer. I'd managed to catch a few hours of sleep here and there, but I couldn't say they had been exactly restful. I couldn't shake the feeling there was something really off with the newcomer claiming to be Conrad's daughter. And no matter how hard I tried, I couldn't convince Hearst that Kody's association with the Sons of Sorrow wasn't anything more than coincidental. The young investigator was like a particularly stubborn dog with a bone, insisting there was a thread there we needed to un-ravel if we wanted to know what had happened to Kody's father. It was hard to sleep knowing Kody was in deep with the bikers, and now there was a sinking feeling settling in my gut that I wasn't going to like whatever Hearst had dug up. I already hated that Kody and Shot had been involved in a romantic relationship, *and* that it was pretty common knowl-edge in Loveless, which gave validation to my temporary partner's suspicions.

"What?" I barked out the word as I jerked open the door. It was a good thing I had quick reflexes, because if I hadn't caught Kody's swinging fist as she started to knock again, I would've ended up with a broken nose.

Kody's eyes popped wide as her gaze drifted over my mostly naked and still-damp body. I heard her inhale.

"Are you always half-naked when you're in your room?" She pulled her hand free and stepped back to fidget with her hair.

I lifted my eyebrows and dryly asked, "Is there a dress code at this motel I don't know about?"

Kody waved a hand in front of her face and purposely averted her eyes. "Can you get dressed?"

I chuckled. "Why are you always telling me to put clothes on lately?" Usually when I was alone with a woman she was telling me to do the opposite.

I heard her clear her throat. "I wanted to ask you about that woman, Presley Baskin. Have you eaten yet? If you put some clothes on, I'll feed you breakfast."

Absently scratching at my bare chest, I told her, "Give me a couple minutes. I wasn't expecting company. I can't do breakfast. I have an appointment out of town I need to leave for soon. But I can grab a cup of coffee if you want to meet me at the diner."

Kody nodded jerkily and turned away. "That works." She started to walk away, but paused and tossed over her shoulder, "You look better than you did the other day. I'm glad."

It wasn't the world's best compliment, but it was an important one, because it was the first one she'd willingly given me. I shut the door and leaned forward so I could rest my forehead on the hard surface. It literally took nothing for Kody to bring me to my knees. Considering all the years I'd tried to train myself to be immune to her, one would think I would have better defenses where she was concerned, but I didn't. Everything she did and said was like an arrow aimed directly at my heart. The damn thing was full of holes because of her.

I took a couple of minutes to towel dry my hair, brush my teeth, and run a razor over my face. I tugged on a pair of jeans, pulled on a lightweight button-up, jammed my feet into my boots, grabbed my weapon and my badge along with my hat, and headed out the door. Hearst called while I was walking across the parking lot to the diner. He wanted to make sure we were still on schedule to meet with Presley Baskin. We'd finally managed to lock the woman into an interview. She was skittish as hell and clearly reluctant to take part in our investigation. It would be very easy to attribute her unease to the recent passing of her mother and the discovery of her new family, but my gut was screaming at me that her behavior had something more serious behind it. Like maybe she knew more about what had happened to Conrad than she was letting on. Either way it was an appointment I couldn't miss, so I had to hear Kody out and be on my way. There was no extra time to spin fantasies around her showing up at my motel room out of the blue and dropping kind words.

She was in the same booth we'd shared before. My coffee

was already sitting on the table, and instead of onion rings, she had a plate full of French toast in front of her.

I slid in across from her. Gave her a quick once-over, noticing she seemed anxious. Her fingers were tapping on the table and her knee was bouncing up and down. Her eyes couldn't seem to decide where to land and her mouth kept shifting between a flat line and a deep frown. Kody always sort of seemed electric and vibrant with energy, but today the invisible vibration was buzzing with something darker and angrier than usual. I had a feeling this wasn't the friendly chat Kody had led me to believe it would be.

"So what do you want to ask? You know I can't tell you anything related to the case. I don't know how much I can tell you about Dr. Baskin." I picked up my coffee and stared at her over the rim. "I have her contact info. You can reach out and learn about her directly from the source. Don't you think that might be best?"

Kody stabbed at her breakfast with her butter knife. "Have you spoken with her since the funeral?" Those neon-green eyes of hers sliced into me like lasers.

"No, not yet. I'm supposed to meet with her today for the formal interview. Hearst ran basic background info on her over the last few days. Nothing unusual popped up other than the fact that she's an incredibly smart individual and has been on the fast track in her career field for quite some time. She was recently offered a promotion to the lead medical examiner position in her county. She's about to be the youngest lead ME in the state." I didn't mention that there had been some hiccups after Dr. Baskin was offered the position, or that her mother's death had coincided with the sudden career advancement.

I watched as Kody's fingers tightened around the knife in her hand. Her grip was so tight her knuckles turned white.

"So, she's smart. Smart enough to plan and execute my father's murder?"

I leaned back in the booth. "Maybe. But in my experience you don't always need to be smart to commit murder. I told you, if she's involved in any way, I will find out and I will hold her accountable." I arched an eyebrow at her. "Do you know something I don't, Kody? You seem a little on edge today."

She dropped the knife with a clatter and purposely smoothed her frowning features out. "I'm just trying to compartmentalize. Case always says you have great instincts, so I thought maybe you had some new insight which would make dealing with all of this easier."

It sounded good, but Kody had never been a good liar. Her face was too expressive, her body language too easy to read. She was digging for something, but I had no clue what it might be.

"I can let you know what my impressions are after I speak with her today. I still think it might be a good idea for you to sit down and talk to her yourself. She's the only one who can really fill you in on how she feels about finding out Conrad is her father and that she has a bunch of half siblings she never knew about. And if she doesn't want to talk to you, then I guess you have your answer as to how she feels about it."

Kody flattened her hands on the tabletop and asked in a very fake, calm voice, "Where are you meeting her today? Here in town?"

That tingle warning me she was up to something pricked at the back of my neck. "No. We agreed on a spot halfway between Loveless and Ivy." I didn't think giving her the exact location was a good idea. I was missing a huge piece of this puzzle. It was easy to see the vague reply annoyed her, but Kody didn't say anything.

I glanced down at my cell phone and quickly finished my coffee. "I actually need to get going if I don't want to be late. Thanks for the coffee."

Kody nodded absently, but put up a protest when I tossed a few bills on the table to cover her untouched breakfast.

"I told you I would buy." She glared up at me, but I didn't have time to argue with her over something so trivial. Every instinct I had told me I was looking at a bigger fight with her down the road, and I knew how to pick my battles.

"My treat, since you seem to be having a bad day. I'll check in if I have anything of value to pass on. Try and turn the rest of your day around, Kody." I didn't like how her pretty face had seemed permanently set in a scowl since I'd been back in Loveless.

She muttered something I was sure I didn't want to hear under her breath as I walked away. I shot a text off to let Hearst know I was on the way in case I hit traffic and ended up being a little late. I listened to the radio, ignored two calls from my mother, and wondered about Kody's odd behavior as I drove the forty-five minutes it took to reach the busy truck stop off the highway where Presley had finally agreed to meet with us. The location seemed deliberately chosen. It was busy, nondescript, and filled with both state patrol officers and local law enforcement traveling between counties. It was a good place for a woman to feel safe. Especially if she was scared of something, or someone.

I parked my truck in the busy lot, nodding to a couple of truckers on my way into the building. Hearst was easy to spot with his slicked-back hair in the sea of trucker and cowboy hats. The woman sitting across from him caught sight of me first, and I touched my fingers to the brim of my hat to acknowledge her slight wave. Again I was struck by how similar she looked to Kody, yet how different. It was such a weird sensation to be judged by eyes I knew as well as my own. Only Presley's were impossible to read, where Kody's showed every single feeling.

"Sorry to keep you waiting." I reached out a hand for her to shake and immediately took note of her hesitancy to reach for it. Eventually she wrapped her slim, ice-cold fingers around mine and gave a half-hearted shake.

"No problem. I really don't know what I'm going to be able to add to your investigation. Like I mentioned to your partner, I don't know anything about Conrad or the rest of the Lawton family. My mother made sure I was kept in the dark. This was all as much a shock to me as it was to them."

I took a seat next to Hearst, making note of the fact that the doctor was sitting facing the front door and her eyes tracked each new entry. She was definitely on guard, on the lookout for someone. We were going to have to dig a little deeper into this woman's life, and I could tell she wasn't going to like it one bit.

"You'd be surprised how helpful even the slightest bit of information could be. Conrad's daughter mentioned that her dad seemed like he was anxious to get rid of her the day you visited, like he was expecting someone. Did you tell him you were coming to see him that day? Did he know you'd found out his identity before you showed up on his doorstep? What did you talk about?" I had to hand it to Hearst, he was good. He had just the right amount of charm and charisma to put someone at ease, but his mind was quick and he fired off all the same questions I would've asked had I been the one in charge of the investigation.

The redheaded woman stayed cool as a cucumber. Her composure never wavered. "I didn't tell him I was coming. I found my mother's safety deposit box that had a DNA test in it. I assume the sheriff demanded proof I was his child before paying her. I asked a friend on the Austin police force to track down his address for me. I don't know why I thought showing up unannounced was the way to go, but I wasn't exactly thinking clearly at the time. The sheriff did not seem at all surprised to see me, now that you mention it. When I told him he was my father and I would like to repay every cent my mother took from him, he told me there was no need. He also told me he already had enough kids and wasn't looking for another one. Then he sent me on my way. He made it pretty clear he wasn't interested in seeing me again."

Hearst gave me a look. Without words I knew he was thinking the same thing I was. Someone else had told Conrad that his long-lost daughter knew his identity. That was the only explanation as to why he hadn't been surprised to see Presley on his doorstep.

Hearst leaned forward, crossing his arms on the table in front of him. "Did you tell anyone else about Conrad or the blackmail?"

Green eyes flicked away briefly, indicating silently that she had. For a second I thought she was thinking about how to answer, but a moment later her expression shifted to surprise with a splash of horror. "What is she doing here?"

Confused, Hearst and I shared another look. Presley climbed to her feet just as a flurry of anger and blond curls stormed up to the side of the table, palms slamming out on the surface with enough force to spill the liquid in all the cups resting there.

"What in the hell?" Hearst struggled to get to his feet as Kody suddenly leaned down, glaring at the unsuspecting doctor as she got almost nose-to-nose with the other woman. I ended up on my feet, instinctively trying to get between the two women.

It was easier said than done, because Kody was intently

focused on her target. "He left everything to you! The house! The land! His pension! All of it is in your name! What did you do to my father?" Her voice rose with each sentence.

Kody was causing a scene. Enraged and out of control the way she was now, every eye in the place was on her as Presley fought to gain some space, her hands lifting defensively as she flinched at each word Kody spit out.

"Goddammit, Kody. You're going to get yourself arrested. Knock it off."

"What are you doing? Are you crazy? This isn't how grown women act." The doctor's voice didn't rise, but I could clearly hear the panic laced through it. "I have no idea what you're talking about."

Kody ignored her words, continuing to crowd her. "Why would he change his will?! Why are you so fucking important to him?"

Kody sounded unhinged, but I could also hear the pain in her voice. She wasn't thinking straight, and it was going to get her in massive trouble.

"How did Kody even know where we were meeting?" Hearst was pushing to get out of the booth as I continued to try to push Kody back a few inches so the other woman could breathe.

I grunted when I got an elbow in my jaw for my efforts.

I recalled her surprise visit this morning and her questionable behavior. "She followed me." It hadn't even occurred to me to keep an eye out for someone tailing me to the meeting spot. Who was crazy enough to do that? The answer was the woman wiggling in my tightening hold.

I wanted to get Kody under control before she hurt the other woman, but I couldn't get a solid hold on her from this angle. She was twisting and wiggling like a fish pulled out of a river.

Kody kept screaming about Presley getting everything, and the redhead kept repeating that Kody's behavior was ridiculous. I had no idea how she didn't lose her temper after getting attacked so outrageously, but she remained calm...until she didn't.

Something snapped in the cool doctor, and the next thing I knew Kody was on the floor at my feet, holding her nose as a steady stream of blood trickled down her face. Presley had her fists clenched and her feet placed in a classic boxer's stance. It was unexpected, and the woman seemed shocked at her own actions, as if she'd only learned self-defense recently.

Swearing under my breath, I reached down to pull Kody to her feet, slapping a hand over her mouth when she immediately started to protest.

"I'll take care of her. You take care of Dr. Baskin. I apologize for the way this interview went." I also realized it was a good thing I wasn't in charge of this case, because it would be my ass in my boss's office getting chewed out for dropping the ball like this.

I hauled a still-fighting Kody out of the building, pausing to flash the badge to a couple of watchful state troopers who'd witnessed the whole altercation.

Once outside, I muscled her against the side of my truck, taking a quick look at her nose to make sure it wasn't broken. Kody was still struggling in my hold until I used my sleeve to wipe up the streaks of blood.

"She's got a solid right hook for a doctor. What were you thinking? You can't just do whatever you want, Kody. You know better than this. What are you going to do if you end up in jail? How's that going to look for Case? Come on now, you're better than this."

She pushed against my chest until I stepped back. "I'm

not better than this. Even if you want me to be." She looked down at her feet and took a deep breath. "Why did he love her, Hill? Why be good to her when he was nothing but terrible to us? What's so great about her? He was her dad for a day, mine for thirty years, and she gets everything." Her voice caught, and I watched as she practically deflated in front of me. She slumped back against the truck and looked up at me with wounded eyes. "Why couldn't he love us, Hill? What was so wrong with us?"

I sighed and reached out to push some of her unruly hair away from her face. "Nothing is wrong with you. Conrad was wrong. He was a bad guy, Kody. You know that. You shouldn't let him still control how you feel now that he's gone. That gives him power he doesn't deserve."

She tossed her head back and looked up at the sky. "Why do I even care? I don't want to care."

"I don't know why we care. We just do." If I could have stopped caring about her to the point of distraction, I would've done it years ago. "I've cared about you from the moment we met."

She wrinkled her nose at my words, then groaned and lifted her fingers to touch it. "It hurts."

I chuckled. "Good." She was lucky all she'd gotten away with was a tender nose.

"Hey, Hill." I looked down at her expectantly. "I'm glad you care about me. I know I don't make it easy."

I forgot how to breathe for a second. I tilted my hat back so I could see her face clearly. "I've never minded a challenge." I'd always believed you had to work hard for the things you wanted most in life.

"I'm sorry I screwed up your interview."

I couldn't tell her it was okay, because we both know it wasn't. "You've got to start using your head. You're still reacting without thinking things through. It's going to get you in trouble you can't get out of one of these days."

"You think?"

"I know." And it scared the hell out of me. What if I wasn't there to pull her out of the fire?

"Thinking things through can be highly overrated."

Maybe she was right, because what she did next made it impossible for me to form a single coherent thought.

CHAPTER 9

∞

KODY

Reckless impulses were sort of my thing. I was real good at acting on them, even if the end results weren't going to be in my favor.

I bought a failing bar on a whim.

I fell in love with a troubled boy when my life was already a chaotic mess.

I crushed on that boy's older brother, even though I knew it was wrong.

I got into business with a bunch of bikers because it seemed like a good idea at the time.

And, possibly the most irresponsible and outrageous thing I'd ever done, I kissed Hill Gamble in the parking lot of a truck stop because I couldn't stop myself.

It would take the threat of bodily harm for me to ever admit to anyone else that I'd always wanted to know what it would be like to kiss Hill. That was a secret I planned on taking to my grave. When I was younger, I imagined it would be fun to shake Hill up a little, to watch some of the stony sternness crack and fall away. He was always so in control, so sure of himself and his actions. I was forever wondering if anything ever shook the stoic facade. After everything we'd been through, I now wondered if the man knew how to take pleasure in anything, if he ever took a moment to enjoy the small things in life...like a simple kiss.

Only this kiss was anything but simple.

The minute our lips touched, all the wiring inside my head and my heart short-circuited. The icy shell that kept the center of my chest nice and cool immediately started to melt, sending a warm, slippery sensation all the way through my body and making my fingers and toes tingle. My hands fisted Hill's perfectly pressed shirt, and I wasn't sure if my intention was to push him away or pull him closer. It was pretty much how I felt about the man all the damn time.

Luckily he took the choice out of my hands when one of his wide, warm hands landed on the base of my spine, pressing at my waist until I could feel the metal of his zipper and the undeniable heat and stiffness of the flesh behind it. The shock of encountering obvious evidence of Hill's arousal should have been like a bucket of cold water poured over my rapidly rising desire. This was wrong. We were impossible. But all I could think was that I wanted to get closer, to feel more, to take more and give everything. My all-consuming thoughts forced out a gasp that parted my lips against Hill's.

A moment later I felt the brush of his fingers against my cheek, and his thumb lightly traced the outline of my jaw as his quick, nimble tongue darted inside the cavern of my mouth. Suddenly his tongue tangled around mine, appeasing my curiosity over how the man would kiss. It wasn't controlled or restrained at all. No, it was wet, wild, and breathless. He kissed me back in a way that made me wonder if he'd been secretly fantasizing about this moment for as long as I had. There was a bite of desperation in the way he tried to taste every single part of my mouth. There was a hint of possession in the way his hand held my face still and tilted slightly back so he could devour my lips, turning my head when he wanted to come at me from a different angle. And maybe there was even a shadow of fear lingering between us. His hands were shaking, his heart racing, and I felt like I wanted to cry. But neither of us moved away.

I thought I heard him swear under his breath, but it was possible it was just my name. He often said it like a curse. I thought he was going to move away, be the rational, reasonable one... like he always was. But he never lifted his head. Never gave me an inch to breathe. It felt like he was trying to consume me, devour me, absorb every single sound and sigh. It did my ego good to know Hill was as caught up in the moment as I was. It was a revelation to know he could indeed lose his head when something powerful moved him.

I used my hold on his shirt to pull him even closer and worked my arm up around his impossibly broad shoulders. I liked the solid, strong feel of him. Liked that he seemed unbreakable, because I knew what it was like to love someone fragile, and I never wanted to go down that road again. I instantly wanted to sink into the heat and warmth emanating from his big, hard body. It was addicting to me, since I was always cold. I let my tongue engage in an erotic duel with his, my body reacting instantly when he used his teeth to nip at the curve of my bottom lip and the tip of his tongue to soothe the sting. I knew the flavor of him would likely linger forever.

There was a bitter tang of coffee on his tongue, and behind it something with a hint of spice and bite. The flavors made me tingle and seemed so different from Hill's generally cool and composed personality. There was heat hidden inside him. No wonder he always made me melt. I had to fight back a moan when his wide palm slid up my back and gripped the back of my neck. My nipples tightened to painful points where they were pressed against his chest. My knees felt like they were made of Jell-O, and there was no ignoring the way all my most private and sensitive places were suddenly tingling with awareness. I was fighting the urge to rub against the man like a cat. I wanted him to pet and stroke me in all the places that were clenching and fluttering. I was always telling him to put his clothes on because it was unnerving and bad for my self-control when he walked around half-naked. Now I wanted to pop the buttons on his shirt off one by one and trace every line of muscle and every divot of his corded abs with my tongue.

The spot inside me having the biggest, most dramatic reaction to the kiss was my heart. Usually frozen solid and numb, the dead little thing now felt like it was on fire. Encased in flames. Glowing and illuminated. I wondered if Hill could feel it. If he had any idea how long it'd been a lonely, dark place. Some things were too hot to touch, and my reaction to Hill was one of them.

I dug my fingers into his silky hair at his nape, under his now-askew hat, and tugged until he lifted his head. His gray eyes glittered with silver shards when they met mine, and his handsome face was flushed. It was hands down the most ruffled and unkempt I'd ever seen the man, and possibly the most attractive he'd ever looked. Well, next to how hot he'd looked mostly naked and wet that morning. That was an image I was never going to get out of my brain. I wanted to take pride in the fact that I was the one who did this to him, that I was the one who shook him up and forced him to feel. But panic was steadily rising up inside me.

I pushed Hill back and jumped a few feet away. I touched

trembling fingers to my kiss-swollen lips and watched the man across from me slump back against the side of his truck, posture defeated and resigned.

I cleared my throat and looked down at the toe of my purple sneaker. "I need to get back to the bar. I only asked Lorenzo to watch it for a little while. He's still mad about the deep clean, so I better go before he lets the locals take over."

I was running away. There was a lot going on inside my head and heart that I didn't want to process at the moment, the kiss with Hill now being at the top of the list. I also didn't want to give him the chance to be the one to walk away first. It was my turn to leave him hanging... confused and wondering what had gone wrong. I cringed at how callous my thoughts were, at how defensive I was being. One of these days we really needed to address what had happened between us in the past. I needed to know why he'd disappeared when I needed him most, but that would mean coming clean about how I felt about him. That would mean I'd have to face the fact that I really, really needed him in my life. I wasn't sure I was ready to be that honest with him, or myself. Not to mention I'd once again let my emotions get the better of me and lashed out in front of Hill. As usual he was the one who'd pulled me back from the edge and protected me from my worst enemy... which happened to be myself.

I'd deal with my surprise half sister and the fact that my father had left everything under the sun to her another day. That problem seemed much easier to tackle than the one staring at me with curious gray eyes.

Hill grunted his response and moved to lower the brim of his hat so I couldn't read his expression. I was both thankful and irritated that he didn't try to stop me when I turned on my heel and started to march my way over to my Jeep.

"Kody."

I stopped at the raspy sound of my name. I hesitated before looking over my shoulder at him.

The silver shine in his gaze had dulled out, and his expression was back to being hard and unreadable. "You and your brothers don't have many good memories, aside from your mom, in that house, and you all took those with you when you left. I'd guess Conrad knew none of you wanted anything to tie you to him or his legacy after he was gone. Dr. Baskin is a stranger. A stranger with his blood. He didn't leave the house to her as a gift. It was a gift to you and your brothers. That woman isn't going to be torn open going through the house, cleaning out all traces of your old man. She isn't going to have to relive every horrible mistake and choice he made where you guys were concerned. I don't think he did it to hurt. I think he did it to help."

I took a deep breath as I considered that and gave Hill a small nod. Then I walked to my Jeep without a word.

Hill always seemed to know the right thing to say. He had a way of putting even the most convoluted situations into perspective. Which was why I'd felt so lost and alone when he stopped taking my calls. Sure, I mostly asked him how I should handle Aaron, but during those talks I ended up seeking his guidance on pretty much everything. He was the first person I mentioned the idea of buying the bar to. He was the one I asked for advice when Case and his ex started having problems, and he was the one I went to with concerns when Crew started acting secretive and hiding things from the family. He really had been my security blanket, and when he yanked the comfort away, I'd never recovered.

When Aaron told me Hill probably didn't want to be burdened by the things going on back home, I'd believed him. I'd let the hurt at being one of those things override my instincts, which were screaming that something was wrong not only with the boy I loved, but with his older brother as well. I was mad at myself that I cared one way or another about what Hill was doing while he was away. I was pissed that, even though I loved Aaron with my whole heart, I couldn't quite deny that Hill was the one I couldn't seem to stop thinking about.

After our kiss I drove back to my bar in a daze. I couldn't forget that kiss...would never forget it. But my heart hurt. It hurt because while I'd always wondered what it would be like to kiss Hill Gamble, that desire was never fair to Aaron. I felt dishonest and guilty. I felt like, even though I'd gotten what I'd wanted, it had still been wrong to wish for it. I wondered if there would ever be a time in my life when I wasn't going to be a conflicted mess when it came to how I felt about the Gamble brothers. God, I hoped so. I'd like to be able to think clearly at least once.

When I walked inside the bar, I was surprised to see several butts already in the seats, and I realized it was getting close to happy hour. Lorenzo was behind the bar, head bent as he spoke to a customer, and Shelby was running around taking orders and flirting with the customers. It was nice to see a crowd. There had been a solid year or two after I'd opened the doors when I'd wondered if I was going to be able to keep the place afloat. The worry was less now, but there were still months when I had to get creative when it came to keeping the lights on and the liquor stocked.

Grateful for the distraction, I immediately jumped into work mode and started to help Shelby on the floor, since Lorenzo seemed to have the bar under control. I sold a pitcher of beer and some nachos to a table of tourists passing through, poppers and a whiskey sour to a rancher on his way back to his property, and sliders and sweet tea to a couple who were obviously on their first date, and I forced water and some artichoke dip on a group of young college kids who'd obviously overdone it on the two-for-one well shots deal. Shelby was getting ready to switch out with the night shift crew when Lorenzo suddenly called my name.

I looked over at the bar and noticed a man dressed like a soccer dad staring at me as he nervously tapped his fingers on the bar.

I didn't recognize him, but the nervous, anxious energy he was putting out I was all too familiar with. He looked like a man who was doing something wrong, knew it, and was desperate not to get caught.

Sighing, I asked one of the night cocktail servers to keep an eye on the potentially problematic frat boys and made my way to the bar. The suburban father looked me over nervously and spun his wedding ring around his finger multiple times. I walked around so I was on the other side of the bar and stopped in front of him. Arching an eyebrow, I asked, "What can I do for you today?"

The man in the wrinkled polo continued to play with his ring as he gazed down at the bar.

"I...uh...came in to try one of your specialty drinks." He lifted his head and muttered, "Barney sent me in."

I sighed and pushed some of my hair back from my face. Barney was the current name Shot and I used when someone wanted to come in and place a bet. The name changed every week or so. Shot and I were the only ones who ever knew what it was, to minimize the risk of getting busted by any lurking law enforcement agents. I'd had people come in and tell me they were sent by so-and-so, but if they got the name wrong, I knew what was up. So far no one had been able to trip me up.

I leaned on the bar and asked, "What did Barney suggest you get?"

The dad nearly fell off his stool. This was obviously new to him, and I could practically feel how anxious he was.

"He said I should get a double of the special reserve whiskey, and...uh...one for my friend when he gets here."

I sighed again and rapped my knuckles on the wooden bar. "The special reserve is pricey. You sure you don't want to start out with top shelf and work your way up?"

When I started acting as the middleman for people who wanted to place bets with the Sons of Sorrow, I'd told Shot the most money I would take from any one customer was five grand. I made him float me the cash to purchase the most expensive booze I could find, so if I ever got inspected by the health department, or the feds, the money in the register matched the product I had on hand. It was a pretty slick system that worked well and kept my conscience semiclean. If I wasn't taking hundreds of thousands of dollars from people, I still managed to sleep okay at night. And I always, always tried to talk the newbies out of getting in over their heads.

The dad sat up straighter on the bar stool and raked his hands through his thinning hair. "No. I need to try the special reserve."

Okay then. Folks needed to make their own mistakes in order to learn from them.

"All righty. What do you want me to pour you?" If Shot had sent him, he would know which special reserve to ask for. Since it was baseball season it was high-end tequila, and depending on which one he ordered I would know which team or teams he wanted to bet on. Whiskey was for football. Cognac for boxing and MMA. Rum for auto racing. Bourbon for the horses, and gin for basketball.

The nervous dad ordered the Clase Azul Ultra and the Patrón en Lalique. Two bets it was, one for each drink. It was amateurish to spread his bets like that, but when I mentioned it, he waved me off and simply asked for his shots chilled.

I set the very, very expensive shots in front of him after getting the fancy bottles out of the special locked and temperature-controlled room in the back.

I clinked the edge of my water bottle to the rim of his glass and muttered, "Bottoms up. Nothing is the same after you try the special reserve."

The guy nodded solemnly and left right after gulping down thousands of dollars of tequila in seconds.

I watched him go, realizing just how wrong letting myself kiss Hill had been. Not only because I felt guilty for kissing my first love's brother but because Hill was a good man, honest to a fault, with an unshakable sense of right and wrong.

He would never understand how I'd ended up selling outrageously expensive shots and taking money for a bunch of outlaw bikers. I doubted he would ever forgive me if he found out. He was the last man I should be kissing, for so many reasons.

But I felt even worse now that I could truthfully say he was the only man I *wanted* to kiss...

CHAPTER 10

∞

HILL

Do you think she had something to do with my dad's murder?"

I looked up from the text I was reading from Hearst. At this point I should put a welcome mat in front of my motel room for the Lawtons. It seemed like they were going to be visiting me on the regular until someone was behind bars and charged with Conrad's murder. It could be worse, I guessed. At least it was Case and not my mother knocking on my door.

"I think Baskin's hiding something and that she's scared. I'm guessing she found out Conrad was her father and latched on to the thought she was no longer alone after her mother passed away. I don't think she got what she bargained for when she sought him out." I tapped out a quick reply to Hearst and turned all my attention to Case.

My friend didn't look good. He appeared tired and worn out. The silver in his sideburns and temples seemed to be spreading throughout the rest of his dark hair, and his strong features were set in a ferocious scowl. I wanted to have better answers for him, but there simply weren't any. My gut said Dr. Baskin was somehow connected to what had happened to Conrad. But I didn't have any evidence.

"None of us got what we bargained for when she entered the picture. Kody came unglued in the estate lawyer's office. I thought she was going to rip his head off. Both Crew and I tried to keep her from tearing out of the office, but when she's determined..." He shook his head and sighed. "I'm worried she's going to do something really stupid before all of this is over. I want you to find who's responsible before my sister gets herself in the kind of trouble we can't get her out of."

I agreed with him. The texts from Hearst were ordering me to be in our makeshift office at the crack of dawn so we could have a video conference with our boss. No doubt we were going to get an earful about Kody crashing our interview the other day. Possibly even worse if Dr. Baskin had filed a formal complaint. Kody had made us look like amateurs. Made us look like fools in front of the only witness we had.

She had also turned me inside out with that kiss.

It had felt like it'd been a long time coming. Something I'd been waiting for without consciously knowing it. And now that I knew what it felt like to kiss her, to taste her, to hear the sounds she made when she was lost in the moment, there was no going back. The kiss was all I could think about, even though Kody had been doing her best to avoid me in the aftermath. She hadn't answered any of my calls over the last few days, and there had been no more ambush visits at my motel. I was planning on going to the bar to track her down and hash things out, but I'd been caught up in the case and hadn't found a free minute. I was used to chasing after her when she pushed me away, but this time, when I caught her, I wasn't letting go. I had a feeling Kody could feel the way the foundation of our relationship was shifting, which was why she'd been so harsh after the kiss. She was scared, and she was mean when she was afraid.

"I'm doing the best I can, Case. You, better than anyone, know how cases like this go." I felt like a broken record. I kept telling the Lawtons they could count on me, but had yet to prove it. Words carried only so much weight if there were no actions to back them up.

Case swore and started pacing in the small space in front of the bed. Really, I needed to upgrade my current accommodations if I was going to have so much company. My condo in Dallas had plenty of room, but oddly didn't feel any more like home than this motel room.

"I know, I know. I just feel...helpless. And I hate it. I'm used to having all the answers. Used to being the one in charge. It's been hard to take a backseat on something that's affecting my family so deeply."

"I know the feeling." I remembered feeling so confused and ineffective when Aaron had started to decline. Wanting to help but being too far away, and unsure how to do anything or even what the right thing was. I was sure Case was drowning in those feelings too.

Case stopped midstep and suddenly pinned me with a look that made me want to squirm.

"Why don't you step up and keep an eye on Kody? She trusts you, and she's more likely to listen to you than she is to me or Crew." He crossed his arms over his chest, gaze unwavering. "It's never been a secret you have a soft spot for her."

"You trying to push me and your sister together, Case?" He was always subtle when it came to letting me know he would have preferred me as the Gamble brother Kody had picked to give her heart to. This was the first time he'd outright given his stamp of approval to the idea of me being with his little sister in any kind of romantic way.

"I don't know. Maybe. Probably. There's always been a connection between the two of you, and anyone is better than that biker." He made a face and gave an exaggerated shudder. "What I wouldn't give for him to be out of the picture. You know, I'm about seventy-five percent sure Shot's the one who took out Jethro Coleman."

Back when Aspen was being threatened, Jethro Coleman was the former police officer her mother had hired to kill her. The man had gone on a shooting spree, hitting first the hospital, then the local high school. It'd been a dicey, scary situation for all, until a single bullet fired with a sniper's precision took Jethro out. There were only a few men within a thousand-mile radius who could've made a shot like that, and the biker was one of them.

"Oh, I agree." Only I was 100 percent sure Caldwell had been the one who took the killer out. Too bad there wasn't a single scrap of evidence to prove it. "How did the two of them get so close anyways?"

Case shrugged and resumed his pacing. "Not really sure. The club showed up out of the blue. Kody being Kody, she was suddenly thick as thieves with Shot. The guys hang out in her bar a lot on the weekends. I think they help bring business in. I don't like it, but I do have to admit Shot's always been good to her." He lifted his eyebrows in my direction and gave me a smirk. "But I think you would be better. You understand her. You accept her for who she is. You guys have history."

I sighed and scrubbed a hand down my face. "A history that includes my brother. I know it's been a long time, but you can't forget him, Case. He's there, right between us." Just like he always was.

Case grumbled something under his breath and pointed a finger in my direction. "Aaron loved both of you. I think he would want you and my sister to be happy. Even if the only way to get there is by the two of you being together. Aaron couldn't control his emotions, but he was never a bad or vindictive guy."

It was a struggle to think back to a time when Aaron had been happy. I could barely recall what he'd looked like when he smiled. The depression had taken over so much of who my younger brother was, it was nearly impossible to remember what he had been like when he wasn't shrouded in either sadness or anger.

"Well, he's not around to ask for his opinion, and Kody's made hers pretty clear. So while I appreciate the ringing endorsement, I don't think your sister is ever going to see me as more than an annoyance." Even if she had kissed the life out of me and reminded me what it felt like to get lost in the moment, to let go of reality and touch a dream.

Case looked like he was going to argue when his phone suddenly went off. I figured it was Aspen calling to check up on him. I was about to help myself to a beer from the minibar but stopped short when Case suddenly swore loud enough for the folks in the room next door to hear.

"How many people are involved?" He waited for a second, eyes catching mine. "Any injuries reported yet?" He shook his head, swearing again. "No. I'm headed out there now. Send a couple of patrol cars, but tell the officers I'll be on the scene along with a Texas Ranger and we'll both be armed."

I moved toward where I'd left my weapon and my hat. "What's going on?" Case was still barking orders into his cell phone as he headed toward the door, motioning for me to follow.

It wasn't until we were at his marked sheriff's SUV that he put his phone down and growled, "Bar fight out at Kody's place. It happens occasionally, but the Sons of Sorrow are there, which means it can turn into a bloodbath in a second. Shot and his boys don't play nice, and they don't mind spending the night in jail. We need to go bust it up before someone gets hurt."

"Absolutely." Like I was going to miss my chance to toss that biker in the slammer for a night or two. Anything to keep him away from Kody.

Case drove like a madman through the mostly sleepy town. He had the sirens blaring, and he didn't stop the steady stream of swear words under his breath until we reached the parking lot. The SUV screeched to a halt in a cloud of dust, the blue and red lights illuminating the crowd in front of the bar.

It looked as if everyone had spilled out into the parking lot. A circle of people surrounded a smaller group of men who appeared to be trying to put each other on the ground. Even from this distance I could see bloody noses, swollen eyes, and split lips. Two distinct groups of men seemed to be involved in the brawl. One side was dressed in leather and had the SoS logo on the backs of their jackets and vests. The other group looked like a handful of cowboys. They would probably have no trouble holding their own under typical circumstances, but they didn't stand a chance against a bunch of pissed-off bikers.

"How do you want to handle this?" While it'd been some time since I'd had to wade into a bar fight, I remembered how to avoid a broken nose.

Case sighed and reached for the radio attached to the dash of his SUV. A second later his voice boomed out of a speaker.

"Sheriff's department! Break it up or you're all going to jail!"

The announcement was enough to send those on the outskirts of the circle scattering, some to their cars, most back toward the bar. The bikers and the cowboys barely flinched. In fact it seemed like the announcement ramped up their efforts to do as much damage to one another as possible.

"I guess we're going in." I took my hat off and set it on the hood of the SUV.

Case grunted and gave a nod. "Watch your weapon. I wouldn't put it past either side to go for it in the heat of the moment."

It sounded like he was speaking from experience, which made me wonder exactly who watched out for Kody when her customers got out of control. If situations like this were common, someone should be doing something to keep her and her employees safe.

I swore under my breath and followed Case toward the mayhem. He was grumbling about getting too old to keep breaking up bar fights, which made me roll my eyes at his back. He was younger than me, and I could still hold my own. There was no easing into the bedlam. Both of us were immediately drawn into the fray.

I caught a wild punch before it connected with my cheek. I pulled a skinny biker with a green mohawk off a much heavier cowboy and told him to knock it off. I sidestepped a cowboy boot someone had removed and sent flying at my head, slowly and methodically making my way to the center of the dogpile.

Once there, I wasn't surprised to find Shot in the thick of things. He was easy to spot with that skull tattoo on the back of his bloodied fist and the sheer skill with which he fought. He was a weapon, trained and honed to inflict the most damage possible. The guy going up against him didn't stand a chance if Shot really wanted to cause some permanent damage, which it appeared he was holding himself back from doing. There was another, bigger guy, positioned with his back to Shot. It was clear his job was to make sure no one came at his brother while his back was turned. It was also clear he didn't care about the law, because he didn't bother to try to hide the brass knuckles wrapped around both of his hands.

"Caldwell." I called Shot's name, trying to get his attention, and was ignored. I reached out to grab his shoulder and was immediately cut off by the guy with the brass knuckles.

"Back off, cop."

I narrowed my eyes and dodged another fist coming at my face. "Break it up." I pointed to his hands. "Those are illegal, by the way."

The biker gave me a smirk and used one of his metal-wrapped hands to knock out a charging cowboy.

"I know."

Fighting back a sigh, I told him flatly, "You're under arrest."

The biker chuckled and held up his hands in a mocking manner. "Of course I am." He lifted an eyebrow and asked, "Why don't you ask the prez who started this?"

Shot suddenly appeared at my side. His cheek was bleeding and his eyes were hard. "Don't say anything, Top. I'm gonna call our lawyer."

The biker, who I suddenly noticed had a VICE PREZ patch on his worn, battered leather vest, chuckled again. "Good thing we have him on retainer. Seriously, Shot, why don't you tell the cop about how that asshole grabbed Kody? Tell him how he put his hands on her without permission and got pissed when Kody put him in his place. His fragile ego couldn't handle being embarrassed in front of his buddies, so he called Kody a bunch of names and said it was no wonder her fiancé killed himself to get away from her."

I went stiff as a board and felt ice start to form in my veins. I looked down at the cowboy writhing on the ground at Shot's booted feet and had a flash of regret the man was still breathing.

"He threw the first punch when I kicked him out of the bar. We didn't start this shit, but there's no way we weren't going to finish it." Shot wiped the blood off his cheek and narrowed his dark eyes at me. "Do what you have to do, Ranger, but at least someone was here to have her back when she needed it."

Before I could come up with an appropriate response, the parking lot was flooded with deputies from Case's department. Chaos ensued as those who were still able to move tried to flee. Except for the bikers. The majority of them immediately dropped to their knees, hands behind their heads, fingers laced together, like this was old hat.

Moving past Shot, I snapped handcuffs around the tattooed wrists of his second in command, stripping him of the brass knuckles as I did so. Shot stood and watched it all go down with a dispassionate expression, gaze flicking between his brothers and the cops to make sure everyone behaved themselves.

Against my better judgment I asked, "Is Kody okay?"

Shot's eyes narrowed even more. "Has she ever been okay?" He turned and headed toward where Case was arguing with one of the cowboys, effectively dismissing me.

It took around forty-five minutes to get the mess cleaned up and everyone booked and then put in a car or the paddy wagon. There were going to be a lot of regrets tomorrow morning, not that any of Shot's boys looked a bit sorry.

Case told me he had to go to the station after he ran into the bar to check on Kody, but offered to drop me off back at the motel on the way. I waved him off and told him I wanted to see that Kody was all right for myself. I should have kept my mouth shut, because he didn't bother to hide his satisfied smile as he flicked his fingers against the brim of his hat in a hasty goodbye.

The bar was pretty empty after all the ruckus, and Kody was nowhere to be found. I got a dirty look from the same bartender I'd asked to stick around and clean the place. He inclined his chin in the direction of her office and growled, "She probably doesn't want any visitors right now, but since you have a badge, do what you want. You will any-way."

Not bothering to respond to the snark, I took the stairs up to the loft two at a time. I knocked briefly, but went in without waiting for her to say it was okay.

She was sitting on the floor, back to the wall, with her forehead resting on her knees. She didn't look up as I approached her, but she did mumble, "I want to be alone."

I sat down on the hard wooden floor next to her and sighed. "How about we be alone together, then?"

When she lifted her head to look at me, the expression on her face broke my heart. It was one I recognized well. It was the look of someone who really wondered if they were responsible for the death of someone they loved.

"Aaron didn't have to die." Her voice cracked and her lower lip trembled. "I've been thinking about it a lot lately."

"No, he didn't." There was so much more we all could

have done if only we'd known more about what was going on with him.

She released a hiccupping breath and met my gaze with a hard, brittle one of her own. "Sometimes I blame you for him being gone."

It hurt to hear, but I wasn't surprised. "I know you do." It was the main reason I'd kept my distance after he passed away. She used to look at me with something like excitement and admiration. My already tattered heart couldn't take it when she started looking at me with disappointment and doubt.

"I blame you so I don't have to blame myself. It gets exhausting, trying to figure out which one of us screwed up more. We both made so many mistakes."

I reached out and put my hand on top of her folded ones. "There's plenty of blame to go around. But you stayed by his side, stuck with him no matter how bad it got. You tried your best to keep him here. You did the work, Kody. I avoided how bad his condition was getting. I couldn't let go of the idea of having my happy, healthy brother back. You did everything you could, I didn't do nearly enough. I was too busy trying to protect myself, selfishly caught up in my own feelings, I didn't stop to think how staying away would affect you and my brother. I'm always telling you to consider how your actions might hurt the ones you love, and I blatantly ignored my own advice. That's why I've never minded shouldering the blame for what went wrong that night. But I do think it's probably time some of the damn blame lands on Aaron. We both pushed him to get help. Maybe we let him down, but he let us down too."

She exhaled deeply, and I swear I felt the caress of it all along my skin.

"Changed my mind. I don't want to be alone." She tilted her head to the side and asked so softly I wasn't certain I heard her correctly, "Will you stay with me?"

On the off chance that I wasn't hallucinating, I gave her the only response I was capable of.

"Always."

CHAPTER 11

∞

KODY

I wasn't sure how long we sat on the floor in silence. It felt like forever, yet not nearly long enough. There was a lot left to be said between the two of us, but the quiet was nice, and needed. Even with the noise from the bar down below, I was in my own little world. The only thing that existed was the gentle caress of Hill's hand gliding over the top of my head and down to the ends of my hair. I couldn't recall the last time I'd felt like I could breathe this easy, or everything inside of me had felt so still and calm. It was as if his touch was a soothing balm to all my desperately frayed edges.

I might've even drifted off for a minute or two, but when Lorenzo knocked on the door and told me last call was done, I shook off the stupor. Hill offered to close up, but the look of pure horror on Lorenzo's face told me taking him up on it would be a bad idea. I didn't have the time, patience, or trust to bring someone new on staff. I wasn't about to let Hill run off my best bartender, even if his intentions were good.

Once Lorenzo went back downstairs I said, "You can head out." I tried to sound unaffected, but there was a wobble in my voice, and I was sure he could plainly see my fear of being left alone stamped all over my face. Well, it wasn't so much the fear of being alone as it was the fear of him walking away from me just when I decided I wanted to hold on to him.

Hill shook his head and leaned back against the wall, taking his hat off so he could rest his head against the hard surface. He extended his long legs in front of him and closed his eyes.

"I'm going to hang out. Case was my ride and he's long gone. If you don't mind, I'm going to bum a ride back to the motel when you're ready to go." He sounded casual about the request, but there was some kind of deeper emotion in his tone.

Maybe it was a hidden suggestion that I go back to his room with him for the rest of the night. Or maybe that was what I wanted the tone to mean.

I ran down the stairs and helped Lorenzo shut the bar down. He apologized multiple times for not having been there to have my back when the handsy, insulting cowboys got out of control. I assured him it wasn't in his job description to keep me safe. Especially from the people in this town who knew exactly where to hit in order to take me down. I grew up in the shadow of whispers and speculation about my father and what was going on inside my house. I lived with the endless weight of "I told you so" and "You should've known better" after everything that happened with Aaron. I should have a thicker skin by now. I usually pretended I did. But after all that had happened with my father and my newly found half sister, the armor I typically wore was paper thin. It was fortunate Shot had been at the bar to pick up his payment. He'd stepped in to fight for me when I forgot for a second how to fight for myself.

"Business has been picking up lately." Lorenzo made the observation as he placed the stools up on the bar. "Maybe it's time to consider hiring an actual bouncer, or some kind of security on nights we think there might be a full house. Some of the girls mentioned they would feel more comfortable if they had eyes on them when the crowd gets rowdy."

I wiped the back bar with more force than necessary and angrily kicked one of the beer coolers. "Why did they tell you and not me? I'm the boss." Which meant I should know if my employees felt unsafe while on the clock.

Lorenzo shrugged. "Probably because you've been out of it lately. First it was that mess with Crew and the gambling debt, then Case landed himself in the middle of an actual shootout. Before you could catch your breath from all of that, your dad ends up dead, and there's a big, brooding Texas Ranger hanging around all the time. No one blames you for not putting work first all the time."

I kicked the cooler again and threw the rag toward the sink tucked under the bar top. "Maybe I can get a pass for not focusing on work, but the people who work *for* me should always be a priority. It's always been important for me to take care of you guys." I wanted to be a good boss, someone they could rely on. It didn't take a genius to know I tried to save people because I hadn't managed to save the one who mattered most.

"Don't stress too much. I'm sure they would've come to you when things calmed down. After tonight it seemed like a good idea to bring it up. We worry about you just as much as you worry about us." Lorenzo slapped his palm on the bar. "I'm outta here. I want to escape before the Ranger decides to come down and make me scrape gum off the bottoms of all the tables again."

I snorted and waved him off. "I'll protect you from him. And I'll ask Shot if he has anyone he would recommend to watch the door." I figured the biker probably had some scary friends on speed dial looking to make some extra cash.

Lorenzo paused midstep and shot me a look over his shoulder. "You might want to ask the Ranger for a name instead. Something tells me he won't like you asking Shot for any more favors. Unless you want to rile the big guy up." He gave me a wink and disappeared out the door, the quiet click of the lock following him.

I cast a glance up the stairs to where I'd left Hill.

I could only imagine his reaction when he showed up to a full-on biker brawl in front of my bar. I was sure he was disappointed and that it'd taken all his self-control not to jump into a lecture the minute he saw me.

I finished cleaning up, making sure to wash my hands and pull my thoughts together before going back upstairs.

As soon as I hit the threshold of my office I heard the heavy sound of Hill's breathing. My steps automatically lightened when I realized he'd fallen asleep where I'd left him sprawled on the floor. His head was tilted to the side, blond hair messy and mouth slack as a soft snore escaped. *Adorable* wasn't a word I'd typically associate with the rough, rugged man, but right now, when he was unaware and unguarded, he really looked cute. Almost cuddly.

Snickering under my breath at what his reaction would be if he knew what I was thinking, I reached out to brush some of his wayward golden hair off his forehead.

I got an immediate reminder that while he might look soft and gentle, the man was anything but.

He'd been a soldier. He'd been a border patrol agent. He

was now a Texas Ranger. He'd carried a gun since he was eighteen years old and learned how to defend himself long before that.

Hill came awake almost instantly. Gray eyes glittering and dangerous. I gasped as I found myself suddenly thrown backward, landing on the floor with him vibrating and tense above me. Both of my hands were clamped tightly in one of his and pulled above my head. One of his legs slid between mine, effectively pinning me between his body and the hardwood floor. The feel of his weight against me, and the press of all those muscles against all my soft and secret places, made my head spin. I watched him blink slowly, the sleep gradually fading from the sharp silver edge of his gaze.

I figured he was going to immediately apologize for manhandling me. That would be such a Hill thing to do. Take the blame, even though I was the one who'd startled him when I should've known better. It was on the tip of my tongue to cut the apology off. I was opening my mouth to tell him I didn't mean to wake him up, but the words never made it anywhere. As soon as my lips parted, Hill's head descended and his mouth sealed over mine.

I stopped breathing for a solid ten seconds. The kiss was so unexpected, so out of character for him. He was not a man who acted rashly or impulsively. He was the type who thought everything through, who had a plan. But there was nothing routine about the way he moved his mouth over mine.

His tongue immediately swept inside my mouth, tasting, testing, teasing. I was already having a hard time keeping up when he released my hands, and they landed helplessly on his shoulders as he continued to kiss me into oblivion.

I let out a surprised whimper when I felt his warm, slightly rough palm slide under the hem of my shirt. His thumb traced along the raised line of my hip bone, and the rest of his fingers spread possessively across my lower abdomen. It felt like his touch seared my skin. I wondered if I was going to have his handprint permanently there as a reminder of his touch.

I made a strangled, nearly panicked sound low in my throat, and Hill's head immediately lifted. Some of the wild glitter that made his light eyes sparkle appeared to clear, and he shot a look down the length of our bodies, which were perfectly aligned. The bulge at the front of his jeans was clearly visible, as were the twin points of my nipples where they pressed insistently against my bra and the thin material of my T-shirt.

His eyes closed briefly and he let out a shuddering sigh. "Goddammit, Kody." He shook his head like he was trying to clear it and gazed down at me with an intensity I felt all the way down to my toes. "Why is it you—and only you—who makes me lose my damn head?"

I felt him tense against me and watched as the bicep of the arm he was using to brace himself over me flexed. He was going to go. He was going to rein those unchecked, primitive reactions back in. Who knew when I was going to get the chance to see them again?

Before he could fully pull himself away, I locked my arms around his neck and wrapped a leg around one of his strong thighs. He made an oomph sound and sort of collapsed back on top of me. I tugged his mouth back to mine and none too subtly rolled my hips against his. The feel of that hard, rigid flesh trapped behind his zipper made me moan. I wanted to touch it, to get intimately familiar with the weight and width of it. I wanted my hands on his erection. My mouth on it. I wanted to drive him out of his mind until he had no choice but to put the impressive length inside me.

Desire was pushing my common sense into a quiet corner where it was easy to ignore. There was no more keeping control. All there was was the haze of passion and need that seemed to entwine us together.

When I arched my hips up off the floor once again, thrusting my tongue between Hill's teeth, he took advantage of my bowed position to tug my T-shirt up my torso and balanced me with a hand on my spine as I wiggled obediently out of the fabric. I gasped against his mouth when I felt the clasp on my bra pop open and again when my shoulders hit the chilly floor.

Hill lifted his head, and I could clearly see he was willing to give me an out. All I needed to do was tell him to stop, to remind him what a bad idea this was, and he would walk away...probably for good. However, every single cell in my body was screaming I couldn't let that happen. Rarely did I know with absolute certainty the choice I was making was the right one. Right now, I'd never been more sure of anything. I *needed* Hill to keep going.

I threaded my fingers through his hair and pulled his head down until his mouth was hovering enticingly over the tip of one puckered nipple. His breath was hot and damp against the stiff peak, which made me arch my back in an effort to get closer. I closed my eyes and panted incoherent words of encouragement. Then I forgot how to speak when I finally felt the sweep of his tongue against the painfully hard point. The tiniest touch of the tip of his tongue sent a lightning bolt of pleasure shooting down my spine. His palm skated down my ribs, both soothing and seducing, once again tracing my hip bones and pausing briefly when his fingers ran into the top of my jeans. I felt him walk his fingers along the edge of the fabric as his teeth suddenly tightened on the delicate flesh caught between them.

He increased the suction at the same time his skillful fingers delved underneath the denim blocking their way.

My stomach quivered, and the slick, steadily warming spot between my legs fluttered in anticipation. Hill didn't bother to pop the button on my pants or to tug the zipper down. Instead he used the confined space to create more friction across my sensitive skin. When his fingertips glided with purpose through damp folds and across velvety skin, I wondered if I was going to burst into flames. I couldn't think of any other time in my life when I'd been this hot, when I'd felt this alive and electric.

"Hill. I feel like I'm going insane."

I moaned his name and yanked on his hair as he continued to torture my swollen nipple with his teeth.

"This is crazy." I couldn't believe this was happening, and that it was so much better than any of my secret fantasies had ever been.

His response was to feather his fingertips against my anxious and eager opening. My entire body practically levitated off the floor at the contact. My hips rolled and my legs involuntarily spread to give him more room. My fingers spread wide on the back of his head, clamping him in place so he couldn't escape. Not that he was trying to.

Slowly, methodically his fingers were exploring, learning my body. The pressure was delicious and consuming. The only thing I could think about was the pleasure coursing through me. Nothing had ever felt as good as being under Hill's deliberate, steady hands. It was like he knew exactly where to touch, where all my hidden hot spots were. I was mad at myself for running from this level of satisfaction for so long.

"Oh my God." The words tripped on a tongue that felt too big for my mouth. My fingernails dug into the back of his head hard enough to make him grunt. I was going to apologize, but he switched his attention to my other breast, using his teeth to bite and tug. Pleasure mingled with pain in a sharp, delicious spike as his fingers finally sank all the way inside me.

The overwhelming sensation of being stretched and filled sent my vision to bursts of bright, white light. Hill's name came out in a strangled sound as I frantically pulled his head up and away from my breast so I could kiss the life out of him. I could no longer remember any doubt about being with him. This was the only place I wanted to be, where I *needed* to be.

I started to resent the restraint my jeans put on his movements. He had to keep his strokes shallow and light because his hands were big and the space he was working with was small. His touch was slippery and sure as my body reacted with obvious excitement to every twist of his fingers and flick of his thumb across the coiled bundles of nerves hidden by delicate folds. I was making noises I should be embarrassed by, saying things I knew I was going to regret when I could think clearly, but I didn't care. I was too greedy. Too hungry for more of him, for more of the insane feelings he sent spiraling through me. I'd completely forgotten what it felt like to be this close, this connected to someone you cared about.

"I used to dream about being able to touch you like this. It was all I could think about. It was so confusing. I wasn't supposed to think about putting my hands all over my brother's girl." Hill's voice was ragged, and I could hear both longing and guilt laced around every word. It matched my feelings exactly. I pulled him back down for a kiss because I couldn't respond.

He touched my body with unmatched skill, but it was my

heart he managed to get a reaction out of, when no one else had been able to. It was amazing how he managed to be both the calm and the storm in my life.

I wanted to scream when his fingers suddenly scissored apart at the same time that his thumb pressed down in steady circles on my clit. The kiss we were caught up in went sloppy and uncoordinated as his tongue began to mimic the motion of his hand sliding in and out of my now-drenched opening.

When he pulled his head back and looked down at me, eyes molten, it was the longing and pure appreciation in his gaze that pushed me over the edge. I'd never felt more beautiful. More desired. More necessary. It was as if pleasing me was his only purpose and his greatest accomplishment.

My body went liquid and pliant. I succumbed to the rush of pleasure, floating away in a fog of bliss. I felt his fingers stroke through the flood of moisture and watched as a self-satisfied smile broke across his handsome face. It was the first real smile I'd seen on him in ages, and it did something to my heart to realize I was the one who'd put it there. I felt protective of it. Possessive even.

I was thinking of all the ways I could make that smile even bigger. All of them included getting him naked and getting my pants off, but then his phone started to ring.

I grew up with a father in law enforcement, and spent a lot of time with an older brother who'd also vowed to protect and serve. I knew a call this late in the night wasn't anything good.

Hill hastily detangled himself from my embrace, though he kept the hand with wet fingers low on my stomach, tracing an aimless pattern on my skin as he grumbled one-word answers to whoever was on the other end of the line.

He swore viciously, and the look in his eyes shifted from appraising and pleased to shady and dark.

"I have to go. Hearst will be here in a few minutes to pick me up."

I nodded and took my shirt from him when he handed it to me. I knew better than to ask him where he was going. Before I crashed his interview with my half sister he might've told me, but I'd blown that tentative trust out of the water by acting impulsively.

"I wouldn't leave if I didn't have to. You know that, right? There are things that still need to be said."

He sounded genuinely concerned that I was going to lose it when he left. I lifted a hand and cupped his cheek.

"One of these days we're both going to be the same level of undressed, and it's either going to be the best or the worst thing that has ever happened to us." I leaned forward and dropped a kiss on the end of his nose. "Go. Catch the bad guys and don't get hurt. You know where to find me when you get back."

He nodded gravely, reluctance clear in every line of his face and every slow movement he made. When he was gone and I was alone, I flopped onto my back and stared up at the ceiling.

I had no idea what I was doing. I knew down to my soul that if things went south with Hill it would ruin more than our tenuous relationship.

Things were changing. But I couldn't say if they were changing for better or worse yet, and that was terrifying. But not scary enough to keep me away.

CHAPTER 12

∞

HILL

"Why didn't you tell me you had a unit watching the doctor?"

I had taken over driving duty since I was more familiar with the dark Texas roads. Plus Hearst's phone hadn't stopped ringing and dinging since the moment he picked me up. Hearst looked up briefly from the new message coming through and gave me a pointed stare. "Because I'm not sure where your head is at. I know you're only here as a consultant, but you're too close to this case. Or rather, too close to the people involved. If anyone else had crashed an interview with our only witness you would've locked them up for obstruction. I need to keep the doctor within my sights because I'm pretty sure she's connected to the murder, *and* so your little friend doesn't scare her off. The woman is ready to jump at any shadow that moves."

I cringed because he was speaking the truth. My objectivity was shot to hell, had been since I set foot back in Loveless. It was even more blown out of the water now that

I knew how sweetly Kody could say my name when she was losing control. How she looked writhing under my hands and trapped underneath my mouth.

I knocked the side of my fist on the steering wheel and wished there were a reasonable argument I could offer up in my defense. But there wasn't one. After all, he'd had to pick me up from Kody's bar in the middle of the night, and I was sure he'd heard all about the fight I'd helped break up. He was right. I was too close, and it was starting to cause problems.

"Why do the cops think Dr. Baskin is making a run for it?" Baskin was twitchy and nervous, but she didn't seem like the rash sort. She was too calm and methodical—at least that was my impression of the woman so far. Plus, she was on the brink of a huge career advancement opportunity. Now would be the worst time for her to disappear.

"She traded in the Tesla today. Picked up some nondescript four-door sedan from a dealer. Paid cash. When she got back to her friend's place she loaded up the trunk with what seemed like her personal belongings and was visibly upset. The friend was nowhere to be found, so I had the guys watching her look into where the friend might have ended up." Hearst turned his attention back to his phone, rapidly typing out a message as he kept talking. "Turns out, the friend was pushed off a curb in the middle of rush hour in downtown Austin yesterday. She got pretty banged up and ended up with a concussion. She swears it was deliberate, the cops investigating think she had one too many at happy hour. Either way, Baskin is spooked and waited until after midnight before jumping in the new car and hitting the road. She stopped about a hundred miles outside of Austin at a no-tell motel. Our unit asked if they should approach her, but I figured she'd have an easier time talking to us. She has no choice but to explain what's really going on now."

The doctor had literally been caught in the act. Most law enforcement operated with the idea that an innocent person wouldn't run. But I still felt like she was running based on fear rather than guilt.

"I feel like I owe you an apology. I'm supposed to be here to help guide the case and offer insight into the Lawtons and Conrad's life. I got so caught up in the past and how they're all feeling right now, I lost sight of the overall objective." In short, I was doing shit at my job, the one thing I'd always been best at.

Hearst looked up from his phone once again, this time with a quizzical expression on his face. "The objective is to find whoever killed Conrad Lawton. I don't think we'd have gotten as close to the doc without your in with the family. We would still be chasing our tails. It doesn't look like any of the Lawton siblings are involved in their father's death, thank God, but I do worry about them ganging up on Baskin and alienating her. We need her. I don't trust you to pick any side other than the Lawtons' if it comes to a showdown, even if they're in the wrong." His eyebrow winged up, and a smirk twisted the corner of his mouth. "I knew you had history with the sister, but I guess it was never fully disclosed how deep that connection was. You can't see anything or anyone else when she's around. If it wasn't happening in the middle of my murder investigation I'd say it was cute as hell."

I grumbled under my breath. "She loved my brother first." Those words were the brick and mortar of the wall forever standing between the two of us. A wall I might have finally taken a hammer to tonight when I admitted to Kody that she'd been on my mind from the start—as something much more than my brother's girlfriend.

Hearst snorted. "So what? That means she can't love you, or anyone else after...or at the same time? That's not the way love works. There isn't a limited supply that runs out. Love is endless."

I scratched my chin and gave him a look out of the corner of my eye. "Aren't you single, champ? If you're such an expert on love and romance, why aren't you settled down?"

Hearst wiggled his well-groomed eyebrows up and down and a wide grin split his face. "I love love. In all different shapes and forms. I've never met anyone I wanted to give my all to. Plus, I'm gone all the time. It works for me to keep my options open. There's a good time waiting for me no matter where I end up, and I don't mind keeping it that way."

It was such a different outlook from my own. I'd been hung up on Kody for as long as I could remember. The idea of a life with her followed me everywhere I went and blocked my view of anyone else. Maybe he was right and the love I had was endless, but it was always all for one person.

"The motel we're looking for is up here on the left off the exit. The unit I have watching her says she checked in and hasn't left. My guess, this is a pit stop and she's planning on driving as far as she can tomorrow. Probably trying to get out of Texas." Hearst seemed to weigh the validity of his thoughts. "We don't have any direct connection between her and the murder, so we can't tell her she can't go. Our best bet is to get her to finally give us the truth about why she's running. Maybe whatever has her spooked so bad will shed some light on Conrad's case."

I nodded in agreement, parking the rental car behind her loaded-up sedan and wondering what could have had Dr. Baskin skipping out on her entire life in the middle of the night. It reminded me of the situation Aspen had suddenly found herself in. Case's girlfriend was forced to go into hiding because someone wanted her dead. I was curious about whether the doctor had found herself in similar circumstances. She didn't seem to have any enemies—other than Kody—at the moment. So it was obvious we were missing a pretty big piece of the puzzle.

I let Hearst take the lead as we headed toward her room. I stifled a yawn, wondering when I was going to get another full night's sleep. Not that I was ever going to complain about missing out on a few hours of sleep if it meant I got to get closer to Kody Lawton.

The curtains covering the window shifted slightly as we approached. They swished shut as soon as Hearst pounded on the door.

"Dr. Baskin. It's Special Agent Hearst. I need to speak with you." He looked over at me and shrugged. "Sorry, it can't wait until morning."

He wasn't sorry at all. The woman really hadn't given us a choice.

There was the sound of rustling and then a thump on the other side of the door. It took way longer than it should've for the door to open a crack. Even the small peek of Baskin showed she looked haggard and worn. The stress was clear in her tired gaze.

"How do I know I won't be attacked again if I speak to you? Are you sure you weren't followed this time? Maybe I need to call a lawyer." She cleared her throat and went to shut the door, but Hearst was quick and crammed the toe of his Nike in the opening before she could.

"We weren't followed. I picked up during our last meeting that you were on edge about something. We took extra precautions for your safety. I'm hoping you'll explain what's going on, Dr. Baskin, because I have to admit, everything surrounding this murder seems to point to you."

Shock and sadness moved across the woman's face. Her indecision was clear. Hearst waited her out, but it was when she finally looked up at me and I gave her a tiny nod that she backed up a step and reluctantly unhooked the chain on the door.

I held up a hand and inclined my head toward the SUV. "How about we meet in the car?" I didn't want to invade her space. And I didn't want to make her sit in the motel room with the two of us when she was already anxious. "You can leave whenever you want."

The redhead let out a visible breath of relief and asked for a minute. When she came back out of her room she slid into the backseat of the car. I noticed she had a plastic bag clutched in one hand and her cell phone in the other.

"Are you sure no one followed you?" Her voice cracked, and she wrenched her neck around to look out the back window toward the darkened sky.

"As sure as can be. We had a unit watching you, and they made sure you weren't followed when you left Austin as well. Do you want to tell me who you're on the run from?" Hearst gave me a look. "Even if it's one of the Lawtons."

It was on the tip of my tongue to argue, but I bit it back and gave another nod to let the doctor know this was a safe space and we were on her side.

A moment later, she leaned forward and dropped the plastic bag with a thump in Hearst's lap. I reached out to turn on the overhead lights, my breath catching when the contents of the bag became visible.

"I'm betting if you run ballistics, that's the weapon that was used to kill Conrad Lawton." The doctor's voice was barely above a whisper. "That was on the passenger seat of my Tesla this morning. A few hours later my best friend was almost killed. And those are just a few of the things that have been going on over the last month."

Hearst held up the plastic bag and let out a low whistle. "Damn."

The doctor wrapped her arms around herself and sat back in the rear seat. "At first I thought I was just stressed out because of my mother's declining health and then her death. I knew I wasn't at the top of my game. It was little incidents here and there. I'd come home and swear the furniture was different, or I wouldn't be able to find something I was sure I put somewhere. My back door was open one day, and my cat disappeared. It was all so odd I decided to go stay with my friend for a little while. I work long hours and my job is stressful, so I thought maybe I just needed a break and should focus on my mom, but then I missed one of her dialysis appointments because the time and date I had scheduled changed, and I was told one of her insurance payments was never made. I was never, ever careless when it came to her health, so I started to get paranoid and really beat myself up."

She scrubbed her hands over her face and blinked obviously tired eyes at us. "I felt like a terrible daughter, and things at work started to go south as well. Two of my findings on two separate homicide cases ended up getting thrown out because the chain of possession of the evidence was compromised. The paperwork was screwed up, and it seemed like I was the one who dropped the ball. I had a pristine track record at work before I was offered the promotion. I'm one of the best, but more and more mistakes were being made, even though I wasn't the one making them. Those kind of inconsistencies mean murderers and rapists go free, so I was becoming a liability. I took a leave of absence, postponed taking the promotion, and decided to focus on spending time with my mother before I ruined my reputation and career."

She sucked in a deep breath and rubbed her hands up and down her thighs. "My mom was dead a few days later. She'd been sick a long time. I knew it was coming, but no one could really explain why she'd taken such a bad turn overnight. Something wasn't right about it."

"Hold up." Hearst lifted a hand and shook his head. "Are you telling me you think your mother was murdered?"

The doctor shrugged. "I don't know what to think. When I spoke to a colleague in the ME's office they said the results of her autopsy were perfectly normal. I really felt like I was going out of my mind. But then I found out about Conrad, and as soon as I made contact with him, he also ended up dead. I can't help but wonder if it's all because of me."

She pointed a shaking finger in the direction of the gun. "I saw that and knew I wasn't crazy. Someone has been gaslighting me. Someone is trying to set me up for murder. I was planning on taking it to the police, but then Ashby got hurt and I realized everyone around me is in danger. I don't know the Lawtons, but that doesn't mean anything terrible should happen to them because they're suddenly related to me." She dropped her head, her chin practically touching her chest. "I honestly don't know what to do anymore."

Hearst let out a low whistle. "That's some story."

The woman sighed and put a hand to her chest like she was trying to hold her heart in place. "It's true. I don't make mistakes. And I didn't kill Conrad. I have no idea why he changed his will, and I've never seen that gun before it showed up in my car today." She let out a bitter-sounding laugh. "I think in the back of my mind I was hoping maybe Conrad could help me since he used to be a cop. That's how desperate I was. I wanted to rely on a stranger to fix things and I may have gotten him killed."

I grunted. "Conrad wasn't the kind of cop who helped. Did you get around to telling him what was going on with you? Did he know you felt like you were in danger? Did you mention something was strange about your mother's death?" That might have been enough to get him to head to Austin that night.

She paused but shook her head. "No. Like I've said, I told him who I was and explained about my mom keeping my father's identity and the blackmail a secret my entire life. I offered to pay back the money and he turned me down. The conversation was short."

I cocked my head to the side and narrowed my eyes slightly. "When we looked into you, we couldn't find any known enemies. Do you have any idea *why* anyone would be doing all these things to you? Who would benefit from you going away for Conrad's murder?"

The doctor sighed heavily and slowly started to rub her temples. "I don't know. I'm kind of a loner and keep to myself. I've worked on some very high-profile homicide cases in my career, so I suppose it could be tied to that. It was always just me and my mom, so I honestly don't know who would benefit from my downfall."

I cleared my throat. "No scorned lovers or angry ex-boyfriends with an ax to grind?" Love, when it was bad, really did make people act all sorts of unpredictable ways.

She shook her head again. "No."

"What about competition at work? You said you were recently offered a pretty big promotion. Who gets the job if you're suddenly out of the running?" Hearst started to take pictures of the weapon with his phone, careful to make sure he didn't contaminate the evidence in any way.

Presley sat up straighter and narrowed her eyes. "My best friend, the one who nearly died today. Ashby Grant. We went to medical school together. We both decided to work for the medical examiner's office at the same time, instead of going the more traditional route when it comes to medicine. We've been friends for years. She's my rock. I don't know what I would do without her. I'm absolutely sick she's lying in a hospital bed because of me right now." She sounded like she was on the verge of tears.

"I understand why you thought the best option was to run, but I think you need to let us help you. If people are dying around you, there has to be a reason behind it. Also, if someone really went as far as to plant a murder weapon on you, I doubt you've seen the end of this scheme, no matter how far you run. Come back to Loveless with us, let us talk to our boss and see if we can put you in protective custody." Hearst was giving her the hard sell, and I could tell she wasn't really buying it.

I turned in my seat and gave her a steady, even look. "You have family in Loveless. If you honestly think they're in danger, you should tell them that and explain why. Like it or not, you're all connected from here on out."

Her gaze shifted between me and Hearst, hesitation clear on every feature of her face. "Do you really think you can help me?"

I nodded. "We can do our best." I didn't bother to mention that if she was lying and actually had something to do with Conrad's murder, I'd lock her up so fast her head would spin. "I don't think this is a problem you can solve on your own." Regardless of how smart she was.

It was a damn shame she'd gotten off on the wrong foot with the Lawtons. There was no one better to have your back when you were facing the kind of fight this woman was facing. I just hoped things didn't go from bad to worse for her when they found out there was now concrete and irrefutable evidence tying her to what happened to Conrad. No matter how questionable the origins of the evidence might be, the gun was very damning, and enough to blind the Lawtons to anything other than justice for their father.

CHAPTER 13

∞

KODY

"I hooked up with Hill last night."

The words burst out before the door to Aspen's office shut all the way. I saw her paralegal lift her eyebrows and heard her secretary giggle as it swung closed behind my not-safe-for-work announcement.

Aspen sat back in her leather chair and waved me over. I'd asked her secretary if she was busy before barging in. Since it was close to lunchtime I'd thought I might catch her in between clients. I was right. Aspen appeared to be eating a sandwich at her desk. Well, she had been before I burst in and dropped the bomb about me and Hill.

Aspen wiped her hands on a napkin and delicately cleared her throat. "Okay. Let's talk about it. How are you feeling?"

I flopped into one of the chairs across from her fancy desk and kicked my feet up so my boot heels were resting on the edge. "I'm freaking out." More about him telling me he'd had a thing for me all those years ago than about the sex stuff. I felt like Hill had been much better about keeping his feelings hidden than I had. I'd never had a clue he was as torn up over me.

Aspen chuckled and leaned forward so her forearms were resting on the desk. Her dark eyes felt like they were trying to pry every secret I had out of my soul.

"Freaking out because you regret it? Or freaking out because you finally realized you have real, honest feelings for him—feelings he clearly returns?" I hated how calm and composed she sounded.

"Freaking out over everything. Hill and I are not a good match." I curled my hands into fists and knocked them against my thighs. "We have chemistry. He's always been the forbidden fruit I shouldn't want to take a bite of, but that makes my mouth water. It can't go anywhere." Right? Especially while I was still tied into Shot's gambling operation. If Hill found out about that, it wasn't going to end well for anyone. Talk about a disaster waiting to happen.

Aspen made a humming sound and tilted her head to the side as she considered me silently for a long moment. "Why won't it go anywhere? What's keeping you from moving forward? Is it Aaron?"

I opened my mouth to tell her of course it was Aaron, but the words got stuck in my throat. For the longest time it had been easiest to tell myself—and anyone who dared ask—that I hated Hill because of the way things had gone down with Aaron. I'd convinced myself Hill should've been able to save his brother somehow, that he should've been there to save me from heartbreak. I'd convinced myself he was supposed to show up when I needed him the most, even though I was the one constantly pushing him away.

In a quiet, shaking voice I was finally honest with someone about the real reason I'd kept Hill at arm's length for so long. "He left. I thought he was always going to be there no matter what, but he left me. He pushed me away." Aaron had fed into all my worst habits and enabled my destructive side. I needed Hill's unwavering strength in order to keep myself together. When he took it away, I really started to spin out of control, taking Aaron on the emotional ride along with me. I felt like there was no one left to lean on.

Aspen nodded, expression grave, as if she'd been expecting my admission from the get-go.

"Kody, I'm going to ask you a question, and I want you to think about the answer. Really think about it."

I dropped my feet from her desk and sat up straight in the chair. "Okay."

"Why do you think Hill left the way he did? And kept away all these years? What could have possibly caused him to keep his distance, from both his brother and you? What was big enough, powerful enough to cause that divide?"

I stared at her, my mouth slowly falling open as I gaped at her in shock. It'd taken a lot of years for the pieces to fall into place. I'd always assumed he'd run away from me. It had never occurred to me that he might have run away *for* me.

"Love? You think he's in love with me...has been in love with me?" The mere thought of it lifted goose bumps on my arms and raised the tiny hairs on the back of my neck. He hadn't used that word last night, but his hands had touched me with love, and his eyes had practically glowed with it.

Aspen's dark eyebrow darted up. The expression on her face was clearly calling me out for being obtuse. "It's not about what I think. It's about what you think."

Was it possible? While I was busy deciding it would be better to fall in love with Aaron, had Hill fallen in love with me? Could a guy like him, controlled, concise...and, more importantly, honest and law-abiding, even have feelings for someone as messy and reckless as I was? Hill's entire life had been about serving and protecting other people, mine had been about exploiting them and keeping them at arm's length.

"No. You're wrong. There's no way someone like Hill could love someone like me." I pounded the side of my fist on the side of her desk to emphasize my point. "The reason Aaron and I clicked is because we were both creatures of chaos. He never had any kind of expectations of me. I was always good enough for him the way I was." And I'd loved him regardless of his erratic ups and downs. Hill and I were on different levels, practically from different planets. We'd never had any kind of common ground, other than our shared concern for his brother.

But that wasn't really true when I broke it down and looked at things closely. Aaron was the reason we stayed in touch at first, but our conversations quickly evolved into something more personal and intimate. We could talk for hours about anything, and every time I hung up the phone, I was already looking forward to the next call. It'd taken me months and months to stop reaching for the phone when Hill cut me off.

And now that I'd kissed him and he'd taken me apart with his talented touch, I knew I'd never felt as connected to anyone as I did to Hill when all the barriers were dropped between the two of us.

Aspen sighed and threw herself back in her chair. "I imagine Hill saw that. He saw the way you clicked with his younger brother, watched you both fall in love, and did what any good big brother would do in that situation. He backed off, regardless of what he wanted. He put his own needs aside so his brother could be happy, and gave the girl he was in love with exactly what she wanted. Even someone as strong as Hill is no match for a broken heart."

"No." I denied it again, but the truth was getting harder

and harder to ignore. She was right. It would've taken something major to get Hill to step away from both me and Aaron the way he had. Not a crush. Not lingering feelings of fondness and friendship. He wouldn't have done it if there were any other option. I'd hurt him.

Aspen smiled at me, but this smile was full of sympathy and understanding. "I hate to tell you this, but the way Hill feels about you is disgustingly obvious. He's never wanted you to be anyone you aren't. We all know he would prefer you make smarter, safer decisions, but everyone who loves you feels that way. Including me. Anyone with eyes can see he has his heart set on you, and Case has been bemoaning the fact that you're blind to it since I met him. You're the only one who thinks the two of you aren't a good match. You're the only one who believes he can't love you."

Moaning at my own stupidity and stubbornness, I bent forward and let my forehead hit the edge of her desk. "I'm an idiot."

Hill was my first crush, the first boy who caught my eye, but I'd let my own insecurities and issues overrule any of the soft, sweet feelings I'd had toward him. I'd convinced myself I wasn't good enough, smart enough, strong enough...and if that didn't just make me want to puke. If watching my mother constantly getting beat down and demeaned by my father while growing up had taught me anything, it was to know my own worth. But the first chance I'd had to stand by that, I'd failed.

I heard Aspen get up and felt her move next to me. A moment later her hand landed on the center of my back and she patted me soothingly. "Love makes us all do dumb things. I loved your brother for most of my life even though I knew he hated me. It was far from the brightest thing I've ever done."

I banged my head on the desk again. "I have no idea what to do with this information."

She laughed and lifted her hand to stroke my hair. "I'd say make good choices from here on out, but it's you, so . . ."

I cranked my head to the side so I could glare at her, which only made her laugh harder. "Talk to Hill, Kody. I'm not saying you're in any way obligated to be with him, return his feelings, or that you have to try and make a relationship with him work. But you do owe him some honesty. He should know how you really feel, even if you feel like the two of you really have no future together."

Before walking into this office, that was exactly how I'd felt. Now, I wasn't so sure.

"As much as I love you and want to be here for you, my next client is going to be here in about fifteen minutes, and I would like to shove the rest of my lunch in my face." Her gentle touch turned into a tug that brought my head up.

I climbed to my feet and wrapped her in a hug, squeezing her until she squealed from the pressure. "I'm so glad my brother got his head out of his ass and brought you into our family." I was also really happy she had never given up on Case when that was exactly what I would've done.

Aspen hugged me back and whispered, "Me too. No matter what happens, or who you decide to love, I am always on your side. No matter what, you deserve the best."

I didn't want to tell her I wasn't so sure about that.

I waved goodbye on my way out of her office, snickering when Aspen's paralegal loudly whispered, "Get it, girl. Hill Gamble is hot. He was my biggest crush in high school."

He was hot, and he made it hard to think straight. But Aspen was right. I needed to be honest with him, and I needed to give him the opportunity to be honest with me for once. I had to stop hiding behind Aaron's ghost.

Once I was sitting in my Jeep, I thought about shooting him a message to see if he was at the motel. I assumed he'd been up most of the night like I had. If he was back, I figured he was more than likely catching up on some much-needed sleep. Catching up on some sleep and getting my thoughts in order was what I should be doing as well. Instead I felt like I was vibrating with energy. I was like a watch wound up too tight, ready to break from the tension.

As if I'd somehow summoned the man through the sheer force of my thoughts, my cell phone dinged with a new message from Hill.

Are you around this afternoon? I need to talk to you about something.

I stared at the screen, wavering on what to do. We did need to talk. However, I suddenly wasn't sure I was ready. Tapping my phone on the steering wheel, I decided to bite the bullet and get this showdown over with sooner rather than later. I had no clue how things were going to play out between the two of us, but anything was better than this push and pull we'd been engaged in.

I'll come to you if you're at your motel. I'm already in town. Stopped by to see Aspen.

He replied that he'd just gotten back to the motel and he had to meet with Hearst for a few minutes, but should be free by the time I got there. I almost sent him a text telling him to be sure he had a shirt on when I showed up, but refrained. I didn't know how our conversation was going to go, so why would I deprive myself of the enticing view of Hill Gamble half-naked whenever I got the chance?

My anxiety and indecision grew exponentially as I drove to the motel. It felt like I was taking a huge step... off a cliff. I parked next to Hill's truck and made my way to his room. I wasn't sure how long I stood there trying to get up the nerve to knock, but it must've been a while, because Hill sent another message asking where I was. Clearly he was hovering close on the other side of the door, because when my phone went off, he yanked the door open and looked at me quizzically as I stood frozen on the spot.

"What are you doing out there? Come in." He took a step back from the doorway, but I couldn't make my feet move.

He was dressed this time, though his light blue button-down shirt was untucked and the sleeves were rolled up his muscular forearms. It was also unbuttoned to a point below his breastbone, showing off a tanned sliver of skin and hard pecs.

How was I supposed to have a serious conversation with him when all I wanted to do was throw him down on the closest flat surface and lick him from head to toe?

"What are you doing?" One of Hill's hands shot out and latched on to my wrist. He gave a little tug and pulled me into the room. "Get in here."

The momentum sent me directly into his chest. My palms flattened against the hard, warm surface, involuntarily sliding underneath the fabric of his shirt. A blast of heat shot from my fingertips throughout the rest of my body, and coherent thought fled.

"I need to talk to you about something important." He sounded hesitant, but I could feel the way his heart was pounding under my palm.

My brain was buzzing, my skin prickly. I was leaving this room knowing my relationship with this man was going to be fundamentally changed in one way or another. It felt huge, and far more important than so many of the other things I let consume me.

"Talking can wait." I wanted it to wait. I wanted things to be simple, easily understandable for just a little bit longer.

I had no trouble understanding the attraction between us. Was far less frightened over the prospect of giving him my body than I was about handing over my heart.

I kicked the door shut with the heel of my boot and slid my hands out of his shirt so I could work open the rest of the buttons. Hill caught my wrists in his hands to still the frantic movement, his blond brows shooting upward.

"Can wait for what? What are you doing?" He sounded baffled, but also turned on. There was no arguing that when we were together the air got thicker and sparks seemed to fly. I really must've been determined to turn a blind eye to the fireworks happening between us in order to have missed the signs.

"I'm being honest. With myself and with you. I want you, Hill." I shook my hands free and reached for his ornate belt buckle. "Have wanted you for a very long time."

His eyebrows arched up even higher, if it was possible. His jaw dropped and a wheezing breath escaped.

"What are you saying to me right now?" His voice sounded lower than normal and took on a sexy rasp.

I appreciated the quiver in his tone and the suddenly stark look of hunger on his face. I grinned up at him as I pulled the leather of his belt free from the buckle, leaving it to dangle as I went for the button and zipper on his dark jeans.

"I'm not saying anything. I told you we could save the talking for later. I'm going to show you instead." So there was no mistake, no misunderstanding. It was so much easier for me to express my feelings through actions than words. I wouldn't screw up touching him, tasting him. I knew how to do both of those things. Truthfully, I was far more comfortable making him lose his mind with my mouth and my hands than I was baring my soul to him.

"Kody." My name was part warning, part plea.

Hill was a good guy. If he knew exactly why my thoughts were racing, and the reason why my hands were shaking, there was no way in hell he would let things get physical between us without all our cards being on the table. He really was so much better than me in so many ways.

I lifted myself up on my toes so I could give him a hard, distracting kiss as I rushed to slide my hands into the opening of his tight pants.

I wasn't sure who was more surprised when my fingers encountered nothing but hot, hard, very bare skin. I never in a million years would've guessed Hill was the kind of guy who went commando, but what a nice surprise that he was.

My fingers curled around the thick, heated flesh as I grinned against his mouth, which opened in a shocked gasp. It was empowering to have the part of him that was both hard and soft in my hold. It was heady to know I was the one making his breathing shift to shallow and fast. I rarely felt like I had the upper hand with Hill. Right now, there was no question I was the one in charge.

I kissed him again. Slipping my tongue between his lips as I did my best to get his jeans down around his lean hips with my free hand. The hand I had wrapped around his rigid length was busy tracking the silky smooth head and gliding through the sudden rush of wetness decorating the tip. There were a lot of sensations slipping and sliding through my body as he visibly reacted to me. I liked all of them, but it was the fact that bringing him pleasure did more to flip my switch than the practiced seduction of anyone who came before him that I liked the best. Nothing got to me more than being the one to shake his unwavering control.

"Kody, come on. This is going to get out of control really quick." The words sounded as if he had to force them out, and his fingers dug into my shoulders to hold me in place, rather than to push me away. He was saying one thing, but it was clear he wanted another. I was correct in thinking we could lie to one another with words, but our bodies would always be honest.

"I want it out of control. Want you out of control. I promise not to run away afterward. Just let me..." Do things my own way. Show him how I felt in the only way I knew how. I wasn't about to beg him, but I figured he could hear the desperation in my voice. *I* could hear it loud and clear.

His hands left my shoulders and shifted so he was holding my face. His thumbs feathered along the ridges of my cheekbones. His eyes darkened to storm-cloud gray when my hold on the velvety shaft in my hand tightened. After a long, silent moment he let his hands fall, giving me the freedom to move.

I smiled up at him, barely resisting the urge to give him a saucy little wink. His face was flushed. His chest was moving with heavy breaths. His eyes looked dangerous and dark. I loved every bit of it.

I let go of the prize tucked into his pants so I could get the denim fully out of my way. I took a minute to trace the defined lines of his abs, and the deep V cut above his hip bones. He swore softly the second I dropped to my knees in front of him. A moment later, I felt his fingers thread through my hair. I smoothed my palms over his hips, silently urging him closer until I knew that every time I exhaled, my breath was hitting the pulsing vein running along the underside of Hill's impressive, tempting erection. His big body shuddered, and

I bit back a grin when his hold on my hair tightened so he could move my head closer to his straining flesh.

Grasping the wide base in my hand and gently smoothing my other up and down the outside of his tense thigh, I used the tip of my tongue to steal my very first taste of Hill.

He was worth the wait.

His masculine, sharp flavor exploded against my tongue and immediately made my head spin and my insides flutter. His cock flexed in my hand, and I heard him suck in a breath. His abs contracted, and the muscles in his legs locked. This time, when he said my name it was definitely a plea for more. He wasn't one to beg either, but I understood exactly what he wanted.

I was going to do my best to give it to him.

CHAPTER 14

∞

HILL

Kody Lawton was on her knees in front of me.

If I was dreaming, I didn't want to wake up. It was impossible to count how many times I'd dreamed of this scenario. It was also impossible to add up the number of times guilt had woken me up in a cold sweat after I'd pictured her exactly as she was. I wasn't supposed to fantasize about my brother's girl, my best friend's little sister. But I did. Sometimes it was seven nights a week for months at a time. Sometimes it was only once in a while, when I was particularly lonely.

None of those illicit, forbidden thoughts seemed to matter anymore, because my imagination had not come close to the real thing. It was as if my fantasies were dull and monotone, almost colorless. The real thing was Technicolor. Bright enough to burn, with sensations so vivid I wasn't sure I could embrace them all. My heart felt too small to contain all the different emotions I was feeling. And my body, well, it felt like a mixture of fire and water.

My knees were liquid, barely keeping me upright, but my blood felt like lava coursing through my veins.

At the first swipe of her tongue across the rounded crown of my cock, it took every ounce of restraint I had not to melt into a puddle at her feet. I was putty in her hands. I choked on a low moan when I felt her hand encircle the wide base of my erection so she could lower the straining shaft to her parted lips. Her soft breath was like a series of feathery kisses all along my heated skin. I had to make a conscious effort to lock my knees to keep upright. My fingers dug deeper into her wild hair, cupping the back of her head as she slowly, achingly started to move forward.

My head fell back, and her name ripped out of my chest when her lips suddenly locked around the first few inches of my eager erection. If she had been anyone else, there was a solid chance I would've lost my patience with the erotic torture and urged her to go fast, to take more. But this was Kody. She was my dream girl. My first love. My only love. The one I couldn't forget or move on from. Whatever she did, I wanted to savor it. I wanted to be able to remember it when she suddenly decided she shouldn't care about me.

Her tongue lapped at the slippery slit, her hand gliding up and down the shaft to meet her lips as they dropped lower and lower. Her green eyes practically glowed up at me. Her cheeks were stained red, and they hollowed out each time she sucked. The sight was enough to make my cock flex against her tongue and pulse in anticipation. Her fingernails dug into the backs of my thighs, and she made a humming noise that sent vibrations shooting along the already sensitive shaft. Pleasure coiled tightly at the base of my spine. I had enough pride and a big-enough ego to say I wasn't a man who was usually quick on the trigger. But when the woman who had her mouth on me was Kody, all my typical restraint went right out the window. She went to my head faster than a shot of pure moonshine.

I grunted in approval as she leaned farther forward, taking even more of my length into the warm, wet cavern of her mouth. Every time she sucked, my eyes wanted to roll up into the back of my head. She really was going to bring me to my knees—in the best way possible.

"Jesus, Kody." This was probably the closest I'd been to a religious experience in the last decade. I was caught between demanding more and begging her to back off so I didn't embarrass myself.

I let go of my stranglehold on her hair, softening my touch so I could weave her tangled curls around the fingers of one hand. I used the other to trace the line of her jaw, my cock throbbing when I felt the way her mouth was stretched open to accommodate my girth. She exhaled loudly through her nose, eyes going half-mast as she really started to move. Her head bobbed up and down in a perfect rhythm with the advance and retreat of her sliding fist. Every time she reached the base, she squeezed tightly, and it made shivers shoot up my spine. Blood rushed between my ears, my heart hammered so loudly I was sure Kody could hear the beat, and my skin went slick with a thin layer of perspiration. It was taking everything I had to keep myself from losing control and emptying into her welcoming mouth.

One of her hands skated up the back of my leg, stopping when it landed on one of my ass cheeks. I yelped in surprise when she gave the firm muscle a playful little tap, but the sound swiftly turned into a moan when I felt the head of my cock hit the back of her throat. I didn't stand a chance when she was determined to undo me, but I'd been waiting for this girl and this moment for what felt like most of my life, and I didn't want it to end before it really even began.

Using the thumb that was stroking her face, I pressed lightly against her cheek. She let go of my cock with a wet pop and looked up at me with curious eyes. The green glimmered with a sheen of moisture like grass after the rain. I wanted a camera, a sketch pad, something to immortalize the way she looked when she was 100 percent focused on me. When we shut out the rest of the world, it was hard to remember all the reasons she and I weren't always like this. We'd spent so long hurting, it didn't seem like it should be so simple to suddenly make each other feel this good.

I pulled Kody to her feet, using the pad of my thumb to wipe the wetness clinging to her lower lip away. I bent forward and kissed her on the center of her forehead and whispered, "How far into this are we going to go, Kody?"

I'd had my hands on her. She'd had her mouth on me. We knew how to drive each other to the edge, but if we were going to go over, I wanted to do it together. I wanted to free-fall with her, while I was inside her. I wanted to let go of control and throw caution to the wind, at least once. I would worry about the ramifications of our actions later. Just once I wanted to have her, to take what I wanted for myself. I felt like I was always giving her up, letting the way I loved her take a backseat. If she gave me the green light, I was going all in with no regrets and no looking back. I wanted to be as close as I could get so she had no choice but to finally look at me, to see me, to acknowledge what I'd been trying to show her.

She reached up and pushed my shirt off my shoulders. She smoothed her hands across my chest, pausing to tap her fingers in rhythm to the erratic beat of my heart. "Oh, we're going all in, Hill. And there is no going back."

Nodding sharply since she was on the exact same page I was, I took a second to kick my boots off and drop my pants to the floor, and bent so I could hook an arm around her waist and lift her off her feet. She giggled when I picked her up and held her to my chest. She kicked off her shoes as I walked toward the bed. I dropped her on the edge, bending so I could kiss her as she wiggled out of her shirt and bra. I had taken a step back to help her work her jean shorts down her long legs when I realized I needed something I'd left in my own pants, which were puddled on the floor. Muttering that I'd be back in a second, I wasn't prepared to turn back around and find her splayed wantonly on her back, one hand hidden enticingly between her tanned, toned thighs, the other playing with the pointed tip of one breast.

There was something inherently sexy about a woman knowing her own body and taking charge of her own pleasure. If I were more certain of our future, if I believed there was really a shot in hell I might be able to keep her, I would've stood there and watched her for hours. But since I wasn't guaranteed another chance to be with Kody like this, I needed to make the most of every moment.

Stopping at the edge of the bed, I made room for myself between her parted thighs. I tossed the condom I'd retrieved from my wallet on the bed, moving so I could drag my index finger from the base of her throat down between the center of her full breasts and across her flat stomach, stopping where her fingers were playing within her wet, pink folds.

"I'm ready for you. I was ready as soon as you pulled me into the room. Having you in my mouth was almost enough to push me over the edge. You're potent, Hill Gamble." Her voice was husky, and the rasp made the hairs on my arms lift up.

"I just want to take care of you, Kody." It was all I'd ever wanted to do, and here she was trying to take care of herself, just like she always did.

I dropped to my knees between her legs. I placed a kiss

on the inside of her bent knee and gently pulled her hand away from her glistening center. I took a second to lick across her fingers, closing my eyes as her taste landed on my tongue. She lifted her head and moved as if she was going to sit up. I lightly pushed her back and grasped her hips so I could lift her up to my mouth. Her legs obediently curved over my shoulders and one of her hands curled around the back of my head.

I dragged my thumb through her damp folds, spreading moisture around, stopping when I felt the tight little bud of her clit. I circled the sensitive spot until her eyes drifted closed, watching as her fingers aimlessly played with her nipple, the raspberry point playing hide-and-seek under her touch. It was hot. She was hot. There was an inferno raging between us.

She moaned my name the minute I put my mouth on her.

Her thighs clamped down around my ears. Her heels dug into my back, and her entire body quivered where I held her. She made a strangled sound as I guided my tongue through wetness and fluttering muscles. She tasted better than I would've imagined. She was going to be my favorite flavor forever.

I kept up the pressure on her clit, alternating between making sweet circles with my thumb and tugging it with my fingers at the same time that she pulled on her nipple. Her chest flushed a pretty, rosy pink as she wiggled and undulated, moving closer as the pleasure intensified. I could feel the way her body reacted. She went soft and liquid against my mouth. Her moans were breathless, and her legs shifted restlessly. Her fingers started to pull at the hair on the back of my head, and her hips practically levitated off the bed.

I switched up my attack. Moved my mouth to her clit and my fingers inside her, touching and tasting every sweet, intimate inch. I wanted to know her so well I could find her in the dark. I wanted to recognize her from touch and taste alone.

"Hill..." She barked my name out as her legs locked around my head. "I want you. I need you." Her hand was frantic where it pulled on my hair. "Get inside of me... right now."

Who could resist an order like that?

I pulled back, left a sloppy, wet kiss on the inside of her creamy thigh, and took the condom she practically threw at me. I suited up with quick, efficient movements, then slowly kissed my way up her body. She was almost glaring at me by the time I was hovering over her. I braced an arm above her head and used my free hand to guide my aching, throbbing erection into her quivering opening.

We fit seamlessly together. There was no resistance. No adjustment. Just two bodies custom-made to fit together. She wrapped a long leg around my waist, slid her arm across my shoulders, kissed the side of my neck, and ordered me to move.

As if I had a choice.

I'd spent a lifetime keeping my distance, now I was as close to her as I was ever going to get.

I dropped my forehead so it rested on hers and did as she asked, chasing after that white-hot pleasure I could feel starting to wrap around my spine. She met every thrust with a shift and wiggle of her own. We were straining, writhing, impatient against one another. The thing building inside the center of my chest felt larger than life, so intense it was completely overwhelming. I forgot to breathe for a long moment, then gasped to take in air when I felt her inner walls clamp down on my shaft. The gentle squeezing sensation made white lights burst behind my eyelids.

I tilted my head so I could get my teeth on her earlobe, tugging until she whimpered. Her nails left a fiery trail across my shoulders as she let out a high-pitched keening sound a second before her entire body went tight and a liquid rush of heat surrounded me where we were joined. Years of back-and-forth, days of foreplay, we were both primed to go off. Her quick-fire orgasm triggered my own. I lost the steady, deliberate rhythm I'd picked up and started pounding into her like I would die if I didn't catch up to her.

When I hit the brink, it was like getting knocked upside the head with a two-by-four. My head spun. My chest felt too tight. My lungs locked, and my vision blurred out. I'd never experienced anything like it, because I'd never been with anyone who meant as much to me as Kody. It gave a whole new meaning to coming together.

I collapsed on top of her, trying to catch my breath and get my brain back in working order. She squeaked at the weight and playfully pushed at my shoulders to get me to roll off her. When I pulled out of her welcoming warmth, we both made a sound of regret. It felt good to be inside her, really good. It was nice to know it felt good for her to have me there as well.

Rolling onto my back, I ran my hand down my sweaty chest, trying to work up the energy to get up and deal with the necessary things in the aftermath. I let out a loud yawn and rolled my head to the side so I could look at her. Her eyes appeared sleepy and heavy, but there was a slight, very satisfied smile on her face. I felt like the ruler of the entire damn universe for being the one who'd put it there.

I shifted so I could give her a kiss on the cheek. Reluctantly I climbed off the bed, meandering to the bathroom to take care of business. I was putting my discarded jeans back on when Kody suddenly sat up in the center of the bed with the rumpled sheet wrapped around her.

She gave me an indecipherable look and asked, "Do you want to go first?"

I paused, one leg in the denim, one leg out. "Go first?"

She nodded and lifted a hand so she could tug on her lower lip with her fingers. "Do you want to talk first, or do you want to hear what I have to say?"

It was tempting to let her take the lead, but the reality was, I should've told her what was going on with Presley Baskin before falling into bed with her. She wasn't going to like it, and she was going to like what I had to say about it even less. But it was well past time she and I figured out how to be honest with one another. If we couldn't face each other's truths, maybe there wasn't anything more for us than this single, special moment.

I finished pulling on my pants and raked my hands through my hair. I walked over to the end of the bed, stopping when I was directly in front of her. I put my hands on my hips and gave it to her straight.

"We found the weapon that was used to kill your dad."

"What?" Kody sat up, the sheet falling forgotten around her waist. It was hard not to be distracted by her full, high breasts.

"Dr. Baskin had it, and she surrendered it to Hearst."

"Are you kidding me?" She lifted up on her knees and leaned forward eagerly. "Does that mean you arrested her? Did she kill my dad? Did it have something to do with him leaving her everything?"

"She's saying someone set her up. There are things not adding up. She believes someone is trying really hard to frame her for Conrad's death."

Kody flopped back on the bed, pulling her knees up to her

chest. "You believe her?" Her excited tone changed to something frosty and sharp.

"I believe there is more to the story. I arranged to put her in protective custody until Hearst and I can clear a few things up."

"She gave you the gun responsible for my father's murder and you're protecting her? What is wrong with you, Hill? Whose side are you on?"

She scrambled from the bed and made a dive for her discarded clothes, pulling them on in a rush. I tried to stop her, but she shook me off, glaring at me over her shoulder.

"Don't. Just . . . don't. If you push me right now I'm going to say something that hurts you on purpose instead of by accident. You need to back off."

I lifted my hands in a gesture of surrender. "Okay. But you need to know I'm on your side no matter what. That doesn't mean I can ignore the facts, or my own intuition. I don't think Dr. Baskin is a bad person. Or a murderer. I think she's someone who ended up in a bad situation and she's just doing her best to get by. I know that's not what you want to hear."

She glared at me, flipping her hair over her shoulder as she stormed toward the door. "It's not what I want to hear, and it makes me question what I was going to say. Let's just talk later, Hill."

I was always waiting when it came to her. What else was new?

She slammed the door with more force than was necessary. Swearing long and loud, I kicked at my boots on the floor, pausing when I caught sight of Kody's bright pink phone case peeking out from under the corner of the bed. It must've fallen out when I wrestled her out of her clothes.

Sighing, I picked it up and stalked to the door.

She always wanted space, and I was always running after her. It was like an adult game of tag, only I never managed to catch her. I swore to myself the next time I got my hands on her I was going to hold on so tightly there would be no way for her to wiggle away.

CHAPTER 15

❧

KODY

Kody...wait a second."

I didn't stop my angry retreat across the parking lot toward my Jeep. I came here to be honest with Hill about how I felt. But right now I was pissed as hell, and I knew talking to him wouldn't lead to anything good. Walking away was the best option right now, even if it sort of felt like I was taking the easy way out.

"Goddammit, Kody." I turned my head to shoot a glare in Hill's direction. I'd been waiting for the man to come after me for a very long time. It was annoying how happy the sight of him jogging across the parking lot made me—even if he was clearly upset, with his shirt hanging open. I needed a minute to figure out how I felt about this new information, but it was nice to know he wasn't going to let me get too far away anymore when I got lost in my own head.

I caught sight of my pink phone in his hand, and the little bubble of delight in my chest popped. Maybe things hadn't changed as much as I thought. It was entirely possible we were going to have to use actual words to communicate.

Sighing heavily, I paused in my angry march and crossed my arms defensively across my chest as I watched him move toward me. His unwavering determination to be absolutely impartial when it came to my newfound half sister might be aggravating, but it didn't change the fact that I enjoyed watching him move...and I liked it even more when he was moving in my direction.

"Kody!" When he screamed my name this time, it was almost shrill.

I took a step in his direction as his jog turned to a run, my phone falling from his hand as he screamed my name once again.

My head whipped around as the squeal of tires and the smell of burning rubber suddenly hit my nose. I was only a handful of steps away from my Jeep when I caught sight of a white car barreling through the parking lot in my direction. For a split second, I thought maybe it was someone trying to show off, but it became startlingly clear that wasn't the case as the car picked up speed and headed directly toward me.

I'd like to think I'm the type of person who is pretty good in a stressful situation.

I didn't panic when Aspen's stalker tried to run us off the highway.

I didn't lose my cool when her mother took a shot at both of us.

I freaked out only marginally when Crew was stabbed in an FBI sting gone wrong.

And I was willing to stick it out with Aaron no matter how rough things got between us as his illness became harder and harder to handle.

I watched in horror as the sports car zoomed closer and

closer to where I was stuck, immobile, watching my life flash before my eyes. It was all so clichéd. If I hadn't been terrified to the point of being unable to function, I would want to kick my own ass.

An ear-piercing scream blasted through my eardrums. I wasn't sure if it came from me or Hill. It was loud enough that it whipped my head around, just in time for me to catch sight of the tall, blond man flying toward me. I had no idea how Hill had made it from one side of the parking lot to the other in such a short time, but he had. When he slammed into me, the force sent us both soaring through the air. I felt his arms wrapped protectively around me and heard the car's tires squeal even louder. It was so close, a rush of air lifted my hair and tangled it around my head. This time I knew the scream was mine, because it was Hill's name at the top of my lungs as we both rammed into the front of my Jeep. I yelped in pain when my elbow connected with the front bumper, watching as Hill's face flushed from red to an alarming shade of white as he immediately loosened his hold on me and slid to the ground once we were out of the path of the car.

Hill made a sound that was a mixture of a groan and a wheeze, his eyes fluttering closed as his hands flopped to the ground next to him.

I looked to make sure the car wasn't coming back around and caught sight of several people in the parking lot already on their phones. I hoped they were calling 911, because Hill looked far too pale.

I fell to my knees at his side, none too gently tapping his cheek with my palm as I called his name.

"Hill. Hill! Did you hit your head? Open your eyes." I tapped even harder, trying to keep the furious panic at bay.

I couldn't get my head around the thought that he might be dying right in front of my eyes. I couldn't breathe when

I thought about what my life would be like if I really, truly lost him for good. I spent a lot of time being angry—at him, at myself, at the world—but now that Hill was getting paler by the minute, it seemed like such a waste. What if he died and we never got a chance to start over? What if I never got to tell him he wasn't alone in either the love or the guilt he felt when it came to the two of us?

No God would be cruel enough to take both brothers away from this Earth—or me— right?

I jolted a little, almost falling over when Hill's slick-looking partner was suddenly crouched in front of me on the other side of the still man.

"He didn't hit his head. The fender of the car clipped him when he dived in front of it to tackle you to the ground." The man sounded surprisingly calm, but his eyes were huge in his face as he reached to check Hill's pulse and muttered, "You better wake up, Gamble. Don't you dare make me explain this to the brass."

A wheezy groaning sound pushed out of Hill's chest, and his eyelids twitched. "I'm awake."

I gasped in relief and practically threw myself on top of him, only to be pulled immediately off by Hearst. "Be careful. We don't know how badly he's hurt. That was a direct hit and the car was flying." He gave me a pointed look. "It was aiming right for you, Ms. Lawton."

I shot him a narrow-eyed look. "I'm aware." I stroked the backs of my fingers over Hill's cheek and silently prayed for him to open his eyes. My hands were shaking, and a freezing numbness was spreading through my whole body as Hill remained still as stone.

The sound of sirens caught my attention. I waved off a couple of curious bystanders, forcing myself to give Hill a more thorough once-over. I could see his side already blooming with dark bruises under his loose shirt. They dotted his ribs, getting darker and uglier as they reached his hip. His jeans were ripped at the knee, and I could see the skin underneath was torn and bloody, but his leg didn't seem to be twisted, so I was holding out hope it wasn't broken.

I rubbed my thumb along his jawline and whispered, "I guess all those years playing football paid off. That was one hell of a tackle."

Hearst snorted, climbing to his feet to wave to the ambulance and one of the marked patrol cars from my brother's office. Case wasn't going to be far behind once he heard his sister and best friend had been involved in the same incident.

I recognized one of the paramedics from high school, which meant he was probably going to recognize Hill. It made me feel slightly better. One good thing about being in a small town was that people did tend to take care of their own in a crisis. We might gossip and drag that same person through the mud when their back was turned, but we rallied together when need be.

I let the first responders shoo me out of the way, refusing to take my eyes off Hill as his partner caught my elbow, sending a jolt of sharp, white-hot pain up my arm as he pulled me to the side. He handed me my abandoned phone, which now had a shattered screen, as he bent his head and spoke in a rough whisper only loud enough for me to hear.

"Did you catch sight of the driver? Male? Female?"

I shook my head, my entire body stiffening when Hill moaned painfully as the paramedics checked him over.

"It was a Tesla. That's the only thing I could tell you for certain."

Hearst nodded. "Yeah. That was the first thing I noticed as well." He lifted his eyebrows at me and cocked his head to the side. "You know the driver wasn't Dr. Baskin, right? It couldn't be her."

I tossed my head back and glared up at the sky. "I know. Hill told me you guys put her in protective custody."

Hearst nodded. "We did. She's being monitored twenty-four-seven by the Rangers. She's nowhere near Loveless."

"But someone wanted us to think it was her." Hill had mentioned the doctor saying someone was trying to set her up, and it looked like this was empirical proof her theory was right.

Hearst nodded and tilted his head even closer to mine. I couldn't take my eyes off Hill as he was loaded onto a stretcher. His eyes flickered open and immediately sought mine out. I took a step in his direction, only to be brought up short by his partner's hold on my arm.

"Dr. Baskin traded in her Tesla yesterday and went on the run. My guess is whoever tried to run you down doesn't know that. They assumed the car would be recognizable enough to jam the doctor up. Someone really wants her out of the way."

I shook his hold loose and gave him a dirty look as I purposely moved toward Hill. "And who might that be?"

"Not sure yet. But it is no doubt someone the good doctor told about you. Someone who knows how angry you were about the changes in the will. Someone who knows you think the doctor is responsible for your father's murder." He was talking more to himself than to me at that point and I couldn't care less. All I wanted to do was get to Hill and make sure he was all right. "Do you need a ride to the hospital? There's something I need to check on."

"I'm going with Hill." I wasn't exactly family, but I was close, and I would fight to the death if they didn't let me ride with him.

Hearst nodded, walking off with his phone in his hand.

Hill's eyes were on me once I got to his side. His head was immobilized and strapped down, but some of the color was back in his face and he seemed mostly coherent.

"Hey." I was shocked by the press of tears in my eyes and the catch in my throat. Seeing someone so strong, someone I always viewed as invincible, taken down because of me did something to all that ice surrounding my heart. I could feel the cracks splintering through the shell and the heat seeping out.

His mouth twisted into something that was probably supposed to pass as a grin but looked more like a grimace. "I'm okay."

The familiar paramedic snorted. "Mostly okay. We need to see if that hip is dislocated or broken. You won't be running any touchdowns into the end zone anytime soon, Gamble."

Hill grunted. "It's not that bad."

I sniffed a little and reached out so I could pat his hands where they were folded over his bare stomach. I needed to call Case and ask him to grab Hill a change of clothes and whatever else he might need for a few days in the hospital. I wasn't leaving his side until he was back on his feet.

"Bad enough. You scared the shit out of me." My voice cracked, and some of those tears spilled over.

Hill made a noise and whispered, "Don't cry, Kody."

I couldn't seem to help it. Luckily, the paramedics lifted the stretcher and moved Hill to the ambulance, so I had a second to collect myself.

I pictured the scars and imperfections decorating his skin. Remembered the way they'd felt, smooth and raised, under my fingertips when I ran my hands over the rest of his perfect skin. Getting hit by a speeding car was probably nothing to a man who'd been shot at and stabbed more than once, but it was one of the scariest things I'd ever witnessed. I was going to see Hill jumping in front of that car whenever I closed my eyes for a very long time.

Squinting at my phone through my tears and all the spidery screen cracks, I sent Case a text letting him know I was going to the hospital with Hill, and telling him we were both okay. I asked him to pick up some personal things for his friend and scurried to climb into the back of the ambulance before they left me behind. Thankfully, no one put up a fight when I took up a spot on the opposite side of the stretcher from the first responder.

Hill muttered again that he didn't want me to cry over him, but I couldn't seem to stop. I cared about him…so much more than I'd realized. It shouldn't have taken nearly losing him for me to realize it, but it had.

Well, crap.

That meant that not only was I going to have to be brutally honest with him from here on out, but I was also going to have to get myself in order. It was time to stop being so careless. If I couldn't handle seeing Hill incapacitated, it was only fair to make sure I didn't unwittingly put him in that situation. I needed to cut ties with the risky areas in my life so I could make room for this larger-than-life man. The only one I was willing to let take care of me.

The only man I wanted to take care of.

"I'm not going anywhere, Hill. I'm staying right next to you until you're back on your feet." It was a vehement promise I was determined to keep. It was the first commitment I'd made to another person as a grown woman. It was me staking my claim to this man I'd decided was mine.

Hill rolled those pretty gray eyes in my direction, and I caught the crinkle in the corners as he tried to smile.

"Good. Because it looks like you found yourself in trouble again, and if you're right next to me, I can keep an eye on you." His voice was shaky and rough, but his cognition was clear, and he was making perfect sense...even if his words were slightly annoying.

"Trouble found me." I hadn't been the one out looking for it this time.

"Doesn't it always?" He must be feeling okay if he could still sling snark like a pro.

Our banter was broken up by our arrival at the hospital. Hill was rushed into the emergency room, and we were separated as he was wheeled off for X-rays. One of the trauma nurses gave me a wink as she flew by, murmuring that we should get a family discount at this point.

It was true. Crew had spent a few weeks in the ICU not too long ago. Both Case and Aspen had landed in hospital beds for different injuries when her life was in danger, and now Hill, who wasn't *technically* family, was down for the count. We should have one of the emergency room bays reserved at the rate we were going.

I was nervously pacing back and forth, hoping against hope Hill hadn't shattered his hip, when Case popped his head into the room.

I immediately threw myself into my oldest brother's arms and wilted as he comforted me.

"I was so scared, Case. I couldn't move. Hill got hurt because of me." I wanted to sob, but I was all cried out. Instead I shook silently as Case shushed me and ran his hand up and down my back.

"Stop it. You didn't do anything wrong and you know it. No one knows how they're going to respond in a situation like that. I bet if the circumstances were reversed and Hill was the one in danger, you wouldn't have hesitated to do exactly what he did. We tend to be willing to risk everything for the people we love."

I couldn't bring myself to correct him about my feelings toward Hill. This wasn't the same way I'd felt with Aaron. It was bigger. Scarier. Out of my hands.

"All that matters is that both of you are okay." My elbow was bruised up and I had a scratch on my cheek, but nothing that required any kind of medical attention. "Hill might be banged up, but it's nothing he won't bounce back from."

I appreciated the reassurance. Things always felt better when Case said they would be all right. I took a deep breath and collected myself. I pulled back and looked up at him.

"It wasn't Baskin. Someone wants us to think this is all her, but she's innocent." It grated to admit I was wrong, but we couldn't place the blame on someone who didn't deserve it. If we kept doing that, it made us no better than our father. Making sure we never acted like him was the one thing we'd all promised each other we would never do.

Case's eyebrows puckered, and a look of concentration crossed his face. I could see him slipping into investigator mode and wasn't surprised when he told me to stay put because he was going to hunt down Hill's partner so he could ask him some questions.

Hill was rolled back into the room a few minutes later. His torn, bloody clothes had been switched out for a hospital gown, and I could see his leg was wrapped from knee to midthigh and that there appeared to be something bulky circling his torso.

"Hip's not broken. Bruised pretty badly, ended up with some busted ribs, and my knee was dislocated and split open so I needed stitches, but nothing to write home about." He looked tired, but his color was good, and he managed to reach for my hand and tug me over to his bedside. "Everything is all right, Kody. We're all right."

I nodded mutely and squeezed his fingers. "I'm so glad." There weren't really words to cover the amount of relief flooding through me at the moment. "I'm not sure I could've handled it going the other way, Hill. I really don't want to lose you." Not when I'd just realized I had him.

He reached up, wincing at the action, and rubbed his thumb along my lower lip.

"Not gonna happen. I'm not going anywhere."

I hoped to God that was true, because I had a lot to come clean about, and he wasn't going to like most of it.

I was leaning over the safety railing on the bed so I could kiss him when a loud cough interrupted us.

Case and Hearst stood inside the room, both looking a little angry and a little amused.

Hill struggled to sit up the minute he saw their expressions, but I pushed him back down with a hand in the center of his chest and ordered, "Spill it before he climbs out of this bed and really breaks something."

Hearst looked at Hill and lifted his eyebrows. "Figured I'd check on Dr. Baskin's friend who was injured and see if maybe she had any insight into who else Baskin might confide in. Guess who was discharged from the hospital in Ivy the same day she was admitted?"

Hill frowned. "How could she be discharged? Wasn't she under observation? Isn't that what the cops who spoke to her told you?"

Hearst rubbed his jaw. "The cops thought she was drunk. They spoke with a doctor at the hospital, took his word as gospel, and went about their day. No one checked up on the woman. She disappeared."

"Isn't she the one in line for the promotion after Dr. Baskin?" Hill tried to sit up again until I growled at him.

Hearst nodded and answered, "Yep," with a pop on the *p*.

Hill looked dumbfounded. "You're telling me this woman's best friend is the one trying to make her believe she's going crazy? She's the one who killed Conrad and framed Baskin?"

Hearst shrugged. "Starting to look that way."

I snorted, bringing all three heads around to look at me. "Never underestimate a determined woman." There was no end to how dangerous we could be.

CHAPTER 16

∞

HILL

Where's my baby? How come no one called to tell me my son was nearly killed?"

The shrill voice pulled me out of my painkiller-induced stupor. I hadn't wanted to spend the night in the hospital, but Kody had insisted, and I was honestly too banged up and worn out to fight with her. At the moment she was out hunting down something to eat. She hadn't wanted to leave my side, but I'd harassed her to take care of herself because she was going to need to be in better shape than she was if she really planned on taking care of me. I could hardly move. The bumps and bruises were bad, but I'd had so much worse over the course of my career. The dislocated knee was going to be a pain in the ass for a few weeks, but at least all my injuries would heal on their own with time and some gentle care.

I had been planning on a quiet night so I could make my escape as early as possible the following morning, but I should've known better. The paramedic on the scene recognized me, which meant the word was probably spreading all throughout Loveless that I'd landed myself in the hospital. It shouldn't have been a surprise that one of my parents had shown up to make a scene, but I'd been holding out hope that I was going to avoid encountering either of them while I was in town. Dealing with my folks took a lot of effort on a good day, which was not today.

I peeled my eyes open as the sharp click of heels on the laminate floor grew louder and louder. My mother was moving with purpose and was clearly worked up. Neither of those things was good.

I hadn't seen either of my parents in over a year. I found spending time with them exhausting. They hadn't changed much since my childhood, only now, whenever we were all together, it turned into an overly dramatic memorial service for Aaron. They used to see Aaron almost daily, yet neither had stepped up to the plate to help him when they had the chance. But now that he was gone they loved placing blame on one another and outdoing each other when it came to over-the-top mourning. My little brother's death was one more thing they could use as a weapon against one another, but I was the one who always felt wounded after spending time with them.

"Mom." I rubbed my eyes and tried to clear some of my drowsiness. "What are you doing here?" I knew she didn't really care one way or the other if I was injured. She just wanted people to see her, to acknowledge her. She'd wanted to make sure she showed up before my father did so she could tell him he was a terrible parent while seeking accolades for her nonexistent nurturing.

She stopped by the side of the bed, her expression a mask of fake concern. Her expressions were always so exaggerated, as if she were playing a role on TV. She looked older than the last time I'd seen her. Her hair was now fully white, and the lines around her eyes deeper and more pronounced. At the moment her mouth was pulled into a pout I assumed was supposed to look thoughtful and worried.

"My baby got hit by a car trying to save someone. Where else would I be? I can't believe you haven't been able to make time for your poor mother while you've been in town. I don't know anything going on in your life. I have to hear it all from strangers while I'm in line at the grocery store. Do you have any idea how embarrassing that is?" Her eyes, which were the same gray as mine—only a hundred degrees colder—narrowed on me as her hands curled around the rails on the side of the bed. "I know I raised you better than that, Hill Gamble."

I snorted and dragged a hand down my face. "You didn't raise me. I raised myself."

Her knuckles turned white as her grip tightened. "How dare you speak to your mother that way?"

I sighed and sat up. My ribs protested the motion, making me gasp in pain as I instinctively placed a hand over my tender side.

"Be careful, Mom. Your true colors are starting to show." I returned her narrow-eyed look.

"Is it true? Did you really risk your life to save Kody Lawton?" Her chin jutted out and her lips thinned into a tight, disapproving line. "I said it wasn't possible. Not after what that woman did to your brother. My sweet little boy deserved so much better. That family is nothing but trouble." She sniffed. "It's to be expected with parents like theirs."

I clenched my jaw to keep the words that wanted to spill out at bay. I'd been down this road with her before. She was looking for a fight, wanted me to feed into her needling so she could throw a fit. When I was younger, it was a challenge not to get drawn into the games both my parents liked to play. I'd long since grown out of the need to defend myself.

"It's my job to try and save everyone." I rolled my eyes at her and got a dirty look in return.

"So you were just doing your job?" The question was pointed and her tone was sharp.

I sighed and rolled my head around, my neck popping loudly as tension pulled my entire body tight. "No. Keeping Kody safe has nothing to do with my job and everything to do with the fact I've been in love with her since I was a teenager. If anything happened to her..." I shook my head slowly from side to side. "I don't know if I'd be able to function. She means the world to me and I will always do whatever it takes to keep her safe."

An ugly hiss escaped my mother's clenched teeth as she leaned closer to me. I'm sure she was trying to be threatening, but the effort was wasted on me. I'd stopped letting her influence my life and decisions years ago.

"She's the reason your brother is dead, Hill. He was perfectly fine until he got caught up with Kody and the Lawtons. She ruined him, and she'll do the same to you." I had to give it to her, the woman knew exactly what buttons to push to get a rise out of me. It was no wonder she and my father were always fighting, she was damn good at it.

"Aaron isn't with us any longer because he had an illness that wasn't given the attention it needed. He was sick. He needed help but didn't know how to ask for it. We all should've realized he was struggling and done more, but we didn't. You think I don't know what you're trying to do, but I see right through you, Mom. You want me to fight you, to defend Kody, but I'm not going to. The facts are simple. She was there for Aaron when the rest of us weren't. She loved him, took care of him when you didn't, when I couldn't. Who knows what would've happened if she hadn't come into his life when she did? We very well could've lost him much sooner than we did." I pointed at my bum knee. "I know you started this nonsense since I can't walk away, but I'm warning you, keep going this way and this will be the last you see of me for a very long time. Neither you nor Dad is getting younger. You might want to consider picking your battles more wisely from now on."

If you'd asked me a month ago if I ever thought I'd end up back in Loveless, my answer would've been an unequivocal no. Now, I wasn't so sure. There was a lot in my hometown I was going to have a hard time leaving behind if I walked away again. Unfortunately, staying in Loveless would entail seeing my parents.

My mother let out a loud gasp and put a hand to her throat. The expression of horror on her face was damn near comical. It was a shame I was the only one around to witness what might've been her greatest performance to date. She was really going all out today.

"Are you threatening me?" Crocodile tears gleamed in her eyes, and her fingers started to shake. "Who treats their mother this way?"

Tired of the burning sensation firing up and down my injured side, I carefully lay back down in the bed. I closed my eyes and silently wished she would take the hint and leave me alone until I was back in fighting form... or even longer than that.

"It's not a threat, Mom. One of these days we're all going to have to learn how to treat each other better." And if we couldn't, I was done with them. "We've all lost so much along the way. The good memories we have from when we were all together should unite us, not divide us. We're family. It shouldn't be this hard." But it always was and had been for so long, I wondered if things could actually change.

She sniffed, and I could tell without even looking at her that she was gearing up for an even bigger emotional out-burst. Any minute now the room was going to be full of staff asking what was going on, and the damn woman was going to be the center of attention in all the wrong ways.

"Okay. That's enough, Mrs. Gamble. Hill's been a lot more patient and understanding with you than he needed to be. He's the one recovering from nearly getting run over. He's the one who needs attention right now. He's too polite to kick you out of this room, but I'm not. We both know your opinion of me can't get much lower, so I've got nothing to lose by making you leave."

Kody's voice was surprisingly calm as she spoke from the doorway. I opened my eyes and glanced in her direc-tion. She looked ready to throw down with my mom if need be. She wasn't budging.

I saw my mother open her mouth to argue, but Kody held up her hand before the older woman could speak. "If you think you're going to cause a scene and make both of us look bad, I'll remind you my brother is the sheriff. If you don't go quietly, I'm going to call Case and ask him to remove you from this room. I know you like to have all eyes on you, but you won't like it so much when they're watching you be led away in handcuffs. You'll like the rumors following a display like that even less."

She had my mom all figured out. It wasn't that she would hate being the topic of conversation. It was that my father would be able to lord the embarrassing situation over her that made her sniff again but finally head toward the door.

"This conversation isn't over, Hill." She tossed the threat over her shoulder.

But as soon as she got close enough for Kody to grab, she was brought up short by the taller, blond woman, who simply stated, "Yes, it is. If you think I'm going to let him save me and not do everything in my power to return the favor, you're out of your mind. I'm going to get between anything and anyone who tries to hurt him, just like he did for me." I watched as Kody's gold eyebrows lifted threateningly. "Consider yourself warned."

My mom slipped out of the room without another word, leaving me and Kody alone.

I watched as she walked across the room, wondering how things between us could shift so dramatically without the entire world rocking off its axis.

"How much of that did you hear?" I figured it was obvious to her how I felt at this point, but still, I would've liked the chance to tell her my feelings face-to-face and not have her overhear my confession during an argument with my problematic parent. I'd loved her for so long, it seemed like there should be some pomp and circumstance when I finally got the chance to share it with her.

She lowered the safety rail and propped herself on the side of the bed. She reached out to brush my hair off my forehead and gave me a smile tinged with sadness.

"I heard most of it. I want to hear the part about you being in love with me since you were a teenager again, but there are things you have to know first, things I have to take care of before we have that particular conversation." The backs of her fingers rested against my forehead, and her expression turned into a frown. "You feel warm and you look pale. Have the nurses been in to check on you?"

I caught her hand and placed a kiss on the center of her palm. "I'm okay. Just tired. Ready to get out of here." I met her gaze and told her quietly, "You know there is nothing you can tell me that's going to change how I feel about you. If I could've let go of you, I would've done it a long time ago. I never intended to live my life alone. It just turned out that way, because I've never cared about anyone else the way I care about you."

She curled her fingers around the spot I'd kissed and gave me another crooked but sad smile. "We were alone together." I couldn't hide a grin as she used my words from the other night. "I told myself I would never care about anyone the way I cared about Aaron, but it was a lie. I always cared about you as much as I cared about him, more toward the end. It was a different kind of feeling, but it was just as strong. Just as important. I relied on you in a way I could never count on him." She reached out and tapped the end of my nose with her index finger. "I noticed you first, you know. I thought you were beautiful. I also thought you were too good for me. You were the most honest, most real person I'd ever encountered. We always made excuses for what happened at home and tried to hide it. I admired the way you owned your upbringing and were determined to be better than it. And I loved the way you stood by me, and your brother, no matter what. We screwed up a lot, but you were always there for us. Some days you were the only thing holding either of us together. I didn't know what to do with myself when you stopped calling. I really needed you. I still do. I felt like I'd lost a limb, and my heart hurt." She lifted her finger and gently traced the arches of my eyebrows. "I thought you might die today. The idea of losing you..." Her head shook slowly. "It's unbearable. I don't want to ignore how I feel about you anymore." She drew a deep breath, like she was about to say more, but then she changed the subject. "Now I'm going to take care of you when you get out of here. Get ready to be babied and pampered within an inch of your life."

Being pampered sounded unbelievably nice.

"I never thought I would hear you say you cared about me." Even in my dreams she never opened up about her feelings. She was always so guarded and evasive.

"Yeah, well, it was time. I'm so tired of being angry at everyone and everything. I have more to tell you, but it can wait until you get out of here." She looked a little nervous.

I was reaching for her to pull her down for a kiss, because that was the only way I could think to convince her that nothing would change, even when all her skeletons were out of the closet, when we were rudely interrupted.

"Lucky bastard." Kody and I both started at the sudden addition of another voice. Hearst sauntered into the room, looking smug and overly pleased with himself. "If I'd been a couple of minutes quicker, I could be the one playing doctor with a hot blonde."

Kody snorted and crossed her arms over her chest. "In your dreams, city boy."

Hearst chuckled and nodded. "Yeah, I don't look so good in cowboy hats, and that seems to be a requirement to score around these parts." The humor fled his face, and his gaze danced between the two of us. "Can you give me a minute with the hero? I need to talk to him about the case."

Kody grumbled about being left out of things, but reluctantly agreed to leave the room for a few minutes.

Once again I pulled myself into a painful sitting position, aggravated at the inconvenience of this case when things were finally starting to come together with Kody.

"Did you find the doctor who gave the cops the false information on Dr. Baskin's friend, Ashby Grant?" I launched right into the important questions.

Hearst nodded. "I did. Turns out the doctor and Ashby Grant got close while Baskin's mom was in the hospital for treatment for her kidney disease. Grant was there pretty regularly. He admitted to having a personal relationship with Grant, and to lying about the severity of her injuries to the police. When I pressed him, he admitted that she was barely scratched up, but she asked him to make it seem like she was seriously injured if anyone, especially Dr. Baskin, asked how she was doing."

I could barely wrap my head around it. "This woman seriously ruined her best friend's life and tried to make her think she was going crazy because she was jealous over a job promotion?"

Hearst shrugged. "Got to find her so we can ask her. Dr. Baskin keeps insisting it can't be her, but all signs are pointing in that direction. This friend was the only person she confided in once she found out about the Lawtons. She trusts Grant implicitly. Dr. Baskin seems to be in denial. Also, Case went and talked to Conrad's attorney. He asked to see the original will written up by his father. The lawyer got antsy. Case pushed and found out the copy of the will the Lawtons were presented wasn't the original. Seems someone paid the attorney a visit and got him to make the changes, further implicating Dr. Baskin in Conrad Lawton's murder. According to Case, the attorney had a much younger lover who encouraged him to change the will. It shouldn't surprise anyone the woman's description matches Grant's."

I let out a whistle. "She's diabolical, and very thorough."

Hearst nodded. "Yeah. Still haven't figured out how Grant got Conrad to drive out to Austin in the middle of the night, but if her pattern persists, it might've been some kind of promise of a sexual liaison. She's good at getting what she wants through sex and seduction. I'm going to e-mail all the info we have on Grant to you so you can read it while you recover. I'll get you a picture and you can show it to Kody. Don't know if Kody will still be a target, but it's better to be safe than sorry."

"I'm not going to let anything happen to her." I was stating the obvious.

Hearst gave me a grin and reached out for a fist bump. "Sounded to me like she's not going to let anything happen to you either." He arched an eyebrow at me and lowered his voice as he said, "I'm happy for you, partner. But there are some things about your girl you've got to know."

I held up my hand before he could go on. "I know. She told me she'll tell me everything."

And I had to have faith that whatever it was, it wouldn't be bad enough to break us apart.

CHAPTER 17

∞

KODY

I'm sorry the place is kind of a mess. I don't spend much time here." I cast a frantic look around my small, one-bedroom apartment, realizing I couldn't remember the last time I'd tidied up, let alone cleaned the place. I worked such odd hours at the bar, it was common for me to spend the night on the couch in my office. "Are you sure you wouldn't rather go back to your motel?" I had been surprised when he asked me to take him to my place once he was discharged. If I'd had more warning, I could've at the very least made the place look habitable.

Hill peered into the dimly lit room, eyebrows shooting up in obvious disbelief at the stark surroundings. "You sure you live here?" A furrow formed between his gold-colored brows. "This looks exactly like the apartment I had when I was in college. Where are all your colors?"

He wasn't wrong. The place did sort of resemble a bachelor pad. I hadn't done much to decorate because I wasn't sure how long I'd be staying. I always told myself that once the

bar business steadied I'd set some money aside and buy myself a house, but neither of those things ever happened. Days
slid by, and I avoided trying to turn a place I hardly visited
into a home.

"I could try to tell you I was going for a shabby-chic look,
but I think it's pretty clear I got stuck on the shabby part."
I reached for his arm so I could pull him into the room. He
was moving like Frankenstein's monster, all stiff legged and
slow. He insisted he was well enough to be discharged from
the hospital, even though I'd wanted him to stay for at least
one more day. He was black and blue from his hips down,
and he winced every time he took a deep breath. But Hill
wasn't having it. He wanted out of that hospital bed. I personally thought he wanted to leave in part so he wouldn't be
ambushed by his parents again. And I couldn't blame him
for that. "Go lay down on the couch. I think the only thing I
have in the fridge is bottled water. I'll grab you one so you
can take your pain meds."

The couch was a hand-me-down from when Case moved
in with Aspen, so it was one of the few nice pieces of furniture I owned. But it had come from a bachelor's home
and was big, black, and leather. I could see why Hill was
wondering where the colors in my home were. I would typically never own something as neutral and boring as a black
leather couch.

Hill slowly made his way across the room, flopping
down on the couch with a groan. "I hate the water pressure
at the motel. The walls are too thin and the sheets are
scratchy. Normally I can sleep anywhere, in any conditions,
but taking it easy for a few days until I'm back on my feet
sounds pretty great."

I snorted and turned to get his water. "I'm on the sixth
floor. Getting up here is not easy."

He chuckled and tossed his head back as he closed his eyes. "You're right. I just wanted to see where you live. This is the first time you've let me come over."

I managed to avoid answering by sticking my head in the fridge. I never had anyone over. Usually, if I wanted to spend time with my family, I went to one of their perfectly acceptable homes. If I wanted to see friends, I usually met up with them at the bar. The last time I'd had a place that felt like a home, one I wanted to show off and protect, was when I lived in the run-down trailer with Aaron. It was the first place that felt like mine. A place without memories of my mother and without the tarnish of my father. When Aaron died, my idea of *home* went with him.

Walking back toward Hill, I told him, "You've been in my office at the bar. That's more of a peek into my personal space than this apartment is."

He rolled his head on the back of the couch, giving me a look I couldn't really decipher. "I had my condo in Dallas professionally decorated. Every time I'm there I feel like I'm staying at a fancy hotel. I didn't pick out any of the colors for the furniture. The designer told me she was going for something edgy and modern." His eyebrows winged up. "Do I look like an edgy or modern type of guy? It cost a fortune, and I pretty much hate everything about it. I'm never there, so I've never bothered to change it."

Hill had never really had a concept of what *home* should be either. At least I'd had my mom around—even if it was too briefly—to give me enough of an idea that I could recognize what a home should be. Because even black and blue and slightly grumpy, Hill made my sparse and soulless apartment feel full of life and light. He did more for those four walls than any number of throw pillows ever could.

I sat down across from him on the oversize ottoman that

came with the couch and asked, "Do you need anything? Is there anything I can do to make you more comfortable?" He'd mentioned hating the bedding at the motel, so I definitely needed to change my sheets and find my fluffiest blankets for the bed. If he wanted to be pampered, I was going to do my best to make that happen.

He shifted, letting out another groan. "Help me get my boots off, and maybe give me a hand getting into the shower." He rubbed a hand over his flattened hair.

I frowned at him. "You aren't supposed to get the stitches on your leg wet for a few days."

He shrugged. "It'll be fine. Not the first time I had stitches. But I think my ankle is more swollen than I thought. Might need a crowbar to pry these boots off."

When Case brought him a change of clothes, he'd had the foresight to bring sweats and T-shirts, stuff that was easy for Hill to get on and off with his banged-up ribs. Apparently the man didn't own anything but cowboy boots, though. He'd even scoffed at Hearst when he offered to loan him a pair of Nikes. It sounded like he was regretting that decision now.

I carefully lifted his injured leg onto my lap and started to pry the snakeskin boot off his clearly swollen foot. I winced every time he flinched. It took a solid five minutes to free his foot, and once we were done, Hill was covered in a fine sheen of sweat, and his lips were flattened into a tight, fierce line.

I smoothed my palm up the back of his calf, feeling the muscles quake and quiver from strain. He might be putting on a brave face, but he was in more pain than he was letting on.

"Take your pain meds. Let me go make up the bed and grab some stuff to help you clean up. Let's save the shower for when you can actually stand on your own two feet." Not that I would mind getting wet and naked with him in the small confines, but if he fell over, he was too big and heavy for me to get him off the ground.

He wiggled his eyebrows up and down. "Sponge bath?"

I rolled my eyes at his expression. "Something like that. But don't get any ideas. You can hardly move right now."

Something silver and bright lit up his eyes, and he chuckled. "All I have is ideas when it comes to you, Kody. You've taken up every single one of my daydreaming hours for longer than you can possibly know. I could be on the brink of death and still be having all kinds of ideas about you."

Well... wasn't that the nicest thing anyone had ever said to me? I bent down and dropped a kiss on the top of his head. He usually towered over me, so it was rare that I could reach that particular spot. I never would've imagined Hill was so good with his words. Maybe I should've started listening to him a lot sooner.

I left him on the couch to do what I could to make my bedroom as comfortable as possible. At least I had a nice king-size bed, even if I rarely used it. I also had a closet full of fancy linen from my soon-to-be sister-in-law. Della never seemed to know what to get me for birthdays and holidays since I wasn't into makeup or skin-care products. Our styles were also polar opposites, so she settled for getting me things that would help make my sparse space homey. It was probably a good thing she never came over, because I'd yet to use any of the luxury items she gave me.

I found a big beach towel to throw over the couch, and grabbed a washcloth and my least flowery-smelling body wash. It took me longer to track down something to put clean water in, so by the time I made it back to the living room, Hill had managed to strip himself down to nothing more than a pair of obscenely tight black boxer-briefs. I bit the tip of my tongue to hold back the gasp that wanted to escape at the sight of his bruised body. The marks had darkened over the last couple of days. I couldn't believe he was moving as well as he was. His torso and injured leg looked like they'd been trampled by a herd of wild horses. I gulped when I imagined what would've happened to me if he hadn't reached me in time. He literally saved my life and was acting like it was no big deal, kind of the way I'd acted when I overheard him telling his mother he'd been in love with me since we were kids.

Clearing my throat, I helped him move so I could get the towel under him, and the words I'd been holding back every time we were together started to pour out of me. I still believed there wasn't much I could offer him, but the truth was the only thing he'd asked me for.

"When Aaron died I threw myself into running the bar. I had zero experience in running a business and no idea how to turn a profit. All I knew was that I needed a distraction, and I wanted to use the money my mom left for me to do something for myself. I was hoping I'd get lucky and be a natural, but I wasn't. By the time I'd renovated the barn into the bar and restaurant, I was almost broke. I had no clue how expensive a liquor license was, or what kind of bill would come with insuring a place like the Barn. I was in over my head before the first customer walked through the door. Both Case and Crew offered to help, to buy portions of the business to keep me afloat, but I told them no. It was my money. My project. My way to prove I could make it on my own, because after losing Aaron, I swore I was never going to get close to anyone ever again. It hurts too much when you have to let them go."

I dropped a squirt of body wash into my palm, added a little water to work up some lather, and focused on dragging my hands across his well-defined chest. I was careful to avoid the bandage wrapped around his ribs, but chased the shine of sweat along his collarbone and down under his arms with the washcloth. His breathing remained steady and even, but goose bumps lifted on his tanned skin as I leaned closer to him.

"I was desperate...and stupid. I thought I could ask Shot for a loan. I knew who he was from him constantly butting heads with Case when the club moved into town. It was a dumb idea, but the only one I had. I don't know why Shot took me under his wing, but he did. He told me a loan was a bad idea and offered me another way to get my hands on the money I needed to keep the bar open and operational."

It took every ounce of courage I had to meet Hill's gaze. I wasn't surprised to find the gray had gone stormy-looking. The white lines around his mouth were more prominent than before, and I could see he was trying really hard not to say anything.

"Shot has a private distributor I buy very, very expensive alcohol from. Customers can come and order it from me. All the booze goes along with a certain bet, and I pass along that information to Shot." I sighed. "Technically I get a cut of all the liquor sales, and a set fee for keeping the operation running every month. The more I move, the more I get paid. At the beginning it was the only way I could pay the bills. The bar is doing much better now, so I don't have to move as much product, and after all the trouble Crew got into with the bookie back in Vegas..." I shrugged. "I know I need to cut ties, but I haven't figured out a way to tell Shot. I really owe him more than I can say."

I grabbed Hill's hand, refusing to let it go even as he tugged on my hold. I ran the washcloth up and down the firm muscle and braved another look at him. His face was flushed, his breathing was no longer even, and I could tell it was taking all his self-control not to launch into a lecture.

"That's racketeering, Kody. If the feds ever look into the club more closely, you'd end up going to jail. No matter how small a role you play or how close you are to the crime, you're still involved. I can't believe you've been so careless. How can Case look the other way while you're playing bookie for a biker gang?"

"Club. Not gang." The protest was automatic. "Case pretends not to know. Crew knows because I had to tell him. I never wanted to compromise Case's position, but I didn't feel like I had a choice at the time. I'm always very careful about who I do business with. Having Shot and his crew involved has always worked to keep me insulated. I know you're angry, and disappointed, but you have to understand the mind-set I was in. I was willing to do whatever it took to make it on my own."

"Including selling yourself to the president of an outlaw biker club?" The words were nasty, and so was the expression on his face.

"I didn't sell myself, I never would. You know that. I'm going to let your attitude slide right now because I know this is a lot to take in. But you should know me well enough to know that if you continue to treat me like garbage when I'm trying to be transparent, it'll be the last time I'm open with you. Shot and I became friends when business picked up and we were seeing each other pretty frequently. We became more than friends *briefly*, because we were both lonely and not looking for anything serious. I've always been able to rely on him in a pinch, and he's never cared about the fact I'm a Lawton." Or that I was a handful with a less-than-stellar reputation.

I let Hill's hand drop and reached for the other one. There was a tense moment when I thought he wasn't going to put his hand in mine, but eventually he relented.

"Kody." He heaved a sigh, and I watched as he struggled to put together whatever he was going to say. I appreciated that he was taking his time with his words after my warning. Smart man.

I squeezed his hand in mine. "I know you're going to tell me it's got to be you or him, and obviously it's you." It'd always been him, even if I was only now recognizing it.

He shook his head and let it drop forward. "Actually, I'm trying to think of a way to keep you out of jail if this all blows up in your face before you cut ties. This is serious, Kody. Really serious."

I blinked in surprise. "Jail? You're going to turn me in?" The thought had never occurred to me. But it should've. Hill was always a pretty righteous kind of guy, and I'd openly admitted to committing a crime.

He growled under his breath and tossed his head back against the couch cushions. "No. I'm not turning you in. I can't, even if I should. I've waited for you for my entire life, how could I send you away when I finally have a shot at keeping you?"

I didn't realize I'd stopped breathing until he spoke. I'd had no clue that speaking the truth was going to set parts of me free. Hearing his acceptance, and knowing he wasn't going to walk away even when it might be better for him, finally splintered the last shards of the icy cage surrounding my heart.

I set the washcloth on the coffee table next to me and reached for him, but I was brought up short when Hill held out his hand.

"Hold up. I'm not turning you in. I would never do that

to you. But that doesn't mean you're in the clear." He leaned forward, wincing all the way. His face was a mask of pain. He reached for my chin, holding my face still as his gaze bored into mine. "You have to promise me a couple of things, Kody. And if you can't follow through on both of them, I'm limping out that door."

I wasn't the only one throwing down absolutes. He respected mine, so it was only fair I listen to his. "Okay. Tell me what you need me to do."

His thumb feathered along the line of my jaw, and I was suddenly very aware he was mostly naked. Even battered and bruised, he still looked better than any man had a right to. My heart started to flutter, and even though we were in the middle of an intense conversation, all my soft parts started to take notice of all his hard ones.

"First, you get out of the business with the Sons. Walk away, and cut all ties as soon as possible. If Shot has a problem with it, you send him my way and let him know I'm not above getting the feds to start a RICO case against him and the entire club."

It was to be expected. Since I'd already had plans to extract myself from the deal I'd made with Shot, meeting Hill on this particular demand was no biggie.

"I'll walk away." Because I was walking toward something—and someone—better. I was finally figuring out I didn't have to do everything on my own.

He brushed his thumb along the curve of my lower lip and gave me a sad smile. "I know how loyal you are. I know how fiercely you protect the people close to you, and those you care about. So I need you to understand, the only reason I'm asking you to do this next part is because I want to protect you. I want to know you're looking out for yourself, and for any kind of future we might have together."

If that didn't just sound ominous as hell..."Hit me with it."

Hill's eyes locked on mine and his jaw went hard. "I need you to promise me that if anyone makes a move against the club, you'll be on the right side of things. If the law gets involved, you'll need to testify against Shot and the club. It's the only way to keep you out of prison. It's the only way to atone for getting away with blatantly breaking the law for so long." He blew out a breath when I immediately tried to pull away. "I know this might be a deal breaker, but it's the only way we can move forward...together. This is the only way I see us having any kind of future."

It was my turn to growl under my breath. "I had to go and get myself involved with a cop, didn't I?"

The tiny smile on his face fell away, and he moved to sit up straighter. "You had to go and get yourself involved with a gambling ring. That was a choice you made. I'd like to think you were hopeless against falling for a cop, because the cop had no choice but to fall in love with you. I told you, if I could've turned my back on my feelings for you, I would've, but that's never been an option for me." He cocked his head to the side and almost whispered, "It still isn't. Honestly, at this point I don't think there's anything you can do, or say to me, that will convince my heart to let go of you."

He put a hand on the center of his chest and rubbed the spot I'm sure was pounding. "I've cared about you most of my life from afar. It will be hard, but I can do it again if you can't make yourself turn against Shot. It's a very Kody-type thing to suffer so others don't have to. But I can't turn my entire life upside down when there's a chance you might get ripped away from me. Like you said, losing someone you love hurts too much."

And I knew it hurt even worse when that loss could've been prevented, when it was totally unnecessary.

I groaned and lifted my fingers to my suddenly throbbing forehead. Never in a million years had I thought anything would ever get me to turn on Shot and the boys, but when it came down to it, I couldn't bear the idea of having to watch Hill walk away. I'd made this messy bed, and now I was the one who was going to have to lie in it.

"If the time comes for me to save myself by sacrificing Shot, regardless of how he's helped me, I'll do it. I won't let anything come between us again. I promise." The words tasted bitter, and I would be keeping my fingers crossed that things didn't come to that. I didn't want to betray Shot. He'd been a good friend and one of the few people outside my family who stood by me. I wouldn't lie to Hill anymore, about anything, but damn it was going to be hard for me to follow through if the worst-case scenario played out.

We stared at each other in a very tense silence for a couple of minutes, both of us realizing the work it was going to require for us to make some kind of relationship possible. I was going to have to learn to be so much better and wiser than I was, and he was going to have to let a little bit of trouble and chaos into his orderly life.

"I love you, Kody. Always have, always will."

Now that all the secrets were out, and he loved me anyway, I could finally tell him, "I love you too, Hill. For a long time. I know I have definitely never loved you as well as you loved me, but I know it'll always be you who makes me unafraid of those feelings." All my life, love had been hard and unforgiving. He made it seem like something softer, something that could be easy enough if we both put the work in. He was the only one who had managed to finally break through all the anger that had been consuming most of my waking hours, making way for kinder, gentler feelings...ones I'd thought were long lost.

The next thing I knew, I was yanked off the coffee table and onto Hill's lap. I shrieked in both surprise and concern, my hands landing on his chest as I tried to keep my weight off his injuries.

"Hey! Be careful! What are you doing? Let go of me."

He shook his head and dropped a kiss on the tip of my nose. "Never."

The more I squirmed on top of him, the more his body reacted. The thin, black cotton covering his lap was doing little to hide the way he'd responded to my admission. He was hard as steel underneath me, and his eyes were molten with desire.

"I told you, all I have is ideas when it comes to you. You're always on my mind." One of his hands dived into my hair as he pulled me closer for a kiss. "I can get creative if need be."

"You're hurt. This is not a good idea." And I'd just sworn to start making better choices, even if he was the most tempting thing I'd ever come across.

"Really? It feels like one of the best ones I've ever had."

He effortlessly held me still as I perched on his lap so I didn't involuntarily jostle his ribs, then he kissed me senseless. I forgot why I was trying to behave. Being the responsible one went against my basic nature anyway...and somehow, miraculously, he still loved me.

CHAPTER 18

∾

HILL

Kody Lawton was in love with me.

Hearing her say the words, hearing the truth in them, was enough to help me ignore any discomfort coming from the parts of me that were currently a little worse for wear. If I moved wrong, I lost my breath as my side protested. If she moved wrong, I felt it in my injured leg and hip. The timing was not ideal to show her exactly how her words made me feel, but there was also no holding back the emotions, or the response, in every single part of my being.

I wanted all of her, touching all of me, because I felt her love all over. My heart seemed like it was taking up too much space inside my chest. My mind, which was always whirring and buzzing, finally felt still and calm. Every thought, every feeling was focused on the woman in my arms. Obviously my body reacted to having her close. My dick didn't care if my ribs had seen better days. Desire pulsed slow and hard in my belly, overshadowing the flare of pain trying to make itself known.

A smoldering warmth also worked its way underneath my skin. Flickering flames of want blazing along my nerve endings, making me acutely aware of the way we were pressed together and how little clothing I was wearing. I'd never considered myself a tactile person, but as always, Kody was the exception to the rule. I couldn't get enough of her touch, or enough of having my hands on her. It felt like I was holding my entire future in the palms of my hands.

As I moved her, I knew we were going to have to take this slow. Be careful and deliberate. We had to appreciate the little things about one another, the subtle movements, the longing looks and lingering touches. Whenever I got the opportunity to get my hands on her, I felt like it was a race to the finish line. I wanted to cram as much into those moments as possible because there was never a guarantee she wasn't going to pull away, both emotionally and physically. Things between the two of us had always been on Kody's terms. I'd always let her lead and followed behind obediently because I believed it was the right thing to do. I wanted her to be happy. To find love again, even if it wasn't with me. Now that I knew it was *only* with me she could achieve either of those things, I felt like I had time.

Time to savor her.

Time to learn all about her, what she liked, what she didn't.

Time to figure out how to make her lose her mind and beg for more.

Time to make her feel like there was no way she could live without me, because I knew there was no way I could return to the way I'd been living before getting swept up in her. The future was uncertain. I had a bad feeling trouble was going to come back around and bite her in the ass. I would look the other way because I loved her and wanted to protect her. But Hearst was already asking questions about her ties to the club. Being in love with Kody was nothing new. *Actively* loving her and being loved by her was proving to be a little more challenging. But I had been serious when I told her I didn't have a choice in the matter. The love I had for her was such a big part of who I was, who I'd always been, I wasn't sure if I would recognize myself without it.

I couldn't hold back a wince when her knee accidentally knocked against my hip. I hissed a breath out between my teeth and tightened my hands on her waist.

Kody pulled back and gave me a hard look. "The body might be willing, but I don't think it's able." I liked her smart mouth and quick wit. Everything about her kept me on my toes. She was worth the work.

I caught one of her hands in mine and purposely put it on the bulge filling out the front of my dark underwear. There was a lot of heat between her hand and the hard flesh beneath the cotton. It warmed my stomach, made my thighs tense. I lifted her other hand so I could drop a kiss on her black-and-blue elbow. She hadn't complained once about me taking her to the ground. It had been a necessary move, but I hated seeing her fair skin marred.

"The body is able. We just have to be careful with it... with each other. We have all the time in the world. There's no rush." And wasn't that just a dream come true?

Her hand moved to caress the hardness nestled between my legs. Her eyes became heavy lidded and darker than normal. "Are you sure about that? Parts of you seem to be in a pretty big hurry."

She was such a flirt. Who knew?

Not me. I'd never seen this side of her before, and I had to say it was adorable.

"I haven't let that part of me call the shots since I was

sixteen." Though it did tend to have a mind of its own when I was around her. "I'm not going anywhere."

I wasn't sure why she needed that reassurance from me, but it seemed to do the trick.

She tugged her bruised arm free and reached out so she could trace each of the features of my face with the tip of her finger. I felt like she was trying to commit how I looked to memory. She drew an outline around my lips and slowly lowered her head to chase after the sweet touch.

The kiss was languorous. Long and drawn out. Our lips pressed tightly together. Our breath mingled. Tongues tangled together, and things went from seductive and slow to hot and wet really fast. She was potent. A small taste was enough to set off fireworks in my blood and make me forget all about good intentions. Where this woman was concerned I was always going to want more.

More of her flavor on my tongue.

More of her smooth, soft skin under my hands.

More of the greedy, hungry noises she made.

More of her heart.

I was never going to get enough.

I reached for her, wanting to pull her closer, but was instantly reminded why we couldn't tear into one another like wild animals. My vision whited out for a second, and not because I was at the peak of pleasure. I instinctively put a hand on my wrapped side and closed my eyes so I could catch my breath. I could feel Kody's frown and hear her protest, even though she didn't make a sound. I was going to have to keep her distracted, or else she was going to send me to bed alone.

I looked up at her with my heart in my eyes. I needed her to see how badly I needed this. How much I needed her. I pushed my hands under the hem of her shirt and worked it up over her head. She was in a pretty, mint-colored bra that was mostly lace and looked like candy against her skin. As delicate and lovely as the lingerie was, what was underneath took my breath away. Unhooking the clasp without moving either one of us too much put all my dexterity to the test, but I managed. I grinned at her when I felt her sigh of surrender.

She corded her fingers through the hair at my temples and leaned forward super carefully so she could place a kiss on the top of my head. While she was arched over me I took advantage of her position to kiss my way across her collarbone and down the valley between her breasts. I heard her inhale a sharp breath when I moved my mouth to cover one of her pointed nipples. It peaked even tighter against my tongue. I traced her spine with the fingers of one hand and used the other to keep her hips still. She was trying to rock against the hardness between her legs, but I needed to be in control of all her movements, of the agonizingly slow pace.

Kody made a frustrated sound, and a moment later I felt her bite the shell of my ear. The contact made me shiver and tilt my head to give her better access to the sensitive spot. She braced one hand on the back of the couch behind me and dragged the other across my battered chest. She was balanced with her knees on either side of me, and seemed sturdy enough in that position, so I released my hold on her. She took advantage of her freedom to slide her hand underneath the waistband of my boxers so she could wrap her hand around my very hard cock. It jumped at the contact, seeking more of her touch as her palm glided over the extra-sensitive skin.

She panted in my ear as I switched my attention to her other breast. It was a long, slow climb. I was all for the foreplay, even if it was enough to drive me out of my mind.

Kody threw her head back when I started to use my teeth on the tightly coiled bud surrounded by the heat of my mouth. She wobbled a little, and lost the rhythm of her strokes around my stiff shaft. When her fist squeezed tighter around my rigid cock, it made my eyes roll back in my head and my breath catch. The shift of her knee banged against my injured hip, which was enough to make me want to howl, but there was no stopping now.

Luckily, Kody was good at reading my body language. She moved with painstaking care as she slid her hand out of my boxers and lifted herself off the couch. I was going to protest, mostly at the loss of her hand on my straining cock, when she held out her hand and quirked her eyebrows. "Come on. We're not going to get anywhere in here. You need to lie down and get somewhere comfortable. Plus I changed the sheets for you. Can't let my brief venture in domesticity go to waste." She looked down at my erection and the obvious wet spot on the front of my underwear. "Can't let that go to waste either. Let's get creative."

I needed her help to get to my feet and to get down the narrow hallway into her bedroom. The exertion was enough to leave my leg muscles quaking and a cold sweat popping up on my skin. All of that faded into the background when Kody stripped the dark material of my boxer-briefs away from my body. Then she maneuvered me to where she wanted me on the bed. I watched her with hungry eyes as she wiggled out of the rest of her clothes, my hand absently finding my hard length. My hand didn't feel nearly as good as hers had, but it was enough to dull the low hum of discomfort ringing behind all the pleasure.

She took a step toward the edge of the bed, but paused for a second, reaching up to pull on her lower lip as she asked, "Should we talk about protection, or is it too soon?"

Too soon wasn't a thing when it came to her. I had years and years invested in this relationship, even if it was brand-new to her.

"I've been working so much lately, there hasn't been time for there to be anyone in my life. You know how meticulous I am. I've always been careful, and we have yearly physicals at work. If you tell me we're good to go, I believe you. If you tell me we should be careful, then I'll appreciate your honesty and you looking out for both of us." Details and specifics were kind of my thing, but in this instance I wanted to have faith in her . . . in us.

She huffed out a breath and lifted her hands to push her hair back. I loved the way the motion forced her breasts out, loved that she was unashamed of how she looked and who she was.

"I can't say I've been too busy to have any fun. However, I've always been selective as to who I have said fun with, and I've always taken care of myself. I've got things covered on my end if you really do trust me to take care of you." The last words sounded almost shy.

"I wouldn't be in this bed if I didn't trust you." Not when I was vulnerable and weak. Not when I wasn't at my best. I would have never fallen in love with her in the first place if I didn't trust her. Even though I knew she might play fast and loose with the personal information she wanted others to have, I also knew she was always unflinchingly honest about her choices and their consequences.

She went quiet for a second, green eyes glittering, and I wondered if maybe I was seeing my own feelings reflected back at me. If I was, they were beautiful.

She released her breath and gracefully climbed up on the bed next to me. When I went to reach for her, she slapped my hands away and told me to stay as still as possible. Curious how she planned to get things back on track, I let my arms drop and watched her with open curiosity.

I gulped when she climbed over me, straddling me on all fours, her knees near my head and her hands braced on the mattress next to my hips. None of her weight was on top of my battered and bruised places this way, and all I had to do to get to her glistening, soft center was pull her hips down toward my watering mouth. And all she had to do was lower her head to take my very interested cock into hers. Her lips slid down my shaft as her tongue swirled around the head. I had forgotten I was supposed to be focusing on returning the favor when I felt a little flick against the slit.

My fingers dug into her thighs, and my teeth dragged across her clit. I felt her whole body stiffen in response and gave her a flick in return. I wasn't over the moon that I couldn't see her face and read her expression while we simultaneously tried to eat each other alive. But I was eternally grateful I could touch her and taste her without wanting to climb out of my skin to escape the pain knocking against my bones. It was easy to get drunk on her flavor and to lose my head at how good her talented mouth felt wrapped around me.

She sucked hard enough my hips wanted to lift off the bed. I responded with a thrust of my tongue that went deep enough to make her shiver where she was arched above me. Her silky hair brushed along the insides of my thighs as she dipped her head even lower. The sensation was erotic as hell. I couldn't get enough of it. My legs twitched restlessly from pleasure, and her hips started to push back against my face in a small rocking motion.

I ran a hand over the curve of her hip and down the side of her leg. I traced her goose bumps with my fingers, working my way back between her quivering thighs. I might not be able to move much, but I still wanted to give her as much pleasure as possible, wanted her to remember the day we told each other we were in love. Since my fingers and my mouth were among the few parts of my body I could move without wanting to pass out, I used them to the fullest.

I swirled my tongue around her clit and slid my fingers inside her wet heat. Her body clenched around them, and she hummed her pleasure around my cock. She shifted so she was leaning her weight on her uninjured elbow and used her free hand to drag her fingernails up the inside of my thigh. It was a light touch, barely there, but I felt it like an electric shock.

I growled in approval and sucked even harder on the little nub trapped between my lips. I flexed my fingers inside her, pleased when a rush of moisture suddenly swirled around them. I felt Kody's nipples drag across my lower abdomen and couldn't stop myself from thrusting into her mouth when she lowered her head at the same time that she carefully raked her fingernails over my tender sack.

There was no place left untouched or unexplored.

It was hands down the longest I'd ever spent learning another person's body, and every new secret spot I uncovered, every hot button I found, got me a better reaction than the one before it. She was also doing her best to drive me out of my mind, alternating between light, little licks and steady suction. My cock was throbbing intensely against her tongue, and I could feel the rest of my body starting to coil in satisfaction. I wasn't going to be able to hold back much longer, but I wanted to make sure I pushed her over the edge first.

I switched to stroking her with my tongue and thrusting my fingers in and out of her in a deliberate rhythm. Her head lifted and she looked over her shoulder in my direction. Her lashes were lowered and she had twin circles of pink staining her freckled cheeks. She panted a little and whispered, "So close."

Good. I wasn't going to last much longer either. I pulled my fingers away from her body and pushed my tongue back in. I swirled around for a second and was immediately rewarded with my name bouncing off the walls and a rush of wetness. I felt her body tremble as she moaned her way through her orgasm. It was a beautiful sight. One that was going to be seared on my memory forever.

I caught a handful of her and silently urged her to sit up.

"Move down." She shot me a questioning look but followed my direction. It must've been a pretty good orgasm for her to be so docile.

Once she was hovering over my cock, I grabbed the base, lined myself up with her very wet and ready opening, and gruffly told her, "All I need is to get inside of you." It was going to be over for me as soon as I felt her surround my aching cock with nothing between her body and mine. I couldn't remember the last time I'd been with anyone long enough, or trusted them enough, to go in bare. "Just move slowly."

She did.

So slowly I was ready to scream.

It seemed like it took ten years for the tip to breach her entrance. Then another ten for the next couple of inches to make their way inside. Kody was watching me over her shoulder for any sign of distress, but I could see the playful smirk on her face. She knew this was torture and she was enjoying it.

Finally I was seated all the way inside her, drowning in the aftermath of her pleasure. It felt so good. This was the connection I needed to finish expressing my feelings to her.

Everything inside my body was screaming at me to move, to thrust hard and fast into the velvet softness encircling the pulsing length. Kody must've sensed my growing desperation, because she carefully, gingerly moved her hips in a purposeful, precise circle.

That tiny motion was all I needed for all the tension pushing at the threshold to break free. I let out a sound that wasn't human. I could no longer stay still, which I was undoubtedly going to pay for later. My hips automatically kicked up as I thrust against her with a desperation that was raw and unchecked. I shook and moaned my way through the most intense orgasm I'd ever experienced.

It would have been nice to wallow in the afterglow. I wanted a pat on the back for our managing to wreck each other while I could hardly move, but Kody almost immediately slipped back into her role as caretaker.

After getting a quick kiss, she disappeared from sight, only to return a few minutes later with the stuff she'd used earlier for the sponge bath. Now that I'd managed to act on some of my dirty thoughts, it was much easier to lie still and let her fuss over me. She gave me a disbelieving look when she got to the spot between my legs and my cock twitched in renewed interest. All I could do was chuckle and tell her I only ever rebounded that quickly with her.

We exchanged playful banter for a few minutes as she cleaned me up the best she could and tucked me into her now-messy bed. She sat down next to me, brushing some of my hair off my forehead.

"I think I need to talk to Dr. Baskin once all of this is over."

Her quiet words caught me off-guard. It was the last thing I'd expected her to say. "Why?"

She sighed and reached out to put her hand lightly on the

bandage around my ribs. "Because I can't keep blaming the wrong people for the painful things that happen in my life. I heard you tell your mother the reason Aaron died was because he was sick." She squeezed her eyes shut and bit her lip. "It's true. I blamed you. I blamed me. I blamed him. But it wasn't any of us. When you told me my dad died, I did the same thing. Found the easiest person to blame." She shook her head as if to clear it, and when she looked at me again her eyes were clear and her expression was earnest. "She's been through a lot. The loss of her mother. Finding out her father was someone like Conrad. Learning she has a whole new family, one who didn't exactly welcome her with open arms. She was betrayed by someone close to her. I guess I just feel bad about how we treated her. I shouldn't have assumed the worst. The blame needs to be placed where it actually belongs. If I'd learned that lesson earlier, maybe I could've seen what was waiting right in front of me. Blame blinded me to beautiful things. I don't want to make that mistake twice."

"You saw what you needed to see when you were ready to see it."

She grinned at me and leaned forward so that the very tips of our noses almost touched. "The world looks a little different now."

I lifted a hand to cup her cheek. "Oh yeah? What's it look like now?"

She blinked. "You. My entire world looks like you."

It was about time, because mine had always looked like her.

CHAPTER 19

∞

KODY

It's the end of the road for you and me, Trouble."

Shot's voice was softer than normal, and so was the look in his very dark eyes. I nodded from my place behind the bar. I was surprisingly choked up about this conversation.

"It is. I need to stop taking the easy way out. I told everyone I was going to make this bar into something on my own, but you've always been there in the background, like training wheels. It's time to sink or swim for real." I needed to do things the right way if I was going to make a relationship with Hill work.

"I figured this conversation was coming the minute I saw the way you looked at the Ranger." His lips twisted into a smirk. "You never looked at me that way."

I wanted to cringe, but I kept my composure. "I'm sorry."

Shot shook his head, black hair falling into his eyes. "Don't be. I liked you from the start. I liked your fearlessness and your smart mouth. I could've more than liked you if I didn't know it was impossible for us to be anything more than what we were. I knew you would never put your brother in a bind. I knew you were actually a really good girl making bad choices. I don't regret having you in my life and letting you get close to my club." He winked at me and knocked on the bar top with the backs of his ringed fingers. "Hanging around you was never boring."

I gave him a weak grin. "Same." I exhaled a long, slow breath and muttered the hardest part of the conversation I had to have with him. "I promised Hill that if the club gets in trouble with the law, with the feds specifically, I have to be honest about the deal we made. He knows everything, and he's still sticking around, so I have to keep up my end of the bargain. I would never betray you, not after all you've done for me, if I had a choice." I looked him in the eye and ordered, "So don't get busted. I can't be the reason you go to prison, Shot." It would break my heart. But I would do it for Hill.

The rings covering his tattooed fingers tapped on the bar again. "Don't worry about us. You do what you got to do. If the feds start digging, all they're going to find is a liquor distribution company under the club's name, which has incredibly inflated prices. All the patrons who came in to see you bought and paid for that product legally. Don't stress the details. That's my job."

I shoved both my hands through my hair and looked down at the wooden floor. "I want to stay friends. Can we?"

It seemed like maybe I was asking too much of him. I'd severed our business ties and told him flat out I would betray him if it came down to it. If I were in his motorcycle boots, my ass would be out the door with zero plans of coming back.

"Of course we can. I've got your back no matter what. Never doubt it. Plus, the boys and I like the Barn. This place suits us when we need a night out. You make sure your cop knows there's no hard feelings so I don't have to worry about him breathing down my neck all the time, and we'll be cool, just like we've always been."

I was very lucky to have great men on either side of the law standing in my corner. I figured it was the universe's way of evening things out since I'd been saddled with a father like Conrad.

I reached across the bar so I could squeeze his hand. "Thank you."

Shot nodded and pulled his hand free before he leaned back on the bar stool. "How'd you convince the Ranger to let you out of his sight? I figured he would have you under lock and key after you nearly got run over."

I rolled my eyes. "I still have a business to run. My life can't grind to a halt just because some crazy woman suddenly has her sights set on me."

It was the same argument I'd given Hill when he tried to keep me from leaving my apartment that afternoon. I had a feeling his reluctance to let me go was only partly due to me being some kind of target. I was fairly certain he was more than a little uneasy I'd planned to meet Shot alone at the bar before it opened. His jealousy was kind of cute. His high-handedness was not. Ultimately, he knew there was no way to stop me from doing what I had to do. But he refused to let me go unescorted. One quick call to Case and I had a babysitter for the day. It was an okay compromise, all things considered. I wasn't going to hide from the woman who had murdered my father and was doing her best to ruin the sister I'd never known about. I was actually looking forward to getting a chance to face the woman. There was a lot she had to answer for.

Shot chuckled. "You know there are two Loveless deputies parked outside, right?"

I snorted. "Yeah. That's Hill's doing. He's still laid up and moving slow. He asked my brother to put one of his guys on the bar until the woman who killed my father is caught."

Shot nodded his approval. "Good man. You also know the deputy called it in as soon as I pulled up, right? Your Ranger is going to know we're together." He wiggled his dark eyebrows up and down, chuckling when I dug out a piece of ice and threw it at him.

"Hill knows we're together. I don't keep secrets from him." Not anymore. "I've made a lot of mistakes where Hill's concerned. I didn't give him, or myself, enough credit. He loved me, even when I forgot how to love myself. He loved me enough for the both of us." I shrugged. "He's the one." Really, it was as simple as that.

Shot studied me for a long moment before finally nodding and giving me his silent approval. "So tell me about the new sister. What's she like?" His midnight brows danced upward playfully. "She look like you? 'Cause I could be into that. You think I'm her type?"

I couldn't hold back my burst of laughter. "Hell no."

He cocked his head to the side and smiled. "You sure? I'm pretty much everyone's type."

He wasn't wrong. It was hard to resist his wicked charm and badass swagger. There was something about the leather and ink that really worked for him.

"I wasn't very nice to her. None of us were. We were all so caught up in our own guilt and grief, we made her an enemy without giving her a chance to prove whether she was friend or foe." I rested my elbows on the edge of the bar and cupped my chin in my hands. "We do look a lot alike, but I think the similarities are only on the surface. She's freakishly smart. She's very composed and talks like she's narrating a documentary on the Discovery Channel. But she's got a killer right hook, so I guess there are some surprises under all the frost. I told Hill I would like to get a chance to know her. She didn't have to tell us about the blackmail. She could've just brought Conrad's affair with her mother to light and demanded her share of whatever he happened to have, but she seemed sincerely remorseful about what her mother did. And it bugs me that she seems so alone. She's not a Lawton, but she has Lawton blood, and that means something. We take care of our own."

Shot let out a whistle. "You should introduce me. I'm intrigued."

The idea of the two of them together was laughable. I couldn't imagine two people being more opposite than Shot and Dr. Baskin.

"She's a medical examiner. She spends her time with dead people. Like, that's the job she chose for herself on purpose, and she's really good at it. What kind of person chooses to surround themselves with death?"

Shot sighed and climbed to his feet. "Sometimes the dead make better companions than the living. I'm going to head out." His smile shifted and started to look a little sad. "I'm glad to see you looking happy, Kody. Gets me right here." He tapped his fist to his chest and flashed me a flirty wink.

"I'd like to see you happy one day too, Shot." I really would. I couldn't envision the type of woman who would be able to handle his rough, often lawless lifestyle, but I liked to think she was out there and he would find her sooner rather than later.

He waved the statement off, pausing to answer his phone as he walked toward the front doors. The staff would be here any minute to get the bar opened for the day. I needed to sit down and brainstorm real, legal ways to increase business and keep the doors open. It was time to grow up. I'd failed

and fought. Now I had the opportunity to struggle and suc-
ceed. I was surprised at how much I was looking forward to
the challenge.

"A fire? Are you sure?" Shot's voice was sharp, catching
my attention as he turned on his boot heel to look at me.
"Call it in. You guys check out the property. You're probably
looking for a woman. Be careful, she's a killer."

"What's going on?" I scrambled around the bar and
hurried toward him. I didn't like the expression on his face.

Shot barked a few more orders into the phone and grabbed
my elbow in an almost painful grip. "Your dad's house is
on fire. The guys in the club were headed back to the ranch
when they saw smoke coming up over the hill. They went
to check it out and found the place burning." He quirked an
eyebrow. "They wanted to make sure they should call the
fire department. Top thought maybe you'd had enough of the
bullshit and decided to torch the place."

My stomach felt like it dropped into my shoes. I hated that
house, hated the childhood I'd had there, but it was also the
last place I'd seen my mother. The last place she'd hugged
me, kissed me good night. It was the final place she'd told
me she loved me and promised me I was good enough, where
she'd whispered I would find someone to love me exactly the
way I was. God, how I wished I could tell her I'd been lucky
enough to find more than one.

"I have to go. I need to get to the house." I wasn't thinking
clearly, wasn't processing that the house was probably gone
already. All I could think about was the few good memories
of my family going up in smoke.

I shook my arm, trying to get Shot to let me go, but he
held on tight. "You're not rushing off into a dangerous situation like an idiot. You know better, and I'm not about to have
your Ranger all up my ass if something happens to you. Call

him and tell him what's going on. Let him know the club is looking for anyone on the property and I'm taking you to the site. He's going to want you to go with the cop out front, but tell him you need a friend right now."

I nodded absently, like a broken bobblehead doll. I dug my phone out of my pocket and pressed the number to call Hill.

He sounded like I'd woken him up when he answered. "Hey. How did everything go?"

"Hill, Dad's house is on fire! It's going to burn to the ground before the fire department can get out there." The hill country was great for isolation and keeping family secrets buried. It was terrible for any kind of quick emergency response. "I'm losing it. Shot's taking me out to the property, and the boys in the club are looking for Presley's crazy friend." I was surprised when a sob snuck out. "I don't know what to do. I need you."

No questions asked. None of the interrogation Shot had anticipated. Hill simply gave me the support I needed and kept me breathing with a few easy words when I felt like I was going to suffocate. "You've got me. Put Caldwell on the phone."

I wordlessly passed the phone over to Shot, memories of watching my brothers grow up in that house swirling like a kaleidoscope in my mind.

"Let's roll. Hill's going to let your brothers know what's going on, and he'll be out at the house before you know it." The biker pulled me out the door. "I told him I would take care of you until he showed up, so get it together and don't make me look bad, Trouble."

I nodded mutely, following him to his big black-and-chrome monstrosity of a bike. He handed me a helmet, which I must've stared at for too long, because he ended up plopping it on my head and snapping the chin strap.

"Try to look a little less like I'm kidnapping you. Hill said he'd take care of the unit watching you, but if we pass another cop on the way out to the ranch, we don't have time to get pulled over." His hands landed on my shoulders, and he gave me a little shake. "The building might burn to the ground, but everything important that happened inside of it is still right here." He tapped his finger on the rim of the helmet, and then on the center of my chest. "And in here. You aren't going to fall apart on me over a pile of old wood."

I sniffed and forced myself to breathe out slow and steady. "Let's go."

I followed Shot's lead, throwing a leg over the bike and settling in as he gunned it out of the parking lot. One of the deputy cars followed behind us, turning the sirens on as we hit the highway and flew down the road toward hill country.

It didn't take long to see the smoke billowing over the rolling hills. It was thick, black, and ominous-looking. It was an omen foretelling the sight waiting for me when we finally hit the backcountry roads that wound their way to the property.

The house wasn't just on fire.

It was a blazing, roaring inferno.

It looked like something out of a movie. The colors of the flames were so intense, so vivid as they ate up century-old wood and plaster. I couldn't stop the pained whimper, or the way I automatically squeezed Shot so tightly he had to tap my hands to get me to loosen my grip.

The house had an avid audience as it popped and whooshed its way through its last few standing supports. The heat was intense, blistering even from a distance. The air smelled acrid and bitter.

Neighbors—who never once showed up to help us when

they knew good and well what kind of man Conrad was—stood by with almost satisfied looks. Conrad Lawton hadn't been any better a neighbor than he had been a father or sheriff. Several of Shot's boys were gathered around in a semicircle. They all had their arms crossed and were watching the spectacle with somber expressions. It was interesting that they appeared to have more sympathy and compassion than the people I'd lived next to growing up.

As soon as the bike rolled to a stop, I hopped off the back, ripped the helmet from my head, and started running toward the blaze. I didn't have a coherent thought. All I knew was that I wanted to be closer, as if I could save something, do something to prevent all the damage.

A strong arm locked around my waist, and I was immediately pulled backward. Shot's low voice rumbled in my ear. "Not going to happen, Trouble. Behave until your man gets here."

I shook him off. Slapped his hands away as he reached for me again. "Leave me alone."

It was impossible to explain to anyone what it was doing to me to watch my entire painful past go up in flames. I'd barely had time to process the very complicated emotions that went along with losing my father in such a violent and tragic way. Now the only thing left that tied me to him was turning into ash. It made things feel so final.

Sirens screamed in the distance, but they were too late.

Without being aware of it, I sank to my knees in the dirt. I was pretty sure I was crying, but the heat coming from the fire was intense, drying the tears as soon as they hit my cheeks.

I had no idea how much time went by. It could've been a minute or an hour, but between one smoky breath and the next, I was suddenly wrapped up in an embrace that felt like home. I would know the way Hill held me in a dark room filled with a thousand other people. There was something healing in his touch.

I let him pull me to my feet and buried my head in his chest as he stroked my hair and muttered words that were nonsense in my ear. It made no sense, but now that he was here, I knew everything was going to be okay.

"I can't tell you how many times I imagined burning the damn place down when we were growing up." Case's raspy words brought my head up as he suddenly appeared next to us. I was shocked he'd admitted it. Crew was the one who was outright defiant when we were growing up. Case was the one who did his best to hold us all together. "Shouldn't hurt to see the place go, but it does."

I nodded, the top of my head bumping Hill's chin as he pulled me closer. "It really does."

Hill cupped the back of my head and moved his head down until his lips were right next to my ear.

"At least you got to send your mom off. I know you didn't get a chance to tell your old man goodbye. You never got to say what you had to say to him before he was taken out of your life. There was no closure, he remains forever unforgiven. But no matter how you felt about him, he was still your dad. This house is the last thing casting Conrad's shadow in your life. Maybe it's time to put the past to rest." He set me away from him and shot a look at Case, and at Crew, who was now lingering behind our older brother. "Go together. After the house is gone, you're done being nothing more than Conrad Lawton's kids. This place wasn't your home. Your homes are the places you all went out and found for yourselves. It's in the love you found despite Conrad trying to take it from you over and over again."

Case released a shuddery breath and reached out to clasp Hill's shoulder. "I'm glad you're here."

So was I. I wrapped my arms around his waist for a quick hug before letting go so I could reach for my brothers' hands. The fire department was now on the scene, along with what looked like half of Case's deputies. Everyone was giving us a respectful amount of space, but Hill took the initiative to ask everyone to move even farther back. He managed to be imposing and authoritative even though he was using a crutch to keep him upright and off his bad knee, still looking like a boxer who'd lost his last fight.

Case threw his arms around my and Crew's shoulders. He yanked us in until we were huddled together, similar to when we were kids trying to comfort each other.

"It's just a house. A stupid house. A place that housed generations of mean and ugly." Case's voice cracked. "We don't need it. None of us wanted it."

"We've got each other." Crew's voice also sounded shaky. "No matter what, we've always had each other. We got the only thing that mattered out of that shithole."

"We aren't going to forget Mom. Never. We don't need the house to remind us of how much she loved us. We don't need those walls to keep her memory here with us." I closed my eyes as I felt tears catch on my eyelashes. "Who we were when we lived in that house doesn't have to define who we are now." That was a lesson I'd learned from Hill long ago. I should've put it into action before we got to this point.

Case pulled me closer until our foreheads knocked together. "This is the end. This is the last time we're going to let this place make us sad. This is the last time we're crying over what happened here. This is some kind of goddamn purification. We're all moving forward. We're taking every lesson we learned the hard way and we're going to do the Lawton name proud. When people think about Dad, we're going to make them say, 'Look how well those Lawton kids did for themselves.' We're going to do right by us, despite him."

We took a minute to hold each other and silently say goodbye to the kids we used to be and the parents we no longer had. It was emotional. It was tragic. It was healing.

There were a loud crack and a few shouts from the firemen as the last of the structure collapsed in on itself. The house was now nothing more than a memory and a pile of embers. It was as if the Band-Aid we had slapped over all the wounds left from our childhood had been ripped away in one swift move. Now there was air and room for the injuries we'd always kept covered up to mend.

I made my way back over to Hill, who was staring at his phone with furrowed brows and a fierce frown. He looked in my direction when I called his name over the commotion happening behind me.

His expression didn't soften at all when I approached.

"What's wrong?"

He looked at the wreckage of the house and over to where Shot and his boys were gathered.

"You, Case, and Crew are going to have to be extra careful until we get a handle on this woman." He sounded angry and very serious.

"This lunatic can't believe she's going to get away with putting the blame on Presley still." It was absurd.

Hill shook his head. "No. I don't think she's trying to frame Dr. Baskin anymore. Since it didn't work, she's just making her suffer. Now she's demanding to know where Baskin is. She says if we don't disclose the doctor's location she's not going to stop coming after her new family."

I blinked and felt my jaw drop. "What?"

"She called the local law asking to be put in touch with the Ranger in charge of the Lawton investigation. They put her in touch with Hearst. She made the threat directly to him. Told him the fire was just the start." His jaw clenched, and a muscle twitched furiously in his cheek. I could feel the heat of his anger radiating off him. "Her plan to put Presley away didn't work, and now she's gone off the deep end."

I jolted and reached out to grab a handful of his shirt. "My bar!" If my childhood home was a target, there was no way my bar wouldn't be next.

Hill held up the hand he didn't have wrapped around the crutch under his arm. "Hearst took care of it. He sent some of our guys to your bar, to Aspen's office, and out to Crew's place to keep an eye on Della. We're going to take every precaution needed until she's caught. We're about to launch a statewide manhunt."

I nearly collapsed against him. "What's the point to all of this? She's got to be plain crazy."

He kissed the top of my head. "I agree, something isn't quite right with her wiring. I'll figure out her motivation, though. I won't stop until we have answers."

I believed he would, but not before all of us, and mostly our new sister, were put through the emotional wringer by her former friend's vengefulness.

CHAPTER 20

∞

HILL

I was back to being so tired it was a battle to keep my eyes open.

When the Texas Rangers launched a manhunt, it was all hands on deck, even if those hands weren't in the best shape. Between chasing down leads, all of which turned out to be busts, and doing my part at the road checkpoints we'd set up to stop Ashby Grant from leaving Texas, I was exhausted. If there was anything worse than a killer, it was a smart killer. I had no idea what Ashby Grant's story was, but there was no arguing the woman was cunning and elusive. So far no one knew where she was, even with local law enforcement, the Texas Rangers, and a special FBI task force involved in the search. She was outsmarting all of us, remaining one step ahead.

It was frustrating as hell, and not just because she'd made threats toward the people I loved and wanted to protect. It was long hours, tedious police work, and I hadn't been able to get back to Loveless or to Kody in almost two weeks. I spoke to her every day when I got a free minute, but it wasn't the same. This relationship, while feeling solid and secure at its foundation, was still brand-new. We were skipping right over the honeymoon period where everything was supposed to be easy, and were jumping into the harsh reality of how things were going to be between us when I was working a case that took me wherever I was needed. There were going to be times when I would be gone for weeks, maybe even months, which was hard on any relationship, but especially hard on one as shiny and new as ours. Luckily, Kody had thrown herself into work and helping Della plan her wedding. She kept herself occupied, but every time we talked she wanted to know about Ashby Grant. She had as many questions as I did, and I really believed it was that curiosity that drew her to reach out to Presley. She was the only one who had any insight into the woman who had turned the Lawtons' lives upside down. Kody wasn't one to sit idly by while others got their hands dirty. She would find her own answers...if only Presley was willing to cooperate. So far the family reunion had gone less than smoothly. The doctor was in protective custody and refusing any kind of contact with anyone from the outside world who wasn't a vetted member of law enforcement. She was scared to death, and I couldn't say I blamed her. Her former friend was proving to be a formidable foe.

After weeks on the road, I was thrilled to finally be headed back to Loveless. The town I was always trying to get out of was now the only place I wanted to be...because Kody was there. I would walk through the flames of hell if it meant I got to see her, got to spend time with her. I missed her while I was on the job, but it was the best feeling in the world to finally have someone waiting for my return. I'd finally found a place that felt like home. The thought warmed the center of my chest and made me smile from ear to ear regardless of the exhaustion weighing down my steps.

She had no idea I was coming into town today, because I didn't want to get her hopes up. I wasn't sure how long I was going to be back, and I wasn't sure if I was going to get called away again before getting a chance to see her. Ashby Grant was unpredictable and elusive.

Covering a loud yawn with my hand, I pushed through the front doors of the bar, only to be brought up short by a burly-looking man with a red beard and arms the size of tree trunks. He gave me a thorough once-over as he pushed the bill of his ball cap up with his index finger. His gaze lingered on the badge and the gun clipped to my belt. A frown formed between bushy, rust-colored eyebrows.

"The cops are supposed to stay out in the lot. I've got everything under control in here." He crossed his arms over his barrel chest and narrowed his eyes. "Don't need any help making people act right."

The Barn was busy. Much busier than it usually was on a Thursday night. I noticed that at some point while I'd been gone, Kody had had a stage built toward the back of the bar. There were all kinds of musical equipment set up on the platform, and a couple of young guys scrambling around with cords and wires as they set up. The increase in the crowd was probably tied directly to the addition of live music, and the easygoing atmosphere was more than likely tied to the giant guarding the door. Kody hadn't mentioned she'd finally hired security, but I was glad she had.

All the Lawtons still had a protective detail following them around since Ashby Grant was still unaccounted for, so like the giant mentioned, Kody was dealing with a patrol car parked in front of her bar. Help wasn't too far away if something dangerous happened inside, but this behemoth at the door lowered the risk of someone getting inside and getting close enough to Kody to do any damage.

"Not here to make anyone act right. Just here to see my girl." I was too tired to do much beyond that.

The big man's eyes swept over me once again, and his eyes widened when he took a closer look at my badge. "Holy shit. You're Kody's Ranger? I thought she made you up so she had an excuse to turn all those thirsty creeps who ask her out down without hurting their feelings. You're actually real."

"I'm real." I tilted my head to the side and asked on a chuckle, "Where exactly did she find you?"

He stuck out a beefy hand for me to shake. "Harris Donner." He chuckled too and lifted a hand to run it over his wild, vibrant facial hair. "She didn't. Her brother did. I used to be a professional rodeo clown. Got hurt a while back and was having a rough time of things. Ran into Crew at an event in New Mexico and asked him if he knew of any work for a broken-down clown. Day or two later, I had a bus ticket to Loveless and a job working here. Those Lawtons are a special breed. I owe both Crew and Kody the world. Not going to let anything happen to her."

I nodded. "I know the feeling. Been out of town for a while, so I'm glad she has someone watching her back." Specifically someone who wasn't part of an outlaw motorcycle club. I shot a look across the busy bar in search of her distinct golden hair. I didn't see Kody anywhere, but I knew she had to be close by. "Can you tell me where the boss lady is?"

"She's been popular tonight. A woman came in looking for her about an hour ago and they went up into her office to talk." He stroked his beard again. "Pretty gal. Looked enough like Kody to be her sister. But I know Crew only has the one."

I frowned.

Last I'd heard, Presley Baskin was still sequestered away in protective custody refusing to see the Lawtons. She shouldn't be wandering around without some sort of protective detail. And she definitely shouldn't be anywhere near Kody, considering the two of them together made the target on their backs twice as big.

"I'm going to go on up to the office. Nice to meet you, Harris."

I took off toward the stairs, taking them two at a time because I was both excited and anxious to see Kody. I had no idea why Dr. Baskin was here, but I knew the reason better be worth the risk the women were taking by being together.

Just as I reached the top landing, the big sliding door opened and revealed the doctor. A startled expression crossed her face, and she gulped audibly. She blinked those familiar green eyes up at me and lifted a hand to touch her throat nervously.

"Hello, Special Agent Gamble. I thought you were out of town." Behind her, Kody was leaning against her heavy wooden desk. Her eyes were locked on mine, and pure, unfiltered happiness started to spread across her features. Her smile when she caught sight of me was bright enough to light up the darkest night. It was almost enough to make me forget why I'd been ready to launch into overprotective cop mode.

"What are you doing here, Dr. Baskin? You aren't supposed to be anywhere near Loveless or the Lawtons. Unfortunately, we still don't have a solid lead on where Ashby Grant is. You're all still in danger." I couldn't keep the censure out of my voice. They were both smart women, Kody savvy and street-smart, Presley a savant and near genius. They should've known better.

"I'm aware she's still on the loose. That's why I'm here. I decided recently that I can't hide from her forever. I'm the one she wants. I can't stand innocent people being in harm's way because of me. I came to explain to Kody that I would be turning down all further offers of police protection. This has to end, and the only way it ends is if Ashby has a chance to get to her real target, which is me." The doctor cleared her throat and reached up to smooth some of her hair back. "Kody called me an idiot. I don't think I can remember having anyone question my intelligence before."

Kody snorted from behind her and I chuckled before reprimanding the doctor.

"It's not a smart move. This woman is unpredictable and dangerous. She's also someone you were close to, and trusted. Your judgment might not be the best when it comes to dealing with her. It's hard to distinguish between who you thought you knew and the person your former friend really is."

The doctor cleared her throat. "I'll be fine. Thank you for your concern." Icicles practically hung from every word.

I sighed. "None of the agencies involved in this case are going to like you dangling yourself out there as bait."

Presley cleared her throat and narrowed her eyes. "I don't love the idea either, but I don't see what other choice we have. She wants me, and she'll keep hurting people until she gets me."

In that moment she reminded me so much of Kody they could've been twins. That determination to do right by others, to put her neck on the line to protect her newfound family . . . she had Lawton blood in her after all.

I dragged a hand down my face and stifled another yawn. "This all started over a job?"

Presley shrugged, and Kody made a noise. I shook my head and looked at the pretty doctor. "She's jealous. Dangerously jealous, isn't she?"

Presley shrugged. "I guess. We were always pretty neck and neck when it came to job advancement and in school." The doctor frowned. "She did always seem to be interested in the same men as me, and she always befriended whoever I was spending time with. I never understood it. My mother was always sick, and we struggled financially. Her parents were both doctors, so she lived a very affluent lifestyle. I've never considered myself very enviable."

I grunted. "We interviewed her family. They didn't seem very close, or surprised that their daughter was the object of a national manhunt. They did, however, sing your praises. More than once, they mentioned that they were super proud of your success. They seemed very impressed by your recent promotion."

The redhead flashed a confused expression and started to move toward me. "I only met her family a few times. They would only know about the promotion if Ashby brought it up."

That information was interesting. I was going to have to pass it on to Hearst and ask him to look deeper into Ashby's background. Something wasn't adding up.

A moment later, Presley said her goodbyes and slid around me so she could glide down the stairs. The woman was a contradiction across the board. She was terrified, but brave. She appeared outwardly calm, but there was chaos swirling in her eyes.

I closed the door behind me as I made my way into the office. I took my Stetson off, tossing it onto Kody's colorful couch. I'd only taken a couple of steps across the room when Kody suddenly ran toward me, launching herself into my arms. I let out an oomph of surprise, hoping my injured knee was up to the task of keeping us both upright as she wrapped her long legs around my waist and her arms around my neck. I held her up with a hand on her backside as the other wrapped around her and held her close to my chest.

She kissed me hurriedly. It was greedy and messy. Too much tongue and teeth. It was wet and noisy. It was uncoordinated and hungry. It was the kind of kiss that was going to leave lips swollen and achy. It was honestly the best—and only—welcome home I'd ever received.

Kody's fingers dug into my shoulders as she clung to me, as if she never wanted to let me go.

I didn't want to be separated from her either. Unfortunately, keeping us both standing with a leg and hip that were still healing was proving more difficult than I'd anticipated. I started walking with her still in my arms toward her desk. I didn't stop until my knees touched the edge, then bent so I could sit her on the top. She kept her legs wrapped around my waist, but lifted her fingers so she could touch my face.

Her fingers feathered over my eyebrows, traced the slope of my nose, outlined my lips, and dragged across the stubble speckled over my jaw.

"You look tired." Her voice was soft and sweet.

I winked at her. "You look good enough to eat."

Her hands cupped my face and her eyes searched mine intently. "I missed you so much, Hill."

I lowered my head so I could give her a soft kiss. "Missed you too."

"I didn't think you were going to be back in town until next week. Did something happen with the case?" She looked so hopeful I hated that I didn't come bearing good news.

"No. Every lead has been a dead end, and the man-hours searching for her have started getting outrageous. Our boss is considering turning the investigation over to the feds. If that happens, they will be in charge, so Hearst and I have a few days before we know what our roles in the investigation will be." I reached out to tuck some of her hair behind her ears. I sighed and pulled back so I could hold her face between my hands. "We did uncover something I wanted to share with you, but I wanted to wait until we were actually together."

Her eyebrows winged up, and she wrapped her fingers around my wrists, holding me in place. "Oh yeah? Something I'm not going to like?"

"You're not going to like it, but I don't think you'll be surprised by it. During this whole investigation, we were wondering how Conrad got lured to the junkyard in Austin. We know Grant wanted your dad dead so she could pin the murder on Baskin, and she needed him in Austin—near where Baskin lived. But how did she get him out there? When we finally got a warrant and tossed Grant's place, we found out she'd looked deep into Conrad's history after Baskin told her he was her biological father. Grant pulled a lot of your dad's cases, I mean she went way back, to when he was just a deputy. Seeing how she was a trained medical examiner, she took note of any of the cases that had questionable autopsy results. We all knew Conrad played fast and loose with the law, but it appears to be much worse than we thought."

I took a deep breath before continuing. "There were several cases, involving mostly women and minorities, where the cause of death was marked as questionable, but Conrad closed them as accidental deaths with no further investigation. Grant must've threatened to make the documents public if Conrad didn't agree to meet with her. Your dad, being the kind of guy he was, probably didn't believe a woman was capable of setting a trap for him, and he walked right into it." I sighed and dropped my forehead so it touched hers. "Decades of cases are going to have to be looked at now. Your father's entire career is about to be turned inside out and judged. The corruption he fostered while in charge is about to be laid out in front of the whole world."

Kody was quiet for an agonizing moment. When she finally spoke, her voice was a little harsh, but steady. "I'm an idiot. I really thought maybe he went that night because he cared about Presley. He was a cop, he must have looked into who Grant was before going to meet her. I thought maybe he figured out Grant was dangerous, and went to protect Presley. Even now, I want to believe he had a heart, although I never saw it. I really hoped he died because he was finally doing the right thing for someone. I guess I should've known better." She blew out a breath that tickled my lips. "He wouldn't have gone that night if he didn't have something he wanted to keep hidden. All his misdeeds finally caught up to him, and he paid the consequence. It's sad, but it all makes perfect sense."

Karma really was a bitch, and there was no outrunning her.

I huffed out a breath and shifted my position so I could rest my cheek on the top of her head. I used to dream about what it would be like to have someone to come home to... what it would be like to have her waiting for me, instead of me being the one waiting endlessly for her.

"I know she killed your father. I know I can prove it. I think her plans fell apart when pinning Conrad's murder on Baskin didn't work. Then she tried to make it look like Baskin ran you over in the parking lot, but that stunt didn't kill you. All it did was prove that Baskin is innocent in all this. Grant's back was against the wall, and she lost it. Now she's trying to torture Baskin. I honestly believe she wants to hurt her. Leaving protective custody isn't a good move." I sighed. "I wish I could find Grant. I want to put the woman behind bars so you didn't have to have a cop car sitting in your parking lot and a giant guarding your front door. I don't want you living under any kind of shadow anymore. I want your days to be spent in the sun."

Kody wrapped her arms around me in a tight hug. I winced as the squeeze reminded me my ribs were still healing.

She made an apologetic face and immediately lightened her touch. "I'm happy to say all the shadows cast by the past are gone. You chased them all away. Thank you for finding the person responsible for killing my father. As soon as you catch Grant, I know you'll put her away for good." I felt her smile against the hollow of my throat.

She was right. That was exactly what I was going to do.

I moved my head so I could seal my mouth over hers. This kiss was slower, softer. I teased her tongue out to play with mine, her flavor bright and sharp on the tip of it. I'd spent a lifetime putting space between the two of us, but now all I wanted was to get as close to her as humanly possible. Now that I knew what it felt like to fall asleep with her in my arms, and wake up with her unruly curls spread out over my chest, being away had been torture. I missed her dirty looks and smart mouth. I missed the way her freckles popped across her cheeks and the bridge of her nose when she blushed. More than all of that, I missed the way she reached for me in her sleep and the way she held on so tightly it seemed like she was scared I might slip through her fingers.

"I never resented having to travel for work before, but

these last few weeks have been hard. Never realized I hated sleeping alone until I reached for you and came up empty." I kissed her again. "When things settle down, we need to talk about where this thing between us is headed. I want to always be able to come home to you, Kody." Home. Not her nearly empty apartment or my sterile condo. I wanted a place we created together.

She smiled against my mouth and shifted her hands so she could start working open the buttons of my denim shirt. "I want you to come home to me too, Hill." She moved her head so she could drag her lips up the side of my neck, stopping when she got to my ear. Her teeth tugged on the lobe, her tongue darting out and soothing the little nip. "But right now, I want you to show me how much you missed me."

Challenge accepted.

While she finished opening my shirt, I kissed her breathless, using my body to force her backward so she was lying atop scattered paperwork. My shirt hit the floor, and her hands shifted to my belt and the opening of my jeans. I worked my hands under the hem of her gauzy tank top, sliding it up her rib cage and along the sides of her breasts. She shivered slightly under my palms, the caress getting bolder the more of her I uncovered.

I left her lips to nibble my way down the side of her neck, dragging my tongue over her pulse point, which fluttered in excitement.

She shot a look at my naked chest, eyes skimming over my side. I'd taken the soft bandage off a few days ago, so the healing bruises were starkly visible against the rest of my skin. Purple, various shades of blue, and yellows all blended together from under my armpit down to my waist.

"You look like a Van Gogh painting." She gingerly dragged fingers over the colorful skin. "Does it still hurt to breathe?"

Since she'd shifted and lifted herself slightly off the desk, I reached behind her and unhooked her pretty, lacy bra. She gasped a little as it slid down her arms.

"It hurts, but not like it did." And definitely not badly enough to stop me from making this a reunion to remember. "Even the worst wounds heal if they have enough time."

She gave me a look but didn't say anything as I reached for the button on her shorts. She silently complied when I urged her to lift up so I could maneuver her shorts and panties over her hips and down her legs. I left her propped on the edge of her desk as I pulled my belt free of the loops and worked the front of my jeans open. My breath hitched when her hand reached out and her fingertips skimmed over the arrow of hair that darted below my belly button and disappeared into the top of my jeans. I stepped between her legs, forcing her to tilt her head back so I could get at her eager mouth.

I kissed her with every bit of longing I'd felt, not only over the last two weeks, but all the years we'd been apart. She wanted me to show her how much I missed her, so the way I touched her, the way I kissed her, was full of hunger, yearning, and the aching need for more.

"Being away from you hurts. It always hurt, but now it's impossible to ignore. My heart aches." I reached out so I could run the backs of my fingers across her smooth, freckled cheek, then down her neck and across the swells of her breasts.

"I never expected you to be so good with words." She worked her hands between the two of us and tugged on my jeans, working them down around my hips. "Also never expected you to be a no-underwear kinda guy, but I'm pleasantly surprised by both. I love all the new things I'm learning about you, Hill."

I laughed under my breath. I met her glittering green gaze and told her truthfully, "Not a lot of time to take care of laundry when I'm on the road." But I was going to have to go out of my way to keep surprising her if the result was making her soft and dreamy-eyed when she looked at me.

I brushed my fingers over her nipples, watching as they puckered in reaction. I grinned and lowered my head so I could drop a light kiss on the tip of each pretty peak. She curled her leg more firmly around my waist as her heel dug into the top of my ass. I kissed my way down between the center of her breasts and in a straight line down over her stomach, until I could dip my tongue into the little divot of her belly button. Her nails dragged up my back, and her hips shifted restlessly against the desk. I kissed my way back up her body until I got to her parted lips. I devoured her mouth, licking my way inside and nipping at her lower lip until she gasped my name on a short breath.

She was devouring my mouth and demanding satisfaction with her hands as they raced over as much of my skin as she could touch, where I had her pinned to the desk with my weight. She pulled me closer with her heels in my backside and wordlessly asked for what she wanted by lifting her hips and slowly grinding all her soft, warm parts against my rock-hard and rigid one.

I winged an eyebrow up at her. I freed my hand so I could make a circle in the air.

"Turn around." I gave her a smirk. "I'll surprise you again."

She returned my lascivious look with a curious one of her own. I took a step backward so she could slide off the edge of the desk and turn around so the long, elegant line of her back was facing me. I swept her hair away from the nape of her neck and placed a careful kiss on the sensitive spot. She shivered and turned her head to peek at me over her shoulder.

I pressed in closer so there was no space between her body and mine. I kept one hand on her bent leg and used the other to reach around the front of her, so I could cup the delicious weight of one breast in my palm. I rolled the pad of my thumb in slow circles around the tight bud of her nipple, hearing her breath catch and watching the way her body rippled in response. I moved so I could place tiny, light kisses behind her ear. Kody muttered my name as the position pushed my cock up against her sweet center.

I bit back a string of swear words as my cock slid through silky wetness, the head nudging against her dainty opening. It felt so much better than I'd anticipated. I was immediately surrounded by her heat and felt how welcoming and ready her body was. She'd missed me too. I could tell by the way she moaned and moved back against me, trying to get closer, urging me to stop the playful teasing as I rocked against her. It only took a couple of slow thrusts for my length to become slippery and the glide smooth and effortless.

I pushed in with one fluid move, both of us groaning at the contact. I loved the way her body pulled at me, loved the tiny flutters that danced up and down every inch inside her. She must've liked the stretch and slide as I pushed forward, because I heard her breath hitch and watched as her back arched. It was beautiful. She was beautiful, and so was the way she started to press back against me. This position was easier on my ribs, but killer on my bad leg. There was nothing on God's green earth that would stop me from showing her just how much I missed her, how much better things were when we were together.

I grunted as her body squeezed my erection. I leaned forward, sinking deeper inside her as I molded myself to her back and locked the edges of my teeth on the sensitive bend where her neck met her shoulder. I was going to leave a mark. I wanted her to have something to remember me by when I wasn't around. I wanted her to have no choice but to think of me when she looked in the mirror. I wanted her to be able to touch it and feel me, to remember the way I made her feel, inside and out.

Kody rolled her hips back, taking more of me inside her, setting a hurried rhythm that had us both gasping for air and forced me to hold on to her so I didn't collapse when my knees went weak. I panted in her ear, telling her how good she felt, how hot she was, how I could feel every flutter and twitch of her body. I told her no one had ever gotten me going so fast, and I made absent promises to her about lasting longer and rocking her world once my body was fully healed.

"I love you, Kody."

I forced the words out before kissing the back of her neck once again and dropping my forehead so it rested between her shoulder blades.

My hips kicked toward hers as she moved back to meet me. The pace was quick, rough, almost brutal, but it felt exquisite, and it only took a few rushed thrusts for the warmth of pleasure to spread through my body. Kody moaned that she was close and I felt her body quake. I dragged my palm up her ribs and told her to let go.

As soon as I felt the first rush of her release, I followed. My hips stuttered in their movement and my cock kicked in a surge of completion. I sighed against her skin, falling forward as her arms gave out. The sudden shift forced out a yelp of pain as my abused side adjusted to the change. We ended in a sweaty, satisfied heap on top of her desk, her cheek pressed against random paperwork.

Kody started to chuckle. Her cute nose wrinkled and her eyes drifted closed as I nuzzled the soft curls at the back of her head.

"Welcome home, Hill."

CHAPTER 21

∞

KODY

"Kody? What are you doing here?"

As soon as the door to the small apartment cracked open, I used my shoulder to push my way past the person on the other side of it. I heard Presley gasp at the high-handed tactic, but the woman had been doing her best to avoid me for the last month. I was tired of her evasion.

"You know it isn't safe to be anywhere near me, not with Ashby still on the loose. Especially since you and I look enough alike to be mistaken for one another at a glance. You shouldn't be here."

"It would be safer if you hadn't decided to put your neck on the line and refused further police protection. Where's your bedroom?"

She frowned at me, turning to close and lock the door. I didn't miss that there were no fewer than four serious deadbolts lining the apartment door. Presley had said she was trying to draw Ashby Grant out so the police could finally catch her, but it was obvious she was terrified.

"My room? It's at the back of the apartment. Why?" I heard her scramble to follow as I purposely marched toward where I assumed her bedroom was.

"I'm packing you an overnight bag and taking you with me to a slumber party." After being home for a few days, Hill had been called back to continue looking for Ashby Grant. Case was working a possible kidnapping case, and Crew was out of town for a competition. Aspen, Della, and I had gotten into the habit of getting together when our boys weren't around. At first we'd used the excuse that we were bonding over the planning of Della and Crew's wedding, but eventually we realized we just liked each other's company and it was nice not to be alone when the men we'd decided to spend the rest of our lives with were off doing something dangerous. We took solace in one another, relied on each other, and it was well past the point that Presley should be included in the small circle of love and support we had going on.

"A slumber party?" She sounded so confused it made me smile.

"Yeah, a grown-up slumber party. We're going to wear pajamas, eat food that's terrible for us, get sloppy drunk, and complain about how unfair life can be. We're also going to laugh a lot and tell embarrassing stories from our childhoods. It'll be fun, and take your mind off anything that might be troubling you." Lord knew the woman had to be under an incredible amount of stress.

"I didn't get invited to slumber parties when I was young. I've never been to one." She cleared her throat but didn't stop me when I started rummaging through her open closet for an overnight bag to throw some basics in. "I had a hard time making friends when I was a child."

And as an adult, her one and only friend had betrayed her in ways that were too painful to fathom.

"I had a hard time making friends too. Must run in the family. Fortunately, I now have friends who feel more like family, and they would really like a chance to get to know you better. We all would." I gave her a pointed look over my shoulder as I shoved a pair of yoga pants into the black-and-white-striped bag I'd found on a shelf of her closet.

I'd reached out to Presley at first because I wanted to know more about Ashby. But after she visited the Barn a few weeks ago, I realized I wanted to know more about my half sister. She was so different from me and my brothers, so composed and cool, I wanted to figure out what made her tick and learn how we could look so much alike but have polar opposite personalities. Case and Crew also tried to reach out to her. Case kept his contact with her professional because I think he was worried he might spook her. Crew had reached out after I'd begged him to. I wasn't getting anywhere and thought his natural charm and charisma might do the trick. He didn't get much further with the redhead than I had. Presley kept us all at arm's length, warning that she feared we would all be targets until Ashby was caught.

"I don't think that's wise." She reached for the bag I was stuffing a plain black T-shirt into.

"Wise or not, you're coming with me. I'm not giving you a choice. We're going to Case and Aspen's house. Even though Case is on a call and won't be home, it's still the safest place in all of Loveless. No one messes with my big brother, and there are weapons stashed all over the place. A girls' night will do you a world of good." I tugged the bag out of her hold and met her wide-eyed look with a sharp one of my own. "Like it or not, you're one of us. The only way we survived our childhood was by leaning on one another. We've always had each other's backs and that now includes you. There is no reason you have to face having your entire life thrown into disarray on your own. I know you must be scared out of your mind every single time you walk out that door. You don't have to be scared by yourself anymore. I'll be scared with you."

Her hand fell away from the bag, and she blinked at me like I'd suddenly sprouted wings and a halo. She cleared her throat and lifted a shaky hand to her chest. "I've always been alone."

The admission was softly spoken and heartbreaking. She'd had to face her mother's death alone. She'd had to face learning her whole childhood was a lie alone. She'd had to come to grips with the fact that the one person she'd let in and trusted was a fraud and a murderer, all alone. My upbringing had been no picnic, but at least I'd always had Case and Crew suffering alongside me.

"Well, Hill is fond of saying we can be alone together. Come on, one night. It'll be good for you." And good for me. Presley felt like a loose end lingering after I'd finally put everything having to do with my father behind me.

Presley was quiet for a long moment. I could see her weighing the pros and cons of opening up and letting me in. If she didn't give me the answer I wanted, I fully planned on dragging her forcibly from her apartment.

To my surprise the doctor relented and moved to grab what she needed from the bathroom. She stopped to put on a pair of tennis shoes and followed me out the door, trepidation clear on her face.

"You're right. I'm terrified to leave my apartment. I'm walking on eggshells waiting for whatever Ashby has planned for me. I don't sleep. Can barely eat. I don't feel human most days." She sighed and pushed some of her fiery hair out of her face. "I really just want this all to be over."

Leading the way to my Jeep at a fast clip so she didn't feel too exposed, I nodded in sympathy. The thought of living my life according to the rules of someone else's sick and twisted game was my actual nightmare. That was what growing up with Conrad had been like, so I understood exactly where she was coming from.

"We all want it to be over." Because I was worried about her safety, but also so I could have Hill home for longer than a couple days at a time. It seemed like every time he got settled in after being gone, he was called right back out to chase after leads that never went anywhere. He was frustrated beyond belief, and I knew some of the aggravation came from his personal connection to the case. I looked over at Presley and hid a grin at how out of place the prim and proper doctor looked in my Jeep. I tapped my fingers on the steering wheel and told her, "When they say everything happens for a reason, it's really true. It took us losing our dad for my brothers and me to really figure out what being a family means. We were always close, but our dad was like this dark, ugly shadow always hanging over us, reminding us of some of the worst times in our lives. He was standing between us, and we didn't even realize it until he was no longer there. Once he was gone, Case, Crew, and I finally figured out how to live lives we could be proud of. We learned what love should look like. We realized we could make good memories together, and with our own families, to replace the bad ones Dad left behind." We were so much closer now. Like soldiers who had fought and won a war that was dragging on, to finally come out victorious on the other side of things. We'd survived. We'd won. "We'd like you to be around so we can make some of those good memories with you, Presley."

She muttered something under her breath but turned her head to look at me as I pulled into the driveway at our destination. "I don't have very many of those. I'm not really sure what I would do with them if I did manage to make a few."

"You hold on tight and refuse to let them go or let anyone take them from you. Sometimes the good memories are all we have to keep us going."

Once I pulled into Aspen's driveway, I kicked open the Jeep door and hefted her bag over my shoulder so she wouldn't be tempted to make a run for it. She slipped out of the Jeep and silently followed me to the front door. The bright turquoise door was thrown open before I could knock and Aspen immediately caught my arm and pulled me inside. Before I could warn Presley about the overly affectionate attorney, Aspen had the doctor wrapped up in a tight hug. It was almost comical considering Aspen was so tiny and Presley was even taller than me.

"I'm so glad you came. I've been dying to get the chance to know you better. Come in. Make yourself at home." She caught Presley's arm and practically dragged the other woman into the house.

I giggled because Aspen was already dressed in a cute, vintage-looking nightgown with fuzzy slippers. She never did anything by half measures. And neither did Della. The stunning blonde was the next one to wrap Presley up in a hug. She was dressed in an obviously expensive silk pajama set and looked like she had just stepped off the set of a movie. Both women immediately urged my half sister to make herself at home and assured me they would keep an eye on her as my cell rang. I knew "keeping an eye on her" meant plying her with wine and expensive charcuterie, but Hill was the one calling and I made it a rule to answer whenever he called.

Slipping out the back door, I put my cell to my ear and let his low, slow drawl wash over me.

"Hey. Things good?" He sounded tired, and I wanted so badly to take care of him.

"Things are good. I managed to get Presley to come with me to girls' night. She hasn't run yet, so I'm putting a mark in the win column. How about you? Things good?" I knew he was going to tell me they were, even if they weren't. He didn't want me to worry.

"As good as they can be." He sighed, and I could picture him running his hands through his hair and the way he would look after a long day at work. I bet he was walking around half-naked in his hotel room like he tended to do, and I suddenly resented every single mile between us.

After a moment he said my name in a tone that made the hairs on the back of my neck stand on end. "Kody, were you ever going to tell me my mother showed up at your bar and made a scene?"

I gulped nervously and started to pace back and forth on the back patio. The motion sensor lights flickered, casting eerie shadows along the back yard.

"I was going to tell you when you got back to Loveless." It wasn't a conversation that felt appropriate for the phone.

Hill's mother had barged into the bar during happy hour a few days ago and raised hell. Now that it was common knowledge around town that Hill and I were an item, she wasn't happy. Once again she accused me, loudly, of being the reason Aaron was dead. She ranted and raved that she would disown Hill if he didn't leave me, and generally made an ass out of herself. It was one of the greatest pleasures I'd had to instruct Harris to escort her from the premises. She looked ridiculous screaming and yelling while the former rodeo clown frog-marched her to the front doors.

Much to my surprise, her forcible exit was met with a

round of applause, and my relationship with Hill was embraced by most of the town. It seemed Aspen was right and I was the only one who had been foolish enough to miss the way the big Ranger felt about me. There were a lot of *about times*, and very little censure over the fact that I'd loved both Gamble brothers at different times in my life.

Hill let out a long, loud string of swear words. Eventually he seemed to run out of steam and sighed heavily in my ear. "I'm done. She can be terrible to me all she wants, I'm used to it. But I will not tolerate her being terrible to you. She was never much of a mother anyway."

I exhaled a long, deep breath and reached up to tug the ends of my hair, pulling a curl straight and letting it bounce back. "You don't have to be done because of me. You know I can take care of myself. Your mom doesn't scare me."

He sighed again. "I'm done because of her, not you."

I tilted my head back to look up at the stars. "You know I'll always be your family...all of us Lawtons will. You're ours, and we aren't letting you go." I was determined to give him a home to come back to every single time he left Loveless. It was my new goal, rather than making my way on my own. I wanted us to make our way together, no matter where we were headed.

"You've always been more my family than my folks have. I have no reservations about cutting ties with them. I hate the idea of you having to face that kind of ugliness when I'm not around. I should be there to protect you."

It wasn't possible with his job, but I appreciated the sentiment. "I miss you."

"I miss you too. I should be home in a few days. Stay out of trouble until I get back."

I laughed a little and closed my eyes briefly as a wave of longing hit me. "Don't worry about me. Worry about you.

Stay safe and hurry home." I huffed out another breath and told him, "I love you, Hill."

He grumbled something about being gone too much but told me, "I love you too, Kody," before hanging up. I held my phone to my chest briefly, almost like I was taking his voice into my heart. Being apart was challenging, but I'd take it over not having him at all.

Realizing I'd been gone longer than I planned, I hurried back inside to save Presley from Aspen's aggressive hospitality and Della's natural urge to manage everyone.

Except Presley wasn't in the plush living room watching old John Hughes movies, she was in the kitchen standing in front of a very tired-looking Case. None of us had expected him to be home tonight.

"I'm sure it's been stressful, dealing with everything that happened on your own. I'm glad Kody forced her way in...to your apartment and your life." Case crossed his arms over his broad chest and leaned a hip on one of the kitchen counters. "I know you refused further police protection, but if you need anything, if you're scared or worried, please give me a call. I'll show up as an officer of the law...but also as your older brother. I would hate to see anything happen to you when we just found out about you. All of us would like the opportunity to show you that being a Lawton isn't half-bad."

Presley looked nervous, but she slowly nodded. "I appreciate that, Sheriff."

Case grinned at her overly formal way of speaking. "You can call me Case."

Presley nodded again and shifted her weight nervously. "Thank you...Case."

I made my presence known, stomping into the kitchen with more force than necessary. "You're back early. Did you wrap things up already?" He'd been called out on a possible kidnapping case, which I'm sure had been hard on him, considering he had a teenage son of his own he constantly worried about.

Case nodded his dark head and ran a hand over his face. "Kid took off with his girlfriend. Apparently the parents didn't want them to be together. Made it as far as Austin before they ran out of gas and realized they didn't have the cash flow to get very far. Glad it wasn't anything too serious." He gave me a look and cocked his head to the side. "When's Hill coming home? Hayes will be back for winter break soon. I want to get everyone together once he's here." He lifted an eyebrow in Presley's direction. "You're invited, by the way."

The doctor coughed a little in surprise. "Excuse me?"

Case grinned and pushed off the counter. "To all our family events. You're invited, no matter what, or where they are. Crew and I try and hit Kody's bar at least once a week so we can all catch up. You should join us."

I cherished the sibling dates the boys made a point of keeping. Our bond had always been strong, but now it felt downright unbreakable and was definitely tough enough for us to add Presley to the mix.

Seeing the panic on the doctor's pretty face, I grabbed her forearm and started to pull her toward the living room. "I barely got her out the door today. Don't overwhelm her. She can acclimate to our family fun at her own pace." I winked at Case, letting him know I would gladly drag her along even if she was reluctant to spend more time with us. Just like Hill, she was ours, and I had no intention of letting her go.

"No boys allowed. Get gone so we can get drunk and talk about you." He snorted his response and reached out to ruffle my hair. I didn't miss the intense look Presley gave both of us as she watched the easy, familiar interaction. If I wasn't mistaken, there was a glimmer of envy in her emerald gaze. I nudged her with my elbow as I guided her back to the living room. "It doesn't matter how old we get, or what we go through, both of them still take a lot of pride in acting like big brothers. You'll get used to it."

She got a wistful look on her face and said so quietly, "It seems kind of nice."

AN CROWNOVER

EPILOGUE

∞

KODY

Six months later

W hen the front door to the bar burst open mere moments after the last patron had been escorted out by Harris, I automatically reached for the shotgun I kept behind the bar and threw a worried look in Lorenzo's direction. Things at the Barn had picked up steadily over the last few months, now that I had live music and specialty nights geared toward different types of customers. I had college night, ladies' night, and locals-only night. Catering to specific groups managed to bring all of them in fairly regularly. I was never going to be a millionaire, but I was doing well enough to pay the bills every month and still have enough left over to live a decent life. It was all I'd ever wanted, and I knew my mother would be thrilled I was finally figuring out how to take care of myself the right way. There were no more shortcuts on my path to success.

The increase in business meant I was working more

than ever, which also meant I'd had to double the security at the bar in order to get all the overprotective men in my life off my back. Case and Hill never let me forget, not for a minute, that Ashby Grant was still on the loose. Even though months and months had passed with no sign of her, the law enforcement officers in my life refused to believe the threat was gone. So aside from Harris, I'd hired two more former rodeo clowns Crew recommended to keep an eye on the place and the customers whenever the bar was open for business. I'd also agreed to have a marked patrol car do frequent drive-bys on the weekends and when the bar was the busiest. I hated living under the umbrella of constant surveillance, and was sure Ashby Grant had done what any smart criminal did when they got away with murder, changed identities and moved far, far away. But there was no arguing with Hill or Case, and I didn't want Hill focused on me and my safety when he was out in the field doing a job that could easily get *him* killed if he was distracted.

Hill had left a few days ago and was currently working a case all the way across the state. Someone was burning down churches in minority communities. He promised it was mostly legwork, knocking on doors and asking a lot of questions, but I could hear the worry in his voice when he called to check in. There were some parts of his job he couldn't—and wouldn't—share with me, but he was always open about the toll catching the bad guys took on him. I'd learned it was the people he couldn't help that weighed most heavily on him. Hill was still a perfectionist and took each loss personally.

I promised to take all the safety precautions necessary, no matter how burdensome they might be, and he promised to come home in one piece.

It was interesting how our relationship had evolved, which circled back to what had made me fall in love with him in the first place. We were back to talking on the phone or FaceTiming for long periods when he was out of town on a case. He called every night, no matter what. The physical distance meant we spent a lot of time relearning everything about one another. I missed him like crazy when he was gone, but I appreciated that he made it a point to show me that I was the center of his entire world when we were together. We both treated our time together like a precious commodity, because we never knew how much of it we were going to be blessed with. I was independent enough that I managed sharing Hill with the Texas Rangers with minimal fuss, but I was ready for him to get rid of his place in Dallas so we could build a home together in Loveless. He'd put his condo on the market a few weeks ago, and I was already looking for places in Loveless that would suit both our needs. It was the first time since I was a naive teenager that I'd looked forward to building a life with someone.

I let my hand fall away from the hidden weapon when I realized the rushed, frantic men pouring in through the doorway were all wearing Sons of Sorrow cuts. I hadn't seen much of Shot or the boys since ending our business agreement. Occasionally one or two would drop by for a beer, and Shot would pop his head in to say hi, but the days of them hanging around until the bar closed had passed. I missed my friend, but realized I couldn't keep close company with someone who might compromise my relationship with Hill. Without realizing it I'd started putting what was best for us before almost everything.

However, when Top yelled my name across the bar and gruffly ordered Harris to lock the door, I automatically moved toward the commotion. All four of the leather-clad bikers were carrying a fifth member, and the lot of them were covered in scarlet splotches of blood.

"Sorry, boss. I wasn't going to let them in, but Shot..." Harris rubbed his bushy, red beard and looked worriedly at the bleeding man hanging limply in the arms of his brothers. "I figured it was best to get him inside before the patrol car drives by."

I scrambled around the side of the bar, snapping at Lorenzo to go find clean towels and anything else we might have on hand to stop the bleeding.

I looked at Top and noticed he was pale and had a cut above his eye that was openly gushing blood. They all looked like they'd been in an accident of some kind, but Shot was by far the worst off. His limp, bleeding body was being carried by several other members of the club. His entire shirt was covered in blood, and his normally tanned skin was a sickly shade of gray. His lips were shadowed with a tinge of blue, and I could hear how shallow and ragged his breathing was.

I glared at Top, demanding, "What happened?"

The club's vice president shook his head at me as the guys all sort of collapsed on the floor, taking Shot down with them.

"The less you know the better. Shot's got at least two bullets in him. He isn't going to make it back to the club." Top reached for the towels Lorenzo returned with and immediately started putting pressure on the wounds hidden under Shot's bloody clothes. "Can't take him to the hospital 'cause they'll report the gunshot wounds. And that's going to bring all kinds of heat we don't need on us right now."

"Shot's not dying in my bar, Top." My voice sounded accusatory as I anxiously walked around the circle of injured men. "Why did you bring him here?"

Top glanced up at me with a frown. "Because this was the

closest safe place I could think of on the way back to the clubhouse. And I knew you wouldn't let him die."

"Jesus." Hill was going to flip his shit when he heard about this. "He needs medical attention, Top. I'm not going to watch him bleed out on my floor."

Shot's breathing became even more raspy and uneven. The white towels covering his wounds immediately became soaked through with blood.

Lorenzo and Harris were both watching me with wide eyes as the bikers swore and surrounded Shot.

"Call an ambulance. This is ridiculous." My tone was sharp, but the worry was clear in each word. I cared very much about the man bleeding to death on my bar floor. I couldn't stand by and not get him help, even if it meant pissing off the entire club. "He's bleeding too much. He's not going to make it."

"Shut up, Kode. Either help or get lost. We're not letting law enforcement anywhere near him." Top lifted his face, looking like some kind of demon between his scowl and the streaks of blood. "Be part of the solution, or you'll be treated like you're part of the problem."

It was the first time I'd ever felt threatened by the guys in the club. Pointing at Lorenzo and Harris, I ordered, "Get out of here." I wasn't going to let my staff be caught in the line of fire because I'd made some very dangerous friends along the way.

Lorenzo was smart. He immediately nodded and bolted for the back door. One of the bikers tried to get to his feet and follow, but Top shot out a hand and stilled him. "He's an ex-con. He's not going to talk. Let him go."

I looked at Harris, who stubbornly crossed his arms over his wide chest and stood his ground. "Ain't going nowhere. Your brother would skin me alive if I left you alone with these heathens, and I don't even want to think about what Hill would do."

Shot let out a low moan, and his dark eyes briefly flickered open. It was obvious he was in pain and barely clinging to life. My throat closed up, and tears burned the backs of my eyes, but Top was right. I needed to be part of the solution, or Shot was going to die. I ran behind the bar so I could grab a handful of bar towels to try and stop the flow of blood.

Behind the bar I found my phone. I threw the towels to Top and scrolled through my contacts until I saw Presley's new number. The woman was paranoid, changing her number and moving around every few weeks. For all her talk about wanting to bait Grant into showing up, Presley was scared of her own shadow and had let almost her entire life slip away from her while she waited for her nemesis to come out of hiding. She hadn't gone back to work yet and hadn't settled into any kind of new routine. Luckily, the county was holding on to her new job for her. The previous chief medical examiner had agreed to stay on board until Presley was ready to come back. It was apparent her colleagues really respected and admired her.

Presley was hard to pin down, even though she was making a slight effort to welcome me and my brothers into her highly sheltered life. Right now I needed her to get it together and pretend we were as close as family.

She didn't answer the first or second time I called. I was ready to throw my cell against the wall, but luckily she picked up on the third call.

"Kody? Why are you calling me so late?" She'd obviously been asleep, and I could hear the fear in her voice. "Did something happen? Are you okay?"

"I need you." The words burst out in a rush. "I can't really explain what's going on, but I need you."

She made a nervous humming sound. "Need me for what?"

I swore and knocked my fist against my forehead. "I need you to stop someone who's very important to me from dying on my bar floor."

"Kody." Her voice shook. "You know I can't do that." Or, more accurately, she was too afraid to do it.

I hiccupped a little sob and whispered, "Please, Presley. He can't die."

"Call an ambulance. Get him to a hospital." Her voice continued to shake. "I really can't get involved...and you shouldn't be involved either."

"He doesn't have time for me to convince the guys who brought him here to get an ambulance. I really wouldn't have called you if you weren't my last resort. I know this is asking for a lot—for too much—but you're literally the only person on the planet who can help me right now."

She muttered something I couldn't make out and eventually whispered, "I can't. I'm sorry."

A second later the call disconnected and I really did throw my phone against the wall.

"Shot!" Top's voice echoed in the empty bar. "Come on, man, don't do this. You got to fight. Shot!" Chills raced up my spine as all the big, badass bikers suddenly started to panic, screaming at their leader while he got paler on my floor. There was just so much blood, and Shot was looking so lifeless.

I bent to find my phone where it bounced after the toss. I was going to have to call 911, regardless of the outcome. I couldn't stand by and do nothing. Couldn't lose someone else who mattered to me because I didn't do the right thing. If it meant making enemies of the club, then so be it.

The screen on my phone was cracked, but not so badly I couldn't use it. I was swiping, getting ready to dial, when a text popped up.

I'll be there in ten minutes.

I blinked at the message from Presley, feeling my knees get wobbly with relief.

"Fuck. He's not breathing." Top sounded hysterical, his deep voice cracking as he smacked Shot on the cheek. "Shot, come on, man. This is just a scratch. This ain't nothing compared to what you went through when you were enlisted. Wake up, asshole. Open your eyes. Right now." Uneasy murmurs moved through the rest of the bikers as I raced back around the bar.

I grabbed Harris by the arm and told him, "Go in the parking lot and wait for my sister." Once he nodded and hurried off, I made my way to Shot's side, dropping down on my knees and looking directly into Top's watery, wild eyes. "Help is coming. No first responders, and I don't know when the last time she worked on a living patient was, but she's our best shot at keeping him with us. Let's do CPR until she gets here. We just need him to hang on long enough for Presley to help."

Top blinked at me in confusion. "You have a sister? Since when?"

I puffed out a breath and shifted so I could move Shot's head into position for CPR. His skin was alarmingly cold, and his lips now looked purple. "Long story. I'll fill you in later. Right now, let's focus on him."

We moved the bar towels covering him so we could start CPR. Top was breathing for Shot and making his heart work for him. It felt like we hovered over him for hours. My hands ended up covered in blood, and I couldn't imagine how graphic and gory the scene was when Presley finally walked into the bar, Harris following close behind.

I expected her to look like a frightened rabbit, to be

freaked out the way she'd been since finding out her former best friend had systematically dismantled her life. But the woman striding confidently across the bar—even though she was dressed in pajamas—seemed calm, cool, and collected. This was the woman who had punched me in the nose and fought back, not the one who was cowering, waiting for the other shoe to drop.

Without saying a word, she walked right up to the carnage and dropped to her knees next to me. I noticed she had a large black bag with her that she immediately started digging through.

"He's lost too much blood. He's going to need a transfusion." She looked over at Top, who was intimidating when he wasn't bloody and on edge, and told him flatly, "This man needs medical care. He's going to die if he doesn't get it."

Top narrowed his eyes and pointed at one of the other bikers over Presley's shoulder. "Go to the clubhouse and get what we need." His eyebrows lifted and a smirk crossed his face. "Not the first time one of us has taken a bullet and lost a little blood. You just get him stable enough that we can move him to the club. We'll take care of the rest."

Presley blinked suddenly huge eyes, looking over at me. I shrugged when she muttered, "They have their own blood supply?"

Now was not the time to be impressed or curious about what the club had going on behind closed doors.

"Just do your best, Presley. That's all I'm asking for." I went to reach for her hand so I could give it a reassuring squeeze, but pulled it back when I realized Shot's blood was smeared on my fingers.

She nodded, reached into the bag, and pulled out a pair of clear goggles, a face mask, and latex gloves. It was like I was watching her become Dr. Baskin right in front of my eyes. Then she used a weird pair of scissors to cut off Shot's saturated shirt before she pulled out a stethoscope, and after wrapping it around her neck and hooking it into her ears, she started running it all over his chest and stomach.

"I think the bullet nicked his lung. That's why he can't breathe. Because of the gunshot wound, there's too much blood in his chest cavity. It's putting pressure on his heart. He's going to go into shock. The rest of his organs sound okay, but I can't be sure without the proper equipment." She reached into the bag and pulled out a syringe and a couple bottles of what appeared to be sterilized water.

Quickly and efficiently, she got Shot's torso cleaned off and injected whatever was in the syringe into his tattooed arm.

She reached into the bag and pulled out something that looked like a torture device. The needle on the end of it was huge. I felt my eyes widen and looked at her in alarm.

"What are you going to do with that?"

She barely glanced at me. "I'm going to put a chest tube in so I can drain the blood, then I'm going to try and inflate his lung before he goes into shock." She looked up at Top and coolly told him, "The blood transfusion needs to happen sooner rather than later."

Top nodded stiffly and whipped out his phone.

I heard Presley suck in a breath, but her hands were steady and her gaze was laser sharp as she started working.

I nearly threw up when she inserted the gigantic needle between his ribs. Even half-dead, the man moaned in pain and started to thrash around. Presley ordered the bikers to keep him still as she attached a clear plastic tube to some kind of bag of fluid, and the end of the hose in her hand to the tip of a massive, scary-looking needle. Slowly but surely a stream of dark blood started to fill the bag. Shot's breathing was still ragged, but not as shallow. Presley listened to his chest once again, nodding at whatever she heard.

A couple minutes later, one of the bikers burst through the door with a cooler full of IV bags filled with blood. Presley's eyes widened even more, but she stayed silent as she got a feed line into the crook of Shot's arm and started the transfusion.

Gulping, I quietly asked Top, "Are you sure that blood is a match?" We were trying to minimize the damage, not escalate it.

"It's his. We all have a stash in case something like this happens."

All I could do was shake my head and whisper, "Holy hell."

"He needs surgery. The bullets need to be removed. He needs to be checked for internal damage. He should be in a sterile environment under a doctor's care." Presley sniffed in a supremely prim way.

"If he's stable enough to move, we got a place and someone to take care of him."

"You can't move him unless that lung reinflates, and there's no guarantee that's going to happen, since he's still bleeding." She reached out a gloved finger and used it to push some of Shot's wavy black hair away from his forehead. "I'm surprised he lasted this long."

It was an agonizing wait for the blood to stop dripping into the bag at his side. While we all held our breath and hoped for the best, Presley kept poking and prodding Shot, trying to stem the bleeding using a coagulating cloth. She kept touching him, muttering to him in a voice so low none of us could hear what she was saying. It seemed to take an eternity, but eventually Shot gasped for breath, his body arching up off the floor in a scary spasm.

Presley pushed him back down, not looking at Top as she

muttered, "You can move him now, but I'm going to go with you. His condition is serious. I don't know how long he's going to be semistable."

I put a hand on her shoulder and told her, "It's too dangerous. You can't go with them." Outsiders weren't allowed in the clubhouse, not ever. I wasn't about to let her get involved with the club more than she already was.

"I have to go. I'm the only one who can keep him alive." She gave me a weak smile. "It'll be okay."

I gritted my teeth, turning to glare at Top. "Harris is going with you guys. He brings her back in one piece or I swear to God I will have Hill and my brother rain hell down on you and everything you hold dear. Do you understand me, Top?"

The burly biker grumbled in agreement, and in a flurry of activity almost as hectic as their arrival, they swept Shot and my sister out the door.

Once they were gone, I was left alone in eerie silence with a bar covered in blood. I was going to have to keep the place closed tomorrow while I figured out how to get it properly cleaned up and sanitized.

I dragged myself to the back so I could scrub my hands nearly raw. Suddenly tired down to my bones, I dug my broken phone out of my pocket and tapped Hill's picture.

It was close to dawn, so he was either still up working from the day before or catching a few fleeting hours of shut-eye. Either way, I shouldn't be calling this late...early...but his was the only voice I wanted to hear.

"Hey. You okay?" He answered after the first ring.

I closed my eyes and let his slow drawl comfort me. "Not even a little bit. You would not believe the night I had."

"Do you need me to come home?" I knew he would, no questions asked.

"No. There's no need for that." Obviously I'd take any

chance I could get to see him, but he had a job to do and lives to save. He didn't need to come running every time trouble seemed to find me. "I just miss you. I already feel better hearing your voice." I let out a little laugh. "I'm going to tell you a story, but you have to promise not to freak out."

He groaned, and I could picture him running his hands through his hair. "That's a guarantee I'm going to freak out."

I laughed for real and closed my eyes. "Just remember you promised to love me forever no matter what."

"I've told you a thousand times, I've always loved you. I don't know how to not love you. Now tell me what happened."

I sighed, sinking into the quiet assurance that he wasn't going anywhere no matter how much trouble I got into. So I started talking and didn't stop.

"You see, these bikers walked into the bar...and it all went downhill from there."

ACKNOWLEDGMENTS

This is where I shamelessly beg and plead with you to drop a short review of *Unforgiven* on any retail site. Good, bad, or ugly...any review is so, so helpful to a new release and to the author. Your review is far more likely to attract a new reader than anything I say or do! Please help a gal out. <3

I just want to thank everyone who picked up *Unforgiven* and is following along with the shenanigans in Loveless. As someone who grew up in a very small town in the middle of the mountains in Colorado, I've always been fascinated by the ties and legacies that linger in such a close-knit community. Loveless has all the gossip and complicated dynamics I grew up witnessing...but obviously exaggerated and over the top to go with the Lawtons and how larger-than-life they all are. I really hope you all are enjoying these hardheaded but huge-hearted siblings and their very brave and patient love interests...lol. I really can't thank my readers enough for following me along whatever creative path I choose to walk at any given time. I honestly believe I have some of the most diverse and brave readers in all of romancelandia. I promise to always do my best to never let you down and to reward the risks you're willing to take with me.

In romance there are few things I love more than the longing and ache associated with unrequited love. It is hands down one of my most favorite tropes. I especially love it when it's the boy who has been left wanting for so long. Seeing a big, tough, alpha guy be brought to his knees by his too-soft heart is pretty much the greatest thing ever. Also, giving that same badass dude his much-deserved happy ending is so entirely satisfying. In this case, does anyone deserve to be happy more than Hill Gamble? The guy is just too good, and too hard on himself. I loved finally bringing him some closure, and I think he really, really appreciates all the work he put in so he could finally get the girl.

I loooooooooved writing *Unforgiven*...but I am DYING to write Shot's book. I had no idea my mysterious biker was going to take over my series...can't say I'm mad about it, though. I think he's going to give the good doctor a solid run for her money. And obviously we haven't seen the last of her evil former bestie. Shit's about to GO DOWN! It's going to be so much fun. I'm anticipating those biker boys will be all kinds of the best sort of trouble.

As always, a huge shout-out to anyone who blogs about, posts about, talks about, or shares *Unforgiven*. The heart and soul of any book is in your hands, and I sincerely appreciate every single person who helps give one of my stories life. You da best. <3

A huge thanks to the girl gang that surrounds me and helps me be a better version of myself. I'm a better Jay and a much better writer because of all the women in my life. Shout-out to my editor Lexi. My agent, Stacey. My friend/assistant, Mel. My publicist, Jessica. And my kickass beta team, which still sticks around, even though they know how ugly and terrible my rough drafts tend to be. Any part of the story you love, they made it 1,000 percent better! Thanks for being rad and super-duper helpful, Sarah, Meghan, Terri, Karla, and Pam. Honestly, don't know what I would do without you ladies.

Until next time! If you are interested in keeping up with me, these are all the places you can find me on the web. I strongly suggest joining my reader group on Facebook and following me on Bookbub. Those are the best places for updates!

Bookbub: bookbub.com/authors/jay-crownover
Website: jaycrownover.com
My store: shop.spreadshirt.com/100036557
FB page: facebook.com/AuthorJayCrownover
Twitter: twitter.com/jaycrownover
Instagram: instagram.com/jay.crownover
Pinterest: pinterest.com/jaycrownover
Spotify and Snapchat: Jay Crownover

Link to my reader group if you are interested in joining. I hang out in there a lot and you get pretty much unlimited access to me:

facebook.com/groups/crownoverscrowd

Don't miss JUSTIFIED,
the first in the Loveless, Texas series!

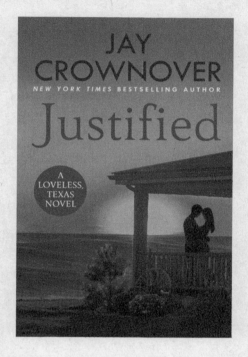

And if you're enjoying the Loveless, Texas series,
don't miss Presley and Shot's book,
Blacklisted,
coming in Autumn 2020!

HEADLINE
ETERNAL

For a bonus story from another author
you may love,
please turn the page to read

Cowboy to the Rescue by A.J. Pine.

All designer Ivy Serrano wants is a fresh start. But instead her Meadow Valley homecoming includes an electrical fire, a trashed custom dress, and a very handsome fireman who knows how to push all her buttons. Lieutenant Carter Bowen may set off sparks of his own, but the last thing Ivy needs now is town gossip...or to risk loving another firefighter.

New to small-town living, Carter is determined to prove himself, both at the station and at the fledgling dude ranch where he volunteers. That means no mistakes, no distractions, and definitely no Ivy. Yet there's something about the sassy shop owner that he just can't resist. As things heat up between them, Carter's more certain than ever that she's the one. But can he convince her they have a future worth fighting for?

CHAPTER ONE

∞

Ivy Serrano smelled smoke.

Not the *Ooh! Someone must be having a bonfire* kind of smoke or the *Mmm! Someone is grilling up burgers* kind of smoke. She smelled the *Shoot! Something's burning* kind of smoke right here, in her new shop, on the day of her grand opening.

She glanced around the small boutique, brows knitted together. She'd been about to flip the CLOSED sign to OPEN for the very first time when it hit her. Something was burning.

After two years of putting her life on hold due to a family tragedy from which she thought she'd never recover, here she was, back home, starting over. And of all things, she smelled *smoke.*

It didn't take long for the smell to be accompanied by sound, the high-pitched wail of a top-of-the-line smoke detector. Although, if anyone was keeping score, *she'd* noticed first. One point for the Ivy, zero for technology.

Except then she remembered that each detector was wired

to the next, which meant that in five, four, three, two, one... a chorus of digital, ear-splitting screams filled eight hundred square feet of space.

Her senses were keen enough, though, that it only took a second to register that the first alarm came from the back office.

Her design sketches! And samples! And *Oh no!* It was opening day!

She sprinted through the door that separated the shop from her office and storage. The only appliance she had back there was a mini refrigerator, because every now and then a girl needed a cold beverage and maybe even a healthy snack and *ohmygod* this was *not* happening.

She gasped when she saw the charred cord and the licking flames dancing up the wall from the outlet. Items on her desk were turning to kindling as the fire reached paper. She grabbed the extinguisher from its prominent space on the wall and, amid the incessant shrieking, snuffed out the fire in a matter of seconds. She yanked on the part of the cord that hadn't been completely cooked and unplugged the appliance.

Problem solved.

Except the design drawing on her desk, the one she'd been working on for the past week, was partially burned and now covered in foam.

No big deal. She'd simply start over—on the first piece she'd been brave enough to attempt that reminded her of Charlie. And now she had to muster that courage again after—of all things—a fire.

Or it would be, once she remembered how to turn the alarms off. Did she rip the battery out of the first one and all the rest would follow? Or did she have to somehow reset each and every one? She spun in a circle, panic only now setting in, because she knew what happened once the first alarm triggered the rest.

She ran back to the front of the shop and pushed through the door and out onto First Street. Sure enough, an emergency vehicle had already pulled out of the fire station's lot, siren blazing.

She dropped onto the public bench in front of her store and waited the fifteen seconds it took for the truck to roll down the street.

"It would have been faster if you all had walked," she mumbled.

Four figures hopped out of the truck in full gear. One who she recognized as her best friend Casey's younger sister, Jessie, started to unfurl the hose while another—yep, that was Wyatt O'Brien—went to open the nearby hydrant. The third was Wyatt's younger brother Shane.

Ivy stood and crossed her arms. "Fire's out already."

The last one—the one she hadn't recognized yet—strode toward her, his eyes narrowed as he took her in.

"Sorry, miss. But we still need to go inside and assess the situation, figure out what type of fire it was, and if you're still at any sort of risk."

She shrugged and cleared her throat, trying to force the tremble out of her voice. "It was an electrical fire. Probably caused by faulty wiring in a mini fridge cord because I had this place inspected a dozen times and know it was up to code. Used a class C extinguisher. I have smart detectors, though. Couldn't get the fire out before you guys were automatically called. Sorry to waste your time."

The fire was out. That wasn't the issue. Fire didn't scare her after the fact, especially now that she was so prepared. It was—*them.* She didn't want them here, didn't need them here, and certainly didn't require anyone's assistance. Just seeing their uniforms made it hard for her to breathe, made it impossible not to think of how Charlie wearing the uniform had cost him his life.

The man in front of her took off his firefighter helmet and ran a hand through a mop of overgrown dark auburn hair. If he weren't wearing the uniform, he'd have been quite handsome. She knew it was backward, that most women found men in uniforms sexy. But there was nothing sexy about a man who risked his life for a living. Noble? Absolutely. That didn't mean she had to find him attractive.

There was something familiar about him, though, even though she swore she'd never met him. Ivy knew just about everyone in town, especially those who worked at the fire station. So who the heck was this stranger?

"You still need to let us inside," he said. "We're not permitted to accept civilian confirmation of fire containment."

Ivy scoffed. "Just tell Chief Burnett it was Ivy's place and that I said everything is fine. He knows me well enough, so that should suffice."

The stranger grinned, but Ivy got the feeling it wasn't because he was happy.

"Chief Burnett is also my new boss, and I don't think he'd take kindly to me slacking off on my first call. But, hey, appreciate the heads-up and the unneeded paperwork I'll have to file when I get back to the station."

Definitely not a happy smile. Well, that made two of them. He wasn't happy to be here, and she wasn't happy to have him here.

He pushed past her and through the front entrance of the store—aptly called Ivy's—while two of his crew assessed the outside of the building's facade and the fourth jogged down to the end of the street and disappeared behind the row of stores that included her own.

"I really do have things under control in here," she called over the continued screech of the multiple alarms. When she received no response, she followed into the back office, where Needed-a-Haircut Man was inspecting the charred cord from the mini fridge and the blackened outlet.

"Don't you turn those off or something?" she yelled, barely able to hear her own voice.

The firefighter stood, pulled off his glove, and climbed onto her office chair. He reached for the smoke detector on the ceiling and pulled it out of its holster. Then he pressed a button, and it and all other alarms ceased.

"Thought you had things under control in here," he said with a self-satisfied grin as he hopped down to the floor, his boots hitting the linoleum tile with a thud.

Her mouth hung open for a second before she regained control.

"I did. I mean, I *do*. The detectors are new. This is the first time I've had to use them." *And I grew up in a firefighter household, thank you very much. So who are you to question what I do and do not have under control?* Of course, she kept all that to herself because her family was her business, but still—this guy had a lot of nerve.

He pointed to a button on the device marked with the word RESET.

"All you have to do is press and hold for five seconds, and they all turn off. But, if you accidentally do the same thing with the TEST button, all alarms will sound for half a minute. So I don't recommend doing that during business hours. Might scare customers away."

Ivy rolled her eyes. "I can read, but thanks for the warning."

"My pleasure," he said, smiling. "I'm gonna grab the rest

of the crew so we can do a full assessment on the outlet, check your circuit breaker. Glad to see you're not using power strips."

"It was the *fridge*. I'm sure of it." That was the last time she took a hand-me-down appliance even if it was still under warranty. "Look, Mr...."

"*Lieutenant* Bowen," he said.

Her eyes widened. "What happened to Lieutenants Russo and Heinz?"

"Nothing. Lieutenant Heinz runs his team, and I run mine. Russo's wife got a really great job in Seattle. They're moving at the end of the month. I'm taking over his team. You new in town?"

She scoffed and smoothed out her A-line blue sundress, then straightened the shoulder straps made of small embroidered daisies she had painstakingly created on her sewing machine. It was one of the few items in the shop that was an Ivy Serrano original. Part of her wanted him to notice. The other part called her out on even considering flirting with him. Firefighters were not her type, yet today she seemed to need extra reminders.

"*No*," she said, indignant. "I was born and raised in Meadow Valley, California. Been here all my life. Mostly. But I can't believe I didn't know Jason and Angie were leaving town." She'd been in her own little world the past couple of months getting the shop ready to open. Had she really been so wrapped up in her own life that she'd missed everything happening around her?

"I might be a little out of touch," she admitted. "But I know *you're* not from Meadow Valley."

He chuckled. Even though it was a small smile, this one was genuine, going all the way to the crinkle of his blue eyes. *Not* that she was noticing his eyes. Or how his broad shoulders shook when he laughed. "Just got here last week from Houston. You're very perceptive, Ms...."

She could hear his light accent now. "Serrano," she said. "Ivy Serrano."

He raised a brow. "Any relation to Captain Emilio Serrano, who practically ran the Meadow Valley Fire Station up until a few years go?"

Ivy swallowed and her eyes burned. "Guess you did your homework. Captain Serrano is my father."

The playfulness left the lieutenant's eyes, but his gaze didn't falter. "I'm sorry to hear about your brother. From what I've been told, he was a hell of a lieutenant himself."

"Thank you." It had been two years since Charlie died in the line of duty, but it still felt like she'd found out only five minutes ago. She cleared her throat. "You were saying something about inspecting the outlet?" She was 99 percent sure the outlet was fine, but right now she'd let him and his crew tear apart the drywall if it meant this conversation would end.

"Right," he said. He pressed a button on a small radio clipped to his collar and called for the other three firefighters. "We should be out of here in less than an hour."

She nodded. "Can I still open the store? Today was supposed to be my first day."

"That'll depend on what we figure out after a short investigation," he said.

The three firefighters she knew poured into her office from the back door.

"Hey, Wyatt," she said.

Wyatt O'Brien, always the gentleman, tipped his helmet. "Hey there, Ivy." Then he turned to Lieutenant Bowen. "All clear out back, sir."

The lieutenant nodded. "Thanks, O'Brien."

"This was a waste of time," Shane said, storming past them all and back out front. That was pretty accurate. Wyatt's younger brother always had a bitterness about him that clung tight. Looked like not much had changed.

The lieutenant's jaw tightened, but he didn't say anything.

"Hi, Ivy," Jessie said.

Ivy forced a smile. She'd known Jessie all the young woman's life. But all she could hope when she saw her in uniform was that Casey would never have to go through what Ivy and her family did.

"Heard you're working the front desk at the guest ranch on your off days," Ivy said. *It's safer there. Maybe you'll like it and sign on full-time.*

Jessie nodded. "Those school loans aren't going to pay themselves off." She looked nervously at the lieutenant. "I'll go check on Shane." And she hurried after him.

Ivy pressed her lips together and forced a smile. "Thanks, gentlemen," she said to the two remaining men. "I guess I'll just wait up front and let you do your job."

She blew out a shaky breath and headed back into her unopened shop—past the checkout counter and the table of baked goods and refreshments she'd set up for her very first customers.

All she'd wanted was to start fresh and instead she'd started with a damned fire and four firefighters bursting her bubble of safety.

A small crowd had gathered outside the store, which meant the gossip mill was in full effect.

She knew to fight an electrical fire with a type C extinguisher. But the only way to fight small town gossip was to shift the focus. The last thing she needed was every person in Meadow Valley talking about poor Ivy and how fire had brought tragedy into her life again.

She squared her shoulders and fluffed out her brunette waves, then pushed through the door and out onto the street.

"Nothing to see here, folks! Just a quick inspection before Ivy's doors are officially open."

"I heard sirens!" a man shouted, and Ivy recognized Lonny Tate, the owner of Meadow Valley's Everything Store. Most small towns had a general store or a small supermarket, but not Meadow Valley. Lonny Tate prided himself on carrying everything from toilet plungers to the occasional bottle of Coco Chanel. The only problem was that because the place was a quarter of the size of the Target the next town over, you never knew for sure if what you needed was in stock.

"Was there a fire?" a woman cried. It was Mrs. Davis from the bookstore. "Oh, poor Ivy. Not another fire."

"I'm fine, Mrs. Davis," Ivy said. "Promise."

"If you're fine, then you'll call me Trudy like I've been asking you to do for decades," the woman said with mild exasperation. "The only Mr. Davis I know is my father."

Mrs. Davis—*Trudy*—was practically family to Ivy, so she understood the worry and wanted to put the woman's mind at ease. But *Poor Ivy*? The whole town would be calling her that before long if she didn't set the record straight.

She kicked off her wedge sandals and climbed onto the bench. A hush fell over the growing crowd of Meadow Valley residents. The town was still abuzz after the annual Fourth of July festival. Ivy had hoped to open up shop before then to capitalize on the event, which was one of their biggest tourist attractions, but—as her good friend irony would have it—her electrical inspection hadn't yet gone through.

"There's no fire," she lied. "Everything is fine. Just a misunderstanding. The store will be open soon. But in the meantime..." She held a hand to one side of her mouth like she was telling them all a secret. "How about that dude ranch on the outskirts of town? I hear we got ourselves some real live cowboys over there."

"Oh!" Mrs. Davis exclaimed. "And I hear they hired that good-looking new fire lieutenant to give some trail tours. Turns out he's a bit of a cowboy himself!"

Suddenly the mumblings changed from the likes of *Poor Ivy* to things like "I've always had a thing for redheads" and "There's nothing sexier than a man on a horse," along with "You mean a redheaded firefighter on a horse."

Funny. Ivy thought the lieutenant's hair was more of a brown with a hint of red. And maybe there was something *slightly* sexy about a rancher on a horse, but not when fighting fires was in the mix. Fire was dangerous. Fire took lives. For the bulk of hers, her family had always worried about her father. But once he hit fifty and still hadn't let any blaze get the best of him, they'd all been lulled into a false sense of security, one that let Ivy and her family believe that Charlie, her brother, would also be immune.

They'd been wrong.

The throng of locals *Oohed*, snapping her back to the present. They weren't looking at her, though. They were looking past her. So she gazed over her shoulder to find the supposed sexy redhead striding through her shop door and out onto the sidewalk, his three cohorts following close behind. While the other firefighters pushed through the crowd and headed back to the truck, Lieutenant Bowen did no such thing.

When he saw her standing on the bench, he crossed his arms and grinned.

"Are you gonna sing or something?" he asked. "And if so, are you taking requests?"

She rolled her eyes.

He thought he was so charming with those blue eyes and that one dimple that made his smile look a little crooked but at the same time really adorable.

Again, all of the *nopes*. Men who played with fire were far from adorable.

"Am I open?" she asked. *Please say yes and then go away.*

"Open for business, Ms. Serrano. Though I think you'll need to retire that pesky appliance of yours."

"You heard the man!" Ivy said. "We are open for business!"

She hopped off the bench, slid back into her shoes, and held open the door, ushering much of the crowd inside.

"So," she said. "I was right?"

He nodded once. "You were right. But it's still my job to make sure."

"And it's *my* job to sell the stuff in there, so I better head back inside," she said. "Thank you, by the way. I know what you do is important. I just wish I could have caught the alarm before you all had to gear up and head over here."

He shrugged. "Beats pulling kittens from trees."

She laughed. He was funny. If he weren't wearing all that gear and the uniform underneath... But he was.

"You obviously haven't met Mrs. Davis yet," Ivy said. "She fosters kittens when she's not at the bookshop. And she's got a big old oak in front of her house. I'm sure you'll hear from her sooner rather than later."

"I'll consider myself warned." He glanced up and down the street, then back at her. "So what do people do around here for fun?"

Her brows furrowed. "I hear there's a new firefighter in town who leads trail rides at the guest ranch. Maybe you can look into that."

He chuckled. "Checking up on me already, are you?"

She brushed her hands off on her skirt. "Not sure how

much you know about small towns, Lieutenant, but around here we don't need to check up. Information is pretty easy to come by, especially when someone new takes up residence."

"Okay, then. When I'm not riding trails or saving kittens, what do you suggest? What are *you* doing tonight?"

She shook her head. "Oh no. I don't date firefighters."

He leaned in close and whispered in her ear, "I wasn't asking for a date, Serrano. Tonight's my first night off since I got to town. Just figured if you were going out, it might mean you knew a thing or two about where someone might let off a little steam."

His warm breath tickled her ear, and a chill ran down her spine.

"Midtown Tavern," she said. "It's the only place open after eight o'clock."

She didn't wait for a response. Instead she headed into the safety of her shop and headed straight for the thermostat.

It was getting hot in here.

CHAPTER TWO

❧

Even though he'd technically had a few nights off in his first week in town, as a new lieutenant—who'd beat someone on his team for the job—he wanted to hang around the station, get the lay of the land, and hopefully ingratiate himself to those who saw him as an interloper. Chief Burnett wanted to keep it under wraps who it was that lost the position to Carter. Regardless, things were tense. And it was never easy being the odd man out.

He'd had a good job back home at the Houston Fire Department. It was the *home* part of the equation that made leaving so easy. There was nothing like a father who disapproved of your life choices. Carter's solution? He left when opportunity presented itself.

Now here he was, a stranger in a strange land who didn't even have a place to live, which meant the firehouse bunk room was the closest thing to home for the time being.

He checked his watch. It was six o'clock on a Saturday evening, and aside from a trail ride he was leading at the

Meadow Valley Ranch tomorrow morning, he had the next forty-eight hours off.

"Hey," he said to Wyatt and Shane, the two guys on his team. "What's the best place to go around here to get a burger and a beer?"

"Midtown Tavern," the two said in unison as they stared at the rec room television watching a baseball game that was *not* the Astros, so he didn't care what it was. But it looked like the consensus was in on nightlife in Meadow Valley. He nodded his thanks to the other two men, whose gazes stayed glued to the screen.

He shrugged, assumed the T-shirt and jeans he'd changed into was proper attire, and headed for the station's front door.

The sun shone over First Street like it was still high noon, which made it easy to spot his destination—right in the middle of the main block. He laughed. *Midtown Tavern* was quite literally *mid* town.

He crossed the street and strolled past the inn. Pearl, the owner—and Carter's great-aunt—had offered him a room when he'd first arrived in town, but he'd preferred the station. She was the reason he was here—the reason he'd learned about an opening for a new lieutenant and possibly part of the reason the chief had even considered an outsider, but both Carter and Pearl were doing their best to keep that under wraps until his one-month trial period was over.

"Secrets don't stay buried for too long around here," Pearl had told him. "So make sure they all realize how good you are at doing what you do before they have a chance to claim favoritism."

Carter knew he was good at his job. Damn good. *That* was why the chief had brought him in and why he was in the running—along with the other lieutenant—to be the next captain when the chief retired in a couple of years. This was it. One false move, and he would have to start from square one again at another station. He couldn't go back to his job in Houston. And truth be told, he needed this distance from home. Going back wasn't an option.

So he was bent on proving himself to everyone at the station, which meant no mistakes, no distractions, and no reason for anyone to say he got the job because of who he knew rather than because of his long list of qualifications.

He passed the Everything Store and chuckled at the signs advertising a flash sale on vegetable peelers in one corner of the window and the release of a romance novel in the other corner.

He sure wasn't in Houston anymore.

It might have looked like noon outside, but when he stepped through the doors of Meadow Valley's Midtown Tavern, it was officially Saturday night.

He grinned at the dark wooden tables and booths that framed a square bar in the center of the space. *This* was what he needed. A place to unwind and mix with the residents of what he hoped to be his new hometown.

He grabbed an empty stool at the bar and cleared his throat to get the attention of the woman behind it. Her back was to him as she typed something into a cash register, so all he could see was the dark ponytail that swished across the back of a black T-shirt that said MIDTOWN SLUGGERS in a baseball-style yellow font. The pockets of her jeans were painted with what looked like pink lily flowers. *Not* that he was paying special attention to the pocket area of her clothing. The vibrant art simply drew his eyes.

His eyes widened when she turned to face him, a receipt and a few bills in her hand.

"Serrano," he said. "And here I thought you owned a clothing store."

She smiled, not at him but at the older man on the stool next to him. "Here's your change, Lonny."

The man waved her off. "Keep it, Ivy. Put it toward repairing the damage from the fire." He shook his head. "Such a shame something like that had to happen on opening day."

Ivy leaned over the bar. "*Nothing* happened, Lonny. The shop opened. I sold a bunch of stuff. There's nothing to repair, but I *will* accept your tip because I was an excellent server."

She brushed off her hands and turned her attention to Carter.

"Evening, Lieutenant. Yes, I do own a clothing store. But sometimes I help out around here."

"You got a thing for flowers?" he asked, remembering the dress she was wearing earlier that day, the straps made of daisies. Or maybe it was *she* who stood out in his mind's eye, and the memory of what she wore simply followed.

Another woman sidled up to Ivy before she could answer, nudging her out of the way with her hip so she could get to the beer tap. "This is the new guy?" she said to Ivy while looking straight at Carter.

"Sure is," Ivy said.

"You're right," the other woman said, blowing blue-streaked bangs out of her eyes. "Totally not as sexy as everyone keeps saying."

Ivy backhanded the other woman on the shoulder. "*Casey!*"

Casey laughed. "Thanks for covering for me while I took that call. I'm good here, so you can—you know—punch out or whatever."

"You don't *pay* me," Ivy said, rolling her eyes.

Casey finished pouring the beer and winked. "Yeah, but I let you drink for free. And I'll add a bonus. You can take *Dreamboat's* order." Then she disappeared around the corner to deliver the drink to a patron on the other side of the bar.

Ivy's jaw tightened, and then she smiled what Carter guessed was her patented customer-service smile. "Yes, I like flowers," she said matter-of-factly. "What can I get for you, Lieutenant?"

"I'm off duty," he said. "You can call me Carter."

"Sure," she said. "Now, what can I get you, *Lieutenant*?"

He laughed. She sure was determined *not* to like him, which was fine by him. It didn't matter that he'd been attracted to her the second he'd hopped out of the truck in front of her store. He could have a drink, blow off a little steam, but that was it. No other distractions.

"I'll have whatever's on tap," he said. "How about you choose?"

She grabbed a beer and filled it with a dark wheat beer, then slid it across the bar to him.

"I didn't call you a dreamboat," she said. "Just for the record."

He nodded. "But there was talk of my sexiness, or I guess lack thereof?"

She shook her head and gave him a haughty lift of her chin. "*No.* I mean, I just don't get what all the fuss is about. So you're cute in a uniform and can supposedly hold your own on a horse. It's not like it's newsworthy." She looked around the bar and rolled her eyes. "Although not much happens in Meadow Valley, so I guess around here it is."

She poured another beer, then took a sip before setting it down. She glanced down each side of the bar, pursing her lips at the occupied stools.

Carter cleared his throat. "There's an empty stool right here." He nodded to the vacant seat on his left. They could sit next to each other and have an innocent beer, right?

She blew out a breath. "Yeah, I know, but—"

"But there's an empty stool. You obviously need a place to sit. You don't even have to talk to me." He took another pull of his beer. "I'm perfectly happy to drink alone."

Ivy groaned, set her beer down next to his, then disappeared the same way Casey had gone. A few seconds later she appeared next to him, hopped on the stool, and took a good long swig from her own mug as she stared straight ahead, not sparing him a glance.

"This is good," she said more to herself than anyone else. "Drinking alone, just me and my thoughts." She sighed. "Me and *myself*."

Carter stifled a laugh. "You don't do alone, do you?" he asked.

She finally shifted her gaze to him. "I do alone just fine. Quiet, though. Quiet isn't my thing."

He laughed out loud this time. "You're in a noisy tavern."

She threw up her hands. "I'm a talker, okay? An extrovert. I get energized by being around others, by interacting with them. If I were sitting over there?" She pointed to the side of the bar on Carter's right. "Lonny and his fishing buddies would be telling me all about what they caught today, and I'd tell them how the highlight of my day was *not*, in fact, the fire but the grand opening of my very own store." She directed him to the row of patrons on the side to their left, a group of women who looked to be about the same age as his mom. "If I were hanging with the knitting guild, we could talk design and what kind of pieces I'm thinking of making for the store when the colder months roll in."

"But instead you're stuck next to me," he said matter-of-factly.

"Exactly." She gasped, her hand covering her mouth. "I didn't mean it like *that*."

But she did, didn't she? And he should be relieved she wanted nothing to do with him, but instead he was—disappointed.

"So you think I'm cute in my uniform?" he asked, brow raised. What was he doing? He wasn't sure, but the urge to flirt with her just sort of took over.

"Of course not," she insisted.

"Like, kitten-hanging-from-a-branch-in-Mrs. Davis's-tree cute?" he added.

"No one is *that* cute." She snorted and took another sip of her beer. "By the way, I'm simply enjoying a drink after a long day. I know you weren't asking me out earlier. This doesn't mean anything. You just happen to be sitting next to the only free seat. So let's just forget whatever this is." She motioned between them.

So they were in agreement. There was *something* between them. Something neither of them wanted, but something nonetheless.

He laughed. "Wow. And here I thought your sunny disposition meant you were a people person." He threw back the rest of his drink.

"I *am* sunny . . . with the right company."

She buried her face in her mug, catching up with him.

"Yeah," he said with a laugh. "About as sunny as a box of kittens."

"You really have a thing for kittens, don't you?" she asked.

"Actually, I'm allergic. You were saying?"

"I wasn't saying *anything*, just that this isn't anything more than two locals drinking a beer at a pub. My opinion of you in your uniform is irrelevant, as is what you think of me. Not that I'm assuming you think anything of me at all or that you're any more or less attracted to me than I am to you. I'm not—by the way—attracted to you." She rolled her eyes, but it seemed more at herself than at him.

"Oh, I'm attracted to *you*, Ivy Serrano," he admitted. "But I don't want to date you."

Her mouth fell open, but she didn't get a chance to respond. A second later, Casey appeared from around the corner carrying a liquor bottle and three shot glasses.

"You know if I comply with your request, I'm enabling you, right?" Casey said.

Ivy nodded. "But a *fire* on grand opening day. Of all things. It destroyed more than my fridge. Got my latest sketches too."

"The ones with the—"

Ivy interrupted Casey's question with another nod. The two women had a language all their own—an immediate understanding between two people who knew each other better than anyone else. He'd had a friend like that once. He also knew loss not unlike Ivy's. How similar they were. If they'd met under any other circumstances... But they hadn't. There was also the issue of her not exactly supporting his career. That was an automatic deal breaker no matter how attractive she was.

Casey blew out a breath, lined up the three shot glasses, and filled them all with a light brown liquid.

Carter lifted his glass and sniffed. "That is *not* whiskey."

Casey shook her head. "No, Lieutenant, it is *not*. It's Ivy's favorite, apple pie liqueur." She groaned, then stared at her friend. "You know it actually pains me to say liq*ueur* instead of liquor, right?"

Ivy smiled. "I know. But it's also how I know you love me." She lifted her glass, her big brown eyes softening as they fixed on Carter's. "You know who my family is, which means you also know I have nothing but respect and admiration for what you and everyone else in that firehouse does. You save kittens and you save lives, and that's a really big thing. But you also risk your own lives, and I've already lost enough for this lifetime."

Casey grimaced at her shot glass. "She, Charlie, and I used to sneak this crap from her parents' liquor cabinet when we were teens. *My* tastes matured. Hers have not."

"To Charlie," Ivy said, and Carter guessed her brother was exactly the reason why she still drank the stuff he couldn't believe he was about to drink. Despite bad timing and the surety that nothing could happen between him and Ivy Serrano, he couldn't ignore the warmth that spread through him at being included in such an intimate act—toasting a loved one who'd been lost in the line of duty.

"To Charlie," he and Casey said together. Then all three of them drank.

The gravity of the moment was quickly lost once his taste buds caught on to what was happening.

"That was *terrible*," Carter said.

"I know," Casey replied.

"One more!" Ivy exclaimed.

Casey shook her head but poured her friend another. Ivy quickly threw back the shot, narrowed her eyes at the almost-empty bottle, then snatched it from her friend.

"Serrano..." Casey said with brows raised.

Ivy looked at her imploringly, her brown eyes wide and her lips pressed together in an exaggerated frown.

Casey relented, and Ivy poured and drank the remaining shot.

"Something stronger for you?" Casey asked him. "She doesn't usually drink like this," she whisper-shouted with one hand covering her mouth.

"I don't usually drink like this," Ivy parroted, her eyes narrowed at her friend. "But today kinda caught me off guard." She turned her attention to Carter. "Anyway, three is good luck, right?"

He held his hand over the top of his shot glass and shook his head in response to Casey's question. "It's my first full day on the ranch tomorrow. How about a burger," he said. "Hear they're pretty good around here."

Casey shrugged. "Probably because it's the only place to get one around here. You want something a little more gourmet—and I stress the *little*—head on over to Pearl's inn. Otherwise, I got you covered."

He laughed and guessed there was some friendly competition between the two main eateries in town. Because if there was one thing he knew for sure, his great-aunt's recipes were a force to be reckoned with. But he was steering clear of Pearl's during the busy hours, and a burger sure did sound good.

"Then I'll have a burger with everything and fries." He nodded toward Ivy. "She should probably eat something, too." He knew a thing or two about some days catching you off guard. Life was funny that way. It never waited for you to prepare for the worst before the worst got handed to you on a silver platter.

"This isn't a date, by the way," she told her friend as she pointed at Carter and then herself. "He finds me attractive but doesn't want to date me, and *I* don't date firefighters, so we have an accord." She hiccupped.

Casey raised her eyebrows. "An accord? Did you two write a treaty or something when I wasn't looking?"

"I'll have my usual, please," Ivy said, ignoring her friend's ribbing.

Casey winked. "A burger and fries for the gentleman

and fried pickles for the lady who are on an *accord* and not a date."

She reached behind the bar and grabbed a tumbler glass, then used the soda gun to fill it with water. "In the meantime, drink this." She set the water down in front of Ivy, who pouted but did as she was told. Then Casey headed out from behind the bar and back toward the kitchen.

"You okay?" he asked.

She nodded, then swayed in her seat.

"Whoa," he said, catching her before she toppled off the side of the stool. "Maybe we should switch to a booth so we don't have another emergency today."

She nodded again, then let him help her down. She wasn't quite steady on her feet either, so he wrapped an arm around her torso and carried her water in his free hand as they made their way to an empty booth. She didn't object but instead responded by wrapping her arm around him.

His palm rested on her hip, and he had the distinct urge to rub his thumb along the curve of her waist. He didn't act on it. But holy hell he wanted to.

Once she was situated in the booth, he slid into the seat across from her. Then he nodded at her half-empty glass.

"Drink more of that." He ran a hand through his hair. He really needed a cut. "You eat anything at all today?"

She drank, both hands wrapped around the glass, and shook her head. When she'd drained the contents, she set the glass down and swiped her forearm across her water mustache.

Damn she was cute. There was nothing wrong with thinking that or wanting to sober her up so he could keep her sitting across from him for as long as this night went on, was there? It was nothing more than two strangers getting to know each other, and where was the harm in that?

"The day just sort of got away from me," she said. "The fridge fire, the first day of the store being open—I kind of forgot to schedule myself a lunch break. I might need to hire on an assistant or something, but the store has to make some money first."

Carter caught Casey looking for them at the bar and waved her over to their booth.

"Pickles were up first," she said. "Figured you wouldn't want me to wait."

Ivy's brown eyes lit up. "Did I ever tell you you're my bestest friend in the whole wide world?"

Casey nodded. "Once or twice."

Ivy pointed at her friend but looked at Carter. "Isn't she beautiful? She broke *all* the hearts in high school, especially Boone Murphy's. Do you know they almost got married?"

For a second Casey looked stricken, but then she laughed. "And now he's getting married, so everything worked out for the best. Speaking of work, I'm closing, which means I need some backup in the friend department." She glanced at Carter. "Can you make sure she gets home okay? It's a short walk from here, ten minutes tops."

Carter nodded. "I'm on it."

Ivy dipped a fried pickle slice into a small bowl of ranch, took a bite, and sighed.

"See?" she said, chewing. "Now I have my best friend and my new friend. Today wasn't so bad after all."

"Atta girl," Casey said, patting her friend on the top of her head. "Also, nothing other than water for you for the rest of the night. You're supposed to open at noon tomorrow, and you don't want to miss the Sunday out-of-towners who want to go home with an Ivy original."

Ivy gave Casey a salute then went back to her pickles.

"Be back with your burger in a minute," she told Carter. "Want another beer?"

He leaned back in his booth and shook his head. "Just a soda," he said. "Coke or Pepsi. Whatever you got."

A second later it was only the two of them again.

"I don't have much of a tolerance," Ivy said.

Carter laughed. "Yeah. I sort of figured that out."

"Thanks for walking me to the table," she added.

"Mind if I try one of those?" he asked, eyeing her food. "If you're looking for a way to repay me, food always works."

Ivy shook her head. "I guess I can spare one. You did keep me from butt planting or face planting at the bar. Not sure which it would have been."

He snagged a pickle disk, dipped it in the ranch, and popped it in his mouth.

"Mmm," he said. "Those aren't half bad. And it would have been a butt plant, judging from the angle of your sway."

Ivy blew out a breath, and a rogue lock of hair that had fallen out of her ponytail blew with it. "I'm not usually half in the bag before seven o'clock," she said. "Today was just—"

"One of those days," he said, finishing her sentence. "I get it. No need to explain. And the pickles and water seem to be helping you crawl back out of that bag, so no worries."

She smiled, and he was sure in that instant that Casey wasn't the only one breaking hearts when they were teens. He'd bet the last fried pickle that her smile alone had devastated a heart or two along the way.

"Food and water," she said with a shrug. "Who knew they were so much better for you than three shots and a beer?"

Casey took a break for dinner and ate with them. When they finished their food and Casey headed back behind the bar, Ivy insisted they head back as well.

"I don't want to hold up a four-top when there's only two of us," she said.

But he knew the truth. She didn't want to be alone with him because that would have been like a date, even if it wasn't. And though he knew that was the right thing to do—to keep Casey as their buffer—he'd have stayed at that table alone with her if she'd wanted. He'd have stayed until the tavern closed, if only to avoid the inevitable for as long as possible—saying good night to Ivy Serrano and good morning to a reality that didn't include terrible liquor or fried pickles or the woman he hadn't stopped thinking about since walking through her shop door that morning. She was beautiful, yes. But she was also strong-willed and funny. What it boiled down to, though, was that simply being in her presence made him forget the stress of the job, of being a new person in an unfamiliar place he hoped to call his permanent home.

He was in big trouble.

Carter had played with fire plenty in his line of work, but never had he felt more in danger of getting burned.

CHAPTER THREE

❧

The sun had finally dipped below the horizon when they left the tavern two hours later. While country music blared inside the bar, as soon as the door closed behind them, all Ivy could hear was the buzz of the cicadas and the occasional chirp of a cricket.

"Wow," Carter said, looking up and down the street. "This place really does shut down at night, doesn't it?"

"Did you live in Houston proper?" she asked. "I imagine this is a far cry from city life. Spent some time in Boston when Charlie and Allison first had the baby and then again after he . . ." She cut herself off and shook her head.

Charlie had thought their parents would flip when he told them he was moving to the east coast to be near Allison's family. Instead they'd seen it as an adventure—a reason to travel more—especially with their father nearing retirement. Ivy hadn't expected them to move there permanently, but then no one expected Charlie to die. After that, her parents couldn't leave the place where their son was buried, and Ivy couldn't blame them. "It's like it's happening for the first time every time I think of it. I wonder if it will ever get any easier."

They walked slowly, Carter seemingly careful to keep his hands in his pockets, which she appreciated. If his pinky accidentally brushed hers, she might do something stupid, like hooking her finger around his.

Why had it been so easy to mention Charlie's name with a man who was a stranger before this morning? To share a sacred shot of apple pie liqueur and even her fried pickles? Opening day was a success, but she couldn't get past how it had started, with a fire and the reminder of what she'd lost. And here was this man who was the embodiment of that loss, and he'd somehow made it better.

"Couldn't you have been a jerk instead of a perfect gentleman?" she mumbled.

"Did you say something?" he asked.

She turned her head toward him, her eyes wide. "What? *No*. Cicadas," she said, protesting a bit too much.

"Cicadas," he mused. "Sure thing, Serrano."

She shifted her gaze back to the sidewalk and tried to ignore the charming lilt of his accent. They ambled along the sidewalk to where it looked like the street hit a dead end at the trees, but she kept on to the right and led him to a small residential area where most of the Meadow Valley locals lived if they weren't farmers or ranchers.

"It'll always hurt," he said as they slowed around the curve. "But after a while the hurt has a harder time clawing its way to the surface. It gets covered up by the good memories of the person you lost and eventually by new joy you let into your life—when you're ready, of course."

She stopped, shoved her hands in the back pockets of her own jeans, and turned to face him.

She stared at him for several long seconds. They were the only two people outside at the moment, but the way he looked at her made it feel like the quiet street was their own little world. If he were anyone else—if he *did* anything else for a living other than risking his life—she would... What would she do? The only relationship Ivy'd had for the past two years was with her own grief. She still wrapped it around herself like a blanket—a reminder to protect her heart from ever having to go through that again.

"You ever lose someone close to you?" she finally asked.

He nodded once but hesitated before saying more.

"It's okay," she said, breaking the silence. "You don't have to tell me. It helps enough simply knowing when people understand."

He cleared his throat. "We already shared my first emergency since coming to town, my first taste of fried pickles, and my first and *last* shot of apple pie liqueur. Why not share personal loss as well?"

His attempt at humor would have sounded callous if she couldn't tell it was a defense mechanism. She was an expert there.

"I'm all ears," she said.

He shrugged. "I was an idiot kid who got in the car after a party with a buddy who shouldn't have been driving. But because I'd been drinking, too, I believed him when he said he was okay to drive. Made it all the way to my street before he lost control and wrapped the car around a light post. Front end caught fire. I got out—and he didn't."

He said the words so quickly and matter-of-factly, like it was the only way he could get them out. It didn't stop her heart from aching, or the tears from pooling in her eyes. He more than understood what she'd been through yet hadn't said a word all night while she'd cocooned herself in her grief blanket tighter than she had in months.

She reached for him but pulled her hand away before making contact. This was too much. Their connection kept getting harder to ignore. She had to make a concerted effort to keep him at arm's length.

"I'm so sorry, Carter. I—you—this whole night you were so nice to me, and I had no idea that—"

There were no right words for wanting to wrap him in her arms while also wanting to run as far from him as possible.

"Hey there," he said, resting a palm on her cheek and wiping away a tear with his thumb.

She shook her head and stepped back, hating herself for doing it. But all she had left was self-preservation, and Lieutenant Carter Bowen was the biggest threat to it.

He cleared his throat, taking a step back himself. "It was more than a decade ago. And I meant what I said. It does get easier. I can talk about Mason now—remember how he was the best at making people laugh, even our teachers. He kicked the winning field goal at our homecoming game junior year. And he had a real future planned, you know? Football was going to take him to college, but he wanted to be a doctor. A pediatrician, actually." Carter laughed. "*He* was the one on the straight and narrow path while I cut class more often than I went."

Her eyes widened. "I don't believe that for a second."

He forced a smile.

"It's true. I never cut for the sake of cutting. It was always for work. My brothers and I knew from the time we were young that our future was already mapped out. After graduation, my two older brothers went to work at my old man's auto body shop. I was supposed to do the same. It wasn't like there was money for college for three kids, least of all the youngest." He shrugged. "I accepted my fate like my brothers had—until Mason died."

Ivy crossed her arms tight over her chest, the urge to touch him—to comfort him—almost more than she could bear. "You changed direction after the accident," she said. It wasn't a question. She knew.

He nodded. "Much to my father's dissatisfaction, but I was done letting others make decisions for me, especially when I know better than anyone else what's right for me."

"What about your mom?" she asked, tentatively.

"She was sort of caught in the middle. She understood us both but wasn't about to take sides. So I got my grades up senior year. Did two years at community college, got my EMT certification, then took out a loan so I could finish my bachelor's in fire science."

"So fighting fires is your penance for surviving when Mason didn't?"

He shook his head. "Maybe it started that way, but the more I learned, the more I realized I could help people in all sorts of capacities. Even did some presentations at local schools about my firsthand experience being in the car with someone under the influence. I hope to set up a similar program in Meadow Valley and neighboring areas."

She let out a shaky breath. "You're a good man, Carter. Your father should be proud of you. I hope he comes around someday." Ivy dropped her hands to her sides. "I'm only a few more minutes this way. You can head back if you want."

He glanced up at the star-studded sky, then back at her. "Don't really have anywhere to be. Plus, I promised Casey, and I don't want to get on the bad side of the person who runs the one nighttime establishment around here."

She shrugged. "Suit yourself."

But she smiled softly as she turned away from him and

strode toward the bend in the road. The safest thing she could do was put as much distance between herself and Carter Bowen as possible, but a few more minutes with him by her side wouldn't hurt anyone.

He didn't say anything for the rest of walk, letting her silently lead him to her porch, where she stopped short of the front door and pivoted to face him once again.

"Can I ask you something?" he finally said.

"Okay," she answered.

He scratched the back of his neck, avoiding her eyes for a moment, then squared his shoulders and set his blue-eyed gaze right at her.

"I've dated plenty. Some relationships got more serious than others, but I've never told a woman about Mason until tonight, and it hasn't even been twelve hours since I met you, Ivy Serrano. Why do you suppose that is?"

Because, Lieutenant, there's an undeniable connection between us.

Because, Lieutenant, if I believed in such a thing, I'd say we were kindred spirits.

Because, Lieutenant, it feels like it's been more than twelve hours. If it didn't sound so crazy, I'd say I felt like I've known you all my life.

But it wouldn't help either of them to say any of that. So she swallowed the knot in her throat. "Because, Lieutenant, I'm simply a good listener. It's my blessing—and maybe my curse. People like to tell me things they wouldn't tell anyone else. I guess I just have one of those faces." She shrugged, hoping it would sell the lie. "I wouldn't read any more into it than that."

Except that I'm a liar, and I want to kiss you, and you scare me, Lieutenant.

She finally gave in and skimmed her fingers along the

hair at his temples and where it curled up above his ear. She couldn't let the night end without any sort of contact, hoping he understood this was the most she could allow herself to give.

"You need a trim," she said. "I could do it. Casey went to cosmetology school right after high school. She used to practice on Charlie, even taught me how to do a simple cut."

He laughed. "And here I thought you were going to break your own rules and do something crazy."

"Like what?" she asked, but she knew. She wouldn't be the one to say it, though. *She* wouldn't break the rules.

"Like kiss me," he said. And even though he was teasing her, hearing the words out loud made her realize how much she wanted them to be true.

Her cheeks flushed. "I don't date firefighters, Lieutenant. And you made it very clear that you don't want to date me."

"Good. Then we're both on the same page. I can't let anything get in the way of work right now. My future rides on everything that happens in the next month. Plus, I've already dated a woman or two who either couldn't handle the hours I worked or the risks I took. I won't change who I am, not for my father and not for any woman, even if it means missing out on something great. On *someone* great. No matter how much you bat those big brown eyes at me."

"I do *not* bat my lashes," she insisted. "Wait, what did you just say?"

She stood there, eyes wide, for a long moment as everything he said registered. Then she held out her right hand.

"Friends, then?" she said, the word leaving a bitter taste in her mouth. But it was all she could offer and all that it seemed he'd be willing to take.

He wrapped his hand around hers, his calloused palm sending a shock of electricity up her arm as he shook.

"Friends it is."

"Well then," she said. "I'm around after five tomorrow if you want that haircut. No charge, of course. Just a favor from one friend to another."

He nodded once, then let her hand go. "Appreciate the offer. I'll get back to you on that. Good night, Ms. Serrano."

"Good night, Lieutenant."

He flashed her a grin, spun on his heel, and then headed off the way he had come.

Ivy leaned against her door and let out a long, shaky breath.

"Friends," she said to herself. "*Friends*."

If she said it enough, she *might* even it believe it was true.

CHAPTER FOUR

Ivy went through the store, checking all outlets. even though she hadn't used any up front. You never could be too careful. Then she went to the back office, where she checked on her new battery-powered mini fridge and powered down and unplugged her laptop. She went to her design table, where she'd been trying out a new pattern, hated it, and went at it with the seam ripper, then unplugged the sewing machine as well. Then she scanned the small space twice, made sure the circuit breaker looked up to snuff, and locked the back door. Once over the threshold and into the store, she doubled back one more time to make extra sure she hadn't left an unknown fire hazard behind.

It was a quarter past five. She remembered her offer to Carter the night before. It had been in the back of her mind the entire day. One minute she hoped she'd make it home to find him waiting on her doorstep while the next minute she prayed he'd forgotten the whole thing.

Why had she even put the offer out there? A haircut,

one-on-one? It was almost as intimate as kissing. It wasn't like she could blame it on the alcohol. By the time he'd walked her home, she was as sober as could be. But the things she'd confided in him about losing Charlie—and what he'd told her about Mason? She'd connected with him in a way she hadn't anticipated.

Shake it off and move on, she said to herself as she turned off all the lights in the shop. *You get close to someone like that and you'll never find peace.* It was why she'd established her rule. And it wasn't just firefighters but police officers, too. She had the utmost admiration for those who put their lives before others, but she couldn't fall for someone like that. No way. No how.

When she'd finally satisfied herself that the shop was safe to leave for the night, she hoisted her bag over her shoulder and slipped out the front door and locked it behind her. After spinning toward the sidewalk to walk home, she gasped to find Carter Bowen leaning against a dusty, beat-up red Ford F-250.

"Evening, Ivy," he said. "Didn't mean to scare you."

She shook her head, half hoping she simply needed to clear her vision and it would be Shane or Wyatt or any other guy she didn't think about kissing the second she saw them. But nope, it was Carter Bowen all right. *Lieutenant* Carter Bowen. And tonight he was wearing a blue-and-white-plaid shirt rolled to the elbows, jeans that looked about as old as his truck, and dirt-caked work boots.

Shoot. He looked as good in clothes that should probably be marched straight to the washer as he did in his uniform. He'd have to take said dirty clothes off, and she'd bet he also looked pretty darn good—

Stop it, Ivy. You aren't doing yourself any favors letting your mind go there.

"Ivy?" Carter said, and she realized she had not offered him any sort of verbal response yet.

"Lieutenant. Hi. What are you doing here?"

He crossed his arms. "First, when I'm not in uniform, Carter will do just fine. Second, are we going to do that thing where we act like you didn't invite me around last night for something as innocent as a haircut?" He ran a hand across the stubble on his jaw. "Could probably use a shave, too. Don't suppose that's included with the cut?"

She swallowed, her throat suddenly dry. "I'm not pretending anything," she said. "Guess I was expecting you at my house, though, rather than outside my shop. My trimmer and barber shears are back at home."

He shrugged. "It's early yet. Sun won't go down for another few hours. Figured we could take a ride first, show you the trail I rode with some ranch guests earlier today. It's real pretty, and there's a great view when you get to the hill. Though I have to admit the view's pretty good right where I am now."

She rolled her eyes and fidgeted with the messy bun on top of her head. Today she wore a chambray linen tunic that had wrinkled the second she'd put it on, but she loved it anyway. It was so comfortable and looked great with her floral leggings and black moto boots. Comfort all around. Maybe she'd been sober when she'd gotten home last night, but that didn't mean waking up this morning was easy after putting away four drinks the evening before. She hadn't had it in her to wear wedges today.

"With corny pickup lines like that, it's a wonder you're still single. Wait, you are single, right? Not that it matters. I mean it might matter to *other* women, but not to *me*."

She winced. She was about as smooth as sandpaper.

Carter grinned. "I'm single. Not that it *matters*, since we are just friends. Is that a yes to the ride, then?"

She opened her mouth, then closed it.

"Everything okay?" he asked. "You said you were free after five. It's after five. It's not too hot, now that the sun is headed west…"

Not too hot. Ha. He was funny. Carter Bowen was an actual riot. Had he looked in a mirror? He was hot on a stick dipped in hot sauce. That was part of the problem. His overall charm didn't help either.

She rolled her eyes again and groaned.

"Okay now I feel like I missed a whole conversation," he said.

She laughed. "Only what's going on in my head. And trust me, you do not want access to what's in there."

He pushed off the side of the truck and took a step toward her. "May I?" he asked, lifting her bag off her shoulder.

"Um, sure," she said.

Now that he had her stuff, she guessed she had no choice but to go with him. Her house keys were in that bag, which meant she was practically stranded. That was sound logic, wasn't it?

He opened the passenger door and held out a hand to help her climb in. She plopped down onto a black leather seat with a stitched-up tear down the middle. The interior was clean as could be, but the dashboard looked like something out of an old movie. There was no USB port and a very minimal digital display for the radio.

When Carter climbed into the driver's seat and pulled his door shut, she gasped.

"Is that a tape deck?" she asked.

He nodded. "Works, too."

"Wait a minute," she said, brushing a hand over the dashboard. "Does this thing even have airbags? Because I'm not sure if you remember my safety setup in the shop, but I don't do risk."

He laughed. "The truck's old, but it's not ancient. Twenty years never looked so good on another vehicle."

She put one hand on the door handle, threatening to get out. "You didn't answer my question, Lieutenant."

He cocked a brow. "I'm not in uniform, Ivy. See how easily I bypassed the Ms. Serrano? I bet you can do it, too."

She sighed. "I can call you by your name." Except that meant they were dispensing with formalities, which also meant they were—what? They'd agreed on friends, but this little after-work activity already felt like something more.

"That's funny," he said. "Because I didn't hear you say it."

"Please, *Carter*, can you confirm that this vehicle is safe by today's standards?" She smirked.

He laughed. "*Yes*. There are airbags. It has four-wheel drive if we ever get stuck in the mud or—highly unlikely for this time of year—snow. Hell, it even has working seat belts. You forget I'm the son of a mechanic. I know a thing or two about maintaining a vehicle."

She pulled her seat belt over her shoulder and clicked it into place, then crossed her arms over her chest. "Tease me all you want, but there's no reason to ride in a death trap when I can walk almost anywhere I need to go around here. Plus, it's enough that you do what you do for a living. The least I can do is make sure you're cruising around town in something safe."

He laughed harder this time. "*Cruising*? Darlin', you don't cruise in a machine like this. You ride, drive, and sometimes even tow, but wherever you're going, it's always with a purpose. Cruising is aimless, and I am anything but."

Damn he was sure of himself. In any other man, that quality would be sexy as all get-out. But she didn't want Carter Bowen to be sexy as anything.

He put the key in the ignition and shifted the truck into

drive. She expected the tailpipe to backfire or the car to lurch forward, but the engine purred quietly as Carter maneuvered smoothly onto the street.

"It's been a few years since I've been on a horse," she said, her heart rate increasing. It wasn't because she was afraid of riding, though. It was being next to him, the thrum of anticipation, but of what she couldn't say. If he'd have kept to the plan and come over for a haircut, she'd have been in control. But Carter Bowen was literally at the wheel, and Ivy had no idea what came next. "Used to ride every summer at sleepaway camp," she continued. With her big brother, Charlie. There he was again, creeping into her thoughts and reminding her of what unbearable loss felt like. Her throat grew tight, and she hoped Carter would fill the silence while she pushed the hurt back into its hiding space.

"Well," he said with a grin. "This is your lucky day. Because in addition to this morning, I've been riding my whole life. My father may be all about cars, but my mother is a rancher's daughter. We spent a lot of time on my grandad's ranch growing up, and our mama made sure we could all handle ourselves on the back of a horse."

This made her smile, the thought of a young Carter and his big brothers, ribbing each other like brothers do, riding around a ranch.

"Sounds like you and your family were really close growing up," she said.

He nodded. "My father always preferred four wheels to four legs, but he managed." His jaw tightened, and his smile faded.

"I feel like there's another *but* in there somewhere," she said.

He blew out a long breath. "He makes a good enough living doing what he does. My brothers do, too. And for a long time I was fine with following along." He shrugged. "Meant I didn't have to take school too seriously and it meant my parents weren't breathing down my neck about grades and stuff like that as long as I was serious about the auto shop. And I was."

She laid a hand on his forearm and gave him a gentle squeeze. "But it wasn't important to you."

He shook his head. "I'd trade everything to have Mason back, even if it meant fixing cars the rest of my life. But I know now that something would have always felt like it was missing if that was the path I took. I wish I'd figured out what I was meant to do in a different way, you know? But I'm happy where I am now. What I do means something to me, just like I'm sure what you do means something to you."

Her hand slid off his arm and back into her lap. "I have a degree in fashion design," she said. "The stuff I sell in the shop comes from a lot of local designers. But—some of it's mine, too." Her cheeks heated. She was proud of the few pieces she had in the shop and would be even prouder when she sold them. But after growing up with a firefighter for a father and watching her brother follow in his footsteps, it was still scary to share her creative side, to run the risk of someone not liking a design or thinking her work wasn't as important, even when it was to her. "It's not saving lives," she blurted. "But it means something to me."

He rounded a corner and came to a halt at a four-way stop sign on a rural road outside the main part of town. She could see the sign up ahead welcoming her to Meadow Valley Ranch, but Carter put the truck in park.

"What are you doing?" she asked.

He turned to face her, one arm resting on top of the steering wheel.

"I'm making sure you can see the truth in my eyes when I say what I'm gonna say so you don't think I'm blowing smoke."

"Okaaay," she said, drawing out the word with a nervous laugh.

"Is making clothes your passion, the one thing in your life you can't live without? Filling your bucket and whatever other mumbo jumbo means you've found your calling?"

She nodded slowly, his ocean blue eyes holding her prisoner so that even if she wanted to look away, she couldn't.

"Then don't ever sound apologetic about it," he said, his face serious. "Because you're never going to change the minds of the naysayers, if there are any. And worrying about what other people think of what you do? All it does is rob you of some of the joy you're due."

He stared at her long and hard until she nodded her understanding, though she knew he was likely trying to convince himself even more than convince her. Still, the power of those words and the intensity in his gaze? No one had ever looked at her like that.

Once he got his response from her, he turned back to the wheel, put the car in drive, and drove them the final thirty seconds to the ranch.

After that speech and the way his eyes had bored into hers, she'd held her breath, thinking he might do something crazy like lean across the center console and kiss her right there. Only when they rolled to a stop in front of a stable and riding arena did she realize she hadn't yet exhaled. Or how much she wished he *had* planted one on her right at the four-way stop.

"You ready?" he asked.

To ride a horse? To find herself even more attracted to him by the day's end? To wonder if he *did* want to kiss her and what she'd do if it happened? Or how in the heck she was going to get this little crush out of her system once and for all? Because Carter Bowen could and *would* break her heart eventually. So no, she wasn't ready for any of it. Not one little bit.

"As I'll ever be," she said instead, and Carter flashed her a smile that knocked the wind straight out of her lungs.

Honey, you are in trouble, she said to herself as he rounded the back of the truck and opened her door.

"Did you say something?" he asked, offering her a hand to help her down. He had a pack over his shoulder he must have grabbed from the bed of the truck.

"Just how much I'm looking forward to an evening ride," she said.

Lies, lies, lies. Her words were nothing but lies. Only the flutter in her belly when her palm touched his spoke the truth. So she pushed it down deep, hiding it where she'd tried to hide her grief for two long years.

"Me, too," he said. Then he laced his fingers with hers and led her toward the stable doors.

And just like that, butterflies clawed their way to the surface without any warning at all.

Trouble with a capital *T.*

CHAPTER FIVE

❦

Carter held the door for Ivy as they entered the stable. Sam Callahan—one of the ranch owners and also a recent transplant to Meadow Valley—greeted them inside.

"Ivy Serrano, this is Sam Callahan. Not sure if you've met him or his brother Ben yet. Or Colt, the third owner of the ranch."

Ivy shook her head and also shook the other man's hand. "I've seen you about town but don't believe I've officially made your acquaintance, Mr. Callahan. It's nice to meet you."

"It's just Sam," he said. "I'm not big on formalities, Ms.—*Ivy*," he said, grinning and catching his own error.

Sam, Ben, and Colt were young transplants to Meadow Valley, just like Carter. When it felt like he didn't yet fit in, which was most days, he at least had them as allies—and a horse to ride if he needed a quick escape.

"Ranch is officially open for business?" Ivy asked Sam.

"Sure is. It's a slow start, but we hope to get things off and rolling in the next several months. First year in a new business is the most important. Keep your fingers crossed we start drawing more folks into the area."

She smiled. "I'll cross all my fingers and toes that you have a great first year. Business for you means more business for the town, so it sounds like a win-win to me."

Sam shook Carter's hand as well. "Glad to have you back. You did a heck of a job this morning, even if we only have ten total guests at the moment."

Carter laughed. "Yeah, but those ten will tell ten more about it, and then *those* ten will tell ten more. You see where I'm going here?"

Sam shook his head ruefully, then waved his index finger at Carter. "I sure hope so. Building a new business in a new town isn't as easy as I'd hoped."

Carter shrugged. "If your mare treats Ivy well enough, she may just be the person to start spreading the news in town. Heck, when that happens and you're booking my riding services on the regular, I'll lower my commission from fifteen percent to ten."

Sam clapped Carter on the shoulder. "I sure met you at the right time. Someday I may really be able to pay you."

"As long as you let me ride the trails, consider me paid," Carter said.

Sam grabbed a straw cowboy hat off a bale of hay and tossed it on his head. "Have a nice ride, you two. Ace and Barbara Ann are all ready to go. You're welcome to stop by the dining hall when you get back, but I'm guessing by the saddle pack that you might have things under control."

Carter nodded. "Thanks for the offer all the same."

Sam turned back to Ivy. "It was nice to officially meet you. I'm sure we'll run into each other again sooner or later." And with that he strode out of the stable.

Ivy stared after him as he left. And then she stared some

more. If Carter were the jealous type, he'd be—well—jealous. But how could he envy a man who caught her attention when she was nothing more than a friend? Pretty easily, it turned out.

Carter cleared his throat. "Not that it matters, but if I *were* trying to properly court you, would I have just introduced you to my competition?"

She spun to face him, cheeks aflame. "What? No. I mean—competition for what?"

He laughed. "I'm just wondering—and this is only a hypothetical, because this is in no way a courting situation—if I'd have shot myself in the foot by introducing you to someone who not only doesn't fight fires for a living but also must be pretty easy on the eyes for someone such as yourself."

Her throat bobbed as she swallowed, and her blush deepened.

"I'll admit that if anyone ever needed a visual display of what tall, dark, and handsome was supposed to be, it's the cowboy who just strode out those stable doors. And he has a brother? My oh my," she said, fanning herself.

He'd been teasing her initially, but now his confidence began to waiver.

"*But,*" she added, "there's one big problem with all of that."

Her tone encouraged him, so he took a step closer, even had the audacity to skim his fingers across her temple. "What's the problem, darlin'?"

She blew out a breath. "It's this other cowboy. One who, after barely knowing me, helped sober me up after a bad day and even made sure I got home safely. He also *donates* his free time to lead trail rides at a new ranch in town. And truth be told, I prefer something closer to a redhead than a brunette. In fact, if this particular cowboy didn't risk his life for a living, I might very well be developing a little crush on him, which *would* make this a courting situation. But it's not, correct?"

It wasn't, as much as he wanted it to be. He'd thought about her the whole walk home last night, about what it would have been like to kiss her if she could only see him differently. Maybe that was what he hoped to accomplish by taking her out on the trail. All he knew was that sharing the view with ranch patrons earlier that day had been fun, but sharing it with Ivy would be something else. He hoped by the time they made it to the trail's end he'd figure out what that something else was.

He dipped his head, his lips a breath away from her ear. She smelled like the lavender fields from the farm that bordered his granddaddy's ranch, and he breathed her in, this intoxicating scent of home.

"No," he whispered. "It's not." Because a new job in a new town was tough enough. He was being tested by the chief, his captain, and everyone in his company. If he lost focus and slipped up, then where would he go? But the real issue was her. If he lost focus while falling for someone who, in the end, couldn't handle what he did for a living, then he wasn't simply putting his career on the line but his heart, too. He understood that Ivy's fear was based in reality, that she'd experienced a heartbreaking loss. And while he'd never push her into something she didn't want, it was impossible to deny this thing between them.

"Courting you, Ivy, would eventually mean kissing you. And I'm not sure you could handle my kissin'."

"Why's that?" she asked, her voice cracking.

"Because," he said softly, "I'd leave your lips swollen and your brain so foggy you won't remember your own name." Yet he wouldn't push her too far too fast. She had to choose him. Because despite bad timing and he being the type of guy she swore she'd avoid, a part of him had already chosen her.

She sucked in a breath, and it took every ounce of his resolve to straighten and take a step back when all he wanted to do was exactly what he'd said.

"Then I guess we're on the same page," she said, but he could hear the slight tremble in her voice. It matched his quickened pulse and the irregular beat of his heart.

He nodded. "I'll just throw my pack on Ace's saddle, and we'll be good to go." He glanced down at her boots. They weren't riding boots, but they looked sturdy enough for a motorcycle, which meant they were sturdy enough for a horse.

His gaze trailed up her toned legs. He could see every curve of muscle, her round and perfect backside, in those form-fitting pants.

"See something you like?" she teased, having regained her composure.

Good lord did he ever.

How the heck was he supposed to read that? He wanted something other than friendship from her but only under the right circumstances. But after all her protesting—was Ivy flirting back?

"Just making sure you had proper boots for riding. Those will do," he said coolly, doing his best to maintain control.

He got Ace ready to go, then introduced Ivy to Barbara Ann and helped her into the saddle. At least, he *tried* to help her, offering to give her a boost, but she stuck one foot in the mare's stirrup and hoisted herself into the saddle like she'd done it every day of her life.

She shrugged and stroked the horse's mane. "Guess it's like riding a bike. You never really forget." She pulled her sunglasses from the collar of her shirt, batted her big brown eyes at him, and then covered them up. "I'm just waiting on you, cowboy."

He crossed his arms and stared up at her. "You want to take her for a lap or two in the arena before we hit the trail to make sure you've got the hang of it?"

"Sure," she said. "Meet you out there."

He stepped aside, and Ivy led Barbara Ann out of her stall and into the arena with ease.

He laughed and shook his head. She could make clothes, cut hair, put out her own fires, and hop onto the back of a horse like she grew up on a ranch herself. She also seemed to be able to make him forget that there was no room in his life for romance right now, especially with a woman who couldn't support what he did for a living.

He strode to a shelf right inside the stable's entrance and grabbed the cowboy hat he kept in there for his trail rides, then headed back to Ace's stall and mounted his own trusty steed. When they trotted into the arena, Ivy and Barbara Ann were galloping around the track. Damn she looked good on the back of a horse. Maybe this was their common ground. Back in town she was a woman still grieving an incomparable loss, and he was the man who—by the simple nature of his profession—reminded her of it. Maybe out here on the ranch for one perfect evening they could just be Carter and Ivy.

She rounded a turn and pulled on Barbara Ann's reins so she came to a halt beside him and Ace.

"Color me impressed, Ms. Serrano," he said. "You're a natural."

She beamed. "That. Was. Amazing! I've never felt so—so—"

"Alive?" he asked.

She shook her head. "Free. Free of all the worry swirling around my head, you know? Will the shop do well? Will my own designs sell? And everything else that gets me all twisted up in knots." She blew out a breath. "*Thank* you for bringing me here. I don't know if you knew it was what I needed or not, but wow. This is the perfect end to a stressful opening weekend."

"Now you know why I help Sam and the boys out for free. Ain't nothing like being on top of a horse and leaving the rest of the world behind every now and then." He nodded toward a gate on the other side of the arena and a path that eventually forked into three different directions. "You ready? We're going to do the open trail to the right."

"Ready," she said.

And they hit the trail.

* * *

How was it that Ivy had grown up in this town but had never seen these rolling green hills? It probably had something to do with there not having been a Meadow Valley Ranch or a stable full of horses until now. Maybe, though, the town wasn't the only thing she was looking at from a different perspective.

She tugged gently on Barbara Ann's reins and slowed to a stop a few yards behind where Carter was doing the same thing. When she'd met him yesterday, he was a walking, talking, embodiment of her biggest fear—losing someone she loved. But today he was this cowboy who gave her exactly what she'd needed at the end of a weekend that had started off on a very wrong foot.

He looked back at her over his shoulder and tipped his hat.

Her stomach flipped.

"Just a few paces ahead and we can tie off the horses. I brought snacks," he called.

She nodded and followed him over the hill to where it leveled into a small clearing overlooking the ranch and beyond it the main street of town.

A short length of fence was set up—most likely by Sam Callahan and the other ranch owners—that seemed to be there for the sole purpose of making sure you could relax a while without your horse running off.

She hopped down into the overgrown grass and walked Barbara Ann to an open spot on the fence. Carter secured his horse while she did the same with hers. He removed the saddle pack and tossed it over his shoulder.

"Sam said the horses like this spot for grazing, and riders like it for gazing down at the town or up at the stars on a clear night, so I said we should call it Gaze 'n' Graze Hill."

She snorted. "That's the corniest thing I ever heard—but at the same time also kind of cute."

He shook his head. "There you go again with that word. *Cute*. Cute in my uniform. Cute the way I name a hill. I've heard the word so much in the past two days that I'm starting to wonder about that vocabulary of yours."

He nodded in the direction away from the fence, then pivoted and headed that way without giving her time to come up with some sort of witty retort.

"I have a very good vocabulary, I'll have you know," she said when she caught up to him, then rolled her eyes at her less-than-formidable response. She'd never had to work to impress when it came to wordplay, but Carter Bowen threw her off her game. He made her tongue-tied and nervous and anxious to lob witty comebacks without a second thought. She had the undeniable urge to show him how much of her there was to like because—*ugh*—she was really starting to like him.

Where would that get her, though? She didn't want to think about that, not when she was up here, able to let go of the fear, even if it was only for a short while.

He laid the pack on the ground and unzipped one of three compartments, pulling out a blue-and-white-checked picnic blanket.

"Here," she said, motioning to take it, since he was kneeling. "I can do that."

He relinquished the blanket, and she shook it out, spreading it over the grass.

Next he opened a plastic container filled with sliced apples and another with what looked like warm, grilled sandwiches.

"Damn," he said. "I didn't think to ask. You don't have a peanut allergy, do you?"

She sat down across from him and shook her head. "Carter Bowen, did you make me peanut butter and jelly?" she asked with a grin.

"No, ma'am. Pearl did. You know Pearl at the Meadow Valley Inn?"

Ivy gasped. "Did you bring me Pearl's grilled PB and J with brie? Because if you did, I just might have to kiss you." Her hand flew over her mouth. "I meant because of how much I *love* that sandwich, not because—" She greedily grabbed one of the sandwich halves from the container and tore off a healthy bite. Anything to keep her from saying more incriminating statements about kissing. "Mmm. Delicious," she said around her mouthful of food.

Carter laughed and dropped back onto his ass—the ass she'd had her eye on for much of the trail ride. It wasn't like she had a choice. He led the way. And if she was searching her *limited* vocabulary for a way to describe the view, it was a long way from *cute*.

He handed her a thermos of Pearl's equally delicious raspberry iced tea, then picked up his own half a sandwich from the container and took a bite. He unscrewed the lid from his own tea and took a couple of long swigs.

"You know," he said, resting his elbows on his knees, "you don't have to be embarrassed about wanting to kiss me. Hell, you don't even have to use my great-aunt's cooking as an excuse for wanting to do it."

Her eyes widened, and she stopped herself in the middle of taking another bite. "*Pearl*? Pearl Sweeney is your great-aunt?"

He held his index finger to his lips.

"She is, though I'd appreciate you keeping that between us for right now. When she heard the chief might be looking to hire from the outside, she passed him my name. That was it. Her only involvement. I got the job on my own merits. I *know* I'm good at what I do. But I'm an uninvited guest right now, so until I prove myself to the company—which I know I will—I don't want to give anyone reason to doubt my abilities."

She lowered her sandwich onto the lid of the container. "But Jessie, Wyatt, and Shane seemed to respect you just fine when you answered my nonemergency alarm."

He laughed, but the smile looked forced. "That's because I'd just written them up for insubordination before we left the station."

"What? Why?" That didn't sound like either of them.

He shrugged. "Because when they saw where the call was coming from, they argued with me about suiting up and taking the truck. 'It's Ivy's place. That girl knows more about fire than we do. By the time we get there, there'll be nothing left to do but paperwork.'"

Ivy winced because they were right about her. But Carter

was in the right as their superior. "You did everything by the book like you were supposed to. I get it. No one should take shortcuts in a possible life-or-death situation."

He set his sandwich down and leaned back on his elbows, his long legs stretching out in front of him. His cowboy hat cast a shadow over his eyes. "Anyway," he said. "You can see why I don't want anyone claiming favoritism."

She moved the food out of the way and stretched out next to him on her side. The sun was low enough that she didn't need her sunglasses anymore, so she took them off and tossed them toward her feet. "Why'd you tell me all that, then? Aren't you afraid I'll spill the beans? For all you know, I'm the town gossip."

"Nah," he said. "I know the type, and you're not it. Besides, I needed to tell *someone*. Figured I couldn't do much worse than you."

She scoffed and backhanded him on the shoulder. "I don't know if that's a compliment or an insult. But judging from the sound of your voice, I'm guessing it's the latter."

He rolled onto his side to face her, but the hat was still obscuring his eyes. So she grabbed it and tossed it the same way she did her sunglasses.

"There," she said. "Now I can see those baby blues."

"Are they *cute*?" he asked.

Something in the pit of her belly tightened, and she shook her head.

"Then what?" he asked, his eyes darkening with the same mischief to match his tone.

"Okay," she said. "Before *then what*? I need to ask you something, Mr. Bowen."

"Go ahead, darlin'."

She blew out a breath. "There's something about being up here with you, away from everything at the bottom of the hill. It's like I can forget what happens down there, you know? Like nothing matters except for what's up here."

"The Gazin' and Grazin' Hill," he said with a wink.

She rolled her eyes but laughed. "There's something between us, right? I mean, you brought me here with Pearl's best sandwich and—and I'm not imagining any of it, am I?"

"No," he said simply. "I can't be with a woman who doesn't support what I do. So I know my wooing is going to waste, even if I keep saying that's not what this is. But I can't seem to help myself. Guess I was hoping I'd be able to change your perspective."

"I support what you do," she said. "But I just can't put my heart out there like that. You have to understand." She paused and took a steadying breath. "Wait. No, this isn't where this was supposed to be going. What I meant to say is that maybe up here, for today, I *can* forget what's down there. We both can." She propped herself up and squinted over the top of the hill.

"If I say yes, that I'd like the same thing," he said, "then I get to hear what else is in that vocabulary of yours?"

She lowered herself so she was facing him again and nodded. "You'd get to hear me say how sexy your butt looks in those jeans."

He laughed. "And here I thought we were talking about my eyes."

"Those are pretty sexy, too." She grinned. "I might even find you a little bit charming."

He trailed his fingers down the bare skin of her arm. "Darlin', I find you to be too many things to list."

She batted her lashes, and he laughed again. "Why don't you try," she said.

"Hmm, I should get comfortable. This'll take a minute or

two." He rolled onto his back and clasped his hands behind his head. "Smart. Beautiful. A competent rider—"

"I like where this is headed," she interrupted. "Feel free to continue."

"A passion for what you do. Oh, can't forget terrible taste in liquor."

"Hey," she said. "I thought you were supposed to be complimenting me."

He raised his brows. "I said there was too much to list to *describe* you. Never said it was all complimentary." He scrubbed a hand across his jaw. "*And . . .* headstrong." He held up his hands like he was waiting for some sort of physical retribution, but she simply sat up, crossed her arms, and glared.

It was easier to find a reason to be indignant than to admit to herself how much she liked hearing what he was saying— complimentary or not. Because even his ribbing meant he'd noticed her. He'd paid attention to her. And he'd thought about her as much as she'd thought about him since their walk last night.

"That one *was* a compliment," he said, sitting up so she couldn't escape the depths of those blue eyes. "You know exactly what you want and what you don't, Ivy. I admire the heck out of that. Even if it means you *not* wanting to get involved with a catch like me."

Her gaze softened. "And you don't want to get involved with a mess like me."

"You're not a mess," he said. "But no. We already know we're not right for each other. And despite what you're offering up here on the hill, I think we both deserve better than that."

He grabbed his hat, stood, and dropped it back on his head.

She clamored back to her feet. "Wait. That's it? What about forgetting what's down there while we're up here?"

He dipped his head and kissed her. She didn't have time to think because her body melted into his like she was molten metal and he was made to mold her into shape. Her stomach contracted, and her back arched. His hands slid around her waist, and hers draped over his shoulders. His kiss was everything he had promised and everything she'd hoped— firm and insistent while at the same time careful and considerate. Whatever he asked for right now, she was more than willing to give. She parted her lips, and his tongue slipped past, tangling with hers. He was heat and fire and passion like she hadn't known existed.

Erase it all, she thought. *My fear, my hesitation—heck, even my name.* She knew it wasn't that easy, that a kiss couldn't take away two years of grief and how scared she was to even consider putting her heart at risk again. But now that she knew what she'd tried to resist, she wanted all she could take before logic stepped back into the picture.

But before she could catch her breath, he backed away and tipped his hat.

"Are you gonna forget that once we get back to town?" he asked. "Because I sure as hell won't."

CHAPTER SIX

Carter Bowen was on fire. Not literally, of course. In the two weeks he'd been in Meadow Valley, the closest he'd gotten to any sort of real flame was the fire at Ivy's shop—the one she'd put out before he'd probably had his gear on.

No gear today, just a very sweaty Meadow Valley Fire Station T-shirt and a pair of basketball shorts. Lieutenant Heinz's crew took over a few hours early so Carter and his team could spend the last of their twenty-four-hour shift doing a scrub down of the rig.

In a hundred-degree heat, because even in the late afternoon, the day was a scorcher, and they needed daylight to see what they were doing. Carter paused from waxing the front of the truck to take a water break.

"You know this rig never sees any action, right?" Shane O'Brien said. "Other than the occasional emergency room transport—and for that we use the ambulance—I think the last fire Meadow Valley saw was two years ago."

He was on top of the rig, checking the ladder hydraulics and making sure there weren't any leaks.

"Not that I owe you an explanation, probie," Carter said, and Shane scowled at the nickname. "But I know the station's history. I'd expect that, having grown up in Meadow Valley, you'd know that while things have been quiet *here* the past eighteen months, we don't service only our own town. Our company has been called for backup more than a few times for forest fires in neighboring jurisdictions. In a rural area like this, debris from low-hanging trees and falling ash can cause issues over time if the upper level isn't cleared out and rinsed every now and then." He took a long swig from his canteen of water. "Plus a good day of work builds character for someone who might have taken a job because he thought he could sit with his feet up and watch ESPN all day."

He'd actually kill to be inside in the air-conditioning checking the Astros score, but there was no way he was going to bond with his team without working with them, and a clean rig was always the safest rig.

"Thanks for the exaggeration," Shane bit back. "I can count how many times *we've* been called for backup on one hand. And just so we're clear, my probationary period ended months ago. I could put myself in the running for your job if I wanted. We all know about your one-month trial period. You mess up and you're out, Lieutenant *Probie*."

Carter's teeth ground together. He'd been the youngest of three, the button pusher, all his life. But it had all been because he looked up to his brothers. He wanted to be like them. This was different. Shane O'Brien had some sort of vendetta, and Carter was the target.

Jessie popped her head out of the driver-side door.

"Mats and underneath the mats are all clean, Lieutenant!" she called. "Gotta admit, it was pretty nasty in there."

Carter did his best to shake off his interaction with Shane. "Let me take a quick look. If all looks good, you're clear to go."

He rounded the rig and climbed inside. The cab was damn near pristine, like no one had ever used it.

"Excellent work, Morris," he said as he hopped out. "I'll see you in forty-eight hours."

She grinned. "Thanks, Lieutenant." Then she gathered up her portion of the cleaning supplies and headed into the garage.

She and a few others on his team had seemed to come around in the past week, even though he'd been extra surly after the way things had ended with Ivy on Sunday. Maybe it started with his team not wanting to poke the bear, as it was, but now they'd fallen into an easy rhythm that felt good. The way he felt about Ivy Serrano, though? There was nothing easy about that.

It was Thursday now, and he was finishing the second of two twenty-four-hour shifts since he'd seen her. He hadn't been able to shake off how much he'd wanted her that evening and how much he still did even after putting four days between them.

It had meant keeping to the station and avoiding any other stops at the Midtown Tavern. But it seemed the more he avoided his attraction, the more he thought about it and wished he hadn't gone from a father who didn't support his life choices to a woman who drove him all kinds of crazy but also couldn't get behind what he did for a living.

He drained his canteen and then finished the rig's waxing. After that he went around the truck, inspecting stations and dismissing his firefighters as they completed their jobs. Until the only one left was Shane O'Brien—who'd decided to take an extended water break.

Carter climbed up to the roof of the truck and found him nestled into a corner, his baseball cap pulled low to cover his closed eyes. But Carter could tell by the rhythm of his breathing that the guy was asleep.

What the hell was it with his guy? It was one thing to push his buttons, but this was a complete disregard for Carter's authority.

He looked down at the small bag of twigs and branches Shane had collected—and at the untouched bucket of soapy water meant to wipe down the roof and ladder.

Carter picked up the bucket and tossed half the contents at the sleeping rookie.

"What the hell?" Shane growled, startling awake.

Carter checked his watch. "I'm off the clock. So is the rest of the team. Except you." He nodded toward the spilled water. "Clean that up and wipe down the rest of the roof. I'll let Lieutenant Heinz know you're not stepping foot off this property until you're done. See you in forty-eight hours."

He gritted his teeth and climbed to the ground before Shane had a chance to be any more insubordinate than he'd already been. Carter needed a shower. And a drink. But that meant hitting the tavern. Except he was *avoiding* the tavern. And right now he wanted to avoid the firehouse as well.

He pulled out his cell phone and called his great-aunt.

"I need a room," he said when she answered.

"Got one ready and waiting. Rough day?"

"Yeah. Does that Everything Store sell liquor?"

She laughed. "And steal business from Casey's place? Kitchen's still open over here, and I might have a few long-necks hiding in the fridge."

He blew out a breath. "You're a lifesaver. Be there in a few." Then he ended the call.

He grabbed his few belongings from the bunkhouse, hoisted his duffel over his shoulder, and headed straight for the front door. He pushed through to find Ivy Serrano heading up the front walkway. Her eyes widened when she saw him.

"Can I help you, Ms. Serrano?" he said with as much formality as he could muster.

Her hair was in two low braids on either side of her head, and she wore a black baseball cap that said SLUGGERS across the top in yellow, a white tank top under fitted overalls, and a pair of what he guessed used to be white sneakers on which she'd doodled intricate floral designs in vibrant colored marker.

Damn she looked cute.

She hesitated, her hands fidgeting with the bag slung over her shoulder.

"Softball practice was canceled on account of the heat, and I figured since I was free and it looks like you're still in need of that haircut..."

He ran a hand through his hair. The overgrown ends were slick with sweat.

"Ivy," he said, more serious this time. "What are you doing here?"

She shrugged. "You were right. I haven't been able to forget about that kiss." She noticed his duffel. "Are you going somewhere?"

"Decided to take a room at the inn. I need a shower and a cold-as-hell beer."

She worried her bottom lip between her teeth. "I've got a shower. And a six-pack of Coors."

He sighed. Despite having thought about her all week, he had every reason in the world to say no. There was something between them, for sure. But they couldn't be together, not when his job seemed to be growing more complicated, especially after what he'd just done. Not to mention the woman standing in front of him couldn't handle his job to begin with.

He got it. He understood and wouldn't fault her for her grief. But he couldn't be anyone else for her.

No, Ivy. I can't come with you. I can't get deeper into this thing we never should have started because it'll keep getting harder to walk away.

The only problem? He couldn't actually form the word *no*. Not with those big brown eyes fixed on him, those dark lashes batting their way past his defenses—because yes, she batted. And it worked.

"Those are the magic words," he said at last. A free haircut and a beer. He could handle that. "But nothing out of any sort of fashion magazine. Just a trim."

She finally smiled, and he swore it was brighter than the still-blazing sun.

"Deal," she said, then held out her right hand.

He shook it. "And for the record," he said, "I haven't forgotten that kiss either."

They strode off down the street and around the bend. When they got to her porch he texted his aunt.

Change of plans. I'll still need that room but not until later this evening.

Or maybe, if they both threw logic out the window, not at all.

Carter showered quickly and threw on a clean T-shirt and jeans. He'd gotten so used to communal living the past couple of weeks that the quiet of Ivy's house made him feel odd and out of place. After college he'd moved straight into a one-bedroom apartment with another probie at the station.

It was a tight fit, one of them living in the bedroom and the other in the living room, but it had been a necessary inconvenience. After his father decided he was a colossal disappointment, he couldn't live at home anymore. So he worked to pay the rent, picked up any overtime that was offered him, and moved up the ranks as fast as he could.

And then he left.

It had been a long time since he'd been under a roof with quiet, space, and permanence.

He padded barefoot into the kitchen, where she was waiting on a stool at the kitchen island. One frosty longneck sat on the blue-tiled counter while she sipped another.

"Evening, Lieutenant," she said, raising her bottle. Her ball cap hung on the corner of her high-top chair.

"Evening, Ms. Serrano," he said, striding toward the counter to stand opposite her. "But I'm off the clock."

She nodded. "I know. But the title suits you. You've got this air of authority that doesn't seem to go away even when you're off duty."

He blew out a breath and took a healthy swig from his beer. "I guess it's kind of hard to turn it off sometimes." He set his beer down and pressed both palms against the counter, shaking his head. "I lost my cool with one of my rookies this afternoon."

She winced. "Shane?"

"How'd you know?" he asked.

She sighed. "Shane's always had a bit of a chip on his shoulder. Wyatt was—and I guess still is—the big brother whose shoes have been hard to fill. He was the starting quarterback our sophomore year. Took the team to state twice. He was as good a student as he was an athlete, and now he's a uniformed town hero in the making. Shane got in with the wrong crowd in high school and sorta disappeared for a few years. Rumor has it that when he turned up in the county jail, his father gave him an ultimatum—clean up his act and get a job or he wouldn't post bail."

"Damn," Carter said. "How long ago was that?"

She raised her brows. "About a year ago."

He whistled. "That explains a lot. Shoot, I'm guessing I fanned the flames pretty good, then."

"Uh-oh." She took another sip of her beer. "What did you do?"

He shrugged. "Caught him sleeping on top of the truck when he was supposed to be scrubbing it down, so I dumped half the bucket of soapy water on him and told him he wasn't leaving until he cleaned up the mess." He scratched the back of his neck. "This sounds kind of crazy, but I think he might have been the internal applicant for lieutenant. It doesn't make any damned sense from an experience standpoint, but now that I know more about his history? I'm nothing more than a reminder to him of not measuring up."

"Oh, Carter," she said, resting a hand over his as she stifled a laugh. "You've got your work cut out for you, don't you?"

"The thing is," he said, "he and I aren't that different. I'm the youngest of three. I always looked up to my brothers. My father. But when I decided to go down a different path, it was like I lost any chance of filling the shoes I was expected to fill."

She squeezed his hand. "I think maybe you and Shane will be good for each other. You know what it's like to be in his place. Now you get to sort of be the big brother, to show him that the right path can still be his own path."

He flipped his hand over and laced his fingers with hers. "Does this mean you've changed your mind about getting involved with a firefighter?"

She shook her head, nodded, and then groaned.

"What kind of answer is that?" he asked with a laugh.

She slid off her stool and rounded the corner of the island so she was standing right in front of him.

"It's the kind where my heart and my head can't come to an agreement. I felt something with you that first night, Carter, and again up on the hill. I tried to ignore it. Tried to keep my heart safe by staying away, but here we are."

He nodded. "Here we are."

"Something died in me the day we lost Charlie. Loving and losing isn't just about romantic love, you know. No matter which way you slice it, the losing is hard. Too hard. I couldn't take that kind of hurt again."

"I know," he said. "All I can do is promise that if this thing with us turns to something real, I'll do my best not to hurt you."

She pressed her lips together and nodded. "Maybe while we're seeing where this goes, we pretend you have a really boring office job where you sit in a cubicle and crunch numbers at a computer."

He laughed. "Fine. But if I don't get to talk about my passion, you don't get to talk about yours." He wasn't changing who he was, just buying them time for her to be okay with it. Besides, after today, he needed a friendly face. He needed to be with the woman he hadn't stopped thinking about all week.

She scoffed at him imposing this rule on their game, but fair was fair. "But I just opened the shop. This is my fresh start, my future, my—"

He pressed a finger to her lips. "If I have to work in a cubicle, so do you."

She pouted, but there was a smile in her big brown eyes. "Okay. No shoptalk. For now."

She held out her free hand to shake, but instead he slipped both his hands around her wrists and draped her arms around his neck.

"I can think of a better way to seal that deal."

He dipped his head and kissed her, and it was everything he needed after the day he'd had. Her soft lips parted, and he felt her smile against him as he tasted what was far better than a cold beer at the end of a hard day.

"Evening, Lieutenant," she whispered.

"Evening, Ms. Serrano."

He slid his hands behind her thighs and lifted her up. She wrapped her legs around his waist and kissed him harder.

"Can we postpone that haircut?" she asked, her voice breathy and full of a need that matched his own.

"Yes, ma'am," he said, and carried her back down the hall. There were three open doors, and one he could tell just from glancing in was clearly her office or design space. So he strode through the only other door that wasn't the bathroom and carried her toward the bed.

He set her down on her feet. "Wait," he said.

She shook her head and slid her overalls off her shoulders, lifted her fitted tank top over her head, and undid her bra in seconds flat.

"Wow," he said, staring at her breasts. "While this is already way better than a haircut, why are we rushing, Ivy?" Even though he wasn't sure how much time he had with her— how long this would last before she decided she couldn't and *wouldn't* be with him—he wanted to take things slow.

She laughed and lifted his T-shirt up and over his shoulders, then wrapped her arms around his torso and stood on her tiptoes to kiss him again. "Why wait?" she asked. "We're two consenting adults who obviously both want the same thing." She paused and took a step back. "You do want me, don't you?" she asked, the sincerity in her voice too much for him to bear.

"God, Ivy, *yes*. So much it hurts." And likely would hurt for a spell until his body caught up with his brain, but he'd survive. "But I don't want to feel like we're rushing only to get each other out of our systems."

He reached for where she'd tossed his T-shirt on the bed and pulled it back on. For a brief second he wondered if she saw the scarred skin on his left side and simply ignored it or if she was too caught up in the moment to notice. There was also the scar on his right shoulder that had nothing to do with the accident, but she seemed to have missed that one, too. Or maybe it was all a part of their game—of pretending he wasn't fully who he was. That was why he was pumping the brakes. Playing make-believe was fine while they figured out what this was, but he wanted their feelings to catch up with their actions. When and if he and Ivy slept together, he wanted the game to be over.

"I'm sorry," she said, crossing her arms over her chest, and he hated that he'd made her feel self-conscious or guilty. "You're right. I just got caught up, and I—"

He wrapped his hands around her wrists and gently pulled her arms back to her sides.

"You play softball, right?" he said, the corner of his mouth turning up.

She nodded, and he dipped his head down to kiss one breast and then the other. She hummed softly, and he breathed in the scent of lavender and silently swore to himself. Ivy Serrano would eventually be his undoing, but tonight maybe they could simply *be*.

He straightened and grinned when he saw the smile spread across her face. "Well maybe no home run tonight, but I could hit a single or double."

She burst out laughing, then grabbed his right hand and placed it on her left breast, his thumb swiping her raised peak. She sucked in a breath before regaining her composure.

"I think you've already made it to second," she teased. "So what's next?"

He sat down on the bed and patted his knee. She climbed into his lap and wrapped her arms around his neck.

He kissed her and lowered her onto her back, his lips traveling to the line of her jaw, her neck, and the soft skin below. He savored each nibble and taste and watching her react to his touch.

"Who knows?" he asked. "If a good pitch comes along, I might hit a triple."

She pressed her palm over the bulge in his jeans and gave him a soft squeeze.

"Only if my team can, too."

He groaned as she squeezed again, then kissed her once more. "Fair is fair."

"But no home runs," she reaffirmed. "At least, not tonight."

"I predict it'll still be a good game."

"Evening, Lieutenant," she said, echoing her earlier greeting as he slipped a hand beneath the overalls that still hung at her hips. "Thanks for coming over tonight."

He nipped her bottom lip. "Evening, Ms. Serrano. Best night I've had in a long time."

And hopefully the first of many more to come.

CHAPTER SEVEN

∞

Ivy pulled her cap over her eyes and stared at the batter, then glanced at Casey, who was pitching. Her friend gave her a subtle nod, which meant she was sending the ball right over the plate, which in turn would mean a line drive to Ivy, who was covering first base. If she caught the ball, it would be the third out and a win for the Midtown Sluggers. If she didn't, the bases would be loaded, and a grand slam would sink them.

No pressure.

Not like this was the big leagues or anything, but the Main Street Loungers from Quincy—aptly named after the pub who sponsored them—were their biggest rival. The Loungers had creamed them the last time they played each other, and tonight the Sluggers were on their home turf.

Ivy breathed in the fresh scent of the ponderosa pines that rose in the distance. Even in the small residential park, you could see the tree-lined hills that gave Meadow Valley its name. It was more than her grief that had swallowed her up in Boston. It was the city itself. Beautiful as it was and steeped in history, Ivy had longed for the comfort of home—for the place where she and Charlie grew up, where she could feel closer to the brother she still missed.

She wasn't expecting a new reason to solidify Meadow Valley as the place she was meant to be. But there was Carter Bowen, climbing into the bleachers. He said he would come as soon as his shift ended—his boring cubicle office job shift—and there he was. They'd been seeing if this thing between them was real for three full weeks now. She counted the week they avoided each other in there because she'd spent each day thinking about him and wishing they *weren't* avoiding each other.

These days they were very much *not* avoiding each other. Whether it was at her house, his room at the inn, or the afternoon she found him waiting in her office after she closed the shop—he'd snuck back there while she was helping one last customer—they'd pretty much *not* avoided each other all over town.

She smiled at the thought. No one had hit any home runs yet, but they'd been enjoying the game nonetheless.

And now he was here, watching her play softball of all things, and all she could think about was how much brighter Meadow Valley seemed with him around. Others would say it had to do with the incessant sun and lack of rain, but not Ivy. She'd smiled more in the last three weeks than she had in the past two years, and the summer sun had nothing to do with it.

Oof! A burst of pain in her shoulder woke her from her stupor.

"Foul!" she heard the referee call.

She saw Carter bolt up from his seat and then sit back down, like his instinct was to go to her, and despite how much the impact had hurt, her stomach flip-flopped.

"Time out!" Casey called, and she jogged over to first base. "Are you okay?" she asked.

Ivy rolled her shoulder. It would need some ice, but she'd live. "Yeah. I'm fine."

Casey threw her hands in the air, which looked ridiculous, because one was covered by her glove and the other palmed a softball. "Then what the hell was that?" she whisper-shouted. "You could have caught that ball instead of acting as a shield for—I don't know—any stray lightning bugs who might have been in its path."

Ivy groaned. "I know. I'm sorry. I got distracted."

Casey glanced toward the small set of bleachers and then back at Ivy.

"Dreamboat's got you all bent out of shape, doesn't he?" she asked.

"No," Ivy said defensively. "I mean yes. I don't know."

Casey placed her glove on Ivy's shoulder, the one that, thankfully, wasn't throbbing.

"Look, you know there's nothing I want more than to see you smile like you used to. But you know what he does for a living, right? You know where he disappears to every forty-eight hours." Casey cut herself off before saying Charlie's name. Everyone in town pretty much did the same. Unless Ivy got tipsy on apple pie liqueur and toasted her dead brother, everyone played the avoidance game, including herself.

She had lived in the thick of her grief for over a year in Boston with her parents, Charlie's wife, and her niece, Alice. She wanted to leave that grief behind now that she was home and had a soon-to-be-thriving business.

Ivy cleared her throat. "You know how we pretend? Like you just did by not saying—by not saying his name. That's what Carter and I do. As far as I'm concerned, he has a really boring job where he sits in a cubicle and crunches numbers."

Casey's blue eyes softened. "Oh, Ives. Be careful, okay? I like Carter a lot, but I don't want you setting yourself up for heartbreak if you can't handle what he *really* does."

The ref alerted them that their time was up, and Ivy nodded.

"Let's win this damn game, okay?" Casey asked. "Drinks are on me if we do."

Ivy laughed. "I've never paid for a drink at Midtown in my entire life."

Casey shrugged. "Fine. If we lose, I'm starting your first tab."

Ivy narrowed her eyes at her best friend. "You wouldn't."

"Try me," Casey said. "Or catch the damn ball next time, and you'll won't have to see whether or not I'm bluffing." She adjusted her baseball cap and pivoted away, her assured strides carrying her back to the pitcher's mound.

"Make me pay for drinks," Ivy mumbled. "Yeah, right." But when the batter readied himself for the next pitch, Ivy squeezed her eyes shut for a brief moment and pushed everything out of her thoughts except one thing—the game.

When she opened her eyes, Casey was already winding up, so Ivy bent her knees, leaned toward the foul line, and held her mitt open and at the ready.

Again, Casey pitched the ball right over the plate, but this time the batter didn't foul. This time it was a line drive inside first. She barely had time to think before she dove over the plate, arm outstretched. The ball hit her hand hard, and she rolled to the ground, tucking it close to her chest. Nervous as hell to look, she sprang to her knees and glanced down. There it was, the softball that was now the game-ending catch.

She jumped to her feet and held the ball high in the air amid cheers from her team.

"Free drinks for life!" she exclaimed, and Casey barreled toward her, embracing her in a victory hug.

Over her friend's shoulders she saw the small gaggle of Midtown Sluggers supporters cheering in the stands, and among them a gorgeous firefighter cowboy who was striding onto the field with fierce determination.

She pulled out of her friend's embrace, and the two of them stared Carter down.

"I think you're about to get kissed," Casey said with a grin.

"Hell yes, I am."

Ivy jogged toward him, giddy, and jumped into his arms, wrapping her legs around his waist.

"Hell of a catch, Serrano," he said, his deep voice only loud enough for her to hear. And then he kissed her.

"I know," she said when they broke apart. "All I needed was to get the distractions out of my head."

He tilted his head back, and she saw his brows draw together.

"Distractions?" he asked.

She felt heat rush to her cheeks. "I know you said you were coming as soon as your shift ended, but it was the bottom of the seventh, and I figured your shift ran late, and—I don't know. I was really excited to see you. Guess I lost my train of thought."

He lowered her to the ground, then planted a kiss on her left shoulder.

She winced. "There's gonna be one hell of a bruise there by the end of the night."

He nodded. "Come home with me tonight, and I can help you ice it."

She grinned and slid her arms around his waist. "I think that can be arranged. Though I want to know when you're going to stop calling Pearl's inn home and find a more permanent residence."

The corner of his mouth turned up. "You afraid I'm going somewhere?"

Every time you're on a twenty-four-hour shift. Because as much as they pretended out loud, she never really forgot what he did. The only safety was in reminding herself that in her quiet little town, nothing much ever happened. The fire in her shop was the most Meadow Valley had seen in years, and she'd taken care of it with ease. So she convinced herself that it'd be at least a couple years more before something else happened, and other than responding to the station's paramedic services, Carter would be safe.

"Are you?" she finally asked. "Going somewhere?"

He shook his head. "Hope not. But the chief wants to make sure he made the right decision. Fire department is a close-knit team, but most of them are warming up to me. Barring any disasters in the next week, I should be ready to start looking for a real place to call home."

She rolled her eyes. "You make Meadow Valley sound so unwelcoming."

He laughed. "I didn't say the town, just the firehouse. When you're working in a life-and-death profession, trust is the most important thing and—"

He stopped short, likely noticing her wide eyes and maybe the fact she was holding her breath.

"Shoot," he said. "Ivy, it's just a figure of speech. You know every day I've been on duty has truly been about as boring as a cubicle job."

She bit her lip and nodded. Meadow Valley was safe. *He* was safe. But how long could she keep pretending that the potential for danger wasn't there? How long could she pretend that she wasn't afraid?

"Are you breathing?" he asked, brows raised.

She shook her head. Then she let out a breath.

They weren't going to have this conversation now. Not when things were going so well. Not when she couldn't imagine *not* kissing him again tonight or waking up in his arms tomorrow morning.

"Come on," she said, forcing a smile. "Drinks are on Casey."

They didn't last long at the tavern, even when the celebration moved outside to the tavern's back alley, where Casey's dad had set up a good old-fashioned charcoal barbecue and was grilling burgers and dogs. Not when Ivy knew she could be with Carter in his room. Just the two of them. First, though, they made a quick stop at the inn's kitchen, where Pearl was still cleaning up the remnants of the small restaurant's dinner service.

"Well this is a surprise," she said as Ivy and Carter slipped through the door. She opened her arms—and strode straight for Ivy.

"I heard you won the game!" she said.

Carter laughed. "Even with my own flesh and blood I'm still not the favorite around here."

Pearl gave Ivy another squeeze before releasing her. She waved Carter off.

"As soon as I can shout from the rooftop that my grand-nephew is the best lieutenant Meadow Valley could ask for, *then* you'll see some favoritism. Until then it goes to your girl, here."

Your girl. Ivy and Carter spending time together was no secret, but that was the first time anyone had verbalized them as a couple. And Ivy liked the sound of it even more than she'd anticipated.

Carter kissed his great-aunt on the cheek.

"In that case, can we get our star first base player a bag of ice? She took a pretty rough foul ball to the shoulder."

Ivy pulled her T-shirt sleeve over her shoulder, and Pearl gasped when she saw the half-moon purple that had already reared its ugly head.

"Oh, honey. Why didn't you say so in the first place?"

She grabbed a box of gallon-size plastic bags from a shelf over the sink and handed one of the bags to Carter. He headed toward the small ice machine that was next to the combination refrigerator-and-freezer and filled the bag.

"He knows better than I do how to ice a shoulder," Pearl told Ivy. "Did you know he was primed to be the starting quarterback his junior year of high school?"

Ivy's eyes widened as Carter finished at the ice machine and turned to look at her.

He smiled and shrugged, but both movements seemed forced. "Shoulder surgery saw to it that *that* never happened." He let out a bitter laugh. "Turns out a summer of football camp trying to prove myself to the coach combined with my dad putting me on tire changing duty at the shop was the perfect combination for a pretty bad tear in the rotator cuff."

He zipped the bag of ice shut and kissed his aunt again. "Need any help finishing up in here?"

She patted him on the cheek. "You kids head on up. I'm good here. Just need to take out the trash." She nodded toward a door that was propped open into the back alley. "And I'm sorry, sweetheart, if I brought up old wounds."

He shook his head. "You never have to apologize for anything. You're my lifeline, Aunt Pearl. If it weren't for you, I'd have never gotten out of Houston."

"Someday you and your daddy will see eye to eye without

expectations or disappointment getting in the way." She sighed. "Now go on before I *do* put you two to work."

She smiled at them both, then busied herself with rolling a trash can toward the kitchen's back door as if they were never there.

Carter turned to Ivy and raised his brows. "Let's go take care of you."

CHAPTER EIGHT

∞

Whoops. When he'd left for his shift yesterday evening, he hadn't bothered to make the bed. Or clean up the clothes strewn over the desk chair. Or hide the pile of leadership manuals he'd been poring over, since he'd had another setback with Shane earlier in the week, and of course Ivy gravitated straight to where they were spread out across the top of the desk.

"Sorry for the mess," he said. "But I made Pearl promise no inn employee would waste any time on my room when I get to live here rent free. I'm just not the best at keeping up with it myself."

She didn't respond, undeterred as she strode toward her destination.

"*How to Make Friends and Influence People? The Coaching Habit?*" She closed one book that he'd left open to the last page he'd read. Then she covered her mouth but was unable to stifle her laugh. "*The Leadership Secrets of Santa Claus?*"

He grabbed the book and held it protectively to his chest. "Hey. Don't knock it until you try it. Santa leads one of the biggest teams out there. He's gotta have some good secrets."

He tossed the book back down, set the bag of ice on the nightstand, then quickly neatened the bed and propped the pillows up so she'd be comfortable.

"Come here." He patted the bed, then readied the ice pack in his hands.

She glanced down at herself and tried brushing away the infield dirt from the right side of her body. "I'm filthy," she said. "I don't want to get dirt all over your bed. Got a T-shirt I can borrow?"

He moved to the dresser and opened a drawer. Then he tossed her a gray T that had HOUSTON ASTROS emblazoned on the chest in navy blue letters outlined in orange.

She narrowed her eyes. "I can't wear this in public, you know. And neither should you."

He laughed. "Lucky for you, I'm not planning on us leaving this room tonight. Are you?"

She shook her head. "Nope." Then she sauntered with the balled-up shirt into the bathroom. "Just need a few minutes to freshen up, Lieutenant. Maybe you can read some more about Santa's leadership secrets while you wait."

He crossed his arms defiantly. "Maybe I will."

She closed the door behind her.

He heard her turn the sink faucet on, so he collapsed into the desk chair and did exactly as she'd suggested. *Everything* seemed to be falling into place at the station except for Shane. No matter what method he used to try and connect with the guy, Shane always pushed back.

It had only taken seconds for him to get lost in the books, so he hadn't heard the faucet being turned off or the bathroom door opened. He didn't even know Ivy was behind him until her hands began massaging his shoulders.

"I think *you're* in need of more TLC than me, mister." She kneaded a knot below his shoulder blade, and he blew out a long breath.

"Good lord, that feels good," he said.

"Tell me about the books." She worked on all his knots and kinks, the physical manifestation of the pressure he'd felt at the station these last few weeks.

He shook his head, happy she couldn't see the defeat in his eyes.

"I don't get it," he said. "I've tried every approach with that kid. And before you tell me he's a grown man, he's twenty-two. That's barely legal and a kid in my book."

Ivy laughed. "I'm simply here to listen, Lieutenant. Not judge."

"Sorry," he said, scrubbing a hand over his face. "I'm at the end of my rope with him. He couldn't have been serious about going for lieutenant seconds after finishing his probation. But it feels like he has this grudge."

"Some people need someone else to take the blame for their mistakes or shortcomings—or fears. I'm not saying it's right, but it happens."

He spun his chair around to find Ivy standing there in nothing more than his T-shirt and her underwear.

"Well shoot, darlin'. That massage was something, but if I'd have known you were behind me wearing next to nothing, I'd have turned around a lot sooner."

She climbed into his lap, her legs straddling his torso. He slid his hands under the T-shirt and rested his palms on her hips.

"How's his big brother Wyatt doing?" she asked.

Carter shrugged. "Perfect. Best driver engineer I could ask for—should we ever get a real call."

Ivy's throat bobbed as she swallowed, but she didn't change the subject.

"Do you and the captain praise Wyatt for his good work?"

He nodded. "Hell yeah. Chief even singled him out last week to commend him on the CPR training he did for the local mother and toddler group."

Her forehead fell against his. "And what's Shane done to earn anyone's praise?"

Carter groaned. "I swear I've tried, Ivy. I've *tried* to use positive reinforcement with him, but it's like he's determined to buck authority just enough so that he doesn't get let go from the team."

She huffed out a laugh. "Because I'm guessing that dealing with you is a shade or two more bearable than dealing with his father. I'm not condoning his insubordination, but you're right. He's a kid who's still trying to find his place in a very small town that knows he messed up and that puts his brother on a pedestal every which way he turns. To him, you're simply one other person reminding him that he can't measure up, so why should he try?"

"I know how that feels." Carter had realized he was competing with his brothers for his father's approval. But once he chose his own path, his father made it clear that if anyone was keeping score, Carter had lost. Maybe this would be his in with Shane. Maybe it wouldn't. But somehow Ivy made sense of what Carter should have seen on his own.

She cradled his cheeks in her palms and brushed her lips over his. "You're good at what you do. You don't need to prove yourself to him, Carter."

"To who?" he asked.

She kissed his cheek. "To your father." She kissed the other. "To the chief." She kissed his lips. "To yourself." She lifted his T-shirt over his head. "To me," she added. Then she brushed a kiss over the scar on his shoulder. "Why didn't you tell me about football? About losing your spot on the team because of surgery?"

He slid his hands up her thighs until his thumbs hit the hem of her underwear.

"Because it wouldn't have mattered if I'd been able to play anyway. I'd have gotten kicked off the team because of my attendance eventually."

He let his eyes fall closed as she peppered his chest with kisses. Everything was better with her in his arms, with her warm skin touching his. The pain of the past fell further away each time he kissed her, each morning he woke up next to her, and each day he got closer to calling Meadow Valley his home for good.

"Did your dad know how important it was to you?" she asked.

He shook his head. "There wasn't a point. Either my brothers and I took over the garage or the business would eventually go under when my old man's arthritis wouldn't let him work anymore. He was a very proud, self-made man. And I respect that about him. But he can't get past seeing me as ungrateful for not wanting what he made."

She brushed her fingers through his hair. "It's okay that you chose a different path. What you're doing is something that not many men or women would or could. Be proud of yourself."

He let out a bitter laugh. "For my boring cubicle desk job?"

"No," she said, a slight tremor in her voice. "You risk your life for others. And there's nothing boring about that."

She ran her fingertips over the raised and knotted skin on the left side of his torso.

"I wasn't just talking about Shane when I said people

blame others for their own baggage. I've been blaming you, in a way, for my fear of once again losing someone I care about. It's not fair. If you're not ready to be proud of yourself, then know that *I'm* proud of what you've done, of what you continue to do."

He nodded. His throat was tight, and he wasn't sure what it would sound like if he spoke, but he needed to know what this meant. He needed to know where they stood as far as her not being able to deal with his job.

"But can you let go of the fear, Ivy? If you're really proud of me—of how well I do my job—can you accept who I am and what I do, so that this"—he motioned between them— "doesn't have to come to an end?"

A tear slid down her cheek, and she nodded. "I don't want to be afraid," she said. "Because I think I'm falling for you, Carter Bowen."

He grinned and lifted her up. Her legs squeezed tight around his waist, but the vise that seemed to be slowly squeezing his heart for the better part of a decade loosened.

He laid her down gingerly on the bed.

"I'm head over heels and ass over elbow and whatever other phrase you got that says how hard I'm falling for you, darlin'."

He glanced toward the melting bag of ice on the nightstand.

"We forgot about your shoulder."

She tugged him down to her. "Forget about it. I have another one that's in perfectly good condition."

He laughed. Then he lifted the Astros shirt up her torso and over her head. And there she was in nothing other than her underwear—bare and beautiful and falling for him. Everything in his life finally felt like it was clicking into place. She was simply the missing piece he hadn't known he was missing.

"I have a question for you," she added. "Actually, it's more of an observation."

"I'm all ears."

She smiled, and he swore he'd do whatever it took to make her smile the last thing he saw before he went to sleep and the first thing he laid eyes on each morning—for as long as she'd let him.

"I know Midtown won their big game and all, but I think it's *our* turn to hit a home run."

He laughed. "I think that's an excellent observation." Then he brushed a lock of hair out of her eye and stared at her.

"You're so beautiful," he said. "Here..." He kissed each breast. "And *here*." He kissed the skin above her heart. "I didn't plan on you, Ivy Serrano. But I sure am glad your refrigerator cord caught fire—*and* that you were able to put it out so quickly."

He rolled onto his side, and their legs entwined as their lips met, as if this were a choreographed dance they'd learned years ago.

"I sure didn't plan on a cowboy fireman turning my life upside down. I didn't know what it would be like to come home, with my parents in Boston and Charlie gone for good. The past several months have been real hard. And then you showed up."

She kissed him, her breasts warm against his chest. And it was simply right—she and he like this.

"And," she said, "you're wearing too many clothes."

Almost as soon as she had said the words, his jeans and boxer briefs were no more.

He slid her panties to her ankles and over her feet, and she hooked a leg over his.

"I don't want anything between us tonight," she said, wrapping a hand around his hard length.

"But—" He was all for what she was suggesting, but after waiting all this time, he wanted to be careful. Tonight was the start of something bigger than he'd imagined, and he wanted to get everything right.

"I'm on the pill," she said. "Have been for years. And I haven't been— It's only you, Carter. Just *you*."

He knew what she meant on a literal level but wondered if she felt it, too—how hard he was falling for her, how he couldn't fathom it being anyone other than her ever again.

He buried himself inside her, hoping to fill her with all that he was feeling but couldn't yet say.

She arched against him and gasped. He kissed her hard, and she rolled on top of him. He watched her move in a rhythm that was all their own. And he wondered how so much could change in such a short time.

He always thought he was running from a father who couldn't accept his choices, but maybe he was running to her all along.

He woke the next morning before she did, their bodies still tangled and her back against his chest.

He kissed her neck, and she hummed softly, but it was a dreamy hum, one that assured him she was still asleep. Still, it couldn't hurt to check.

"Ivy," he whispered. "You awake?"

She didn't stir.

He knew this was right—that *she* was right. So why deny it any longer.

"Maybe this is too soon, but I'm a man of certainty, and I'm certain that I'm not falling for you, darlin'. I'm not falling because I already fell." He kissed the softball-shaped bruise on her shoulder. "I love you, Ivy."

He wasn't ready to say it to her face, not when a tiny part of him kept whispering that eventually his job would spook her and this would be over. It was better like this, not knowing what she'd say in return. Because if the other shoe dropped, he wanted to be prepared. He could handle her walking away if he never knew that she loved him, too. But if he knew and she still left, that might downright ruin him.

Maybe he risked his life doing what he did for a living, but he realized now that the one thing scarier than walking into a burning building was risking his heart.

CHAPTER NINE

∞

Ivy closed the store at four, since business had been slow. Plus, happy hour at Midtown started at five on Thursdays, and most folks went early to claim their preferred seats, especially those who liked to sit closest to the free appetizers.

"Ow!" Casey said when Ivy accidentally poked her with her hemming pin.

"Sorry," Ivy said with her lips pressed tight around the blunt ends of the remaining pins, so it sounded more like *Srry.*

"I get that you're nervous and all about putting this design on display, but if you poke your very human mannequin one more time, she's quitting. She didn't sign up for acupuncture, *and* she has to get her butt behind the bar soon."

Ivy spit the pins into her palm and sighed.

"Sorry. This is—it's more than the design. It's symbolic, you know? If I can look at the dress in the store—on an actual mannequin who doesn't complain—it'll mean I'm okay. It'll mean that I can remember the good things about Charlie, about growing up here, and be happy instead of—" She trailed off before finishing. Because she would be a horrible person if she said what came next.

"I know," Casey said with more understanding in her voice. She held out a hand, and Ivy grabbed it, letting her friend give her a reassuring squeeze. "It's okay to be angry."

Leave it to her best friend to know exactly what Ivy was thinking.

"He should have known better," Ivy said softly, the tears pooling in her eyes. "They train to know when the building is safe to enter and when they need to get out. He should have gotten out. He should have thought about his wife and his baby and his family and..."

Ivy hiccupped and sobbed. She'd never said any of this aloud, not to her parents or Charlie's wife. She'd grieved as best she could, but she'd never admitted the ugly part of it, the irrational blame she placed on the brother she'd lost.

"I'm the worst," she said. "You don't need to tell me because I already know."

Casey sat down carefully in Ivy's office chair and patted the top of the desk, for her friend to sit. Ivy nodded and complied.

"Hey," Casey said, taking both of Ivy's hands now. "You know this is normal, right? The anger part? I know you've accepted that Charlie's gone, but I think you skipped right over this part. I should have stayed longer in Boston after the funeral. You kept it together for your parents and Allison, but you didn't get to fall apart with your best friend like you should have."

Ivy choked out a tearful laugh. "You mean like now?" She grabbed a tissue from the box on her desk and blew her nose. Then she grabbed two more to try to dry her tear-stained face. "You had a business to run. I never expected you to stay. I never expected *me* to stay as long as I did, but I couldn't leave until I knew they were all okay..." She paused for a long moment. "Or until I could come back here, knowing home would never be the same." She blew out a long breath. "So, I'm really not the worst?"

Casey smiled sadly and shook her head. "Do you really blame your brother for doing a job not many are cut out to do?"

Ivy shook her head.

"See?" Casey said. "Not the worst. This is actually a really good step, Ives. I think you're finally starting to move past the worst of it."

Ivy worried her bottom lip between her teeth, and Casey's brows furrowed.

Once she said what she was about to say out loud, it would be real. Like *really* real. And real with Carter Bowen still scared her half to death.

"There's something else you're not telling me." Casey narrowed her eyes. "This is about more than Charlie, isn't it? *Spill*," she added. "You have ten more minutes before I turn into a pumpkin and this badass dress changes back to jeans and a T-shirt."

Ivy laughed. Casey always could make her feel better about any situation. Venting her anger was cathartic, as far as taking a productive step past her grief, but it wasn't the only thing she'd been thinking about.

"Did I mention that Carter said he loved me?" she asked softly.

"What?" Casey threw her arms in the air. Then she yelped as a bodice pin scraped along her skin. "Ow!"

"Sorry!" Ivy cried, fumbling to fix the pin.

"Screw the apologies!" Casey said with a grin. "Tell. Me. *Everything*."

Her pulse quickened at having said what *he'd* said out loud. She'd sat on the information all week, not sure what to do with it. Hearing those words from him had been everything—shooting stars, fireworks, and a lifetime supply of fried pickles. She'd wound up exactly where she never wanted to be, except for one minor detail... Ivy loved Carter, too. And the realization solidified how much she had to lose if anything ever happened to him.

Ivy cleared her throat. "I spent the night at the inn with him after the game last week," she started.

"Bow-chica-bow-bow," Casey sang.

She rolled her eyes even though she was grateful for a moment of levity. "Yes. I'm a woman in my mid-twenties who has sex."

Casey waggled her brows. "Yes, but unless you stopped telling your best friend *everything*, you're a woman in her mid-twenties who up until meeting Lieutenant Dreamboat had not had sex in quite some time *and* who was taking things slowly with said Dreamboat."

"Nine months," Ivy admitted. "But who's counting? *Anyway.* If you want your best friend to tell you everything, you're going to need to stop interrupting." She paused, brows raised, and waited. Casey made a motion of zipping her lips, so Ivy went on.

"It was the next morning," she continued. "I was sort of asleep, sort of not. So I'm ninety-nine percent sure I didn't dream it. But he said something along the lines of knowing it was probably too early to say it but that he was a man of certainty and that he was certain he loved me."

Casey stared at her, eyes wide and mouth hanging open.

"You can talk now," Ivy said.

"Phew! Okay, first things first. I think it's reasonable to

fall in love with someone in a few weeks. Plus, we're talking you, and you're pretty damn loveable."

"Thank you very much," Ivy said with a grin.

"But the part of the story that's missing is what you said back to him."

Ivy winced.

Casey's eyes narrowed. "Oh my God, Ivy Serrano. Did you pretend you were still sleeping?"

If it was possible for her wince to get bigger, Ivy's did.

"What if I dreamed it?" she asked.

Casey sighed. "You didn't dream it."

"Well, what if he only told me because he thought I was sleeping and didn't *really* want to tell me for *real* for real."

Casey shook her head. "I don't even know what you just said so why don't you tell me this—do you love *him*?"

Ivy sucked in a steadying breath.

"Maybe?"

"*Serrano*..."

"I don't know if I've ever *been* in love before. So how would I know?"

"*Ivy*," Casey said this time, her patience definitely growing thin.

"What if you're wrong and I'm not past the worst of what happened to Charlie? What if I *have* fallen for him and he—?" She couldn't say it. It was one thing for Casey to tell her she was moving past Charlie's death. It was a whole other to be brave enough to risk her heart in an entirely new and terrifying way.

Casey crossed her arms. "You can be scared, Ives. But you have to be able to answer the question. So riddle me this, Batgirl. When you think of your life without him, how do you feel?"

Ivy's eyes burned with the threat of fresh tears.

Casey laughed. "Oh, honey. It's worse than I thought. You fell *hard*, didn't you?"

Ivy nodded as the truth took hold. "I love him, Case. I *love* Carter Bowen."

"Carter Bowen—who is a firefighter." Casey placed a hand on Ivy's leg and gave her a soft squeeze. "Can you handle that?"

Ivy swallowed and placed her hand over her friend's. "I worked it out in my head. We're not a big city like Boston. My dad made it to retirement here without any major injuries. Meadow Valley is safe, which means Carter is safe, even if he's a firefighter."

"And you'll support him if he has to do something you don't deem safe?"

Ivy nodded. She could do this if she held on to her logic—no matter how convoluted—that she couldn't lose Carter like she lost Charlie. Not here.

"I love him," she said again.

"Then you better finish putting this dress together and tell him," Casey said.

"I haven't even seen him all week. I think he's been avoiding me. I went looking for him at Pearl's after his first shift since that night, and she said he'd decided to stay at the station for the week—iron some things out with his unit." It could have been true. He could be working on the situation with Shane. Or he could be taking extra shifts to keep from running into her.

Casey raised a brow. "Honey, the man's in love with you and has no idea if you feel the same way. Even the bravest of the brave get a little gun-shy when it comes to matters of the heart. Luckily, *you* can fix that."

Ivy grinned. "Okay." Then she grabbed her phone and hammered out a quick text to Carter.

Meet me at Midtown tonight?

The three dots appeared immediately, and she held her breath.

Sure. Off at six.

Great. Can't wait to see you.

She waited several seconds, but there was no response after that. It didn't matter. He was coming, and she was going to tell him what she should have said that morning.

Ivy shrugged. "Looks like I'm spilling my heart out at six o'clock. Wish me luck."

Casey waved her off. "You got this, Ives. Home run. Or is it a slam dunk?"

Ivy snorted. "Let's go with basketball for this one."

She finished the final pinning and stitching in record time, fueled by the adrenaline of what she'd been afraid to admit to herself all week. When she was done, she and Casey headed to the tavern to celebrate with a drink and whatever was left of the appetizers while Ivy waited for Carter.

She tried not to look nervous when the clock hit 6:30 p.m. and he wasn't there, *nor* had she heard from him. At 6:45, she started to worry. And at 7:00 she was near to panicking. Not that she thought anything had happened to him. She'd have heard sirens if there had been any sort of emergency. But the kind of panic that said even without telling him how she felt, she'd somehow spooked him. Or maybe he had realized she'd heard what he said and was furious she hadn't reciprocated.

"Hey," Casey said from the other side of the bar. "You *can* call *him*, you know."

"Mmm-hmm," she said, popping a fried pickle into her mouth. Because a stressed-out girl in love needed some comfort food. "Or I could eat my weight in pickles. I think I'm going with option number two." Because wouldn't that be just her luck—to realize she was in love with the guy exactly when he realized he'd made a *huge* mistake saying he loved her?

Casey snagged the basket of fried goodness before Ivy could grab another bite.

"*Hey*!" Ivy said, trying to swipe her prized possession back. But Casey held it over her head. The only way Ivy was getting it back was if she climbed onto the bar and stole it back.

She shrugged. She wasn't above such a move.

Ivy was midclimb when Casey whisper-shouted, "He's here!"

Ivy rolled her eyes. "I want my damn pickles!"

"Ivy?" she heard from behind her. "What are you doing?"

She winced but not before grabbing her food back. Then she slid not-so-gracefully back onto her stool.

She spun to see Carter still in uniform, brows furrowed.

"Just taking back what was stolen from me." She held up her spoils. "Pickle?"

He shook his head, his jaw tight as his confusion morphed to something graver. She forgot her panic and grabbed his hand. "Hey, are you okay? I thought I'd see you at six and was starting to worry."

He climbed onto the stool next to hers.

"Here," Casey said, sliding a mug of beer his way. "No offense, but you look like you need this."

He shook his head. "None taken." And he took a sip.

"I spent the last hour in the chief's office, trying to figure out how to fix things," he said.

Ivy forgot about her fried pickles. "What's broken?"

Carter blew out a breath. "Morale? My team's faith in me? It turns out there have been several complaints turned in about me this week, all pertaining to me not knowing how the station runs and questioning the chief hiring someone based purely on nepotism."

"Nepo-*what*?" Casey asked. When Ivy opened her mouth to answer, she held up her hand. "I know what the word means. I just don't get how it relates, unless Lieutenant Dreamboat is the captain's or chief's long-lost son."

Ivy's eyes widened. "We're calling him Lieutenant Dreamboat to his face now?"

Casey popped a piece of pickle into her mouth. "We are *now*!"

Ivy turned back to Carter. "Okay, so someone found out about you being Pearl's nephew. I really don't get how that's nepotism. Pearl isn't a high-ranking firefighter or anything like that. She put in a good word, and you got the job."

Carter shook his head.

"Turns out I'm not the only one keeping a low profile as far as my Meadow Valley connections. Aunt Pearl is *dating* the chief."

If Ivy had been sipping her beer, this would have been her first ever spit take, which wasn't the kind of thing a girl wanted to do *before* she and her significant other officially declared those three little words to each other. *Win him over and* then *start embarrassing yourself while eating and drinking.*

"I didn't know Pearl dated. Period," Ivy said.

"Go Pearl," Casey said. "Not only dating but a younger man, too. I want to be her when I grow up."

Carter sighed. "She took it so hard when my uncle passed away. I don't think any of us ever thought of her being with anyone else. Not that she doesn't deserve to be happy. It was just sort of a shock. And of all people..."

"Wait, wait, wait," Ivy said. "Put a pin in the whole nepotism thing for a second. Pearl's husband passed away a decade ago."

Carter nodded.

"Does that mean you were here for the funeral? I mean—I'm retroactively sorry for your loss. But were you here?"

He nodded again, and the set of his jaw loosened as realization set in. "He was my mother's favorite uncle. My brothers and I liked him, too. We drove out with my mom and my grandma for the funeral."

Ivy's eyes widened. "*I* was at that funeral. I mean, the whole town was, because that's small town life for ya, but we were both there."

The corner of his mouth turned up, the first hint of a smile since he walked through the door. Something about it made Ivy's breath catch in her throat.

"You didn't wear black," he said matter-of-factly, and she shook her head. "You had on a blue dress with a sunflower print. And I thought, *What is up with this girl who doesn't know anything about funeral etiquette?*"

She laughed, and her cheeks filled with heat.

"It was the first dress I ever made," she said. And the one that inspired her latest design, the one she hoped to actually finish and display in her shop window. "My mom loved planting flowers, and she taught Charlie and me. Our favorite was the sunflowers. Did you know that when they're young, before they bloom, they actually follow the sun across the sky each day?"

"Heliotropism," Carter said with a self-satisfied grin. "Solar tracking." Her eyes widened, and he shrugged. "I had to take a lab science in college. Botany was the only one that fit my schedule."

He knew about sunflowers. He *saw* her in her first dress.

Her stomach flipped. Every new thing she learned about Carter Bowen made it harder to resist the connection she felt with him.

She nodded. "I thought there was nothing more beautiful, and I wanted to wear something beautiful for Pearl. But it was more than that. I liked the idea of the new buds repositioning themselves each night so they faced east again. I admired their determination—their fierce sense of direction." Direction Ivy wanted so badly now that she was home. She wanted to face the grief and move past it. She wanted to wake up in the morning with the sun shining on her face instead of under the cloud where she'd lived for more than two years. "Pearl loved it, by the way." Ivy cleared her throat. "It's where my *thing* for flowers comes from. Haven't been able to bring myself to plant my own garden, but I add a rose here, a lily there—when it suits the design."

"I have no doubt Aunt Pearl loved it," Carter said. His brows drew together. "But I can't believe that was *you*."

Casey waved a hand between them. "Hell*oo*. Before you two start talking about nonsense like *meant to be* or *star-crossed lovers* or whatever, can we get back to the *real* story so I can help actual paying customers? What the heck happened with the chief?"

Carter blinked, and the far-off look in his blue eyes that could have swallowed Ivy whole disappeared.

"Someone who knows about Pearl and the chief also knows about me being Pearl's nephew, and there's a petition going around to get me removed as lieutenant. There are quite a few signatures already."

Ivy gasped. "They can't actually *do* that, can they?"

Carter shook his head. "Technically, no. Family members are absolutely allowed to work in the same company."

"Right," Casey said. "Like Wyatt and Shane."

"Oh no," Ivy said. "*Shane*."

"There's no nepotism clause in the handbook," Carter went on. "But in a job like this, morale is everything. If anyone thinks I got the job because of favoritism from the chief, then they might not trust that I'm up to the task. And if my presence is bringing down the morale of the whole company, then me staying on could be more detrimental than it's worth. Chief won't say who started the petition, but I took a job someone on the inside wanted, and that someone doesn't want me around..."

Casey shook her head. "You really think it was Shane? I mean, the guy carries around resentment like no one's business, but that seems a little over the top even for him."

Ivy winced. "I don't know. He and Carter have been butting heads since the day Carter stepped foot in the station. We were just as shocked when Shane ended up in jail. Maybe this isn't out of character at all."

Carter took another long, slow pull of his beer. "At the end of the day, it doesn't matter who it is if I can't win over the trust of my company."

There was a finality in his voice that made the hair on the back of Ivy's neck stand up.

"So, what does this mean?" she asked.

"It means I'm on leave for the weekend. Captain's taking over my crew. And by the end of next week, I may be out of a job. Leaving Houston for Meadow Valley made sense not simply for the job but also because I had family here. I could find another station in a different city or state, but at my age, a résumé that shows me having already left *two* stations? That doesn't give me a very reliable track record. If I haven't burned a bridge, I could ask for my job back in Houston. But if they say no..." He let out a bitter laugh. "There's always my father's auto shop. I bet he'd love me coming home with my tail between my legs, begging for what I told him I didn't want anymore." He finished his beer in one final gulp, then slapped some bills on the bar.

"Oh you don't—" Casey started, but Carter interrupted.

"It's way less than what I owe you since I got here, but I don't want to fuel the notion that I take handouts. Thanks, anyway," he said. He turned to Ivy. "I'm not gonna be good company tonight." Then he kissed her, his lips lingering on hers even after the kiss ended. "But I sure am happy I got to do that," he finally added. "I'm glad you texted."

Then he stood, pivoted toward the door, and left.

Ivy sat there, dumbfounded, staring at the door for several long moments after it closed behind him. She'd been so scared to lose Carter in the worst way possible that she never had considered him having to leave town.

"You okay?" Casey asked, breaking the silence.

"No," she said, turning to face her friend. "Case, what if he leaves?"

Casey nodded. "What if you go out there and tell him how you feel and see if that makes a difference? Maybe if you let him know you're willing to fight for him, he'll fight for a way to stay. All I know is *not* telling him how you feel will make you always wonder what would have happened if you did."

Ivy's eyes widened. "Are we still talking about me and Carter, or does this have something to do with Boone Murphy's recent engagement?" Ivy had been so wrapped up in everything Carter that she'd forgotten Casey's high school sweetheart was marrying someone else.

Casey rolled her eyes. "You're deflecting, Ives. What this is *about* is not regretting a missed opportunity. If you love the guy, *tell* him. It's as simple as that."

She swallowed the lump in her throat. Casey was right. She *loved* Carter, and he loved her. Once they said it aloud for real, everything would be different, wouldn't it? They could figure this job thing out together.

"I said I was going to tell him, which means I have to go tell him."

Casey nudged her shoulder. "Then get off your ass and go do the thing instead of talking about doing the thing."

She glanced down at Carter's cash on the counter, then back at her friend. "You're okay if I don't make a similar monetary gesture, right? I'll cover your next closing shift for free."

Casey raised her brows. "Yeah, you will. Now *go!*"

Ivy hopped off her stool and bounded toward the door just as she started to smell smoke. She pushed the tavern door open to the blaring sound of sirens filling the street. Along with it came the ringing of the firehouse bell, which meant only one thing.

For the first time in years, there was a real fire in Meadow Valley. And even though he was off duty, amid the ensuing chaos she saw Carter Bowen running across the street, straight toward the firehouse.

CHAPTER TEN

This was bad. He could already smell the smoke, and the air had taken on the type of haze that meant whatever was burning was feeding a fire that was growing.

"Carter!" he heard from behind him, and spun to see Ivy running toward him.

"I have to go, Ivy!" he called back.

She was out of breath when she stopped in front of him. "But you don't," she insisted. "You're—you're off duty. Lieutenant Heinz and his team will take care of whatever's happening."

"Ivy. You don't have to be a firefighter to know that *whatever's happening* probably needs more than one crew. Even when I'm off duty, I'm still on call. And I'm answering the damn call."

She pressed her hands to his chest as the first emergency vehicle pulled out of the station. The engine would be next, which meant he needed to hurry.

"Please," she said, her brown eyes shining. He wasn't

sure if it was the threat of tears or because of the smoke in the air.

"Are you asking me *not* to do my job? Because I thought we were past this. I thought you were okay with what I did." Yet he didn't really trust her, did he? Or he'd have said how he felt to her face rather than when she was still asleep.

"And I thought you were done trying to prove yourself. You just told me you were on leave for the weekend, which means you don't *have* to go. I can't—" She swiped underneath one eye. "When you said you might have to go back to Houston, I knew right then that I'd beg you to stay, that I couldn't lose you. And now?" She pressed her lips together and shook her head. "I can't do it, Carter. I can't watch you run head on into a life-threatening situation when there are plenty of others who are prepared to do so. It's selfish of me to ask, and I have no right to do so, but I am begging you, Carter—begging you to stay *safe*."

The chief's voice sounded on his radio. "All available crews report. I repeat, all available crews report."

"I have to go, Ivy," he said firmly. "And you're wrong. I *do* need to prove that I'm what this company needs, that I'm capable of leading my crew into any situation and bringing them all home—safe, myself included. *This* is what I do. We're not tying up horses on the top of a hill and acting like what's down here doesn't exist. I can't pretend for you anymore."

"I love you," she said. It wasn't another plea or a last-ditch effort to get him to stay. He could hear the sincerity in the tremor of her voice. And God, he *knew* what she'd already lost and how she'd never quite be over it. It was the same for him with Mason. But this was who he was. This was what he did. He couldn't be what she needed if that meant sitting on the sidelines when there were lives at stake.

"I love you, too," he finally said face-to-face, like he should have all along. "And I understand that this is too much for you. But I need you to understand that it's what I'm meant to do."

He kissed her, tasting the salt of her tears on her lips.

"Maybe, after you've had more time, and they haven't shipped me back to Texas..."

She said nothing after his pause, and he wouldn't finish the rest. Because even though he was done pretending for her, maybe he could do it for himself. Maybe he could pretend for tonight that they hadn't said those three words and then followed it up with a kiss that meant good-bye.

He pivoted toward the firehouse and strode up the walkway and inside to where he was met with the type of organized chaos he was meant to control. The chief saw him and nodded, so Carter started barking orders as he jogged into the engine room and suited up just in time to hop on.

All he had to prove was that he was bringing everyone on this crew home safe tonight. Then she'd see.

* * *

The street was filled with people by the time Ivy woke from her daze and turned around.

Patrons spilled out of Midtown Tavern, and she started to cross back that way. But then the engine's siren roared as the truck pulled out of the firehouse, around the corner, and onto First Street, causing her to jump back onto the curb. She stared at Wyatt in the driver's seat, then past him to where a pair of bright blue eyes stared back. Carter sat in the passenger seat, his jaw set and determined.

Her stomach roiled, and she thought she might be sick.

When the engine passed, she saw Casey coming toward her, her face pale.

"It's Mrs. Davis's house," she said. "The whole thing is up in flames."

"Oh my God," Ivy said. "Is she still inside?"

Casey shook her head, and for a second Ivy was relieved. But then Casey said, "I don't know. A neighbor called 911, not her." She sniffled. "Jessie called. She's on paramedic duty and said she'll give us an update as soon as she can. This is really bad, Ives."

Ivy hugged her friend. Mrs. Davis lived up the hill from Ivy's childhood home. She was like a second mother to her and Casey. As far as they knew, the woman had never married. At least she never said she had. But she was always adopting rescues from Dr. Murphy, the vet just outside of town, which meant she was never really alone. Today that would mean three cats, two dogs, and a cockatoo.

"I told him not to go," Ivy said, squeezing her friend tighter. "I told him I loved him and that he didn't have to go."

Casey stepped back, her hands still on Ivy's shoulders. "Charlie was in an office building whose roof collapsed. This isn't the same thing. It's Meadow Valley. Tragedies don't happen *in* Meadow Valley."

"It's a *fire,* Case. A fire brought that roof down and trapped my brother. Houses have roofs, too." She was arguing like a petulant child. She *knew* she was. But Casey didn't get it. *No* one seemed to get it. "He was my best friend, and he left us. Me, my parents, Allison, and the baby. He left us, and for what?"

Casey swiped her thumbs under Ivy's eyes, then crossed her arms. "My sister's on the scene of that very same fire. Am I scared? Hell yes, I'm scared. But there's a reason Jessie's there instead of me. She's *trained* for this, and because of *her* training and Carter's and the whole company's, Mrs. Davis and her home have their best chance."

Ivy swallowed. "I'm sorry. I'm the worst. I know you're worried about Jessie, and—"

"How many people lived that day because Charlie did his job?" Casey interrupted.

Ivy shook her head.

"How many, Ives?"

Ivy squeezed her eyes shut. She'd thought leaving Boston and coming home to start fresh would mean that her grief stayed out east. But it followed her back to Meadow Valley and reared its ugly head without so much as a warning. And it made her forget how good Charlie was at his job—how safe his company was under Charlie's leadership. How even when he lost his own life, he saved so many others.

"Seven," Ivy finally said. "Seven civilians lived because Charlie was an expert firefighter." But even experts can't plan for every contingency. Charlie's company got him out in time so that he didn't have to die alone. His closest buddies rode with him in the ambulance and stayed with him at the hospital until the end. It was the one piece of the story she and her family held on to like a life raft. Charlie wasn't alone.

The sound of sirens clamored in the air once more. This time it was the ambulance coming back from the opposite direction. It whizzed by them at a speed not normally seen on their quiet little street. Then it rounded the corner in the direction of the highway and likely the hospital.

Ivy's stomach sank.

"It's probably Mrs. Davis in there with my sister, but Jessie hasn't sent any updates," Casey said, and for the first time Ivy detected a note of panic in her friend's voice. "There's no way to really get any answers unless..."

"Unless we get as close as we can to Mrs. Davis's house." Ivy didn't think she had it in her to see the danger into which Carter had walked. But the not knowing felt even worse.

"Let's go," Ivy said.

They headed down the street, following the throng of curious folks who were likely trying to get close enough to marvel at the spectacle. One person who wasn't following the herd, though, was the older woman standing on the front porch of the inn.

Pearl.

She locked eyes with Ivy and gave her a reassuring nod. "I wouldn't have brought my nephew here if I didn't know he was damned good at his job." She stared wistfully down the street, and Ivy suddenly remembered about Pearl and the chief. Pearl had already lost one great love of her life. There was no way the universe would let that happen again or be so cruel as to take her nephew, too. That's what Ivy hoped and what she guessed gave Pearl her stoic strength.

"I'll text you when we get word about any of them," Ivy said.

Pearl nodded again, and Ivy and Casey kept on.

Ivy's heart thudded in time with the rhythm of her feet pounding the concrete. But all she could think about was what Carter had said about life-and-death situations and needing the trust of your team.

Maybe he was good at his job, but who had his back when there was a list of signatures who wanted to send him packing? And how could she let him go, thinking that he couldn't rely on *her*?

She started walking faster until she was in a slow jog and then close to a sprint.

She had Carter Bowen's back. If no one else did, it had

to be her. Because though she was terrified for him, she also loved him. He needed to know he wasn't alone in this. She would be there. No matter what.

It was only minutes before she reached the blockade in front of Mrs. Davis's house, but it felt like hours.

"Hey!" Casey called. And Ivy turned around to see her friend halfway up the hill, her hands on her knees as she struggled to catch her breath. "What the hell was that, Flo Jo?" She lumbered the rest of the way until she made it to Ivy's side. Casey slung her hand over Ivy's shoulders and held up a finger while she tried to get her breathing in check. "Seriously," she finally said. "We run bases, not long-distance uphill."

An earsplitting crack followed by a crash cut their conversation short. Both startled and pivoted toward the sound. Half the town stood in front of them, so they could barely see over everyone's head. But they could *feel* the heat, the evidence that not too far away, Mrs. Davis's house burned.

"Screw it," Ivy said and grabbed Casey's hand, tugging her forward. "Excuse us!" she said as she pushed through the crowd. "Coming through! Sorry!" she cried as she stepped on someone's toes. But she wasn't stopping. Not until she made it to the barricade and got some answers. All the while, she held tight to Casey's hand, and Casey did the same with hers.

"Oh my God," Casey said when they got to the front.

Ivy couldn't speak. Her hand flew over her mouth, but no sound escaped.

Mrs. Davis's bright blue bungalow stood there at the top of her driveway like it always had. The front porch—decorated with potted plants and flowers, looked exactly the same. If you only stared at the porch and didn't look up, it was the same house Ivy had known for almost thirty years.

But they did look up, and out of the white-trimmed attic window poured livid orange flames. The place was burning from the top down.

Two firefighters controlled the front of the hose. Actually, one manned the hose while the other held him or her steady by the shoulders. She realized that she'd never seen her father or brother in action, had never truly understood what it meant to work as a team the way they did.

The chief rounded the back of the engine and spoke into his radio. When he finished his conversation, Ivy waved wildly, hoping to get his attention.

"Chief Burnett! Over here!" she cried. She'd known the chief most of her life. He and her father were rookies together. If anyone could ease her mind about what was going on inside Mrs. Davis's house, it was him.

Casey grabbed her arm and yanked it down. "I know how badly you want some information, but I think he's a little busy, Ives."

The chief looked up, though, and strode toward the barricade.

"Who was in the ambulance?" Ivy blurted. "Is Mrs. Davis okay? Is—are all your firefighters safe?"

He scratched the back of his neck.

"Mrs. Davis is being treated for smoke inhalation and some minor burns. Looks like she was going through some old boxes in her attic and dozed off while a scented candle was lit. We're guessing one of the animals knocked it over, and once the drapes caught—"

"The animals!" Ivy said. "Are they out?"

The chief blew out a breath. "It may not look like it, but we have the blaze contained. It's gonna be a while before it's out, though. Lieutenant Bowen and a small team are inside, trying to round up the animals."

Ivy had joked about Carter having to rescue one of Mrs. Davis's cats from a tree. The irony of this situation, though, was far from amusing. It was as dangerous as anything Meadow Valley had ever been.

She nodded and tried to swallow the knot in her throat. "What—what was that sound? Is the structure stable enough for them to be inside?"

"One of the ceiling beams in the attic was torn free." He glanced back toward the house. "We've got every available man and woman on the job. Got another engine from Quincy running a hose with some of our crew from the back and a second and third ambulance at the ready in front of our truck. We assess the situation as best we can, making predictions on what we know about the fire and how we believe it will behave. But there's always risk."

Casey squeezed Ivy's hand and pointed toward the house. "Look!"

A parade of firefighters exited the front door, one carrying Mrs. Davis's cocker spaniel, Lois. Another had a box of kittens. And the third held Butch Catsidy, the three-legged foster cat she'd had since he was a kitten—and had kept when no one adopted him. The crowd of onlookers applauded, but Ivy knew Mrs. Davis's beagle was still missing. Frederick was old and prone to hiding, and he was no doubt burrowed somewhere he thought was safe.

A voice sounded on the chief's radio, and he turned his back to listen and respond.

Ivy let go of Casey's hand and pulled out her phone and fired off a quick text to Pearl.

With the chief. He's outside. Mrs. Davis at the hospital but will be okay. No word on anyone else yet.

She couldn't bring herself to say Carter's name. The not knowing was making it hard to breathe. She started slipping her phone back into her pocket but then changed her mind. Even though there was no way he'd see it now, she hoped with everything she had he'd see it soon. So she brought up her last text exchange with Carter and typed.

I'm here. If you'll let me, I will always be here for you. I love you.

She pocketed her phone just as the chief turned back around.

"They found Frederick," he said.

Ivy breathed out a sigh of relief. But it was short-lived.

"He's under Mrs. Davis's bed. Two of them are trying to coax him out while another keeps watch on the soundness of the structure." He shook his head. "I wanted everyone off the second floor by now." He pulled his radio out again. "Lieutenant, you have two minutes to get your team out of there, dog or no dog. Do you copy?"

"Copy that, Chief. Two minutes. But we're coming *with* the dog. Over."

Ivy's heart lifted. That was Carter's voice. Carter was okay. The team was still okay.

The firefighters on the ground had now moved to the bucket ladder just outside the fiery attic window.

"Who else is inside?" she asked.

"It's just Lieutenant Bowen, O'Brien, and O'Brien."

Carter. Wyatt. Shane.

"The dog is secured, sir. We're coming out. Over," Carter said over the radio.

Ivy choked back a sob. In seconds he'd be out of the building and she'd be able to breathe again.

But instead she heard another screech followed by a crash and then the unmistakable sound of the PASS device, a firefighter's personal alarm that meant he or she was in distress.

Seconds later, one of the firefighters and Frederick ran out the front door, but whoever was carrying the dog set him down on the lawn and ran back inside.

Casey hooked her arm through Ivy's and pulled her close. "He's gonna come out, Ives, okay? This is Meadow Valley. We don't do tragedy here. Plus, you've already had your fill for one lifetime, so this is only going to end with Carter Bowen walking out of that house."

Ivy nodded, but she couldn't speak. Maybe she'd had her share of tragedy, but had she played a role in setting herself up for more? She shook her head, a silent argument with her thoughts. She could let her fear close her off from risk—and also happiness—or she could be here for Carter, believing in him and in what Casey said: This was going to end with Carter Bowen walking out of that house.

"What if that's not how it ends, Case?" she asked, her voice cracking with the reality of the situation.

Casey looked at her, the tears in her best friend's eyes mirroring her own.

"Then you will fall apart, and I will be here to put you back together again. You're not alone in this, okay? You will *never* be alone."

Ivy nodded and held her breath.

"Lieutenant, what's your status? Over," the chief said, somehow maintaining his calm.

"Sir, this is Shane O'Brien. Part of the attic ceiling came down over the stairs. Lieutenant Bowen and my brother— I was already at the bottom with the dog—got knocked down by a burning beam." He went silent for a few seconds. "They're under the beam and neither of them are moving."

Ivy could see the fiery beam through the window. It stretched halfway down the length of the stairs.

The PASS alert ceased, and the chief's radio crackled.

Carter's voice sounded over the radio. "The rest of the ceiling's gonna go, Chief. Don't send anyone else in. O'Brien's got this. Shane?" Carter sounded pained, and Ivy stopped breathing altogether. "Shane can you hear me?"

"Copy that. I hear you, Lieutenant Bowen," Shane said. "But—I can't do this. I can't—"

"I need you to stay calm but act fast. Your brother's unconscious and my arm is broken, and my hand is pinned under the corner of the beam. All you need to do is unpin me, and I can help you carry your brother out."

"This shit isn't supposed to happen here," Shane said. "*Nothing* happens here."

"You can do this, Shane," Carter said. "But it has to be fast. The rest of the ceiling is starting to buckle."

The radios went silent after that. Ivy swore she could hear her own heartbeat. Her hand was in Casey's again, the two of them squeezing each other tight yet not laying voice to what they were both thinking.

This was Charlie all over again. They got Charlie out but not in time to save him from the internal injuries the paramedics couldn't treat.

The firefighters on the outside still worked tirelessly, and the flames began to retreat. But Ivy knew that did nothing for the internal damage or the safety of the structure. The ceiling was already compromised, and the extra weight of the water would expedite its complete collapse.

A buckling sound came from within the house, and Ivy knew their time was up.

"Come on. Come on. Come on," she chanted.

Then the roof of the house dipped. Less than a second later, it folded in on itself as two figures burst through the front-door opening with a third figure's arms draped over their shoulders.

Shane and Carter ran with the toes of Wyatt's boots scraping across the grass until they were far enough from what once was Mrs. Davis's home and paramedics were able to retrieve Wyatt and get him onto a stretcher. Carter held his right arm against his torso, and when he tore off his hat and mask, she could see an expression wrought with pain as another paramedic escorted him to a third ambulance.

Ivy dropped down to the ground and crawled under the barricade.

"Go get him, Ives!" Casey called after her.

And Ivy ran. She ran past the chief, who called her name, but she didn't stop to listen. She ran past a police car where she recognized Daniela Garcia, who'd graduated high school with Charlie, standing against the bumper. Except she was Deputy Garcia now, and although Ivy didn't think she was breaking any laws by bypassing the barricade, at the moment she didn't care if she had, as long as she made it to Carter.

"You can't be back here, Ivy!" Deputy Garcia yelled. But Ivy still didn't stop.

Not until she was breathless and banging on the already closed back door of the emergency vehicle did she come to a halt.

A paramedic swung the door open, and she climbed inside without being invited. Carter sat on the gurney still in his protective boots and pants, but his jacket had been removed and a ninety-degree splint was affixed to his right arm from shoulder to wrist. A clear tube that led to an IV bag hanging from the ceiling of the vehicle was taped to his left hand.

"Hi," she said, barely holding it together. "All right if I ride along?"

CHAPTER ELEVEN

❧

Carter looked at the paramedic who was closing the door, a younger guy from his team named Ty. "You think you could give us some privacy?" he asked.

The other man hesitated. "With all due respect, Lieutenant—and that's a mighty fine thing you did talking O'Brien through that situation—you know I can't leave you alone back here." He had to give it to the kid for following procedure. He wondered, though, if Ty's name was on that petition.

The ambulance lurched forward, and Ivy fell into the seat meant for the paramedic.

"Guess that means you're staying," Carter told her.

"I can sit here," Ty said, taking a spot on the bench to Carter's right. "And the best I can do about privacy is this." He pulled a pair of wireless earbuds out of his pocket and stuck them in his ears. "Just tap my shoulder if you need something!" he said, already too loud over whatever music he was playing, and Carter laughed.

"Looks like it's just you and me," he said. "Which means that now I can ask you what the hell you were doing so close to the fire. Dammit, Ivy. Don't you know how dangerous that was?"

Her eyes widened. "Me? You're *mad* at me when I came here to show you that I support you no matter what? To tell you that I love you and that you're not alone in this?"

She threw her hands in the air, but with such limited space, she had to keep her arms close to her body. The whole gesture made her look like an exasperated T. rex, and Carter had to bite the inside of his cheek to keep from laughing.

"Are you—laughing?" she said. "I just heard you over the chief's radio say that you were trapped under a burning ceiling beam and that your arm was broken, and you're *laughing*?"

Her voice trembled, and a tear slid quickly down her cheek.

He wasn't laughing anymore.

"Jesus, Ivy," he said. "You heard all that? How long were you out there?"

She sucked in a steadying breath and blew it out slowly.

"Long enough to know that you are really good at your job. Long enough to know that even in the worst situation, you were still in control and knew what to do." She shook her head and pressed her lips together. "I will always be scared when you have to leave that firehouse with sirens blaring. But I also know that you're the best shot your team has at coming home safe whenever you do."

He cupped her cheek in his palm. IV or not, he didn't care. He needed to touch her, and he needed her to know the truth—that as good as he was at his job, he was scared, too, scared that he couldn't guarantee he'd always walk away from a situation like today.

"I can't promise you that'll be the case 100 percent of the time. If we hadn't gone back in for that damn dog, no one on my command would have left in an ambulance. I mean, hell, if Shane wasn't there—if he didn't listen to me?" He dropped his hand and let out a bitter laugh. "You were right," he told her. "The whole month I've been here I've been so hell-bent on proving myself. What if that clouded my judgment? What if—"

"No what ifs," Ivy interrupted. "I heard everything. You listened to the chief's orders. You're alive. Wyatt's alive. And Shane saved you both. I've spent the past four weeks promising myself I wouldn't let you get too close because of what happened to Charlie. Because of *What if?* I never should have told you not to go tonight. And I never will again."

His brows furrowed. "You'll never tell me *not* to go again or you'll never *not* tell me not to go. Either the pain meds are kicking in or there are too many negatives in what you said that I'm not sure if you meant what I think you meant."

This time she was the one to laugh, and the effect of the pain meds paled in comparison to her smile. He could live with being unsure about the future as long as it meant she was in it.

"Just to clarify," he said, "are you saying that if I stay in town, you're not going to turn the other way if you pass me on the street?"

She let out something between a laugh and sob. "If you weren't all busted up, I'd punch you in the shoulder or something."

"Well then, I guess I'm safe from any further *physical* distress," he said. "But are you gonna break my heart, Ivy Serrano?"

She shook her head, then rested it on his shoulder. "Nah. I love you too much to do that." She tilted her head up, and her brown eyes shimmered in the normally unpleasant fluorescent light.

"That's a relief," he said. "Because I don't think I could walk by you without wanting to do this." His lips swept over hers in a kiss that felt like the start of something new. He couldn't wrap her in his arms, and maybe the bumps in the road made the whole gesture a little clumsy, but she was here. And she was staying. And petition or not, dammit, so was he.

Carter waited outside the chief's office, anxious more about being late for Ivy's fashion show than he was about what would be said behind the office doors. If he was being let go, he was being let go. He was damned good at his job, and he didn't need anyone's approval anymore to know that was true.

Okay, fine, so he needed the chief's approval to *keep* his job but not to know that he did everything he could for this company in the month he was here.

The door swung open, and Chief Burnett popped his head out.

"Come on in, Lieutenant. Sorry to keep you waiting."

Carter stood and brushed nonexistent dust from his uniform pants. His right hand had cramped, so he flexed it, still getting used to the air cast.

He walked inside, expecting to find the chief alone waiting for him, but instead he saw Shane O'Brien standing in front of the chief's desk.

The chief cleared his throat. "Lieutenant Bowen, I hope you don't mind, but I thought it best for Firefighter O'Brien to speak first."

Carter nodded. "O'Brien," he said. "Heard your brother is being discharged today."

"Yes sir, Lieutenant. It was a pretty bad concussion, but thanks to you, he's going to be fine."

Carter's brows drew together. The formality from Shane confused him. Not that he'd expected the guy to mouth off, but this was a complete one-eighty from what Carter had seen from him.

"He's going to be fine, O'Brien, because of *you*," Carter said. "Neither of us would be here right now if you hadn't gotten us out of that house before the roof caved in."

Shane's jaw tightened. "With all due respect, Lieutenant, I never wanted to be here. And I made sure everyone knew it. And then I made your life a living hell because I knew I wasn't good enough, and it was your job to remind me of that." He squared his shoulders. "The signatures on the petition were forged. Every one of them but mine. I am not proud of my behavior and need some time to regroup."

Carter opened his mouth to say something, but Shane cut him off.

"I need to figure things out without everything that's been hanging over my head since I was a kid. I'm leaving town, sir. And the company. Effective immediately."

Shane held out his hand to shake but then realized that was Carter's broken arm and dropped it back to his side.

"O'Brien," Carter said. "You don't have to do this."

"It's already done," the chief said. "I tried to talk him out of it, but I think his mind was made up the second he rode away from the Davis fire with his brother in an ambulance."

Shane nodded once, his eyes dark and expression stoic.

"You're a good firefighter, O'Brien," Carter added. "I'd have been proud to keep you on my team."

"Thank you, Lieutenant," he said. He nodded toward the chief. "You too, Chief."

The chief clapped Shane on the shoulder. "You always have a place here if you ever decide to come back."

Shane pressed his lips together but didn't say anything else. Then he strode through the door, closing it behind him.

Carter blew out a long breath. "You think he's going to get into trouble again?"

The chief shook his head. "If you'd have asked me that a month ago, I'd have said yes. But something changed in him since you've been around. And the way you handled things in the Davis fire? We're damn lucky to have you, Lieutenant."

He was staying in Meadow Valley. This was—home.

"Thank you, sir. I feel damn lucky to be here."

After a long moment, Carter turned to head for the door.

"One more thing, Lieutenant," the chief said, stopping him in his tracks. "Your family was notified of your injury, and your father has called your aunt four times in the past two days to check on you. I thought you should know."

Carter swallowed hard but didn't turn back around. "Appreciate the information," he said. "But he knows my number."

"Give him time," the chief said. "Father-son relationships can be a tricky thing."

Carter thought about Shane, who was leaving town to deal with his own tricky thing, and the weight on his shoulders lifted, if only a fraction of an inch.

"Yes, sir. I suppose they are."

Then he was out the door and down the steps two at a time. When he pushed through the station's front door, Ivy was there on the sidewalk, right where he'd left her on his way in. The sky was overcast, but she was a vision in her bright yellow sundress, brown waves of hair falling over her shoulders.

He only needed one arm to lift her up and press his lips to hers.

"I'm home, darlin'," he said.

"Good," she said through laughter and kisses. "Because I wasn't letting you go without a fight. Now come on. I need to show you something."

She led him down the street to her shop. She bounced on her toes as they slowed in front of the window where a single mannequin stood displaying a dress that could only be described as a field of sunflowers.

"You made that?" he said. "It's like nothing I've ever seen, Ivy. If I didn't know any better, I'd say those were live flowers."

She smiled the biggest, most beautiful smile he'd seen since the fire.

"I made them," she said, and he could hear how proud she was. "It's my version of my and Charlie's garden. I don't think I'd have ever finished it if I hadn't met you, which is why I wanted you to be the first to see it."

She beamed—a ray of sunshine on an otherwise cloudy day.

He stepped closer and wrapped his arm around her waist. "Are you calling me your muse?" he teased, and she laughed.

"I'm calling you my everything, if that's okay," she said, then kissed him.

He smiled against her. "That's about the okayest thing I've ever been called, darlin'. So yeah, I think I'm good with that. As long as you're good with me spending the rest of my days making good on that title."

She kissed him again, and he took that as a yes.

* * *

Ivy and Carter tied Ace and Barbara Ann to the fence. She stared at the beautiful, stubborn man she loved and shook her head.

"What would the doctor say if he knew you were on a horse three days after breaking your arm?" she asked. She'd tried to stop him, but he'd threatened to ride off without her if she didn't join him.

He opened and closed his right hand. "Arm's broken," he said. "Thanks to Shane O'Brien, the hand's just fine. Besides, who's snitching on me to the doctor?"

She removed the pack from Barbara Ann's saddle and tossed it on the ground. They'd get to that shortly. Then she wrapped her arms around him and kissed him in the place where they'd kissed for the first time. When they finally parted, he spun her so her back was against his torso, his hands resting on her hips.

From the top of the hill above town, Ivy could see the ruins of Mrs. Davis's home. She could also see the inn where Pearl would give her—and her animals—a place to stay for as long as it took for her to rebuild. She could see the bell above the firehouse, the one that would forever remind her of the day she *didn't* lose the man who held her in his arms right now.

"Can you see that?" he whispered in her ear. "I don't mean the town. I mean what's right in front of you."

Her brows furrowed, and she shifted her gaze from the tapestry of Meadow Valley to a shock of color just a little way down the hill. A sunflower.

She spun to face him. "I don't understand. How did it—I mean, those don't sprout up in a matter of days."

He laughed. "I talked to Sam Callahan, and we thought it

might be fun to start a community garden up here between locals and ranch guests. It's public property, so there are permits involved, but I'm sure you can point me in the right direction of who to talk to."

"You want to build me a garden?" she asked, her eyes wide.

"I want to build you everything," he said. "But if the garden's too painful—if the memories are too much..."

She shook her head.

"It *is* painful," she admitted. "But it's also wonderful and thoughtful." She pressed her palms to his chest. "I don't want to forget the painful stuff. And I don't want to wrap myself in a bubble of fire extinguishers and interconnected smoke detectors and—and loneliness to protect myself from getting hurt again. I want to start something new—with this garden and with you. I will always be scared, but I don't have to be alone. *We're* not alone."

"Although fire safety *is* important," he teased. "So don't abandon your extinguishers just to make a statement."

She laughed.

"You know," he said, looking past her and down at the town, "if you need to when things get tough, we can always come here to forget the rest of the world for a little while, pretend it doesn't exist."

She shook her head. "I want to experience it all, the good and the bad. With you."

She gave him a soft kiss and ran her hands through his hair, smiling against him. "Starting with a hilltop haircut," she said. "Are you ready, Lieutenant? Brought all my tools."

He laughed and stepped away. "At the risk of you miscalculating and lopping off my ear, I need to ask you one quick thing before I potentially lose my hearing."

Ivy crossed her arms. "Cut off your ear? Please, Lieutenant. And here I thought you trusted—"

He dropped down to one knee, and Ivy lost the ability to form words.

"I know there's supposed to be a ring and everything, but I'm kind of doing this out of order. It's as simple as the text you sent me the night of the fire. Everything's been so crazy the past few days I didn't even see it until later the next day. I'm here, Ivy. If you'll let me, I will always be here for you. I love you. Say you'll marry me, plant gardens with me, and build a life with me, and *then* I'll let you cut my hair."

She wasn't sure if she was laughing or crying because the tears were flowing, but she was smiling from ear to ear.

She clasped her hands around his neck and kissed him and kissed him and kissed him some more.

"Yes," she said against him, and she felt his smile mirror hers. "Yes. Yes. Yes."

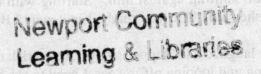